THE LADIES OF MISSALONGHI

TIM

The Ladies of Missalonghi

Tim

COLLEEN McCULLOUGH

BOOK CLUB ASSOCIATES LONDON

This omnibus edition published 1987 by
Book Club Associates
by arrangement with Century Hutchinson Ltd
and Angus & Robertson Publishers.

Typeset by Rowland Phototypesetting Ltd,
Bury St Edmunds, Suffolk.
Printed and bound in Great Britain by
Richard Clay Ltd, Bungay, Suffolk.

CONTENTS

The Ladies of Missalonghi

'Can you tell me, Octavia, why our luck never seems to change for the better?' asked Mrs Drusilla Wright of her sister, adding with a sigh. 'We need a new roof.'

Miss Octavia Hurlingford dropped her hands into her lap, shook her head dolefully and echoed the sigh. 'Oh, dear! Are you sure?'

'Denys is.'

Since their nephew Denys Hurlingford ran the local iron-mongery and had a thriving plumbing business as well, his word was law in such matters.

'How much will a new roof cost? Must it be a whole one? Couldn't we have the worst sheets replaced?'

'There isn't one sheet of iron worth keeping, Denys says, so we're looking at about fifty pounds, I'm afraid.'

A gloomy silence fell, each sister cudgelling her brain in search of a source for the necessary funds. They were sitting side by side on a horsehair-stuffed sofa whose better days were so far in the past that no one remembered them. Mrs Drusilla Wright was hemstitching pulled threads around the border of a linen cloth with microscopically fine, meticulous skill, and Miss Octavia Hurlingford was occupied with a crochet hook, the work dangling from it as exquisitely done as the hemstitching.

'We could use the fifty pounds Father put in the bank for me when I was born,' offered the third occupant of the room, anxious to make amends for the fact that she saved not a penny of her egg and butter money. She was also working, sitting on a low stool producing lace from a tatting shuttle and a ball of ecru thread, her fingers moving with the complete efficiency of a task known so well it was sightless, mindless.

'Thank you, but no,' said Drusilla.

And that was the end of the only conversation occurring during the two-hour work period of Friday afternoon, for not long afterwards the hall clock began to chime four. While the last vibrations still lingered in the air, all three ladies proceeded with the automatism of long custom to put away their handicrafts, Drusilla her sewing, Octavia her crocheting, and Missy her tatting. Each lady disposed of her work inside an identical grey flannel drawstring bag, after which each lady disposed of her bag inside a battered mahogany sideboard sitting beneath the window.

The routine never, never varied. At four o'clock the two-hour handwork session in the second-best parlour came to an end, and another two-hour session began, but of a different kind. Drusilla moved to the organ which was her only treasure and only pleasure, while Octavia and Missy moved to the kitchen, there to prepare the evening meal and finish off the outside chores.

As they clustered in the doorway like three hens unsure of the pecking order, it was easy to see that Drusilla and Octavia were sisters. Each was extremely tall and each had a long, bony, anaemically fair face; but where Drusilla was sturdily large and muscular, Octavia was crabbed and diminished by a longstanding bone disease. Missy shared the height, though not so much of it, being a mere five feet seven to her aunt's five feet ten and her mother's six feet. Nothing else did she have in common, for she was as dark as they were fair, as flat-chested as they were fulsome, and owned features as small as theirs were large.

The kitchen was a big bare room at the back of the dim central hall, its brown-painted wooden walls contributing their mite to the general atmosphere of gloominess.

'Peel the potatoes before you go out to pick the beans, Missy,' said Octavia as she strapped on the voluminous brown pinny which protected her brown dress from the perils of cooking. While Missy peeled the three potatoes considered sufficient, Octavia shook up the coals smouldering in the firebox of the black iron range which occupied the whole frontage of the kitchen chimney; she then added fresh wood, adjusted the damper to cull more draught, and put a huge iron kettle on to boil. This done, she turned to the pantry to get out the raw materials for next morning's porridge.

'Oh, bother!' she exclaimed, emerging a moment later to display a brown paper bag whose bottom corners bled a flurry of oats that floated to the floor like turgid snowflakes. 'Look at this! Mice!'

'Don't worry, I'll set some traps tonight,' said Missy without

much interest, putting her potatoes into a small pot of water, and adding a pinch of salt.

'Traps tonight doesn't get our breakfast on the table, so you'll have to ask your mother if you can run to Uncle Maxwell's to buy more oats.'

'Couldn't we do without for once?' Missy hated oats.

'In *winter*?' Octavia stared at her as if she had gone mad. 'A good big bowl of porridge is cheap, my girl, and sets you up for the whole day. Now hurry, for goodness sake!'

On the hall side of the kitchen door the organ music was deafening. Drusilla was an appallingly bad player who had never been told other than that she was very good, but to play with such consistent ineptitude required remorseless practice, so between four and six every weekday afternoon, Drusilla practised. There was some point to it, as she inflicted her lack of talent on the largely Hurlingford congregation at the Byron Church of England each Sunday; luckily no Hurlingford had an ear for music, so all the Hurlingfords thought they were very well served during service.

Missy crept into the parlour, not the room where they did their handwork, but the one reserved for important occasions, and where the organ lived; there, Drusilla was assaulting Bach with all the clangour and thunder of a jousting knight his rival in the lists, seated with her back straight, her eyes closed, her head tilted, and her mouth twitching.

'Mother?' It was the smallest whisper, a filament of sound in competition against whole hawsers.

However, it was enough. Drusilla opened her eyes and turned her head, more in a spirit of resignation than anger.

'Well?'

'I'm sorry to interrupt, but we need more oats before Uncle Maxwell shuts. The mice got at the bag.'

Drusilla sighed. 'Bring me my purse, then.'

The purse was fetched, and sixpence fished from its flaccid recesses. '*Bulk* oats, mind! All you pay for with a proprietary brand of oats is the fancy box.'

'No, Mother! Proprietary oats taste much better, and you don't have to boil them all night to cook them, either.' A faint hope entered Missy's breast. 'In fact, if you and Aunt Octavia would rather eat proprietary oats, I'll gladly go without to make up the difference in expense.'

Drusilla was always telling herself and her sister that she lived for the day her timid daughter showed signs of defiance, but this present humble bid for independence only ran up against an authoritarian wall the mother didn't know she had erected. So she said, shocked, 'Go without? Most definitely not! Porridge is our winter staple, and it's a lot cheaper than coal fires.' Then the tone of her voice became friendlier, more equal-women. 'What's the temperature?'

Missy consulted the thermometer in the hall. 'Forty-two!' she called.

'Then we'll eat in the kitchen and spend the evening there!' shouted Drusilla, beginning to give Bach another belting.

Wrapped up in her brown serge overcoat, a brown fleecy scarf and a brown knitted bonnet, with the sixpence from her mother's purse tucked down into the finger of one brown woollen glove, Missy let herself out of the house and hurried down the neat brick path to the front gate. In a small shopping bag was her library book; opportunities to sneak in an extra trip to the library were few and far between, and if she really scampered, no one need ever know she had done more than go to Uncle Maxwell's in search of oats. Tonight her Aunt Livilla would be manning the library herself, so it would have to be an improving sort of book instead of a novel, but in Missy's eyes any sort of book was better than no book at all. And next Monday Una would be there, so she could have a novel.

The air was full of a soft, fine Scotch mist that dithered between fog and rain and covered the privet hedge along the boundary of the house named Missalonghi with fat round drops of water. The moment Missy stepped out into Gordon Road she began to run, only slowing to a rapid walk at the corner because that wretchedly painful stitch was back in her left side, and it really did hurt. Slowing down definitely eased her discomfort, however, so she trotted along more sedately and began to experience the glow of happiness which always came when she was offered this rarest of treats, a chance to escape on her own from the confines of Missalonghi. Picking up her pace again the minute the stitch disappeared, she commenced to look around her at the familiar sights Byron had to offer on a misty late afternoon of a short winter's day.

Everything in the town of Byron was named after some aspect

of the poet, including her mother's house, Missalonghi, christened after the place where Lord Byron had expired untimely. This bizarre urban nomenclature was the fault of Missy's great-grandfather, the first Sir William Hurlingford, who had founded his town hard on the heels of reading *Childe Harold*, and was so pleased that he had actually discovered a great work of literature he could understand that ever after he had rammed indigestible amounts of Byron down the throats of everyone he knew. Thus Missalonghi was situated in Gordon Road, and Gordon Road ran into Noel Street, and Noel Street ran into Byron Street, which was the main thoroughfare; on the better side of town George Street meandered for several miles before plunging over the edge of the mighty Jamieson Valley. There was even a tiny cul-de-sac called Caroline Lamb Place, situated of course on the wrong side of the railway line (as was the house named Missalonghi); here dwelled a dozen very brassy women divided between three houses, and here came many masculine visitors from the fettlers' camp just up the line, as well as from the huge bottling plant that marred the town's southern outskirts.

It was one of the more puzzling and interesting facets of the first Sir William's intriguing character that on his deathbed he had firmly enjoined his surviving progeny not to interfere with the course of Nature by changing the function of Caroline Lamb Place, which in consequence had remained distinctly shady ever since, and not just due to its chestnut trees. In fact, the first Sir William had been addicted to what he always described as 'an orderly system of naming things', and had called all his daughters by Latin names because they were popular in the higher ranks of society. His descendants kept the custom up, so there were Julias, Aurelias, Antonias, Augustas; only one branch of the family had tried to improve upon this policy by starting, with the arrival of their fifth son, to call their boys by Latin numbers, thereby glorifying the Hurlingford family tree with a Quintus, a Sextus, a Septimus, an Octavius and a Nonus. Decimus died at birth, and no one wondered at it.

Oh, how beautiful! Missy stopped to marvel at a huge spider's web beaded by the soft feelers of mist that trailed pulsating up out of the invisible valley on the far side of Gordon Road. There was a very large sleek spider at the webs middle, apologetically escorted by her tiny mate-of-the-moment, but Missy felt neither fear nor revulsion, only envy. Not merely did this lucky creature own her world intrepidly and securely, but she flew the original suffragette banner by not only dominating and using her husband, but also by eating him once his purpose was scattered over her eggs. Oh, lucky, lucky spider-lady! Demolish her world, and she would serenely remake it to inborn specifications so lovely, so ethereal, that impermanence could never matter: and when the new web was finished, she would arrange the next series of consorts upon it like a movable feast, the modestly robust husband of today just off-centre, and his successors getting littler and littler the farther they were from Mother at the hub.

The time! Missy began to run again, turning into Byron Street and heading for the row of shops which marched down either side of one block in the centre of the town, just before Byron Street became grandiose and produced the park and the railway station and the marble-fronted hotel and the imposing Egyptian façade of the Byron Waters Baths.

There was the grocery and produce store, owned by Maxwell Hurlingford; the ironmongery, owned by Denys Hurlingford; the millinery shop, owned by Aurelia Marshall, née Hurlingford; the smithy and petrol pump, owned by Thomas Hurlingford; the bakery, owned by Walter Hurlingford; the clothing emporium, owned by Herbert Hurlingford; the newsagency and stationery shop, owned by Septimus Hurlingford; the Weeping Willow Tea Room, owned by Julia Hurlingford; the lending library, owned by Livilla Hurlingford; the butchery, owned by Roger Hurlingford Witherspoon; the sweet shop and tobacconist, owned by Percival Hurlingford; and the Olympus Café and Milk Bar, owned by Nikos Theodoropoulos.

As befitted its importance, Byron Street was sealed with tarmacadam as far as its junctions with Noel Street and Caroline Lamb Place, provided with an ornate polished granite horse-trough donated by the first Sir William, and possessed of proper hitching-posts right along its awninged section of shops. It was lined with very beautiful old gum trees, and contrived to look both peaceful and prosperous.

There were very few private dwellings in the central part of Byron. The town made its living from summer visitors anxious to escape the heat and humidity of the coastal plain, and year-round visitors who aspired to ease their rheumatic aches and pains by soaking in the hot mineral waters some geological freak had placed beneath Byron ground. Therefore all along Byron Street were many guest-houses and boarding-houses – mostly owned and run by Hurlingfords, of course. The Byron Waters Baths provided a most agreeable standard of comfort for those not precisely penny-pinched, the vast and prestigious Hurlingford Hotel boasted private baths for the exclusive use of its own guests, while for those whose pecuniary resources just stretched to bed and breakfast in one of the cheaper boarding-houses, there existed the clean if spartan pools of the Byron Spa, just around the corner on Noel Street.

Even those too poor to come to the town of Byron at all were catered for. The second Sir William had invented the Byron Bottle (as it was known throughout Australia and the South Pacific); a one-pint, artistically slender, crystal-clear bottle of Byron's best spring water, gently effervescent, mildly but never disastrously aperient, distinctly tasty. Vichy water be damned! said those fortunate enough to have travelled to France. The good old Byron Bottle was not only better, it was also a great deal cheaper. And there was a penny refund on the empty too. Judicious buying of shares in the glassworks had put the final polish on this extremely inexpensive to run but remarkably lucrative local industry; it continued to thrive and to make enormous sums of money for all the male descendants of the second Sir William. The third Sir William, grandson of the first and son of the second, currently presided over the Byron Bottle Company empire with all the ruthlessness and rapaciousness of his earlier namesakes.

Maxwell Hurlingford, in direct line from the first Sir William and therefore a hugely wealthy man in his own right, did not need to run a grocery and produce store. However, commercial instinct and acumen in the Hurlingfords died hard, and the Calvinistic precepts which governed the clan dictated that a man must work to have grace in the eyes of the Lord. Rigid adherence to this rule should have made Maxwell Hurlingford a saint on earth, but instead had only managed to create a street-angel cum house-devil.

When Missy entered the shop a bell tinkled raucously, that being a perfect description of the sound Maxwell Hurlingford had devised in order to gratify his ascetics as well as his prudence. He emerged immediately the bell summoned him from the nether regions out the back, where resided the bran and chaff and wheat and barley and pollard and oats in towering stacks of hempen bags; not only did Maxwell Hurlingford cater to the gastronomic needs of the human population of Byron, he also victualled its horses, cows, pigs, sheep and chooks. As one local wit said when his grass failed, Maxwell Hurlingford got you going and coming.

His face bore its normal expression, sour, and his right hand a big scoop whiskered with webby strands of fodder.

'Look at this!' he snarled, waving the scoop at Missy in an uncanny imitation of his sister Octavia bearing her mouse-pillaged bags of oats. 'Weevils all over the place.'

'Oh, dear! The bulk oats too?'

'The lot.'

'Then you'd better give me a box of proper breakfast oats, please, Uncle Maxwell.'

'Just as well horses aren't fussy,' he grumbled, putting the scoop down and squeezing behind the grocery counter.

The bell erupted into agitated life again as a man came through the door with a huge swirl of cold misty air and a dazzling briskness of purpose.

'Bloody hell, it's colder than a stepmother's tits out there!' gasped the newcomer, slapping his hands together.

'Sir! There are *ladies* present!'

'Oops!' said the newcomer, neglecting to follow this sop with an apology proper. Instead, he bellied up to the counter and grinned wickedly down at the gaping Missy. 'Ladies in the plural, man? I can only see half a one!'

Neither Missy nor Uncle Maxwell could work out whether this was merely an insulting reference to her lack of height in a town of giants, or whether he was grossly insulting her by implying she was not really a lady. So by the time Uncle Maxwell had collected the use of his famously acid wits and tongue, the stranger was already well embarked upon his list of requirements.

'I want six bags of bran and pollard, a bag of flour, a bag of sugar, a box of twelve-gauge cartridges, a side of bacon, six tins of baking powder, ten pounds of tinned butter, ten pounds of raisins, a dozen tins of golden syrup, six tins of plum jam, and a ten-pound tin of Arnott's mixed biscuits.'

'It is five minutes to five, and I close at five on the dot,' said Uncle Maxwell stiffly.

'Then you'd better hop to it, hadn't you?' asked the stranger unsympathetically.

The box of proprietary oats was sitting on the counter; Missy milked her sixpence out of the finger of her glove and tendered it, waiting in vain for Uncle Maxwell to give her any change and quite lacking the courage to ask him whether a small quantity of a basic commodity could cost so much, even dolled up in a fancy box. In the end she picked up the oats and left, but not before stealing another glance at the stranger.

He had a cart drawn by two horses, for such was tethered outside the store, and had not been there when Missy entered. A good-looking equipage too; the horses were trim and sleek with a sensible dash of draft in them, and the cart seemed new, the spokes of its wheels picked out in yellow on a rich brown background.

Four minutes to five. If she reversed the order of their arrival in Uncle Maxwell's shop, she could plead the stranger's rudeness and vast order as an excuse for being late, and thereby manage to fit in a dash to the library.

The town of Byron possessed no public library; few towns in Australia did in those days. But there was a privately owned lending library to fill the gap. Livilla Hurlingford was a widow with a very expensive son; economic need allied to the need always to appear respectable had driven her to open a well-stocked book room, and its popularity and profitability had led her to ignore the general blue laws which closed the shops of Byron at five on weekday afternoons, for the bulk of her patrons preferred to exchange their books in the evenings. Books were Missy's only solace and sole luxury. She was permitted to keep the money she made from selling Missalonghi's excess eggs and butter, and she spent all of this pittance borrowing books from her Aunt Livilla's library. Both her mother and aunt disapproved strongly, but having announced some years earlier that Missy should have an opportunity to put something by above and beyond the fifty pounds her father had bestowed upon her at her birth, Drusilla and Octavia were too fair to rescind their decree simply because Missy turned out a spendthrift.

Provided she did her allotted share of the work – and did it properly, without skimping by a whisker – no one objected if Missy read books, where they objected strenuously if she voiced a desire to go walking through the bush. To walk through the bush was to place her debatably desirable person smack in the path of murder or rapine, and was not going to be permitted under any circumstances. Drusilla therefore ordered her cousin Livilla to supply Missy only with *good* books; no novels whatsoever, no scurrilous or scandalous biographies, no sort of reading matter aimed at the masculine gender. This dictum Aunt Livilla policed rigorously, having the same ideas as Drusilla about what unmarried ladies should read.

But for the last month Missy had harboured a guilty secret; she was being supplied with novels galore. Aunt Livilla had found herself an assistant to run the library on Monday and Tuesday and Saturday, thus enabling Aunt Livilla to enjoy a four-day respite from the grizzling importunities of locals who had read everything on her shelves and visitors whose tastes her shelves did not cater for. Of course the new assistant was a Hurlingford, though not a Hurlingford from Byron; she hailed from the fleshpots of Sydney.

People rarely took any notice of the tongue-tied and sadly inhibited Missy Wright, but Una, as the new assistant was named, had seemed instantly to detect in Missy the stuff of a good friend. So from the beginning of her tenure, Una had drawn Missy out to an amazing degree; she knew Missy's habits, circumstances, prospects, troubles and dreams. She had also worked out a foolproof system whereby Missy might borrow forbidden fruit without Aunt Livilla's finding out, and she plied Missy with novels of all kinds, from the most adventurous to the most wildly romantic.

Of course tonight it would be Aunt Livilla on duty, so her book would have to be of the old kind. Yet when Missy opened the glass door and came into the cheery warmth of the book room, there sat Una behind the desk, and of the dreaded Aunt Livilla there was no sign.

More than Una's undeniable liveliness, understanding and kindness had endeared her to Missy; she was a truly remarkable looking woman as well. Her figure was excellent, her height sufficient to mark her out as a true Hurlingford, and her clothes reminded Missy of her cousin Alicia's clothes, always in good taste, always in the latest fashion. always verging on the glamorous. Arctically fair of skin and hair and eye, still Una contrived not to appear half bald and wholly washed out, which was the fate of every Hurlingford female except Alicia (who was so ravishingly beautiful that God had given her dark brows and lashes when she grew up) and Missy (who was entirely dark). Even more intriguing than Una's positive brand of fairness was a curious, luminous quality she owned, a delicious bloom that lay not so much upon her skin as inside it; her nails, oval and long, radiated this lightfilled essence, as did her hair, piled in the latest puffs all around her head and culminating in a glittering topknot so blonde it was almost white. The air around her took on a sheen that was there and yet was not there. Fascinating! Lifelong exposure to none save Hurlingfords had left Missy unprepared for the phenomenon of the person with an aura; now within the space of a single little month she had met two of them, Una with her luminescence, and today the stranger in Uncle Maxwell's with his fizzy blue cloud of energy crackling around him.

'Goody!' cried Una at sight of Missy. 'Darling, I have a novel you're going to adore! All about a young noblewoman of indigent means who is obliged to go governessing in the house of a duke. She falls in love with the duke and he gets her into trouble, then refuses to have anything to do with her because it's his wife has all the money. So he ships her to India, where her baby dies of cholera just after it's born. Then this terrifically handsome maharajah sees her and falls in love with her on the spot because her hair is red-gold and her eyes are lime-green where of course all his dozens of wives and concubines are dark. He kidnaps her, intending to make her his plaything, but when he gets her into his clutches he finds out he respects her too much. So instead, he marries her and casts off all his other women because he says she is a jewel of such rarity she must have no rival. She becomes a maharanee, and very powerful. Then the duke arrives in India with his regiment of hussars to quell a native uprising in the hills, which he does, only he's fatally wounded in the battle. She takes the duke into her alabaster palace, where he finally dies in her arms, but only after she forgives him for so cruelly wronging her. And the maharajah understands at last that she really does love him more than she ever loved the duke. Isn't that a wonderful story? You'll just adore it, I promise!'

Being told the entire plot never put Missy off a book, so she accepted *Dark Love* at once and tucked it down on the bottom of her shopping bag, feeling as she did so for her own little money-purse. But it wasn't there.

'I'm afraid I've left my purse at home,' she said to Una, as mortified as only someone very poor and very proud can be. 'Oh, dear! I was sure I put it in! Well, you'd better have the book back until Monday.'

'Lord, darling, it's not the end of the world to forget your money! Take the book now, otherwise someone else will grab it, and it's so good it'll be out for months. You can pay me next time you're in.'

'Thank you,' said Missy, knowing she ought not embark upon a course of action utterly against the precepts of Missalonghi, but helpless in the face of her lust for books. Smiling awkwardly, she began to back out of the shop as fast as she could.

'Don't go yet, darling,' pleaded Una. 'Stay and talk to me, do!'

'I'm sorry, I really can't.'

'Go on, just a wee minute! Between now and seven it's as quiet as the grave, everyone's home eating tea.'

'Honestly, Una, I can't,' said Missy wretchedly.

Una looked mulish. 'Yes, you can.'

So, discovering that to refuse favours to those who held one in debt was quite impossible, Missy capitulated. 'Well, all right then, but only for a minute.'

'What I want to know is if you've set eyes on John Smith yet,' said Una, her sparkling nails fluttering about her sparkling topknot, her blue-white eyes glowing.

'John Smith? Who's John Smith?'

'The chap who bought your valley last week.'

Missy's valley was not actually her valley, of course, it simply lay along the far side of Gordon Road, but she always thought of it as hers, and had told Una more than once about her longing to walk through it. Her face fell.

'Oh, what a shame!'

'Pooh! It's a jolly good thing, if you ask me. Time someone got his foot in the Hurlingford door.'

'Well, I've never heard of this John Smith, and I'm sure I've never seen him,' Missy said, turning to go.

'How do you know you've never seen him when you won't even stay to hear what he looks like?'

A vision of the stranger in Uncle Maxwell's shop rose in front of Missy's eyes; she closed them and said, more positively than usual, 'He's very tall and solidly built, he has curly auburn hair, an auburn beard with two streaks of white in it, his clothes are rough and he swears like a trooper. His face is nice, but his eyes are even nicer.'

'That's him, that's him!' squeaked Una. 'So you have seen him! Where? Tell me all!'

'He came into Uncle Maxwell's shop a few minutes ago and bought a great many supplies.'

'Really? Then he must be moving into his valley.' Una grinned at Missy wickedly. 'I think you liked what you saw, didn't you, little Missy Sly-Boots?'

'Yes, I did,' said Missy, blushing.

'So did I when I first saw him,' said Una idly.

'When was that?'

'Ages ago. Years ago, in fact, darling. In Sydney.'

'You *know* him?'

'Very well indeed,' said Una, sighing.

The last month's spate of novels had vastly expanded Missy's emotional education; she felt confident enough to ask, 'Did you love him?'

But Una laughed. 'No, darling. One thing you can be absolutely sure of, I never loved him.'

'Does he come from Sydney?' asked Missy, relieved.

'Among other places.'

'Was he a friend of yours?'

'No. He was a friend of my husband's.'

This was news indeed to Missy. 'Oh, I am sorry, Una! I had no idea you were widowed.'

Una laughed again. 'Darling, I am not a widow! The saints preserve me from wearing black! Wallace – my husband – is still very much alive. The best way to describe my late marriage is to say that my husband divorced himself from it – and me.'

In all her life Missy had never before met a divorcée; Hurlingfords did not sunder marriages, be they made in heaven or hell or limbo. 'It must have been very difficult for you,' she said quietly, on her mettle not to appear prim or shocked.

'Darling, only I know how difficult it was.' Una's light disappeared. 'It was a marriage of convenience, actually. He found my social standing convenient – or rather his father did – and I found his pots and pots of money convenient.'

'Didn't you love him?'

'My whole trouble, darling – and it has wound me up in a lot of trouble – is that I have never loved anybody half so well as myself.' She pulled a face and down went her inner light again, having just regained its normal intensity. 'Mind you, Wallace was very well schooled in all the proper things, and very presentable to look at. But his father – ugh! His father was a dreadful little man who smelled of cheap pomade and even cheaper tobacco, and didn't know the first thing about manners. However, he had a burning ambition to see his son sitting right on top of the Australian heap, so he'd poured a great deal of his time and money into producing the kind of son a Hurlingford wouldn't baulk at. Where the truth was that his son liked the simple life, didn't want to sit on top of the heap, and only tried because he loved that awful old man quite desperately.'

'What happened?' asked Missy.

'Wallace's father died not long after the marriage came crashing down. A lot of people reckoned the cause was a broken heart, including Wallace. As for him – I made him hate me as no man should hate any woman.'

'I can't believe that,' said Missy loyally.

'I daresay you genuinely can't. But it's true, all the same. Over the years since it happened, I've been forced to admit that I was a greedy selfish bitch who should have been drowned at birth.'

'Oh, Una, don't!'

'Darling, don't weep for me, I'm not worth it,' said Una, hard and brilliant again. 'Truth's truth, that's all. So here I am, washed ashore for the very last time in a backwater like Byron, doing penance for my sins.'

'And your husband?'

'He's come good. He's finally found a chance to do everything he always wanted to do.'

There were at least a hundred other questions Missy was dying to ask, about Una's obvious change of heart, about the possibility she and her lost Wallace might patch things up, about John Smith, the mysterious John Smith; but the small pause which ensued after Una finished speaking brought time back with a jolt. A hasty goodbye, and she fled before Una could detain her further.

She ran almost all the five miles home, stitch or no stitch in her side, and her feet must have grown wings, for when she came breathless through the kitchen door she discovered mother and aunt perfectly ready to accept the story of John Smith's huge order as sufficient excuse for tardiness. Drusilla had milked the cow, Octavia's bones being unequal to the task, the beans were picked and simmering on the back of the range, and three lamb chops sizzled in a frying pan. The ladies of Missalonghi sat down on time to eat their dinner. And afterwards came the final chore of the day, the darning of much-laundered and much-worn stockings and underwear and linens.

Her mind half on Una's painful story and half on John Smith,

Missy listened rather sleepily to Drusilla and Octavia as they indulged in their nightly dissection of whatever news might have come their news-starved way. Tonight, after an initial period of mystified discussion about the stranger in Maxwell Hurlingford's shop (Missy had not passed on what she had gleaned from Una), they proceeded to the most interesting event looming on the Byron social calendar – Alicia's wedding.

'It will have to be my brown silk, Drusilla,' said Octavia, winking away a tear of wholehearted grief.

'And it will have to be my brown grosgrain, and it will have to be Missy's brown linen. Dear God, I am so tired of brown, brown, brown!' cried Drusilla.

'But in our straightened circumstances, sister, brown is the most sensible colour for us,' comforted Octavia, not very successfully.

'Just once,' said Drusilla savagely, jamming her needle into her reel of thread and folding the invisibly mended pillowcase with more passion than it had known in its entire long life, 'I would so much like to be silly rather than sensible! As tomorrow is Saturday, I shall have to listen to Aurelia endlessly vacillating between ruby satin and sapphire velvet for her own wedding outfit, asking my opinion at least a dozen times, and I would – I would dearly love to *kill* her!'

Missy had her own room, timber-panelled and as brown as the rest of the house. The floor was covered in a mottled brown linoleum, the bed in a brown candlewick spread, the window in a brown Holland blind; there was an ugly old bureau and an even older, uglier wardrobe. No mirror, no chair, no rug. But the walls did bear three pictures. One was a faded and foxed daguerrotype of an incredibly shrivelled, ancient first Sir William, taken about the time of the American Civil War; one was an embroidered sampler (Missy's earliest effort, and very well done) which announced that THE DEVIL MAKES WORK FOR IDLE HANDS; and the last was a passe-partouted Queen Alexandra, stiff and unsmiling, but still to Missy's uncritical eyes a very beautiful woman.

In the summer the room was a furnace, for it faced south of west, and in the winter it was an ice-box, taking the full brunt of the prevailing winds. No deliberate cruelty had been responsible for Missy's occupying this particular chamber; simply, she was the youngest and had drawn the shortest straw. No room in Missalonghi was truly comfortable, anyway.

Blue with cold, she shed her brown dress, her flannel petticoat, her woollen stockings and spencer and bloomers, folding them neatly before placing the underwear in a drawer and the dress on a hook in the wardrobe ceiling. Only her Sunday-best brown linen was hung up properly, for coat-hangers were very precious commodities. Missalonghi's tank held only 500 gallons, which made water the most precious commodity of all; bodies were bathed daily, the three ladies sharing the same scant bath-water, but underwear had to last two days.

Her nightgown was of prickly grey flannel, high to the neck, long-sleeved, trailing on the floor because it was one of Drusilla's hand-me-downs. But the bed was *warm*. On Missy's thirtieth birthday her mother had announced that she might have a hot brick during cold weather, since she was no longer in the first flush of youth. And when that happened, welcome though it had been, Missy abandoned forever any hope she might have cherished that she might one day find a life for herself outside the confines of Missalonghi.

Sleep came quickly, for she led a physically active life, however emotionally sterile it was. But the few moments between lying down in this blessed warmth and the onset of unconsciousness represented her only period of utter freedom, so Missy always fought sleep as long as she could.

She would begin by wondering what she really looked like. The house owned only one mirror, in the bathroom, and it was forbidden to stand and gaze at one's reflection. Thus Missy's impressions of herself were hedged with guilt that she might have stayed too long gazing. Oh, she knew she was quite tall, she knew she was far too thin, she knew her hair was straight and dark, that her eyes were black-brown, and her nose sadly out of kilter due to a fall as a child. She knew her mouth drooped down at its left corner and twisted up at its right, but she didn't know how this made her rare smiles fascinating and her normal solemn expression a clownlike tragicomedy. Life had taught her to think of herself as a very homely person, yet something in her refused to believe that entirely, would not be convinced by any amount of logical evidence. So each night she would wonder what she looked like.

She would think about owning a kitten. Uncle Percival, who ran the combined sweet shop and tobacconist and was by far the nicest Hurlingford of all, had bestowed a cheeky black kitten upon her for her eleventh birthday. But her mother had taken it from her immediately and found a man to drown it, explaining to Missy with undeniable truth that they could not afford another mouth to feed, even one so small; it was not done without compassion for her daughter's feelings, nor without regret, but nevertheless it had to be done. Missy had not protested. She had not cried, either, even in her bed. Somehow the kitten had never been real enough to trigger desperate grief. But her hands could still, all these long and vacant years later, could still remember the feel of its downy fur and the vibrating thrum of its pleasure at being held. Only her hands remembered. Every other part of her had managed to forget.

She would dream of being allowed to walk through the bush in the valley opposite Missalonghi, and this was always the waking dream that passed tranquilly into sleeping dreams she could never recall. If she wore clothes they did not hamper her, nor did they get wet when she waded cascading streams, nor did they become soiled when she brushed against mossy boulders; and they were never, never brown. Bellbirds flew chiming round her head, butterflies flickered gorgeously coloured amid canopies of giant tree-ferns that made the sky seem satin under lace; everywhere was peace, nowhere did another human soul intrude.

Lately she had begun to contemplate death, who appeared to her more and more a consummation devoutly to be wished. Death was everywhere, and visited young and in-between as often as old. Consumption, fits, croup, diphtheria, growths, pneumonia, blood-poisoning, apoplexy, heart trouble, strokes. Why then should she be exclusively preserved from his hand? Death was not an unwelcome prospect at all; he never is, to those who exist rather than live.

But this night she remained wakeful through the gamut of looks, kitten, bush walks and death, in spite of an extreme weariness resulting from that scamper home and the painful stitch in her left side she seemed to be suffering more and more. For Missy had made herself save some time to devote to the big wild stranger named John Smith who had bought her valley, or so Una said. A wind of change, a new force in Byron. She believed Una was right about him, that he did intend to take up residence down in the valley. Not her valley any more; his valley now. Eyelids nearly closed, she conjured up an image of him, tall and heavy-set and strong, that lovely luxuriant dark red hair all over scalp and jaws, and two startling white ribbons in his beard. Impossible to tell his age accurately because of his weather-beaten face, though she guessed him to be somewhere on the wrong side of forty. His eyes were the colour of water that had passed over decaying leaves, crystal-clear yet amber-brown. Oh, such a *nice* man!

And when to round out this nocturnal pilgrimage she went once more upon her bush walk, he walked with her all the way into sleep.

The poverty which ruled Missalonghi with such cruel inflexibility was the fault of the first Sir William, who had sired seven sons and nine daughters, most of whom had survived to produce further progeny. It had been Sir William's policy to distribute his worldly goods among his sons only, leaving his daughters possessed of a dowry consisting of a house on five good acres of land. On the surface it seemed a good policy, discouraging fortune-hunters whilst ensuring the girls the status of land-owners as well as a measure of independence. Nothing loath (since it meant more money for them), his sons had continued the policy, and so in their turn had their sons. Only as the decades passed, the houses became steadily less commodious, less well built, and the five good acres of land tended to become five not-so-good acres of land.

The result two generations later was that the Hurlingford connection was sharply divided into several camps; uniformly wealthy males, females who were well off due to fortunate marriages, and a group of females who had either been tricked out of their land, or forced to sell it for less than its real value, or struggled still to subsist upon it, like Drusilla Hurlingford Wright.

She had married one Eustace Wright, the consumptive heir to a large Sydney accounting firm with good interests in some manufacturing concerns as well; naturally enough, at the time of her marriage she had not suspected the consumption any more indeed than had Eustace himself. But after his death only two years later, Eustace's father, surviving him, had elected to leave his property entirely to his second son rather than divert part of it to a widow with no better heir than a sickly girlchild. So what had started as an excellent essay into matrimony ended dismally in every way. Old man Wright had taken into consideration the fact that Drusilla had her house and five acres, and came from a very wealthy clan who would be obliged to look after her, if only for appearance's sake. What old man Wright failed to take into account was the indifference of the Hurlingford clan to those of its members who were female, alone, and without power.

So Drusilla eked out an existence. She had taken in her spinster sister Octavia, who sold her own house and five acres to their brother Herbert in order to contribute cash to Drusilla's household. Therein lay the rub; it was inconceivable to sell to an outsider, yet the male Hurlingfords took gross advantage of this. The ungenerous sum Herbert gave Octavia for her property was immediately invested by him on her behalf, and, as investments masterminded by Herbert had a habit of doing, this particular one yielded absolutely nothing. The few timid enquiries Octavia had made of her brother were brushed aside at first, then treated with outraged anger and indignation.

Of course, just as it was inconceivable that any female Hurlingford should dispose of her property to an outsider, so also was it inconceivable that she should disgrace the clan by going out to work, unless work could be found for her safely within the bosom of the immediate family. Thus Drusilla, Octavia and Missy stayed at home, their utter lack of capital preventing their sanctifying work through the medium of owning a business, their utter lack of useful talents meaning the immediate family regarded them as unemployable.

Any pipe-dreams Drusilla might have harboured about Missy's growing up to snatch the ladies of Missalonghi out of penury via a spectacular marriage died before Missy turned ten; she was always homely and unprepossessing. By the time she turned twenty, her mother and her aunt had reconciled themselves to the same remorselessly straightened circumstances all the way to their respective graves. Missy in time would inherit her mother's house and five acres, but there would be none of her own to swell that, as she was a Hurlingford only on the distaff side, and therefore ineligible.

Of course they did manage to live. They had a Jersey cow which produced wonderfully rich and creamy milk as well as splendid calves, a Jersey heifer they had kept because she was superlative, half a dozen sheep, three dozen Rhode Island Red fowls, a dozen assorted ducks and geese, and two pampered white sows which farrowed the best eating-piglets in the district, as they were allowed to graze instead of being penned up, and ate the scraps from Julia's tea room besides the scraps from Missalonghi's table and vegetable garden. The vegetable garden, which was Missy's province, produced something all year round; Missy had a green thumb. There was a modest orchard too – ten apples of various kinds, a peach, a cherry, a plum, an apricot, and four pear trees. Of citrus they had none, Byron being too cold in winter. They sold their fruit and butter and eggs to Maxwell Hurlingford for a lot less than they could have got elsewhere, but it was inconceivable that they should sell their produce to any but a Hurlingford.

Food they did not lack; money was what beggared them. Prevented from earning a wage and cheated by those who by rights should have been their greatest support, they depended for the cash which meant clothing and utensils and medicines and new roofs upon sale of a sheep or a calf or a litter of piglets, and could permit of no relaxation in their eternal financial vigilance. That Missy was dearly loved by the two older women showed visibly in only one way; they let her squander her egg and butter money upon the borrowing of books.

To fill in their empty days the ladies of Missalonghi knitted and tatted and crocheted and sewed endlessly, grateful for the gifts of wools and threads and linens that came their way each Christmas and birthday, giving back some of the end results as their gifts in their turn, and stockpiling a great deal more in the spare room.

That they acquiesced so tamely to a regimen and a code inflicted upon them by people who had no idea of the loneliness, the bitter suffering of genteel poverty, was no evidence of lack of spirit or lack of courage. Simply, they were born and lived in a time before the great wars completed the industrial revolution, when paid work and its train of comforts were a treason to their concepts of life, of family, of femininity.

Her genteel poverty was never more galling to Drusilla Wright than each Saturday morning, when she came on foot into Byron and through it and out to where the most prosperous of the Hurlingford residences hunched across the flanks of the magnificent hills between the town and an arm of the Jamieson Valley. She went to have morning tea with her sister Aurelia, never forgetting as she trudged that when they were girls and engaged to be married, she, Drusilla, was considered to have made by far the better bargain in the matrimonial marketplace. And she made the pilgrimage alone, Octavia being too crippled to walk the seven miles, and the contrast between Missy and Aurelia's daughter Alicia too painful to be endured. Keeping a horse was out of the question, as horses were destructive grazers and Missalonghi's five acres had to be safeguarded against drought at all times. If they couldn't walk, the ladies of Missalonghi stayed home.

Aurelia had also married out of the family, but far more judiciously, as things turned out. Edmund Marshall was the general manager of the bottling plant, having a talent for practical administration every Hurlingford lacked. So Aurelia lived in a twenty-roomed imitation Tudor mansion set within four acres of parkland planted with prunus and rhododendron and azalea and ornamental cherry that transformed the place into a fairyland each late September and lasted for a month. Aurelia had servants, horses, carriages, even a motorcar. Her sons Ted and Randolph were apprenticed to their father in the bottling plant and showed great promise, Ted on the accounting side and Randolph as a supervisor.

Aurelia also had a daughter, a daughter who was everything Drusilla's daughter was not. The two possessed only one fact in common; they were both thirty-three-year-old spinsters. But where Missy was as she was because no one had ever dreamed of asking her to change her single status, Alicia was still single for the most glamorous and heartrending of reasons. The fiancé she had accepted in her nineteenth year was gored to death by a maddened work elephant only weeks before their wedding, and Alicia had taken her time about recovering from the blow. Montgomery Massey had been the only child of a famous family of Ceylon tea planters, and very, very rich. Alicia had mourned him in full accordance with his social significance.

For a whole year she had worn black, then for two more years she wore only dove-grey or pale lilac, these being the colours referred to as 'half-mourning'; then at twenty-two she announced the period of retirement was over by opening a millinery boutique. Her father purchased the old haberdashery shop that time and Herbert Hurlingford's clothing emporium had made redundant, and Alicia put her one genuine talent to good stead. Convention demanded that the business be placed in her mother's name, but no one, least of all her mother, was under any illusion as to whose business it was. The hat shop, called Chez Chapeau Alicia, was a resounding success from the moment it opened its doors, and drew customers from as far afield as Sydney, so delightfully attractive and flattering and fashionable were Alicia's confections in straw and tulle and silk. She employed two landless, dowerless female relations in her work room and her spinster Aunt Cornelia as her aristocratic sales dame, confining her own share of the enterprise to design and banking the profits.

Then, just when everyone had assumed that Alicia was going to wear the willow for Montgomery Massey until she too died, she announced her engagement to William Hurlingford, son and heir of the third Sir William. She was thirty-two, and her prospective bridegroom was only just nineteen. Their wedding was set for the first day of this coming October, when the spring flowers would make a garden reception *de rigeur*; the long wait would finally be over. That there had been a long wait was the fault of the third Sir William's wife, Lady Billy, who on hearing the news had attempted to flog Alicia with a horse whip. The third Sir William had been forced to forbid the couple to marry until the groom turned twenty-one.

So it was with no joy in her at all that Drusilla Wright marched up the well raked gravel drive of Mon Repos and applied the knocker to her sister's front door with a vigour born of mingled frustration and envy. The butler answered, informed Drusilla loftily that Mrs Marshall was in the small drawing room, and conducted her there imperturbably.

The interior of Mon Repos was as charmingly right as its façade and gardens; pale imported wood panellings, silk and velvet wallpapers, brocade hangings, Axminster carpets, Regency furniture, all perfectly arranged to show off the lovely proportions of the rooms to best advantage. No need to use brown paint here, where economy and prudence so patently did not reign.

The sisters kissed cheeks, more alike in every way than either of them to Octavia or Julia or Cornelia or Augusta or Antonia, for both of them possessed a certain brand of haughty frostiness, and their smiles were identical. In spite of their contrasting social circumstances they were also more fond of each other than of any of the rest; and only Drusilla's implacable pride prevented Aurelia from assisting her financially.

After the greetings were over they settled on either side of a small marquetry table in velvet-covered chairs, and waited until the maid had served them from a tray of China tea and two dozen fairy cakes before getting down to business.

'Now it's not a scrap of use being proud, Drusilla, I do know how desperately you need the money, and can you give me one good reason why all those lovely things should pile up in your spare room instead of in Alicia's glory box? You can't plead that you're saving them for Missy's glory box when we both know Missy said her last prayers years ago. Alicia wants to buy her household linens from you, and I am in full accord,' said Aurelia firmly.

'I am of course flattered,' said Drusilla stiffly, 'but I cannot *sell* them to you, Aurelia. Alicia may have whatever she wants as our gift.'

'Nonsense!' countered the lady of the manor. 'One hundred pounds, and let her take her pick.'

'She may have her pick gladly, but only as our gift.'

'One hundred pounds, or she will have to spend several times that buying her linens from Mark Foy's, for I will not permit her to take anything like as much as she needs from you as a gift.'

The argument went on for some time, but in the end poor Drusilla was obliged to give in, her outraged pride warring with a secret relief so great it finally vanquished pride. And after she had drunk three cups of fragrant Lapsang Souchong and eaten her confection-starved way through almost the entire plate of perfectly iced pink and white fairy cakes, she and her sister had passed from the awkwardness of their social disparity to the cosiness of their social consanguinity.

'Billy says he's a jailbird,' said Aurelia.

'In *Byron*? Good God, how did Billy let this happen?'

'He couldn't do a thing to prevent it, sister. You know as well as I do that it is a myth, the Hurlingfords owning every acre of land between Leura and Lawson. If the man could buy the valley, which apparently he has done, and if he has paid his debt to society, which apparently he has also done, then there is nothing Billy or anyone else can do to drive him out.'

'When did all this take place?'

'Last week, according to Billy. The valley has never been Hurlingford land, of course. Billy assumed it was Crown land – a mistaken impression dating back to the first Sir William, it seems, so no one within the family has ever thought to verify the fact, more's the pity. Had we only known, a Hurlingford would have bought it long since. Actually it has been a Master of Lunacy estate for donkey's years, and then this chap bought it at auction in Sydney last week without our even learning it was for sale. The whole valley, if you please, and *dirt* cheap! Wouldn't it? Billy is livid.'

'How did you find out about it?' asked Drusilla.

'The fellow arrived in Maxwell's shop yesterday just on closing time – Missy was there too, apparently.'

Drusilla's face cleared. 'So that's who he was!'

'Yes.'

'Maxwell found out, I take it? He could prise information out of a deaf mute.'

'Yes. Oh, the fellow wasn't at all backward, he talked about it very frankly – too frankly, in Maxwell's judgement. But you know Maxwell, he thinks any man a fool who advertises his business.'

'What I fail to understand is why anyone other than a Hurlingford would *want* to buy the valley! I mean, to own it would have significance for a Hurlingford, because it's in Byron. But he can't farm it. It would take him ten years to clear enough to put to the plough, and it's so wet down there that he couldn't keep it cleared. He can't log it because the road out is too dangerous. So why?'

'According to Maxwell, he said he just wants to live alone in the bush and listen to the silence. Well, if he isn't actually a jailbird, you must admit he's certainly a bit of an eccentric!'

'What exactly makes Billy think he's a jailbird?'

'Maxwell phoned Billy as soon as the fellow had loaded up his cart and gone. And Billy set enquiries going at once. The fellow calls himself John Smith, if you please!' Aurelia snorted derisively. 'Now I ask you, Drusilla, would anyone call himself John Smith unless there was real dirty work at the crossroads?'

'It might be his proper name,' said Drusilla fairly.

'Pooh! One is forever reading about John Smiths, but have you ever actually *met* one? Billy thinks the John Smith is an – an – what do the Americans call it?'

'I haven't the faintest idea.'

'Well, not that it matters, this isn't America. A false name, anyway. Billy's investigations have revealed that the man has no records with any official body. He paid in gold for the valley, and that's as much as can be found out.'

'Perhaps he's a lucky strike miner from Sofala or Bendigo?'

'No. Every gold field in Australia has been in company hands for years, and there have been no big finds by a private individual, Billy says.'

'How extraordinary!' said Drusilla as she absently reached for the second-last fairy cake. 'Did Maxwell or Billy have anything else to add?'

'Well, John Smith bought a very large quantity of food, and he paid in gold. Out of a big money-belt under his shirt, and he not wearing an under-garment, either! Luckily by then Missy had gone, for Maxwell swears the fellow would have pulled up his shirt just the same. He *cursed* in front of Missy, *and* he said something or other that implied Missy was no lady! With *no* provocation, I assure you!'

'I believe that,' said Drusilla dryly, taking the last fairy cake from the plate.

At which point Alicia Marshall came into the room. Her mother beamed at her proudly and her aunt gave her a wry little smile. Why oh why couldn't Missy have been like Alicia?

A truly exquisite creature, Alicia Marshall. Very tall and built on voluptuous yet disciplined lines, she was angelically fair of skin and hair and eyes, with beautiful hands and feet, and a swanlike neck. As always, she was dressed in perfect taste, and wore her ice-blue silk gown (eyelet embroidered, its shorter overskirt fashionably pointed) with incomparable flair and grace. One of her own hats, a tumbled mass of ice-blue tulle and ice-green silk roses, adorned her profusion of palest gold hair. Miraculous, that her brows and lashes were a definite, visible brown! For naturally Alicia did not tell the world that she darkened brows and lashes any more than Una did.

'Your Aunt Drusilla would be happy to provide your household linens, Alicia,' announced Aurelia triumphantly.

Alicia removed her hat and stripped off her long ice-blue kid gloves carefully, unable to answer while she concentrated on these enormously important tasks. Only when she had placed the shed articles on a table well out of harm's way and seated herself nearby did she activate her disappointingly flat and unmusical voice.

'How very kind of you, Aunt,' she said.

'Kindness does not enter into it, my dear niece, since your mother is determined to pay me,' said Drusilla stiffly. 'You had better come to Missalonghi next Saturday morning and pick out whatever you want. I shall host morning tea.'

'Thank you, Aunt.'

'Shall I order some fresh tea for you?' Aurelia asked Alicia anxiously; she was just a little bit afraid of her big, capable, ambitious and driving daughter.

'No, thank you, Mother. I really came in to see what if anything you've discovered about the stranger in our midst, as Willie insists upon calling him.' Her lovely lip curled.

So the news was given again and discussed again, after which Drusilla rose to go.

'Next Saturday morning at Missalonghi,' she adjured her relatives, giving herself into the butler's custody.

All the way home she mentally catalogued the contents of the spare room and various cupboards, terrified that the amount and variety were not going to prove sufficient for the honest sale of one hundred pounds. One hundred pounds! What a lovely windfall! Of course it must not be *spent*. It must go into the bank and begin to accrue its minuscule interest, there to reside until disaster struck. Just what disaster, Drusilla did not know; but every blind corner on life's road concealed a disaster – illnesses, property damages and repairs, increased rates and taxes, deaths. Part of it would have to pay for the new roof, certainly, but at least they would not have to sell the Jersey heifer now to pay for that; stretched into the future with numerous as yet unconceived offspring to her credit, the Jersey heifer was worth a lot more than fifty pounds to the ladies of Missalonghi. Percival Hurlingford, a kind man with a kind wife, had always allowed them the services of his very valuable Jersey bull without charge, and had besides been responsible for the gift of their original Jersey cow.

Yes, it was most satisfactory! Perhaps Alicia, a notable trendsetter, would start a fashion among the girls of the Hurlingford connection; perhaps in future other brides-to-be would come to the ladies of Missalonghi to buy their household linens. This would be condoned as an acceptably ladylike form of business venture, where simple dressmaking would never be condoned, for that would have exposed them to the whims of anyone and everyone rather than the whims of the family.

'So, Octavia,' said Drusilla to her crippled sister that night in the kitchen after they had settled to their handwork while Missy buried her head in a book, 'we had better spend next week really going through everything we have, to make sure it's fit for Aurelia and Alicia to see. Missy, you will have to cope with the house and garden and animals on your own, and since you have the lightest hand with flour, you will have to make the refreshments for morning tea. We'll have pikelets with jam and cream, a sponge, some little butterfly cakes, and a sour-apple tart cooked with cloves.'

This sorted out to Drusilla's satisfaction, she then passed to a spicier topic, the advent of John Smith. For once the conversation attracted Missy more than her book did, though she pretended to continue reading, and when she went to bed she carried this additional information with her to integrate and correlate among what Una had told her.

Why shouldn't his real name be John Smith? Of course the real basis for so much Hurlingford mistrust and suspicion was his acquisition of the valley. Well, John Smith, good for you! thought Missy. It's high time someone shook up the Hurlingfords. She fell asleep smiling.

The fuss of preparation which preceded the visit of the two Marshall ladies was largely futile, a fact of which all three Missalonghi ladies were well aware. However, none of them minded the change of pace, for it had the virtues of novelty and misrule. Only the housebound Missy felt any pangs of regret, and her pangs were due to a combination of booklessness and fear that Una would think she had defected upon payment for the novel taken out last Friday.

The delicacies Missy had taken such pains to prepare were not eaten by the ladies for whom they were intended; Alicia 'watched her figure', as she phrased it, and so too these days did her mother, who wanted to cut a figure of high fashion at her daughter's wedding. However, the goodies were not wasted upon the pigs, for later on Drusilla and Octavia gobbled them up. Though they both adored sweet things, they rarely ate them because of the additional expense.

The amount of linen displayed for Aurelia and Alicia staggered them, and after a pleasant hour spent discussing the final choices, Aurelia pressed not one but two hundred pounds into Drusilla's reluctant hand.

'No arguments, if you please!' she said, at her most imperious. 'Alicia is getting a bargain.'

'I think, Octavia,' said Drusilla later, after the visitors had driven off in their chauffeured motorcar, 'that now we can all afford new dresses for Alicia's wedding. A lilac crêpe for me, with a beaded bodice and beaded tassels around the overskirt – I have just the right beads put by! Do you remember the ones our dear mother bought to sew onto her new best half-mourning gown just before she passed away? Ideal! And I think you might purchase that powder-blue silk you so admired in Herbert's material department, don't you? Missy could tat up some lace insertions for the neck and sleeves – very smart!' Drusilla stopped to ponder, brow furrowed, looking at her dusky daughter. 'You're the really difficult one, Missy. You're too dark for pale colours, so I think it will have to be . . .'

Oh, let it not be brown! prayed Missy. I want a *scarlet* dress! A lace dress in the sort of red that makes your eyes swim when you look at it, that's what I want!

'. . . brown,' Drusilla finished at last, and sighed. 'I understand how disappointing this must be, but the truth of the matter is, Missy, that no other colour *becomes* you half so well as brown! In pastels you look sick, in black you look jaundiced, in navy you are at death's door, and the autumn tones turn you into a Red Indian.'

Missy said not a word, the logic of this being inarguable, and not knowing how much her docility pained Drusilla, who would have welcomed a suggestion at least – though of course scarlet would not have been countenanced under any circumstances. It was the colour of tarts and trollops, fully as much as brown was the colour of the respectable poor.

However, nothing could keep Drusilla's spirits oppressed for long tonight, so she cheered up again rapidly. 'In fact,' she said happily, 'I think we can all have new boots as well. Oh, what a dash we're going to cut at the wedding!'

'Shoes,' said Missy suddenly.

Drusilla looked blank. '*Shoes?*'

'Not boots, Mother, please! Let us have shoes, pretty dainty shoes with Louis heels and bows on the front.'

It is possible that Drusilla may have considered the idea, but Missy's cry from the heart was smothered immediately by Octavia, who, in her invalidish way, did quite a lot of the ruling at the house called Missalonghi.

'Living all the way out at the end of Gordon Road?' Octavia snorted. 'You're not right in the head, girl! Just how long do you think shoes would last in the dust and the mud? Boots are what we must have, good sturdy boots with good sturdy laces and good sturdy thick heels on them. Boots *last*! Shoes are not for those who must go on Shank's pony.'

And that was that.

By the Monday following the visit of Aurelia and Alicia Marshall, life had returned to normal at Missalonghi, so Missy was allowed to take her habitual walk to the lending library in Byron. Of course it wasn't all selfish pleasure; she went armed with two large shopping bags, one for either hand to balance the load, and she did the week's marketing as well.

Quiescent for the week she had stayed at home, the stitch in Missy's side came back in full force. Odd, that it only seemed to bother her on long walks. And it was painful, so wretchedly painful!

Today her own purse had joined company with her mother's, and her mother's purse was unusually fat, for Missy had been commissioned to buy the lilac crêpe and the powder-blue silk and her own brown satin at Herbert Hurlingford's clothing emporium.

Of all the shops in Byron, Missy hated Uncle Herbert's the most, for he staffed it exclusively with young men, sons or grandsons naturally; even if one were purchasing stays or underdrawers, one had to suffer the attentions of a sniggering cad who found his task exquisitely funny and his customer the embarrassed butt of his jokes. However, this sort of treatment was not meted out to everyone, only to those whose means were sufficiently pinched to make shopping in Katoomba or – God forbid! – Sydney an impossibility; it was also chiefly reserved for Hurlingford women who had no men to exact retribution. Old maids and indigent widows of the clan were uniformly regarded as fair game.

As she stood watching James Hurlingford bring down the bolts she indicated, Missy wondered what he would have done had her own brown satin been a request for scarlet lace. Not that the clothing emporium stocked such a fabric; the only reds it offered were cheap and vulgar artificial silks kept for the denizens of Caroline Lamb Place. So along with the lilac crêpe and the powder-blue silk, Missy bought a length of very beautiful delustred satin in the shade known as snuff. Had the material been any other colour she would have loved it, but since it was brown, it may as well have been jute sacking. Every dress Missy had ever owned had been brown; it was such a serviceable colour. Never showed the dirt, never went in or out of fashion, never faded, never looked cheap or common or trollopy.

'New dresses for the wedding?' asked James archly.

'Yes,' said Missy, wondering why it was that James always

succeeded in making her feel so uncomfortable; perhaps it was his exaggeratedly womanish manner?

'Let's see, now,' burbled James, 'how about a weeny game of guessies? The crêpe is for Auntie Drusie, and the silk is for Auntie Octie, and the satin – the *brown* satin – must therefore be for little brown Cousin Missy!'

Her brain must still have been filled with the image of that impossible scarlet lace dress, for quite suddenly Missy saw nothing but scarlet, and out of the recesses of her memory she dredged the only insulting phrase she knew.

'Oh, go bite your bum, James!' she snapped.

He would not have been so shocked had his wooden dress dummy come to life and kissed him, and he measured and he cut with a hitherto unknown alacrity, thereby unintentionally giving each lady an extra yard of fabric, and he couldn't get Missy out of the shop fast enough. The pity was that he knew he couldn't confide his dreadful experience to any of his brothers or nephews, because they would probably echo Missy's words, the bastards.

The library was only two doors down, so when Missy went in she was still flying the flags of her anger in her cheeks, and she banged the door after her.

Una looked up, startled, and began to laugh. 'Darling, you look absolutely splendid! In a paddy, are we?'

Missy took a couple of deep breaths to calm down. 'Oh, just my cousin James Hurlingford. I told him to go bite his bum.'

'Good for you! Time someone told him.' Una giggled. 'Though I imagine he'd much rather someone else bit it for him – preferably someone masculine.'

This sailed straight over Missy's head, but Una's burst of merriment did the trick, and Missy found herself able to laugh too. 'Dear oh dear, it wasn't very ladylike of me, was it?' she asked, sounding more surprised than horrified. 'I don't know what came over me!'

The radiant face turned up to her looked suddenly sly, not the slyness of dishonesty but the slyness of someone fey, away with the fairies. 'Straws and camels,' intoned Una in a singsong voice, 'eyes of needles and days of dogs, revolving worms and well reaped whirlwinds. There's a lot in you, Missy Wright, that you don't even know is there.' She sat back and hummed like a gleeful naughty child. 'But it's started now, and it can't be stopped.'

Out came the story of the scarlet lace dress, the terrible longing to wear something other than brown, the defeat of having to admit no other colour than brown suited her, so that on this glorious day when she might actually have attained a dress in some other colour, still she must wear brown. Her feyness quite vanished, Una listened sympathetically, and when Missy had got it all out of her system, she looked her up and down deliberately.

'Scarlet *would* suit you beautifully,' she said. 'Oh, what a pity! Still, never mind, never mind.' And she changed the subject. 'I've saved another new novel for you – two pages into it, and I promise you won't even remember your red dress. It's all about a drab young woman who is utterly downtrodden by her family until the day she finds out she's dying of heart trouble. There's this chap she's been in love with for years, only of course he's engaged to someone else. So she takes the letter from the heart specialist telling her she's going to die to this young man, and she begs him to marry her rather than the other girl, because she's only got six months to live and after she's dead he can marry the other girl anyway. He's a bit of a wastrel, but he's just waiting for someone to reform him, only he doesn't know that, naturally. Anyway, he agrees to marry her. And they have six heavenly months together. He finds out that under her drab exterior she's an entrancing person, and her love for him reforms him completely. Then one day when the sun is shining and the birds are singing, she dies in his arms – I love books where people die in each other's arms, don't you? – and his old fiancée comes round to see him after the funeral because she got a letter from his dead wife explaining why he jilted her. And his old fiancée says she forgives him and she'll marry him the minute he's out of mourning. But he jumps up, wild with grief, rushes to the river and throws himself in, calling out his dead wife's name. And then his old fiancée throws herself in the river, calling out his name. Oh, Missy, it's so sad! I cried for days.'

'I'll take it,' said Missy instantly, paid up all her debts, which made her feel a lot better, and tucked *The Troubled Heart* into the bottom of one of her shopping bags.

'I'll see you next Monday,' said Una, and went to the door to wave at her until she disappeared from sight.

As long as she walked it on her own, the five miles from Byron's shops to Missalonghi never seemed half so much. For as she walked, she dreamed, fantasising herself into roles and events and characters far beyond her real ken. Until Una had come to the library these characters had all looked exactly like Alicia, and the antics they got up to revolved around hat shops or dress shops or tea rooms of awesome gentility, and the men in their lives were a composite Hurlingford beau ideal, Siegfrieds in boots, bowlers, and three-piece suits. Nowadays her imagination had better grist to work on, and whatever character she played through whatever adventure it might be bore far more resemblance to the latest novel Una had smuggled her than to any aspect of Byron life.

So for the first half of her walk home that Monday, Missy metamorphosised herself into a divinely beautiful strawberry blonde with amazing lime-green eyes; she had two men in love with her, a duke (fair and handsome), and an Indian prince (dark and handsome). In this guise she shot tigers down from the howdahs of richly caparisoned elephants without assistance, she led an army of her husband's subjects against Muslim marauders without assistance, she built schools and hospitals and mothers' institutes without assistance, while her two lovers drifted vaguely in the background rather like the little male spider consorts not permitted into the wife's parlour.

But halfway home, where Gordon Road branched off from the long straggle of Noel Street, began her valley. At this point Missy always stopped daydreaming and looked about her instead. It was a beautiful day, as late winter days on the Blue Mountains can be when the wind takes time off to rest. Answering the lure of the valley, she crossed to the far side of Gordon Road and lifted her face to the kindly sky and swelled her nostrils to take in the heady tang of the bush.

No one had ever produced a name for the valley, though from now on it would in the way of Byron folk come to be known as John Smith's Valley, no doubt. Compared to the Jamieson Valley or the Grose Valley or even the Megalong Valley it was not very big, but it was perfect, a bowl some fifteen hundred feet lower than the three thousand foot ridge upon which Byron and all the other towns of the Blue Mountains were built. In shape it was a symmetrical oval, one narrow curving end lying just beyond the place where Gordon Road petered out and the far end some five miles away to the east, where its otherwise uninterrupted wall was dramatically broken by a chasm through which flowed its nameless river on its way to join the Nepean-Hawkesbury system of the coastal plain. All the way round the margin was a stunning drop of dull orange sandstone cliff a thousand feet high, and below this sheer precipice a tree-covered skirt of fallen rock curved down to the course of the river which had made the valley aeons before. And the valley was, looking across it, stuffed with lush native forest, a blue ocean of gums that sighed and whispered ceaselessly.

On winter mornings the valley was filled with brilliant white cloud that sat like turning milk below the level of the cliff tops, and suddenly as the sun increased in warmth it would lift up in a moment and vanish. Sometimes the cloud would come down from above, fingers seeking out the tree tops far below until it succeeded in covering them from sight under a spectral blanket. And as sunset approached, winter and summer, the cliffs began to take on deeper, richer colour, glowering rose-red, then crimson, and finally the purple that faded into night's mysterious indigo. Most wonderful of all was the rare snow, when all the crags and outcrops of the cliffs were picked out in white, and the moving leafy trees shook off their powdering of icy moisture as fast as it fell upon them, unwilling to accept a touch so alien.

The only way down to the valley's floor was a terrifyingly steep track just wide enough for a large wagon, a track that emerged onto the top of the rim just beyond the end of Gordon Road. Fifty years earlier, someone had made the track in order to plunder the rainforest below of its massive cedars and turpentines, but after a whole team of eighty oxen, their driver, two loggers and a dray bearing a mighty tree trunk had gone over the edge, the plundering had ceased abruptly. There were easier forests to log. And gradually the track had been forgotten, as indeed had the valley; visitors preferred to go south to the Jamieson than north to this less awesome cousin, bereft as it was of kiosks and properly landscaped lookouts.

That wretched stitch came back just as Missy rounded the corner not far from Missalonghi, and ten seconds later the pain struck at her chest like a blow from an axe. She faltered and dropped her loaded shopping bags, her arms flying up to pluck at this terrifying agony; then she saw the neat hedge of Missalonghi through her terror, and ran for home. At precisely the same moment John Smith rounded the corner from its other side, striding along with his head down in thought.

Only ten yards short of the gate in the hedge, she pitched headlong. No one inside Missalonghi saw, for it was about five o'clock, and the rolling chords of Drusilla's organ were erupting into the outside air like a suffocating fall of hot volcanic ash.

But John Smith saw, and came running. His first thought was that the odd little soul had tripped after bolting to escape meeting him, but when he knelt and turned her face upwards, one look at her grey skin and sweat-soaked hair told him differently. He half-sat her against his thigh, rubbing her back helplessly, wishing he knew of some way to force air into her lungs. That much knowledge he had, not to lie her flat on the ground, yet farther than that his knowledge did not extend. She put up her hands to clutch at his arm where it lay lightly across the front of her shoulders, supporting her; the whole of her body was heaving with the fight to breathe, and her eyes were turned up to his, silently beseeching him for an aid he was incapable of giving. Caught mesmerised, watching the extraordinary cavalcade of an inner horror and bewilderment and pain pass through those eyes, he began to think she was going to die.

Then with startling swiftness the grey colour faded, a warmer and healthier tinge crept into her skin, and her hands relaxed on his arm.

'Please!' she gasped, struggling to rise.

He got to his feet at once, slipped one arm under her legs and scooped her up. Though he had no idea where she lived, there must surely be some assistance in the dingy house behind the hedge, so he carried her through the gate and down the path, calling for help at the top of his voice and praying he would be heard above the bellowing of the organ.

Apparently he was heard, for two ladies came out of the house immediately, both unknown to him. There was no nonsense about them, which he appreciated deeply; one pointed wordlessly to the front door, while the other slipped around ahead of him and ushered him into the parlour with his burden.

'Brandy,' said Drusilla curtly, bending to loosen her daughter's clothes. She wore no stays, having no need of them, but her dress was tightly belted and high to the neck.

'Do you have a telephone?' asked John Smith.

'I'm afraid not.'

'Then if you give me directions, I'll go for the doctor right now.'

'The corner of Byron and Noel, Dr Neville Hurlingford,' said Drusilla. 'Tell him it's Missy – she's my daughter.'

He went immediately, leaving Drusilla and Octavia to administer the brandy every prudent household kept in the sauce cupboard in case of heart trouble.

Chapman

By the time Dr Neville Hurlingford arrived some sixty minutes later, Missy had almost fully recovered. John Smith did not return with him.

'Very puzzling,' said Dr Hurlingford to Drusilla in the kitchen; Octavia was helping Missy into bed.

The experience had shaken Drusilla badly, used to assuming that everyone she knew enjoyed the same rude health she did herself; Octavia's bones were such old friends they didn't really count. So soberly and quietly she made a pot of tea, and drank from her own cup more gratefully than Dr Hurlingford did from his.

'Did Mr Smith tell you what happened?' she asked.

'I must say, Drusilla, that in spite of the tall stories going around at the moment, Mr Smith seems to me to be a good fellow – a sensible and practical man. According to him, she grabbed at her chest, ran across the road in a panic, and collapsed. She was grey and sweating and having great trouble breathing. The attack lasted about two minutes, and her recovery was quite sudden. Her colour came back, so did her breath. That was when Mr Smith brought her inside, I gather. I could find nothing wrong with her a minute ago, but I may find more when I do a proper examination once she's in bed.'

'There's no heart trouble in our branch of the family, as you know,' said Drusilla, feeling betrayed.

'She takes after her father's family in the rest of her bodily makeup, Drusilla, so she may have inherited a bad heart from that side too. She has had no other attack like it?'

'Not that we know of,' said Drusilla, properly rebuked. '*Is* it her heart?'

'I honestly don't know. It's possible.' But he sounded doubtful. 'I'll go in and see her again now, I think.'

Missy was lying in her narrow little bed with her eyes closed, but the moment she heard Dr Hurlingford's unfamiliar step she opened them and looked at him, then unaccountably seemed disappointed.

'Well now, Missy,' he said, sitting gingerly alongside her. 'What happened, eh?'

Drusilla and Octavia hovered in the background; he would dearly have liked to dismiss them, sensing that their presence inhibited Missy, but decency and convention forbade it. In all of Missy's life he had only seen her two or three times, so he knew only the little about her that everyone knew; she was the sole dark Hurlingford in history, and she had been doomed to spinsterhood before she was into her teens.

'I don't know what happened,' lied Missy.

'Come now, you must remember something.'

'I got short of breath and fainted, I suppose.'

'That's not what Mr Smith says.'

'Then Mr Smith is wrong – where is he? Is he here?'

'Did you experience any pain?' pressed Dr Hurlingford, not satisfied, and not bothering to answer Missy's question.

A ghastly vision of herself reduced to the status of a chronic invalid at Missalonghi rose up in front of Missy's mind; the awful additional monetary burden she would become, the guilt she would in consequence feel every day of her bedbound life, the impossibility of ever getting away on her own to walk past her valley into Byron and the library – no, it could not be borne!

'I had no pain at all,' she insisted.

Dr Hurlingford looked as if he didn't believe her, but for a Hurlingford he was fairly perceptive, and he too knew what sort of life Missy would lead from the moment she was diagnosed a case of heart trouble. So he forebore to press the poor girl further, merely got out his old-fashioned funnel-shaped stethoscope and listened to her heart, which was beating quite normally, and to her lungs, which were clear.

'Today is Monday. You had better come and see me on Friday,' he said as he rose. He patted Missy reassuringly on top of her head and then walked into the hall, where Drusilla lurked in wait. 'I can't find anything wrong,' he said to her. 'Lord knows what happened, I don't! But mind she sees me on Friday, now, and if anything else happens in the meantime, send for me at once.'

'No medicine?'

'My dear Drusilla, how can I prescribe medicine for a mystery illness? She's as skinny as a wormy cow, but she seems healthy enough. Just leave her alone, let her sleep, and give her plenty of good nourishing food'

'Should she stay in bed until Friday?'

'I don't think so. Let her stay in bed tonight, but let her get up tomorrow. Provided she only does light duties, I can see no harm in her leading a normal and active life.'

With that Drusilla had to be satisfied. She ushered her uncle the doctor out, tiptoed across the hall to the door of Missy's room and peeped in, saw that Missy was asleep, and so retreated to the kitchen, where Octavia was sitting at the table polishing off the last of the doctor's pot of tea.

Actually Octavia looked very shaken; the hands that both were needed to lift her cup to her lips trembled badly.

'Uncle Neville doesn't seem to think it's serious,' said Drusilla, sitting down heavily. 'Missy is to stay in bed for what's left of this evening, but she can get up tomorrow and move around, though only light duties until Uncle sees her again on Friday.'

'Oh, dear!' A large pale tear rolled down Octavia's large pale cheek as she looked down at her gnarled fingers. 'I will try in the garden, Drusilla, but I really cannot milk the cow!'

'I'll milk,' said Drusilla. She put her hand to her head and sighed. 'Don't worry, sister, we'll manage somehow.'

The disaster! Drusilla saw her precious two hundred pounds frittering itself away on a series of doctors and hospitals and treatments, none of which would she grudge for a moment; what depressed her was the disappearance of her tail just when she thought she had caught up with it at last. If she had not already cut out the lilac crêpe and the powder-blue silk and the snuff-brown satin, back they would have gone to Herbert's emporium on the morrow. *Wouldn't* it?

At dinner time Drusilla brought Missy a huge bowl of beef-and-barley broth and sat by the bed until Missy managed to struggle through it; but after that she was left mercifully alone. The long sleep of the earlier part of the evening had left her wakeful, though, so she settled to think. About the pain and what it might mean. About John Smith. About the future. Between the pain and the future, two deserts of appalling dreariness, John Smith stood lit up and glorious. So she abandoned all thought of pain or future, and concentrated upon John Smith.

Such a nice man! Interesting too. How easily he had lifted her off the ground and carried her inside. The recent avalanche of second-hand knowledge Una's smuggled novels had tipped on top of her was suddenly of genuine benefit; Missy understood that she was in love at last. But hope was not present at all in the sweet and smiling train of thought this realisation of love triggered. The Alicias of this world might scheme and plot to attain their ends, but the Missys could not. The Missys didn't know enough about men, and the smidgin they did know lay in the realm of generality. All men were untouchables, even jailbirds. All men had choices. All men had power. All men were free. All men were privileged. And presumably jailbirds had more of everything than men like poor Little Willie Hurlingford, sheltered as he had been from every adverse wind that might have blown a little stiffening into him. Not that she believed John Smith was really a jailbird; Una had known him during her years in Sydney, and presumably that meant he had moved at least on the fringes of the highest society – unless of course despite his friendship with Una's husband he had delivered the ice, or the bread, or the coal.

Oh, but he had been nice to her! Nice to a nonentity like Missy Wright. Even through that hideous and frightening pain she had been conscious of his presence, felt too some strange passage of strength from him to her that had, she fancied, tossed death aside like so much chaff.

John Smith, she thought, if I were only young and pretty, you would stand no more chance of escaping me than poor Little Willie did Alicia! I would chase you remorselessly until I caught you. Wherever you went, there I would be, with my best foot forward to trip you up. And once I had you in my toils, I would love you so much and so well that you would never, never want to get away from me.

John Smith came in person the next day to enquire after Missy, but Drusilla dealt with him at the front door and did not permit him sight or sound of Missy. It was merely a courtesy call, as Drusilla perfectly understood, so she thanked him nicely but not profusely and then stood watching as he strode off down the path to the gate with his hands swinging loosely and his lips whistling a saucy tune.

'Fancy that!' said Octavia, coming out of the parlour, where she had been hiding to watch John Smith through a lifted curtain edge. 'Are you going to tell Missy he called?'

'Why?' asked Drusilla, surprised.

'Oh, well . . .'

'My dear Octavia, you sound as if you've been reading those penny dreadful romances Missy's been bringing home from the library recently!'

'*Has* she?'

Drusilla laughed. 'You know, until I realised what a dither she was in trying to hide the covers of her books, I'd forgotten all about our original rule as to the kind of books she might read. After all, it was fifteen years ago! And I thought, why should the poor little wretch not read romances if she wants? What has she to enjoy the way I enjoy my music?'

Nobly Drusilla refrained from adding that Octavia had her rheumatics to enjoy, and Octavia, who might under different circumstances have implied aloud how bereft she herself was of things to enjoy, wisely decided to leave the subject of enjoyment alone.

'Aren't you going to tell her she may read romances?' Octavia asked instead.

'Certainly not! If I did that, it would remove most of her pleasure, you know. Pure freedom to read them would only give her sufficient detachment to see how dreadful they are.' Drusilla frowned. 'What intrigues me is how Missy managed to persuade Livilla of all people to let her borrow them. But I can't ask Livilla without letting the cat out of the bag, and I wouldn't spoil Missy's fun for the world. I see it as a wee bit of defiance, and that gives me hope that there's some starch in Missy's backbone after all.'

Octavia sniffed. 'I can't see anything laudable about a sort of defiance that necessitates her becoming *underhanded*!'

A small sound halfway between a growl and a mew escaped Drusilla's lips, but then she smiled, shrugged, and led the way into the kitchen.

Drusilla accompanied Missy to the doctor the following Friday morning. They went off on foot in good time, warmly clad – naturally – in brown.

The surgery waiting room, dim and fusty, was empty. Mrs Neville Hurlingford, who did service as her husband's nurse, ushered them into it with a cheery word for Drusilla and a rather blank stare for Missy. A moment later, the doctor poked his head round his consulting room door.

'Come in, Missy. No, Drusilla, you can stay there and talk to your aunt.'

Missy went in, sat down, and waited warily, her guard up.

He commenced with a frontal attack. 'I do not believe you were merely short of breath,' he said. 'There had to be pain, and I want to hear all about it, and no nonsense.'

Missy gave in, told him about the stitch in her left side, the way it only bothered her on long walks if she hurried, and the way it had ushered in that sudden, terrifying onslaught of severe pain and breathlessness.

So he examined her again, and afterwards sighed. 'I can find absolutely nothing the matter with you,' he said. 'When I examined you last Monday there were no residual signs to indicate heart trouble, and today is the same. However, from what Mr Smith told me, you certainly did have some sort of genuine turn. So, just to make sure, I'm going to send you to a specialist in Sydney. If I can arrange an appointment, would you like to go down with Alicia on her weekly Tuesday trip to the city? It would save your mother having to go.'

Was there an understanding twinkle in his eyes? Missy wasn't sure, but she looked at him gratefully all the same. 'Thank you, I'd like to go with Alicia.'

In fact, Friday was a very good day, for in the afternoon Una drove up to Missalonghi in Livilla's horse and sulky, and she had half a dozen novels with her, discreetly wrapped in plain brown paper.

'I didn't even know you were ill until Mrs Neville Hurlingford told me this morning in the library,' she said, sitting down in the best parlour, to which Octavia had ushered her, dazzled by her elegance and composure.

Neither Drusilla nor Octavia offered to let the two young women talk alone, not because they were consciously spoilsporting, but because they were always starved for company, especially when the company took the form of a brand new face. Such a lovely face too! Not beautiful like Alicia, yet – disloyal though the thought was, they fancied Una was perhaps the more alluring of the two. Her arrival pleased Drusilla particularly, since it answered the vexed question as to how Missy was suddenly managing to borrow novels.

'Thank you for the books,' said Missy, smiling at her friend. 'The one I brought home last Monday is nearly worn out.'

'Did you enjoy it?' asked Una.

'Oh, very much!' As indeed she had; its dying heroine with her dicky heart could not have come at a more appropriate moment. Admittedly the heroine actually had managed to die in her beloved's arms, but she, Missy, had had the good fortune merely *almost* to die in her beloved's arms.

Una's manners were perfect. By the time she had partaken of a cup of tea and some plain home-made biscuits, she had won Drusilla and Octavia over completely. To have no better fare to offer was humiliating, but Una's appreciation turned the despised biscuits into an inspired guess as to what the visitor really liked and wanted.

'Oh, I get so tired of cream cakes and asparagus rolls!' she exclaimed, smiling with dazzling effect at her hostesses. 'How clever of you, and how considerate! These little biscuits are delicious, and *so* much better for my digestion! Most Byron ladies swamp one in oceans of jam and cream, and as a guest it is of course impossible to refuse refreshments without offending.'

'What a lovely person,' said Drusilla after Una had gone.

'Delightful,' agreed Octavia.

'She may come again,' said Drusilla to Missy.

'Any time,' said Octavia, who had made the biscuits.

On Sunday afternoon Missy announced that she didn't care to read, she was going for a walk in the bush instead. So calm and decided was her tone that for a moment her mother just stared at her, at a loss.

'A walk?' she asked at last. 'In the *bush*? Most definitely not! You don't know who you might meet.'

'I won't meet anyone,' said Missy patiently. 'There has never been any kind of prowler or molester of women in Byron.'

Octavia pounced. 'How do you know there's never been a prowler, madam? It's that ounce of prevention, and never do you forget it! If a prowler is prowling hereabouts, he never finds anyone to molest, because we Hurlingfords keep our girls safe at home, which is where you ought to be.'

'If you are set on the idea, then I suppose I must come with you,' said Drusilla in the tones of a martyr.

Missy laughed. 'Oh, Mother! Come with me when you're so engrossed in your beading? No, I'm going on my own, and that's final.'

She walked out of the house wearing neither overcoat nor scarf to protect her from the wind.

Drusilla and Octavia looked at each other.

'I hope her brain's not affected,' said Octavia dolefully.

So secretly did Drusilla, but aloud she said stoutly, 'At least you can't call this bit of defiance *underhanded*!'

In the meantime Missy had let herself out of the front gate and turned left instead of right, down to where Gordon Road dwindled to two faint wheelmarks meandering into the heart of the bush.

A glance behind her revealed that no one was following; Missalonghi's squat ugliness sat with front door firmly closed.

It was a still clear day and the sun was very warm, even filtering through the trees. Up here on top of the ridge the bush was not thick, for the soil was scanty and whatever did grow mostly had to scrabble for an unloving hold on the sandstone substrate. So the eucalypts and angophoras were short, stunted, and the undergrowth sparse. Spring had arrived; even high up in the Blue Mountains it came early, and two or three warmish days were sufficient to bring the first wattle popping out into a drift of tiny fluffy yellow balls.

The valley went on to her right, glimpsed through the trees; where was John Smith's house, if house he had? Her mother's Saturday morning visit to Aunt Aurelia's yesterday had elicited no further information about John Smith, save a wild rumour that he had engaged a firm of Sydney builders to erect him a huge mansion at the bottom of the cliffs, made out of sandstone quarried on the spot. But Missalonghi could offer no evidence to support this, and Missalonghi sat plump on the only route such builders would have to use. Besides which, Aunt Aurelia apparently had more important worries than John Smith; it seemed the upper echelons of the Byron Bottle Company were becoming extremely alarmed about some mysterious movements in shares.

Missy had no expectation of meeting John Smith on top of the ridge, as it was Sunday, so she decided to find out where his road went over the edge of the valley. When at last she stumbled upon the spot she could see the logic behind the site, for a gargantuan landslide had strewn boulders and rocks in a kind of ramp from top to bottom of the cliff, thus decreasing the sheerness of the drop. Standing at the commencement of the track, she could just glimpse it twisting back and forth across the landslide in a series of zigzags; a perilous descent, yes, but not an impossible one for a cart like John Smith's.

However, she was far too timid to venture down, not from fear of falling but from fear of walking into John Smith's lair. Instead, she struck off into the bush on top of the ridge along a narrow path that might have been made by animals going to water. And sure enough, as time went by a sound of running water gradually overpowered the omnipresent sound of the trees talking in that faint, plaintive, fatigued speech gum trees produce on calm days. Louder and louder was the water, until it became a bewildering roar; then when she came upon the stream, it offered her no answer, for though it was quite deep and wide, it was sliding along between its ferny banks without a flurry. Yet the roar of rushing water persisted.

She turned to the right and followed the river, inside her dream of enchantment at last. The sun glanced off the surface of the water in a thousand thousand sparks of light, and the ferns dripped tiny droplets, and dragonflies hovered with rainbow-mica wings, and brilliant parrots wheeled from the trees of one bank to the trees of the other.

Suddenly the river vanished. It just fell away into nothing, a smoothly curving edge. Gasping, Missy drew back quickly, understanding the roar. She had come to the very head of the valley, and the stream which had cut it was entering it in the only way possible, by going down, down, down. Working cautiously along the brink for a good quarter of a mile, she came to a place where a great rock jutted far out over the cliff. And there, right on its end, legs dangling into nothingness, she sat to watch the waterfall in awe. Its bottom she could not discover, only the beautiful untidy tangle of its flight through the windy air, and a rainbow against a mossy place on the cliff behind it, and a chilly moistness that it exhaled as it fell, like a cry for help.

Several hours slipped away as easily as the water. The sun left that part of the ridge. She began to shiver; time to go home to Missalonghi.

And then where her path joined the road leading down into John Smith's valley, Missy met John Smith himself. He was driving his cart from the direction of Byron, and she saw with surprise that the cart was laden with tools and crates and sacks and iron machinery. Somewhere was a shop open on Sunday!

He pulled up at once and jumped down, smiling broadly. 'Hello!' he said. 'Feeling better?'

'Yes, thank you.'

'I'm glad to catch you like this, because I was beginning to wonder if you were still in the land of the living. Your mother assured me you were when I called, but she wouldn't let me see for myself.'

'You came to see how I was?'

'Yes, last Tuesday.'

'Oh, thank you for that!' she said with fervour.

His brows rose, but he didn't attempt to quiz her. Instead, he left his conveyance where it was, and turned to walk back with her towards Missalonghi.

'I take it there was nothing serious wrong?' he asked after some minutes during which they just paced along together without speaking.

'I don't know,' said Missy, recognising the emanations of pity and sympathy his obviously healthy being was giving off. 'I have to see a doctor in Sydney quite urgently. A *heart* specialist, I believe.' Now why did she say it like that?

'Oh,' he said, at a loss.

'Whereabouts exactly do you live, Mr Smith?' she asked, to change the subject.

'Well, further around in the direction you've just come from is a waterfall,' he said, not at all reticently, and in a tone of voice which told Missy that, whether because of her sickly condition or because maybe she was so manifestly harmless, he had decided she could be counted a friend. 'There's an old logger's hut near the bottom of the waterfall, and I'm camping in that for the time being. But I'm starting to build a house a bit closer to the waterfall itself – out of sandstone blocks I'm quarrying on the site. I've just been down to Sydney to pick up an engine to drive a big saw. That way I can cut my blocks a lot faster and better, and mill my own timber too.'

She closed her eyes and heaved a big unconscious sigh. 'Oh, how I envy you!'

He stared down at her curiously. 'That's an odd thing for a woman to say.'

Missy opened her eyes. 'Is it?'

'Women usually don't like being cut off from shops and houses and other women.' His tone was hard.

'You're probably right for the most part,' she said thoughtfully, 'but in that sense I don't really count as a woman, so I envy you. The peace, the freedom, the isolation – I dream of them!'

The end of the track came into sight, and so did the faded red corrugated iron roof of Missalonghi.

'Do you do all your shopping in Sydney?' she asked, for something to say, then chastised herself for asking a silly question; hadn't she met him first in Uncle Maxwell's?

'I do when I can,' he said, obviously not connecting her with Uncle Maxwell's, 'but it's a long haul up the Mountains with a full load, and I've got only this one team of horses. Still, Sydney's definitely preferable to shopping in Byron – I've never encountered a place so full of Nosey Parkers.'

Missy grinned. 'Try not to blame them too much, Mr Smith. Not only are you a novelty, but you've also stolen what they have always regarded as their exclusive property, even if they never thought about it, or wanted it.'

He burst out laughing, evidently tickled that she should bring the matter up. 'My valley, you mean? They could have bought it, the sale wasn't secret – it was advertised in the Sydney papers and in the Katoomba paper. But they're just not as smart as they think they are, that's all.'

'You must feel like a king down there.'

'I do, Miss Wright.' And he smiled at her, tipped his battered bushman's hat, turned and walked away.

Missy floated the rest of the way home, in perfect time to milk the cow. Neither Drusilla nor Octavia made reference to her bush walk, Drusilla because she had been more pleased at the display of independence than worried about the outcome, and Octavia because she had convinced herself Missy's cerebral processes were being affected by whatever ailed her.

In fact, when by four o'clock there had been no sign of Missy, the two ladies left at Missalonghi had had a small tiff. Octavia thought it was time to inform the police.

'No, no, no!' said Drusilla, quite violently.

'But we must, Drusilla. Her brain's affected, I know it is. When in her whole life has she ever behaved this way?'

'I have been thinking ever since Missy had her turn, sister, and I'm not ashamed to say that when Mr Smith carried her in, I was terrified. The thought of losing her to such an unfair, unjust thing – I was never more glad than when Uncle Neville told me he didn't think it was serious. And then I began to wonder what would happen to Missy had it been me? Octavia, we must *encourage* Missy to be independent of us! It is not her fault that God did not endow her with Alicia's looks, or my strength of character. And I began to see that a whole lifetime's exposure to my strength of character has not been good for Missy. I make the decisions about everything, and it is her nature to acquiesce without a fuss. So for far too long I have gone on making her decisions. I shall do so no longer.'

'Rubbish!' snapped Octavia. 'The girl's got no sense! Shoes

instead of boots! Romances! Bush walks! It is my opinion that you must be more severe in future, not less.'

Drusilla sighed. 'When we were young women, Octavia, we wore shoes. Father was a very warm man, we lacked for nothing. We rode in carriages, we had plenty of pin-money. And ever since those days, no matter how hard life has been, at least you and I are able to look back and remember the pleasure of pretty shoes, pretty dresses, coming-out parties, *gaiety*. Where Missy has never worn a pair of pretty shoes, or a pretty dress. I'm not castigating myself for that, for it isn't my fault, but when I thought she might be going to die – well, I decided I was going to give her whatever she wanted, so long as I could afford it. Shoes I cannot afford, especially if there are going to be heavy doctor's bills. But if she wants to walk in the bush, or read romances – she may.'

'Rubbish, rubbish, rubbish! You must go on as you have in the past. Missy needs strong direction.'

And from that viewpoint Drusilla could not budge her.

Unaware of her mother's soul-searching, Missy decided she had better not read one of the new novels after dinner; she elected to tat instead.

'Aunt Octavia,' she said, fingers flying, 'how much lace do you plan to set into your new dress? Is this going to be enough, do you think? I can easily make you a lot more, but I'll need to know now.'

Octavia held out her knobby hand and Missy deposited the bunched-up lace in it, leaving her aunt to spread out each piece on her lap.

'Oh, Missy, it is beautiful!' breathed Octavia, awed. 'Drusilla, do look!'

Drusilla plucked a scrap out of her sister's lap and held it up to the weak light. 'Yes, it is beautiful. You're improving all the time, Missy, I must say.'

'Ah,' said Missy gravely, 'that is because I have finally learned to unknit the sleeve of ravelled care.'

Both older ladies looked utterly blank for a moment, then Octavia cast a significant glance at Drusilla and ever so slightly shook her head. But Drusilla ignored her.

'Quite so,' she said majestically.

Cutting a dash at Alicia's wedding won out; Octavia put Missy's brain storm aside. 'Is it enough lace, Drusilla?' she asked anxiously.

'Well, for what I had originally planned it's enough, but I've had a better idea. I'd like to let in some of the same lace all the way around the hem of the overskirt – *so* fashionable! Missy, would you mind doing so much extra work? Do be frank if you'd rather not.'

Now Missy looked blank; in all her life her mother had never deferred to her before, nor stopped to think whether what she asked was excessive. Of course! It was the heart trouble! How amazing! 'I don't mind in the least,' she said quickly.

Octavia beamed. 'Oh, thank you!' Her face puckered. 'If only I might help you with the sewing, Drusilla. It's so much work for you.'

Drusilla looked at the heap of lilac crêpe in her lap and sighed. 'Don't worry, Octavia. Missy does all the fiddly bits like buttonholes and hems and plackets. But I do admit it would be wonderful to have a Singer sewing machine.'

That of course was out of the question; the ladies of Missalonghi made their clothes the old-fashioned hard way, every inch of every seam sewn by hand. Drusilla did the main sewing and the cutting, Missy the fiddly bits; Octavia could not manage to hold an instrument so fine as a sewing needle.

'I am so very sorry your dress has to be brown, Missy,' said Drusilla, and looked at her daughter pleadingly. 'But it is lovely material, and it will make up very well, you wait and see. Would you like some beads on it?'

'And spoil the cut? Mother, you cut superbly, and the cut will carry it without any adornments,' said Missy.

That night in bed Missy lay in the darkness and remembered the details of the loveliest afternoon of her entire life. For not only had he said hello to her, he had climbed down from his cart and actually chosen to walk along with her, chatting to her as if she was a friend rather than a mere member of that tiresome gang called Hurlingford. How nice he had looked. Homespun, but nice. And he smelled not of stale sweat, like so many of the oh-so-respectable Hurlingford men, but of sweet expensive soap; she had recognised it immediately because whenever the ladies of Missalonghi received rare gifts of such soap, it was not consumed upon their bodies (Sunlight was quite good enough for that!), but inserted between the folds of their clothes as they lay in drawers. And his hands might be toil-roughened, but they were clean, even beneath the nails. His hair too was immaculate; no trace of pomade or oil, just the healthy gloss one saw on the fur of a freshly licked cat. A prideful and scrupulous man, John Smith.

Best of all she liked his eyes, such a translucent golden brown, and so laughing. But she couldn't, *wouldn't* believe any of the tales hinting at dishonesty or baseness. Instead, she would have staked her life upon his intrinsic integrity and fiercely defended ethics. She could see such a man doing murder, perhaps, if goaded beyond endurance, but she could not see him stealing or cheating.

Oh, John Smith, I do love you! And I thank you from the very bottom of my heart for coming back to Missalonghi to see how I did.

With only a month left until her wedding, Alicia Marshall came day by day closer to the most perfect manifestation of her long and glorious blossoming, and she meant to enjoy even that final frantic month to the top of her bent. The date had been set eighteen months previously, and it had never occurred to her to doubt the season or the weather. Sure enough, though occasionally springs on the Blue Mountains might be late, or wet, or unduly windy, this one, obedient to Alicia's whim, was coming in with the halcyon dreaminess of Eden.

'It wouldn't dare do otherwise,' said Aurelia to Drusilla, a nuance in her tone suggesting that just once Alicia's mother might enjoy Alicia's plans going awry.

Missy's Sydney appointment had been set up, but a week later than had been hoped; which was lucky for Missy, because on the Tuesday that Dr Hurlingford had planned she should see the specialist, Alicia did not make her customary weekly trip to town. For on the Thursday of this week Alicia had scheduled her bridal party, and the preparations for it allowed of no other consideration, even hat shop business. The bridal party was not a humble sort of affair where modest kitchen gifts and girlish chatter prevailed; it was instead a formal reception for Alicia's female relatives of all ages, an occasion upon which everyone would have an opportunity to see and hear what would be expected of them on the Great Day. During the course of the festivities Alicia intended to announce the names of her bridesmaids, and show the designs and fabrics for the bridal party and the church décor.

The only blight came from Alicia's father and brothers, who

brushed aside her attempts to enlist their help with a brusque impatience hitherto unknown.

'Oh, for God's sake, Alicia, go away!' snapped her father, more passion in his voice than she certainly could ever remember. 'Have your wretched bridal party, by all means, but leave us out of it! There are times when women's affairs are a flaming nuisance, and this is one of them!'

'Well!' huffed Alicia, staylaces creaking dangerously, and went to complain to her mother.

'I'm afraid we must tread very carefully at the moment, dear,' said Aurelia, looking worried.

'What on earth's the matter?'

'I don't really know, except that it's something to do with shares in the Byron Bottle Company. I gather they've been disappearing.'

'Nonsense!' said Alicia. 'Shares don't disappear.'

'Out of the family? Is that what I mean?' amended Aurelia vaguely. 'Oh, it's quite beyond me, I have no head for business.'

'Willie hasn't mentioned it to me.'

'Willie mightn't know yet, dear. He hasn't had much to do with the company yet, has he? After all, he's just finished at university.'

Alicia dismissed the whole tiresome business with a snort, and went off to instruct the butler to the effect that only female servants would be allowed in the front of the house, as it was a party purely for ladies.

Of course Drusilla came, and brought Missy with her; poor Octavia, dying to go, was obliged at the last moment to remain behind in all her best clothes, as Aurelia had forgotten to arrange the promised conveyance for the ladies of Missalonghi. Drusilla wore her brown grosgrain, happy in the knowledge that to do so would not be exposing this tried-and-true outfit to an early encore at the wedding itself. And Missy wore her brown linen, on her head the old sailor hat she had been forced to don on every occasion demanding a hat for the last fifteen years, including church each Sunday. New hats would be forthcoming for the wedding, though not, alas, from Chez Chapeau Alicia; the basics were already bought from Uncle Herbert's emporium, and the final furbishings would be done at Missalonghi.

Alicia was looking stunning in a delicate apricot crêpe dress trimmed with lavender-blue embroidery and bearing a huge bunch of lavender-blue silk flowers on one shoulder. Oh, thought Missy, just this once I would love to be able to wear a dress like that! Now I *could* survive that apricot colour, I am positive I could! And I could survive that shade of blue too, it's halfway to pale purple.

Over a hundred women had been invited to the party. They wandered about the house in little clutches, catching sight of faces and catching up on gossip. Then at four o'clock they settled like roosting hens in the ballroom, where they partook of a magnificent tea of scones with jam and cream, petits fours, cucumber sandwiches, asparagus cornucopias, éclairs, cream buns and deliciously gooey Napoleons. There was even a choice between Darjeeling, Earl Grey, Lapsang Souchong and Jasmine tea!

Hurlingford women were traditionally fair, and traditionally tall, and traditionally incapable of frank speech. Looking around the gathering and listening to its chatter, Missy saw for herself the truth of these observations. This was the first occasion of its kind she had ever been invited to, probably because it would have been impolite not to invite her when so many women less closely related were coming. Somehow in church on Sunday the awesome presence of Hurlingford women en masse was watered down by the presence of a roughly equal number of Hurlingford men. But here in Aunt Aurelia's ballroom the breed was undiluted and overwhelming.

The air was thick with participles properly tucked away and exquisitely spliced infinitives and a great many other verbal delicacies largely gone out of fashion fifty years before. Under the splendour and graciousness of Aurelia's roof, no one dared to say 'can't ' or 'won't ' or 'didn't '. And, noted Missy, she herself was literally the only dark-haired woman there. Oh, a few borderline mouses glimmered (the greys and whites did not stand out at all), but her own jet-black hair was like a lump of coal in a field of snow; she quite understood why her mother had instructed her to keep her hat on throughout. Obviously, even when a Hurlingford man or woman married out of the family, he or she chose a blond partner. Indeed, Missy's own father had been very fair, but his grandfather, according to Drusilla, had been as dark as a dago, this term then being conventional and acceptable.

'Dearest Augusta and Antonia, it is the Saxon in us,' fluted Drusilla to the sisters she saw least of.

Aurelia was devoting herself almost exclusively to Lady Billy, who had been amputated from her horse for the afternoon, not without bitter protest. And Lady Billy was sitting looking encephalitically expressionless, for she had no daughters of her own and no interest whatsoever in women. En masse they both frightened and upset her, and the greatest grief of her life had been the acquisition of Alicia Marshall as a prospective daughter-in-law. Undeterred by the fact that she fought a lone battle, Lady Billy had loudly opposed Little Willie's betrothal to his second cousin Alicia, declaring that they would never run together as a team, and would breed very poor stock. However, Sir William (called Billy) rode roughshod over her, as indeed he did over everybody; he had always had an eye for Alicia himself, and was delighted at the prospect of looking down his dining table every night to see Alicia's shining flaxen head and lovely face. For it had been arranged that the newlywed couple would reside at Hurlingford Lodge with Sir William and his lady for some months at least; Sir William's wedding present was prime land, ten acres of it, but the house built upon it was nowhere near finished.

Left very much to her own devices, Missy looked around for Una. She found Aunt Livilla, but no Una. How odd!

'I don't see Una here today,' said Missy to Alicia when that ravishing creature drifted by with a bright and wonderfully condescending smile.

'Who?' asked Alicia, stopping.

'Una – Aunt Livilla's cousin – she works in the library.'

'Silly girl, there's no Hurlingford by that name in Byron,' said Alicia, who had never been known to read a book. And off she went to spread her glorious presence as thinly across the surface of the gathering as the layer of jam on a boarding school pudding.

At which point the penny dropped. Of course! Una was *divorced*! An unheard-of sin! Stirred to the extent of providing a roof over her cousin's head Aunt Livilla might have been, but her humanitarian instincts would never extend to allowing that cousin – that *divorced* cousin – to enter Byron society. So it seemed Aunt Livilla had decided to keep quiet about Una altogether. Come to think of it, Una herself had been the sole source of Missy's information; on the rare occasions since Una's advent that Missy had found Aunt Livilla in the library, Aunt Livilla had never mentioned Una's name, and Missy, who was afraid of Aunt Livilla, had not mentioned Una either.

Drusilla bustled up, her sister Cornelia in tow. 'Oh, is this not splendid?' she asked, speech patterns perfect.

'Very splendid,' said Missy, shifting up on the sofa she had found behind a large potted Kentia palm cluster.

Drusilla and Cornelia sat down, replete with at least one specimen from every kind of delicacy offered at the buffet.

'So kind! So considerate! Dear Alicia!' waffled Cornelia, who regarded it as a great privilege to be permitted to work for a pittance as Alicia's sales dame, and had no idea how cynically Alicia traded on her gratitude and devotion. Until Chez Chapeau Alicia had opened its doors, Cornelia had worked for her brother Herbert in his alteration room, so there were grounds for her illusions; Herbert was so stingy he made Alicia look like a lady bountiful. In the same way as Octavia, and with the same result, Cornelia had sold her house and five acres to Herbert, only in her case it was to help her sister Julia pay her tea room off when Julia bought it from Herbert.

'Hush!' breathed Drusilla. 'Alicia is going to speak.'

Alicia spoke, cheeks glowing, eyes sparkling like bleached aquamarines. The names of the ten bridesmaids were greeted with squeals and claps; the chief bridesmaid fainted clean away from the honour of it, and had to be revived with smelling-salts. According to Alicia, the dresses for her attendants were to be paired in five shades of pink, from palest through to deep cyclamen, so that when the white-clad bride stood at the altar she would be flanked on either side by five attendants who gradually shaded from palest pink at the bride's end to rich dark pink at the farthest end.

'We are all very nearly the same height, all very fair, and of much the same figure,' explained Alicia. 'I think the effect will be remarkable.'

'Is it not a brilliant concept?' whispered Cornelia, privileged to have been a party to the preliminary planning of the entire bridal. 'Alicia's train will be of Alençon lace, twenty feet long, and cut on the full circle!'

'Magnificent,' sighed Drusilla, remembering that the train on her own wedding gown had been of lace and even longer, but deciding not to say so.

'I notice Alicia has kept her choice to virgins only,' said Missy, whose stitch had been bothering her ever since the seven-mile walk from Missalonghi, and now was growing worse. To leave the room was impossible, but nor could she sit still and silent a moment longer; to keep her mind off the pain, she started to talk.

'Very orthodox of her,' she continued, 'but I'm *definitely* a virgin, and I didn't get picked.'

'Ssssh!' hissed Drusilla.

'Dearest little Missy, you're too short and too dark,' murmured Cornelia, feeling very sorry for her niece.

'I'm five feet seven in my stockinged feet,' said Missy, making no effort to mute her voice. 'Only among a collection of Hurlingfords would that be called short!'

'Ssssh!' hissed Drusilla again.

In the meantime Alicia had passed to the subject of flowers, and was informing her enthralled audience that every bouquet would consist of dozens of pink orchids that were coming down in chilled boxes on the Brisbane train.

'Orchids! How ostentatiously vulgar!' said Missy loudly.

'Ssssh!' from Drusilla, despairingly.

At this moment Alicia fell silent, having shot her bolt.

'You'd wonder that she's happy to give the whole show away at this early stage,' said Missy to no one in particular, 'but I suppose she thinks if she doesn't, half the details she's so proud of won't even be noticed.'

Down swept Alicia upon them, laughing, glowing, her head full of limelight and her hands full of bridal sketches and swatches of fabric.

'It's such a pity you're so dark and so short, Missy,' she said, very prettily. 'I would have liked to ask you, but you must see that you wouldn't fit in as a bridesmaid.'

'Well, I think it's a pity that *you're* not dark and short,' said Missy, equally prettily. 'With everyone around you of similar height and colouring, and all that gradual shading of pink, you're going to fade into the wallpaper.'

Alicia gasped. Drusilla gasped. Cornelia gasped.

Missy got up in a leisurely manner and attempted to shake the creases out of her brown linen skirt. 'I think I'll be off now,' she said chirpily. 'Nice party, Alicia, but utterly undistinguished. Why does everybody have to serve the same old food? I would have appreciated a really good curried egg sandwich for a change.'

She had gone before her audience managed to regain its breath; when it did, Drusilla was forced to hide a smile, and turn a deliberately deaf ear to Alicia's demand that Missy must be fetched back to apologise. Served Alicia right! Why couldn't she have been kind just this once, marred her perfect bridal group by including poor Missy in it? How amazing! Missy's analysis was spot on; Alicia *would* fade into the wallpaper, or rather into the pink and white bows and bouquets and bunting with which she intended to deck the church.

Just outside the front door of Mon Repos, the awful pain and airlessness struck. Deciding she would rather die in decent seclusion, Missy left the gravel drive and darted round the side of the house. Of course Aurelia Marshall's notions of garden layout did not permit a hint of thicket, so there were very few places wherein Missy might huddle undetected. The closest of these was a large clump of rhododendrons beneath one of the downstairs windows, so into the middle of the clump Missy crawled, and half-sat, half-lay with her back against the red brick behind the shrubs. The pain was unbearable, yet had to be borne. She closed her eyes and willed herself not to die until she could die in John Smith's arms, like the girl in *The Troubled Heart*. What a depressing place to be found all stiff and stark, Aunt Aurelia's rhododendron bushes!

She didn't die. After a little while the pain began to recede, and she began to stir. There were voices nearby, and, since the rhododendrons were still rather bare from their autumn pruning, she didn't want the talkers to come round the corner and find her. So she rolled over onto her knees and started to get up. That was when she realised that the voices were coming from the window just above her head.

'Did you ever see such a monstrosity of a hat?' asked a voice Missy recognised as belonging to Aunt Augusta's youngest daughter, Lavinia; of course Lavinia was a bridesmaid.

'All too often, in Church every Sunday to be exact,' said Alicia's tonelessly harsh voice. 'Though I think the person underneath the hat is a far worse monstrosity.'

'She's so *drab*!' came a third voice, belonging to the chief bridesmaid, Aunt Antonia's daughter Marcia. 'Honestly, Alicia, you're according her far too much importance by calling her a monstrosity. Nonentity is a much better word for Missy Wright, though the hat, I grant you, is indeed a monstrosity.'

'You have a point,' conceded Alicia, who was still smarting from the unexpected flick of Missy's observation about fading into the wallpaper. Of course she was wrong! And yet Alicia knew that never again would the visual splendour of her wedding quite

please her; Missy had planted her barb with more deadly skill than she realised.

'Do we really care about Missy Wright one way or another?' asked a more distant cousin called Portia.

'Due to the fact that her mother is my mother's favourite sister, Portia, I'm afraid I have to,' declared Alicia in ringing tones. 'Why Mama persists in pitying Auntie Drusie so, I don't know, but I've given up hoping I'll ever wean her from it. Oh, I daresay Mama's charity is laudable, but I can tell you that I try never to be at home on Saturday mornings, when Auntie Drusie comes to gorge herself on Mama's cakes. Lord, can she eat! Mama has Cook make two dozen fairy cakes, and by the time Auntie Drusie has gone, so have the fairy cakes, every last one.' Alicia produced a brittle unamused laugh. 'It's become a regular joke in our house, even among the servants.'

'Well, they are dreadfully poor, aren't they?' asked Lavinia, who had been good at history at school, so aired her superiority by saying, 'It always puzzled me why the French rabble guillotined Marie Antoinette, just because she said they should eat cake if they had no bread. It seems to me anyone dreadfully poor would adore the chance to eat cake for a change – I mean, look at Auntie Drusie!'

'Poor they are,' said Alicia, 'and poor I am afraid they are going to remain, with Missy their only hope.'

That raised a general laugh.

'A pity one cannot have people condemned the way one can have houses condemned,' said another voice, a mere fourth or fifth cousin, by name of Junia; disappointment at not being chosen as a bridesmaid had concentrated all her natural venom down to one or two deadly drops.

'In this day and age, Junia, we are too kind for that,' said Alicia. 'Therefore we must all go on putting up with Auntie Drusie and Auntie Octie and Cousin Missy and Auntie Julie and Auntie Cornie and the rest of the spinster-widow brigade. Take my wedding. They will quite spoil it! But Mama rightly says they must be invited, and of course they will come the earliest and be the very last to go home. Haven't you noticed how pimples and boils always pop up when they're least welcome? However, Mama did have a brain-wave that will spare us from those hideous brown dresses. She bought my household linens from Auntie Drusie for two hundred pounds. And I will admit that they do the most remarkably fine and dainty work, so Mama's money was not wasted, thank God. Embroidered pillow-slips closed with little covered buttons, and every last button embroidered with a tiny rosebud! Very beautiful! Anyway, Mama's scheme worked, because Uncle Herbert slipped the word to her that Missy came in and bought three dress-lengths – lilac for Auntie Drusie and blue for Auntie Octie. Any guesses what colour for Cousin Missy?'

'*Brown*!' chorused every voice, and then there was a gale of laughter.

'I have an idea!' cried Lavinia when the merriment ceased. 'Why don't you give Missy one of your own cast-offs in a shade that will suit her?'

'I'd rather be dead,' said Alicia scornfully. 'See one of my lovely dresses on that dago-looking scragbag? If you feel so strongly about it, my dear Lavinia, why don't you donate her one of your cast-offs?'

'I am not,' said Lavinia tartly, 'in your cosy financial position, Alicia, that's why! Think about it, since you're so peeved at her appearance. You wear a lot of amber and old gold and apricot. I imagine anything in that sort of range would look all right on Missy.'

At which point Missy managed to get herself on hands and knees out of the rhododendrons and onto the path. She crept on all fours until she was well clear of the window, then got to her feet and ran. The tears were pouring down her face, but she wasn't about to stop and dry them, too angry and shamed to care who might see.

She hadn't thought anything anybody might say about her could hurt, for a thousand thousand times in her imagination she had catalogued the various pitying or contemptuous things that might conceivably be said about her. Nor did it hurt, really. What stabbed to the quick were the dreadful things Alicia and her friends had said about her mother and all those poor spinster aunts, so decent and honourable and hard-working, so grateful for any attention, yet so proud they would accept nothing they suspected might be charity. How dared Alicia speak of those infinitely more admirable women so scathingly, so unfeelingly! Let Alicia see how she would fare if she were placed in the same pinched shoes!

As she hurried through Byron with the stitch again burning in her side, Missy found herself praying that the library would be open, for Una would be in occupation. Oh, how she needed Una tonight! But the premises were dark, and a sign on the door simply said CLOSED.

Octavia was sitting in the kitchen of Missalonghi, changed back into her workaday clothes, with the small provender of their meal simmering away in a pot on the stove. Stew. Her misshapen hands were busy with knitting needles, magically producing the most fragile and cobwebby of evening shawls as a wedding present for the ungrateful Alicia.

'Ah!' she said, laying her task aside when Missy walked in. 'Did you have a nice time, dear? Is your mother with you?'

'I had a wretched time, so I left ahead of Mother,' said Missy briefly, then seized the milk bucket, and escaped.

The cow was waiting patiently to be let into the shed; Missy reached out to stroke the velvety dark muzzle, and looked deeply into the big sweet brown eyes.

'Buttercup, you're *much* nicer than Alicia, so I just don't understand why it's such an unforgivable insult to call a woman a cow. From now on, the women others call cows, I shall call Alicias,' she told it as she led it into the shed, where it moved of its own accord into the milking stall. Buttercup was the easiest cow to milk, letting down without a struggle, never complaining if Missy's hands were cold, as they often were. Which of course was why its milk was so good; nice cows always gave nice milk.

Drusilla was home when Missy returned. It was customary to pour most of the milk into the big flat pans which lived on the shady side of the back verandah; as she poured, she could hear her mother enthusiastically regaling her aunt with a full description of Alicia's bridal party.

'Oh, I'm so glad one of you had a good time,' said Octavia. 'All I could get out of Missy was that she'd had a wretched time. I suppose her trouble is lack of friends.'

'True, and no one is sorrier for it than I. But dear Eustace's death removed any chance of brothers and sisters for Missy, and this house is so far out of Byron on the wrong side that no one ever wants to come and see us regularly.'

Missy waited for her sins to be divulged, but her mother made no reference to them. Courage seeping back, she went inside. Ever since the heart trouble came on it had become easier for her to assert herself, and apparently also easier for her mother to accept these signs of independence. Only it wasn't really the heart trouble that caused the change. It was Una. Yes, everything went back to Una's advent; Una's forthrightness, Una's frankness, Una's unwillingness to be sat on by anyone. Una would have told a supercilious twerp like James Hurlingford to go bite his bum, Una would have given Alicia something verbal to remember if she condescended,

Una would always make sure people treated her with respect. And somehow this had rubbed off on such an unlikely pupil as Missy Wright.

When Missy walked in, Drusilla leaped up, beaming.

'Missy, you'll never guess!' she cried, reaching round to the back of the chair where she had been sitting and plucking a very large box off the floor. 'As I was leaving the party, Alicia came and gave me this for you to wear at her wedding. She assured me that the colour would suit you beautifully, though I confess I would never have thought of it for myself. Only look!'

Missy stood turned to stone while her mother scrabbled in the box and unearthed a bundle of stiff and crushed organdie which she proceeded to shake out and hold up for Missy's dazed inspection. A gorgeous dress of a pale toffee shade, not tan and not yellow and not quite amber; those in the know would have understood that its frilled skirt and neckline put it at least five or six years out of date, but even so it was a gorgeous dress, and with extensive alterations it would suit Missy down to the ground.

'And the hat, only look at the hat!' squeaked Drusilla, clawing a huge cartwheel of pale toffee straw out of the box and twitching its artless piles of matching organdie into place. 'Did you ever see a more beautiful hat? Oh, dearest Missy, you shall have a pair of shoes, no matter how impractical they are!'

The stone dropped away from Missy's limbs at last; she stepped forward, arms extended to receive Alicia's bounty, and her mother placed dress and hat in them at once.

'I'll wear my new brown satin and my home-made hat and good sturdy boots!' said Missy through her teeth, and took to her heels out the back door, the masses of organdie billowing up about her like the skirts on a swimming béche-de-mer.

It was not yet fully dark; as she raced for the shed she could hear the frantic cries of her mother and aunt somewhere behind, but by the time they caught up with her, it was too late. The dress and hat were trampled beyond repair into the muck of the milking stall, and Missy, a shovel in her hands, was busy heaping every pile of dung she could find on top of Alicia's grand gesture.

Drusilla was unspeakably hurt. 'How could you? Oh, how could you, Missy? Just this once in your life, you had a chance to look and feel like a belle!'

Missy laid the shovel against the shed wall and dusted her hands together in complete satisfaction. 'You above all people ought to understand how I could, Mother,' she said. 'No one's pride is stiffer than yours, no one I know is quicker than you to interpret the most wellmeaning gift as charity in disguise. Why then are you denying me my share of that pride? Would you have taken the gift for yourself? Why then take it for me? Do you honestly think Alicia did it to please me? Of course she didn't! Alicia is determined to have her wedding perfect down to the last guest, and I – I *spoiled* it! So she decided to make a silk purse out of Missy Wright the sow's ear. Well, thank you very much, but I'd rather be my own sow's ear in all its natural homeliness than any silk purse of Alicia's making! And so I shall tell her!'

And so indeed she did tell her, the very next day. Though Drusilla had crept out in the dead of night armed with a lamp, the dress and hat had disappeared from their vile resting place, and she never saw them again; nor did she ever discover what had happened to them, for no one who knew remembered to tell her, so shocking were the other events of that memorable Friday morning in the Marshall residence.

Missy arrived at the front door of Mon Repos about ten o'clock, hampered by a large and exceedingly well wrapped parcel which she carried rather gingerly by a string loop. Had the butler any idea of the consternation already reigning in the small drawing room, it is doubtful whether Missy would have got any further than the front stoop, but luckily the butler did not have any idea, and so was able to contribute his mite to the general atmosphere of disaster.

The small drawing room, not really small, was nonetheless rather full of very large people when Missy sidled round the door with her parcel on its string. Aunt Aurelia was there, and Uncle Edmund, and Alicia, and Ted and Randolph, and the third Sir William, and his son and heir, Little Willie; Lady Billy was not there, as she was assisting a mare to foal.

'I don't understand it!' Edmund Marshall was saying as Missy gave the butler a smile and a gesture which indicated she would announce herself as soon as maybe. 'I just don't understand it! How could so many shares escape us? *How*? And who the hell sold them and who the hell bought them?'

'As far as my agents can gather,' said the third Sir William, 'every share not held by a Hurlingford proper was bought up for many times its actual value, and then the mystery buyer began to make inroads on shares held by Hurlingfords. How or when or why I don't know, but he managed to discover every Hurlingford in need of money and every Hurlingford not tied to Byron, and he made offers no one could refuse.'

'It's ridiculous!' cried Ted. 'For the sort of money he's been paying, there's absolutely no way he can ever recoup his outlay. I mean, the Byron Bottle Company is a very nice little enterprise, but it's not gold we're taking out of the ground, nor is it the elixir of life! Yet the prices he's been paying are the sort of prices a speculator might pay on receipt of an infallible tip that the ground is solid gold.'

'I agree with all that,' said Sir William, 'but I can't give you an answer, because I just don't know it.'

'Are we reduced to minority shareholders, Uncle Billy, is that what you're trying to say?' asked Alicia, who was fully acquainted with the practices and terminology of the business world – and a not inconsiderable shareholder in the Byron Bottle Company herself, since Chez Chapeau Alicia had put capital in her hands and an acquisitive nature had tempted her into the safer realms of speculation.

'Good God, no, not yet!' cried Sir William; then, with less confidence, he added, 'However, I admit it's going to be touch and go unless we can either stem the tide of shares we're losing, or buy more ourselves.'

'Aren't there any stray small shareholders living here in Byron whom we can get to first?' asked Randolph.

'A few, Hurlingfords on the distaff side mostly, and two or three of the old maids who accidentally inherited shares they weren't really entitled to. Naturally they've never been paid a dividend.'

'How did you manage that, Uncle Billy?' asked Randolph.

Sir William snorted. 'What do they know about shares, silly old biddies like Cornelia and Julia and Octavia? I didn't want them thinking they were hanging onto something valuable, so as well as never paying them a dividend, I told them the shares were worthless because they belonged by rights to Maxwell and Herbert. However, rather than make a big fuss, I merely told them they could best rectify the mistake by willing the shares to the sons of Maxwell and Herbert.'

'Clever!' said Alicia admiringly.

Sir William gave her one of his hot lusting glances; she was beginning to wonder privately how easy it was going to be to keep Uncle Billy at arm's length after she married and moved into Hurlingford Lodge – but cross that bridge later.

'We'll have to acquire the old maids' shares now,' said Edmund Marshall, looking very gloomy. 'Though, Billy, I must be frank and admit that I don't know how I'm going to find any ready money. I'd have to retrench drastically, which would be most disagreeable for my family – Alicia's wedding, you know.'

'I'm in the same boat myself, old man,' said Sir William, the words sticking in his gullet. 'It's all this flap over a big war in Europe, dammit! Rumour-mongering is all!'

'Why *buy* the shares?' asked Alicia, just the smallest tinge of contempt for their stupidity in her voice. 'All you have to do is go to Auntie Cornie and Auntie Julie and Aunti Octie and *ask*! They'll hand them over without a murmur!'

'All right, we can do that with those three, and with Drusilla as well, I imagine. What on earth possessed Malcolm Hurlingford to leave shares to his daughters, I ask you? He always was soft over his girls, though thank God Maxwell and Herbert don't take after their father in that regard.' Sir William sighed impatiently. 'A pretty pickle we're in! Even if, as Alicia says, the old biddies hand over their shares without a murmur, we've still got to deal with the various ne'er-do-wells and half-Hurlingfords who most certainly won't want to part with what shares they have for nothing. Oh, we'll manage, I have no doubt, just as long as they don't get wind of the mystery buyer. Because we can't match his prices.'

'What can we sell in a hurry to raise cash?' asked Alicia crisply.

They all turned to look at her, and Missy, as yet quite unnoticed, shifted stealthily from her spot in front of the door (against which her brown dress and person didn't show at all) to a safer spot behind one of the potted Kentia palms Aunt Aurelia had placed everywhere inside her lovely house.

'There's Lady Billy's bloody horses, for a start,' said Sir William with relish.

'My jewels,' said Aurelia with great resolution.

'And my jewels,' said Alicia with a nasty look at her mother for getting in first.

'The thing is,' said Edmund, 'that this mystery buyer, whoever he – or they – might be, seems to know more about who owns shares in the Byron Bottle Company than we do, and we're the board of directors! When I consulted our list of shareholders I discovered that in a great many cases the shares had passed from the person listed as owning them into other hands, mostly sons or nephews, admittedly, but strange hands nonetheless. It never occurred to me that *any* Hurlingford would sign away his birthright this side of death!'

'Times are changing,' sighed Aurelia. 'When I was a girl, Hurlingford clannishness was a legend. Nowadays it seems as if some of the young Hurlingfords don't give a tuppenny bumper about the family.'

'They've been spoiled,' said Sir William. He cleared his throat, slapped his hands on his thighs, and said with great decision, 'All right, I suggest we leave matters as they stand over the week-end, then on Monday we get down to raising some cold hard cash.'

'Who is to approach the aunties?' asked Ted.

'Alicia,' said Sir William instantly. 'Only not until a bit closer to her wedding, I think. That way she can hoodwink them into thinking they're giving her a wedding present.'

'Won't the mystery buyer get to them first?' asked Ted, who always worried about everything, and so had drifted into accounting quite naturally.

'One thing you can be absolutely sure of, Ted, is that none of those silly old chooks would dream of parting with anything Hurlingford to anyone outside the family without first asking me or Herbert. The buyer could offer them a fortune, and they'd still insist upon consulting me or Herbert first.' So positive was Sir William of his ground on this point that he smiled when he said it.

Taking advantage of the general mêlée as several worried and overwrought people endeavoured to find the right way to break off their meeting, Missy slid out the door and came back inside very noisily. And they all noticed her at once, though none of them looked pleased to see her.

'What do you want?' asked Alicia rudely.

'I came to show you how I feel about your charity, Alicia, and to tell you that I am happy to come to your wedding in good old brown,' said Missy, marching across the room and dumping her

parcel on the table in front of Alicia. 'There! Thank you, but no thank you.'

Alicia stared at her much as she might have stared at a dog turd she had almost stepped in. 'Please yourself!'

'I intend to, from now on.' She glanced up at the much taller Alicia (who admitted to five feet ten but was actually six feet one) with a puckish grin. 'Go on, Alicia, open it! I dyed it brown just for you.'

'You what?' Alicia began to fumble with the knots in the string, so Randolph came to her rescue with his pocket knife. After the string was cut the wrapping parted easily, and there lay the beautiful organdie dress and the ravishing hat, unspeakably smirched with what looked – and smelled – like fresh, sloppy, healthy cow and pig dung.

Alicia let out a squeak of horror that kept on growing and swelling until it became a long thin screech, and jumped away from the table as her mother, father, brothers, uncle and fiancé crowded round to see.

'You – you disgusting little trollop!' she snarled at the beaming Missy.

'Oh, I am not!' said Missy smugly.

'You're worse than a trollop! And you may count yourself lucky indeed that I am too much of a lady to tell you exactly what I do think you are!' gasped Alicia, hardly knowing which had shocked her most, the deed, or the doer of the deed.

'Then you may count yourself unlucky that I am not too much of a lady to tell you exactly what I think you are, Alicia. I am only three days older than you which puts you a lot closer to thirty-four than it does to thirty-three. Yet, here you are, mutton dressed up as lamb, brazen as brass, about to marry a boy hardly more than *half* your age! His father's years are more suitable! And that makes you a cold-blooded cradle-snatcher! When Montgomery Massey died before you could haul him to the altar – thereby escaping a fate worse than death – you couldn't see anyone on your horizon who was a tenth as good a catch. And then you spied poor Little Willie, still with all his baby-curls, playing with his hoop in his sailor suit, and you decided to be Lady Willie one day. I have no doubt that had the circumstances changed, you'd have been just as happy to be Lady Billy instead of Lady Willie – happier maybe, since the title's already there. I admire your gall, Alicia, but I do not admire you. And I feel very sorry for poor Little Willie, who is going to lead a wretched life, a bone between his wife and his mother.'

The object of her pity was standing, with the rest of his relatives, gaping at Missy as if she had jumped stark naked out of a gigantic cake and proceeded to do the can-can. Aurelia had mercifully gone into hysterics, but so mesmerised was the rest of Missy's audience that it had failed to notice the fact.

Sir William recovered first. 'Get out of this house!'

'I'm on my way,' said Missy, looking very pleased.

'I will never forgive you for this!' cried Alicia. 'How dare you? How *dare* you?'

'Oh, go bite your bum!' said Missy, and laughed. 'It's big enough,' she added, and departed.

This was the proverbial last straw; Alicia stiffened until she became utterly rigid, gave a gurgling moaning shriek, and fell over with a crash to join her mother on the floor.

Oh, how *satisfying* that had been! But as she walked away down the gradual hill of George Street that led into the main thoroughfare of Byron, Missy's elation faded. Compared to the topic under discussion during her first and unnoticed tenure of the drawing room, the presentation of Alicia's violated clothing was picayune. Those poor women! Missy knew as little about the world of company business as her mother and aunts, but she was fully intelligent enough to have caught the drift of Sir William's words. She even knew of the shares, for Drusilla kept hers and Octavia's both in the small tin cash-box that lay inside her wardrobe and held things like the deeds to her house and five acres of land. Ten shares each, twenty shares altogether. Which meant that Aunt Cornelia and Aunt Julia probably had ten shares each as well. Dividend. That was obviously some sort of periodic payment, a share in the company's profits.

How very despicable most of her male relations were! Sir William, eager to keep that disgraceful policy of the first Sir William's going, so that the hapless female members of his family who pinched and scraped in grinding but genteel poverty should have none of the fruits that accrued from the bottling of what was, after all, in God's gift rather than in any Hurlingford's. Uncle Maxwell, who was the worst kind of thief, rich in his own right, yet stealing the eggs and butter and orchardings of his poor relations because he had bullied them into believing that to sell elsewhere would be an unforgivable act of disloyalty. Uncle Herbert, who had bought up many of those houses on five acres in his time, always for a great deal less than they were worth, being the same kind of bully as his brother Maxwell. Only he was worse, because he stole back the little he paid out as well, by telling his victims that the investment schemes designed to make that little a little more had failed.

Not only the male relations were despicable, Missy amended, in a mood to dish out criticisms fairly. If the Aurelias and Augustas and Antonias had brought pressure to bear, having married on the inside of the clan fortunes, maybe they might have succeeded in changing things, for the worst bully is vulnerable to being bullied by his wife.

Well, something must be done. But what? Missy debated carrying her tale home, then decided she would not be believed, or if believed, that her mother and aunts would still end in being bullied out of their just due. Something *had* to be done, and done soon, before Alicia came smarming round to secure the shares, as secure them she undoubtedly would.

The library was open today; Missy glanced through the window expecting to see Aunt Livilla's grim form behind the desk, but there instead was Una. So she slowed down, turned round, and backtracked.

'Missy! What a treat! I didn't expect to see you today, darling,' said Una, smiling as if she really did think it a treat to see the family trollop cum scragbag.

'I'm so angry!' cried Missy, and sat down on the hard chair provided for browsers, fanning herself with her hand.

'What's the matter?'

Suddenly realising she couldn't possibly expose that small clutch of close blood-relations to the contempt of a person as remotely connected to the Byron arm of the clan as Una, she had to compromise with a lame, 'Oh, nothing.'

Una didn't attempt to probe. She just nodded and smiled, that lovely radiance emanating from skin and hair and nails subtly soothing rage.

'How about a cup of tea before the long hike home?' she asked, getting up.

A cup of tea assumed the proportions of a life-giving elixir; 'Yes, please!' said Missy with fervour.

Una disappeared behind the last bookshelf at the back of the room, where in a small cubicle there lay facilities for making tea; there was no toilet, the norm in Byron shops, for everyone was expected to use the toilets in the Byron Waters Baths, and be quick about it.

To investigate the novels while she waited seemed like a good idea to Missy, so she moved to the back of the room and inched along the shelf that came hard up against the edge of Aunt Livilla's desk. And her eye in moving sideways round the desk to where the shelf continued on its far side encountered a familiar-looking sheaf of papers lying there. A packet of share certificates in the Byron Bottle Company.

Una emerged. 'Kettle's on, but it takes time to boil from scratch on a spirit stove.' Her eyes followed Missy's, then came to rest on Missy's face. 'Isn't it lovely?' she asked.

'What?'

'The money that's being offered for Byron Bottle Company shares, of course. Ten pounds a pop! Unheard of! Wallace had a few shares of mine, you know, and when we separated he gave them back to me – said he didn't want anything that reminded him of the Hurlingfords. I only have ten shares, but I can definitely use a hundred quid at the moment, darling. And just between you and me, Auntie Livvie is a bit on the short side too, so I've persuaded her to give me her twenty shares to sell while I'm selling mine.'

'How did Aunt Livilla manage to acquire shares?'

'Richard gave them to her when he couldn't pay her back in cash the time he needed money so desperately he actually borrowed from her. Poor Richard! He never can bet on the right horses. And she's such a stickler for repayment of loans, even when it's her only beloved son on the borrowing end. So he signed over a few of his shares in the Byron Bottle Company to her, and that shut her up.'

'Has he got more?'

'Naturally. He's a male Hurlingford, darling. But I do believe he may have sold out completely, because it was Richard put me onto this godsend of a buyer.'

'How can you sell someone else's shares?'

'With a Power of Attorney. See?' Una held up a stiff foolscap form. 'You get it at the stationer's, like a will form. And you fill it out with the details, and you sign it, and whoever is giving you permission to act on her behalf signs it, and someone signs it as a witness.'

'I see,' said Missy, forgetting all about perusing the novels. She sat down again. 'Una, do you have an address for whoever is buying Byron Bottle shares?'

'Right here, darling, though I'm taking the whole kit and kaboodle down to Sydney in person on Monday to sell them, it's safer. That's why I'm minding the library today, so I can have Monday off.' She got up and went back to make the tea.

Missy thought hard. Why couldn't she, Missy, have a try at getting hold of the aunts' certificates before Alicia came asking for them? Why should Alicia fill her with defeat when in their sole clash just concluded, Alicia had been the loser?

By the time Una came back with the tea tray, Missy had made up her mind.

'Oh, thank you.' She took her cup gratefully. 'Una, is it imperative that you go to Sydney on Monday? Could you possibly make it Tuesday instead?'

'I don't see why not.'

'I have an appointment with a Macquarie Street specialist next Tuesday morning,' Missy explained carefully. 'I was going with Alicia, but . . . . . I don't think she's going to want my company, somehow. It's possible I may have some of these shares to sell, and if I could go with you, it would be easier. I've only been to Sydney a couple of times when I was a child, so I don't know the place.'

'Oh, what fun! Tuesday it is.' Una fairly glittered, so bright had the light in her become.

'I'll have to ask you for another favour, I'm afraid.'

'Of course, darling. What?'

'Would you mind going next door to the stationer's and buying me four of these Power of Attorney forms? You see, if I go myself, Uncle Septimus is sure to want to know what I need Power of Attorney forms for, and the next thing he'll mention it to Uncle Billy, or Uncle Maxwell, or Uncle Herbert, and – well, I'd rather keep my business to myself.'

'I'll go the minute I finish my cup of tea, while you're here to mind the shop for me.'

And so it was arranged, including Una's driving out to Missalonghi on Sunday afternoon at five o'clock to witness the signing of the forms. Luckily this time Missy had her own little money-purse with her, and luckily it contained two shillings; the forms were expensive, at threepence each.

'Thank you,' said Missy, stowing the rolled-up forms in her shopping bag.

She had decided upon some books as well.

'Good lord!' exclaimed Una, glancing at the titles. 'Are you sure you want *The Troubled Heart*? I thought you said you read it to death all last week.'

'I did. But I still want to read it again.' And into the bag alongside the forms went *The Troubled Heart*.

'I'll see you at Missalonghi on Sunday afternoon, and don't worry, Auntie Livvie never minds lending me her horse and sulky,' said Una, accompanying Missy to the door, where she deposited a light kiss on Missy's unaccustomed cheek. 'Chin up, girl, you can do it,' she said, and pushed Missy out into the street.

'Mother,' said Missy that evening as she sat in the warmth of the kitchen with Drusilla and Octavia, 'have you still got those Byron Bottle shares Grandfather left you and Aunt Octavia in his will?'

Drusilla looked up from her beading warily; though the altered pecking-order was of her own making, she still found it a little difficult to accept the fact that she was no longer the boss-chook. And she had learned very quickly to spot the more subtle, oblique approach Missy employed, so that she knew something was in the wind now.

'Yes, I've still got them,' she said.

Missy put her tatting in her lap and looked across at her mother very seriously. 'Mother, do you trust me?'

Drusilla blinked. 'Of course I do!'

'How much is a new Singer sewing machine?'

'I don't honestly know, but I imagine at least twenty or thirty pounds, perhaps a great deal more.'

'If you had yet another hundred pounds besides the two hundred pounds Aunt Aurelia paid for Alicia's linens, would you buy yourself a Singer sewing machine?'

'I would certainly be tempted.'

'Then give me your shares in Byron Bottle and let me sell them for you. I can get you ten pounds a share in Sydney.'

Both Drusilla and Octavia had ceased working.

'Missy dear, they're worthless,' said Octavia gently.

'No, they are not worthless,' said Missy. 'You've been duped by Uncle Billy and Uncle Herbert and the rest, is all. You should have been paid what's called a dividend upon them every so often, because the Byron Bottle Company is an extremely prosperous concern.'

'No, you're wrong!' insisted Octavia, shaking her head.

'I'm right. If you two and Aunt Cornelia and Aunt Julia had only taken yourselves off to a disinterested solicitor in Sydney years ago, you might be a lot richer today than you are, and that's the truth.'

'We could never go behind the menfolk's back, Missy,' said Octavia. 'It would be a breach of faith and trust in them. They know better than we do, which is why they look after us and watch out for us. And they're *family*!'

'Don't I know it?' cried Missy from behind clenched teeth. 'Aunt Octavia, your menfolk have been trading on the fact that they're family ever since the Hurlingfords began! They *use* you! They exploit you! When have we ever got a fair price from Uncle Maxwell for our produce? Do you honestly swallow all those hard-luck stories of his about being done down in the markets himself, so how can he afford to pay us more? He's as rich as Croesus! And when have you ever seen proof that Uncle Herbert actually did lose your money in an unlucky investment? He's richer than Croesus! And didn't Uncle Billy tell you in person that those shares were worthless?'

The fixity of Drusilla's silent regard had passed from shock to doubt, from unwillingness to listen to a distinct desire to hear more. And by the end of this impassioned speech, even Octavia was visibly wavering. Perhaps had it been the old Missy sitting there destroying the old order, they might have dismissed what she said without a qualm; but this new Missy possessed an authority which lent her words the ring of unequivocal truth.

'Look,' Missy went on more quietly, 'I can sell your shares in the Byron Bottle Company for ten pounds each, and I know that kind of opportunity is as rare as hen's teeth, because I was there when Uncle Billy and Uncle Edmund were talking about it, and that's what they said. They didn't know I was listening, otherwise they'd not have said a word of it. They spoke of you as they think of you, with utter contempt. Believe me, I did not misinterpret what I heard, and I do not exaggerate. And I made up my mind that there was going to be an end to it, that I was going to see that you and Aunt Cornelia and Aunt Julia got the better of them for once. So give me your shares and let me sell them for you, because I'll get you ten pounds each for them. But if you offer them to Uncle Billy or Uncle Herbert or Uncle Maxwell, they'll bully you into signing them away for nothing.'

Drusilla sighed. 'I wish I didn't believe you, Missy, but I do. And what you say comes as no surprise, deep down.'

Octavia, who might have battled on in blind loyalty, instead decided to switch allegiances; for she was a little bit of a child, and craved firm direction.

'Think what a difference a Singer sewing machine would make to you, Drusilla,' she said.

'I would enjoy it,' admitted Drusilla.

'And I must confess I would enjoy having a hundred pounds all of my own in the bank. I would feel less of a burden.'

Drusilla capitulated. 'Very well, then, Missy, you may have our shares to sell.'

'I want Aunt Cornelia's and Aunt Julia's as well!'

'I see.'

'I can sell their shares for the same amount of money, ten pounds each. But like you, they must be prepared to give me their shares without one word to Uncle Billy or any of the others – not one word!'

'Cornelia could certainly do with the money, Drusilla,' said Octavia, feeling more cheerful every moment, and consigning her male relatives to limbo because it was better to do that than grieve over their perfidy, bleed from their hurtfulness. 'She could afford to have her feet done by that German bone specialist in Sydney. She does so much standing! And you know how desperate Julia's case is, now that the Olympus Café has put in that extra room out the back, with marble-topped tables and a pianist every afternoon. If she had an extra hundred pounds, she could afford to make her tea room even swankier than the Olympus Café.'

'I'll do my best to talk them into it,' said Drusilla.

'Well, if you do talk them into it, they have to be here at Missalonghi on Sunday afternoon at five o'clock, with their shares. All of you will have to sign a Power of Attorney.'

'What's that?'

'A piece of paper that authorises me to act in your name.'

'Why at five o'clock on Sunday?' asked Octavia.

'Because that's when my friend Una is coming to witness the signing of the documents.'

'Oh, how nice!' Inspiration struck Octavia. 'I shall bake her a batch of my plain biscuits.'

Missy grinned. 'For once in our lives, Aunt Octavia, I think we can treat ourselves to a slap-up Sunday high tea. We can have plain biscuits for Una, of course, but we'll have fairy cakes and melting moments and cream puffs iced with toffee, and – *lamingtons*!'

No one gave her any argument about that menu.

When Missy arrived at the Byron railway station at six o'clock on Tuesday morning, she carried forty shares in the Byron Bottle Company, and four duly signed and witnessed Powers of Attorney. Una, it turned out, was a proper Justice of the Peace in spite of her sex (she said it happened in Sydney from time to time), and had fixed a most official-looking seal to the documents.

She was waiting on the platform, and so was Alicia. Not together, for Alicia was at the engine end, where the first class carriages would stand, and Una was at the guard's van end, where the second class carriages would stand.

'I hope you don't mind travelling second class,' said Missy anxiously. 'Mother has been most generous, I have ten shillings for my expenses and a guinea for the specialist, but I don't want to spend any more of it than I can help.'

'Darling, my first class days are long over,' soothed Una. 'Besides, it's not a terribly long journey, and at this time of a cold morning, no one is going to insist that the windows be opened to let in the soot.'

Missy's eyes encountered Alicia's; Alicia sniffed and deliberately turned the other way. Thank heavens for that, thought Missy unrepentantly.

The rails began to hum, and shortly afterwards the train came in, a huge black monster of an engine with a stubby stack clunking past in torrents of grimy smoke and fierce gushes of thick white steam.

'Do you know what I like to do?' asked Una of Missy as they found themselves a couple of vacant seats, one a window.

'No, what?'

'You know the overhead bridge at the bit of Noel Street near the bottling plant?'

'I do indeed.'

'I love to stand right in the middle on top of it, and hang over

Chapman

the edge of the parapet when a train goes underneath. Whoosh! Smoke everywhere, just like descending to hell. But oh, such fun!'

And so are you fun, thought Missy. I've never met anyone like you, nor anyone so full of life.

By the time the train drew into its terminus at Central Station, the hands of the platform clock said twenty minutes to nine. Her appointment in Macquarie Street was for ten, but Una said that left them plenty of time for a cup of tea in the railway refreshment rooms. Alicia swept by them in the main concourse; she must have been lurking in wait just to do it, for the first class passengers were normally well ahead of those at the back of the train.

'Isn't that the famous Alicia Marshall?' asked Una.

'Yes.'

Una made an untranslatable sound.

'What do you think of her?' asked Missy, curious.

'Obvious and flashy, darling. Keeps all her goods in the shop window, and you know what happens to goods in shop windows, don't you?'

'I do, but tell me in your own words.'

Una giggled. 'Darling, they *fade*! Constant exposure to the glaring light of day. I give her another year at most. After that, no amount of lacing her stays tighter will keep her figure trim. She'll grow enormously fat and lazy, and she'll develop the most dreadful temper. I believe she's going to marry a mere lad. Pity. What she needs is a man who will make her work very hard, and treat her like dirt.'

'Poor Little Willie is too limp, I fear,' sighed Missy, and had no idea why Una found that remark so exquisitely funny.

In fact, Una laughed in fits and starts all the way down Castlereagh Street on the tram, but she refused to tell Missy why, and by the time they reached the building on Macquarie Street where the specialist had his rooms, Missy had given up.

At ten on the dot, Dr George Parkinson's haughty nurse took her into a room plentifully endowed with movable screens of terrifying cleanliness and whiteness. She was directed to remove all her clothes, including her bloomers, place an indicated white wrap around her scrawny person, and lie down on the couch to wait for Doctor.

What an odd way to meet anyone, she couldn't help thinking when Dr Parkinson's face loomed over hers; she was left to wonder what he looked like when the hairy caverns of his nostrils were not his most prominent feature. With his nurse in silent attendance, he thumped her chest, stared at her pitifully under-developed breasts with the rudeness of utter indifference, listened to her heart and lungs through a far sleeker stethoscope than Dr Hurlingford's, took her pulse, stuck a spatula down her throat until she gagged dangerously, felt both sides of her neck and under her chin with impatient hard fingers, then went rolling round her flinching belly with his palms.

'Internal examination, Nurse,' he said curtly.

'Pee ar or pee vee?' asked Nurse.

'Both.'

The internal examinations left Missy feeling as if she had undergone some sort of major operation without benefit of chloroform, but there was worse to come. Dr Parkinson flipped her over onto her front and then went poking and prying along the cordillera of her backbone until, somewhere around the spot where her shoulder blades stuck out like pathetic wings, he grunted several times.

'Ahah!' he exclaimed, striking treasure-trove.

Without any warning, Missy was grabbed around head and heels and hips by doctor and nurse combined; what they did was over so quickly she had no positive idea what they did, except that there came the sound of a grinding, sickening crunch all the more horrifying because she heard it inside her ears as well as outside them.

'You may get dressed now, Miss Wright, and then go through that door,' ordered Dr Parkinson, and went through that door himself with his nurse still in attendance.

Shaken and diminished, Missy did as she was told.

The right way up he turned out to have a very pleasant face, and his light blue eyes were kind and interested.

'Well, Miss Wright, you may return home today,' he said, fingering a letter that lay on his desk along with quite a number of other papers.

'Am I all right?' asked Missy.

'Perfectly all right. There's absolutely nothing wrong with your heart. You've got a badly pinched nerve near the top of your spine, and those vigorous walks of yours kinked it into a vigorous protest, that's all.'

'But – I couldn't breathe!' whispered Missy, aghast.

'Panic, Miss Wright, panic! When the nerve kinks the pain is very severe, and it is just possible that in your case it inhibits some of the respiratory musculature. But there's really no need to worry. I manipulated your spine myself now, and that should fix it up as long as you slow down the pace of your walking a little when you're going some distance. If it doesn't clear up, I suggest you rig yourself up a sort of chinning bar, have someone tie a couple of house-bricks to each of your feet, and then try to lift yourself up to your chin on the bar against the weight of the bricks.'

'And there's nothing else wrong with me?'

'Disappointed, eh?' asked Dr Parkinson shrewdly. 'Come now, Miss Wright! Why on earth would you prefer to have heart trouble instead of a kinked spinal nerve?'

It was a question Missy had no intention of answering aloud; how could one die in John Smith's arms of a kinked spinal nerve? It was as romantic as pimples.

Dr Parkinson sat back in his chair and regarded her thoughtfully, tapping his pen on the blotter. It was obviously his habit to do this, for the blotter was pocked with many little blue dots, and at times, perhaps from boredom, he had begun to join up the more scattered dots into a meaningless cat's cradle.

'Periods!' he said suddenly, apparently feeling he ought to cheer her up a little by investigating every avenue. 'How often do you have a period, Miss Wright?'

She blushed, and hated herself for blushing. 'About every six months.'

'Lose much?'

'No, very little.'

'Pain? Cramps?'

'No.'

'Hmmmm.' He began to join up some dots. 'Headaches?'

'No.'

'Are you a fainter?'

'No.'

'Hmmmm.' He pursed his lips so successfully that the top one actually managed to caress the tip of his nose. 'Miss Wright,' he said at last, 'what really ails you can only be effectively cured if you find yourself a husband and have a couple of babies. I doubt you'd ever have more than a couple, because I don't think you'll fall easily, but at your age it's high time you got started.'

'If I could find someone willing to start me, Doctor, believe me I would start!' said Missy tartly.

'I beg your pardon.'

At this precise and uncomfortable moment Dr Parkinson's nurse thrust her head around the door and wiggled her brows.

He rose immediately, semaphored away. 'Excuse me.'

For perhaps a minute Missy sat immobile in her chair wondering whether she ought to get up and tiptoe out, then she decided she had better wait for a formal dismissal. Dr Neville Hurlingford's name leaped at her from the top of a letter on the desk, midway between a constellation of joined dots and a globular cluster of unjoined dots. Quite independently of her brain, Missy's hand reached out, picked up the letter.

'Dear George,' it said,

'Odd that I should have to send you two patients within the same week, when I haven't sent you any in six months. But such is life – and my practice – in Byron. This letter is to introduce Missy Wright, a poor little old maid who has had at least one attack of chest pain and breathlessness following on a long, brisk walk. The single attack witnessed was rather suggestive of hysteria except that the patient was grey and sweating. However, her return to normal was dramatically sudden, and when I examined her not long afterwards, I could find no sequelae of any kind. I do indeed suspect hysteria, as her life's circumstances would make it a most likely diagnosis. She leads a stagnant, deprived existence (vide her breast development). But to be on the safe side, I would like you to see her with a view to excluding any serious illness.'

Missy put the letter down and closed her eyes. Did the whole world see her with pity and contempt? And how could pride contend with so much pity and contempt when it was so wellmeaning? Like her mother, Missy was proud. 'Stagnant'. 'Deprived'. 'A poor little old maid'. 'With a view to excluding any serious illness', as if stagnation and deprivation and old maidenhood were not serious illnesses within themselves!

She opened her eyes, surprised to discover that they contained not one tear. Instead, they were bright and dry and *angry*. And they began searching through the litter on Dr Parkinson's desk to see if among the pieces of paper there might be at least the start of a report on her condition. She found two reports, neither distinguished by a name; one had a list of findings on it that all said 'normal', the other was a technical litany of disaster, all to do with the heart. And she discovered the beginning of a letter to Dr Hurlingford.

'Dear Neville,' the letter said,

'Thank you for referring Mrs Anastasia Gilroy and Miss? Wright, whose Christian name I am afraid I do not know, as everyone including yourself seems to add a "y' to her marital status and leave it at that. I am sure you will not object if I send you my opinion about both patients in this one' –

And there it ended. Mrs Anastasia Gilroy? After sifting through a few of the non-Hurlingford faces in Byron, she came up with a sickly-looking woman of about her own age who lived in a run-down cottage beside the bottling plant with a drunken husband and several small, neglected children.

Was the second clinical report about Mrs Gilroy, then? Missy picked it up and tried to decipher the jargon and symbols which filled the top half of the sheet. Though the bottom half was clear enough, even to her.

It said, 'I can offer no course of treatment able to change or modify this prognosis. The patient is suffering from an advanced form of multiple valvular disease of the heart. If no further cardiac deterioration takes place, I give her six months to one year of life. However, I can see no point in recommending bed rest, as I imagine this patient would simply ignore the directive, given her nature and home situation.'

Mrs Gilroy? If only there was a name on it! But it would be hers, saved to put in with the letter to Dr Hurlingford. There were no other reports amid the confusion. Oh, why wasn't Missy Wright's the bad report? Death, snatched from her, seemed suddenly very sweet and desirable. It wasn't fair! Mrs Gilroy had a family who needed her desperately. Where Missy Wright had no one to need her desperately.

Voices sounded on the other side of the door; Missy folded up the report still in her hand neatly and swiftly, and stuffed it into her purse.

'My dear Miss Wright, I am so sorry!' cried Dr Parkinson, breezing in with sufficient flurry to send the papers on his desk flying in all directions. 'You can go, you can go! Leave it a week before you go back to see Dr Hurlingford, eh?'

Sydney was warmer and moister than the Blue Mountains, and the day was fine and clear. Emerging onto Macquarie Street with Una at her side, Missy blinked in the brightness.

'Nearly half past eleven,' said Una. 'Shall we go and sell our share certificates first? The address is in Bridge Street, which is only round the corner from here.'

So they did that, and it was remarkably easy. However, the small office and its surly clerk offered no clue as to the identity of the mystery buyer; the most intriguing aspect of the sale was that they were paid in gold sovereigns rather than in paper money. And four hundred gold coins were very heavy, as Missy discovered once she had put them in her bag.

'We can't walk far loaded down like this,' said Una, 'so I suggest we lunch at the Hotel Metropole – we're only a hop skip and jump away from it – then catch a tram back to Central and just go tamely home.'

In all her life Missy had never eaten in a restaurant, even her Aunt Julia's tea room, nor had she ever been inside the Hurlingford Hotel. So the opulent vastness of the Metropole staggered her, with its crystal chandeliers and marble columns; it also reminded her of Aunt Aurelia's house, because it was beautifully greened and silenced with potted Kentia palms. As for the food – Missy had never tasted anything as delicious as the crayfish salad Una ordered for her.

'I think I might be able to get fat, if I could eat food like this every day,' said Missy ecstatically.

Una smiled at her without pity, but with a great deal of understanding. 'Poor Missy! Life has passed you by, hasn't it? Now me, life ran over like a through train. Bang boom crash, and there's our Una flat on her face in the water. But cheer up, darling, do! Life won't always pass you by, I promise. You just hang onto the thought that every dog has its day, even the bitches. Only don't let life run you over, either – that's equally hard to deal with.'

Wanting to tell Una how very much she liked her, but too inhibited to do so, Missy sought around for an acceptable topic of conversation. 'You haven't asked me what the doctor said.'

Una's bright blue eyes gleamed. 'What did he say?'

Missy sighed. 'My heart is as sound as a bell.'

'Are you sure?'

Knowing exactly what Una was implying, she smiled. 'All right, yes, it is a bit affected. But not by a disease.'

'I think it's the worst disease in the world!'

'Not in a doctor's book.'

'If you like John Smith so terribly much, why don't you show him you like him?'

'*Me*?'

'Yes, darling, you! You know, your real trouble is that you've been brought up – along with that whole town – to think that if you don't look and act like Alicia Marshall, no man could ever be interested. But my dear, Alicia Marshall does not slay every man who meets her! There are many men with more taste and discrimination than that, and I happen to know that John Smith is one of them.' She smiled impishly. 'In fact, I think you'd suit John Smith extremely well.'

'Is he married?'

'He was at one time, but he's respectably single now – his wife died.'

'Oh! Was she – was she nice?'

Una thought about that. 'Well, at any rate *I* liked her. There were plenty who didn't.'

'Did he like her?'

'I think he probably liked her well enough in the beginning, but not nearly well enough in the end.'

'Oh.'

Una commandeered the bill and would hear none of Missy's protests. 'Darling, your transactions this morning have been quite without personal reward, where mine have netted me one hundred wonderful pounds that I intend to fritter away like a king's mistress. Lunch is therefore my treat.'

A very exclusive-looking dress shop occupied the corner where they waited for the tram, but to Missy's surprise, Una displayed no interest.

'First of all, darling, a hundred pounds wouldn't buy the smell of an oil rag in there,' she explained. 'Besides which, their clothes are as deplorably dull as their prices are deplorably expensive. No red dresses! It's far too respectable a shop.'

'One day I shall have my scarlet lace dress and hat,' said Missy, 'no matter how unrespectable I look.'

'So I don't have heart trouble at all,' said Missy to her mother and aunt. 'In fact, my heart is perfect.'

Both the big pale faces turned anxiously to Missy fell instantly into repose.

'Oh, that is good news!' said Octavia.

'What is the matter, then?' asked Drusilla.

'I have a pinched nerve in my spine.'

'Good heavens! Does that mean there's no cure?'

'No, Dr Parkinson thinks he may already have cured me. He almost screwed my head off, there was a horrible sort of crunch, and I should be quite well from now on. He referred to what he did as a manipulation, I think. But if I do get more attacks, I have to get you to tie two bricks to each of my feet, and I have to hang in the air with my chin resting on a bar!' She grinned. 'The mere thought is enough to cure any complaint!' Only with a hefty swing did she manage to deposit her handbag on the table. 'Here's something a lot more important – look!' And she withdrew four neatly wrapped cylinders. 'One hundred pounds for you, Mother, all in gold. And the same for Aunt Octavia, Aunt Cornelia, and Aunt Julia.'

'It's a miracle,' said Drusilla.

'No, it's a little tardy justice,' contradicted Missy. 'You will buy that Singer sewing machine now, won't you?'

Prudence warred with desire in Drusilla's breast until she declared a temporary truce with the outcome undecided. 'I said I would think about it, and I will.'

When bedtime came around Missy found herself sleepless, despite the day's novel exertions; she lay contentedly in the dark and thought about John Smith. So he had been married, but his wife was dead. There could surely have been no children, or he would surely have them with him for at least part of the time. That was sad, so too was Una's opinion of the union, that he had not liked his wife nearly well enough in the end. Sydney society, decided Missy, was not conducive to happy marriages, what with Una and her Wallace, and John Smith and his dead wife. Still, Mrs John Smith had not had to suffer the stigma of divorce; at which point, Missy wondered for the first time in her convention-hedged life whether the stigma of divorce might not be preferable to the finality of death.

By midnight her plan was all worked out, and her mind was made up. She would do it, and she would do it tomorrow. After all, what did she have to lose? If her scheme did not bear fruit, she would simply have to continue for the next thirty-three years as she had gone on for the last thirty-three years. Certainly it was worth a try.

Somewhere in her suddenly sleepy brain a little thought was

spared for John Smith, the unsuspecting victim. Was it fair? Yes, came the answer. Missy turned over and went to sleep with no further misgivings.

Drusilla elected to bear the four hundred pounds into Byron without assistance, and set off the next morning at nine o'clock, the heavy burden of her bag seeming as a feather. She was very happy, not only for herself, but for her sisters also. In the last few weeks more good fortune had come her way than in the last almost four decades, and she was beginning to dare to hope that the good fortune was a trickle building into a rivulet rather than a splash draining into the sand. But it cannot be for me alone, she vowed. Somehow I must ensure it embraces *all* of us.

While Octavia pottered happily in the kitchen, Missy quietly packed her scant clothing into the battered carpetbag which served all the ladies of Missalonghi on the rare occasions a bag was needed. On the top cover of her bed she left a note for her mother, then she let herself out of the front door, walked down the path to the gate, and turned left, not right.

This time she didn't timidly explore the start of the descent into John Smith's valley; she walked down it with decision and purpose, using a strong stick and the carpetbag to keep her balance on the treacherous rubble. At the bottom of the landslide the going became easier as the road plunged into the forested flanks below the cliffs. It was not nearly as cold as she imagined it might be, for the ramparts far above took the brunt of the wind; down on the valley floor, all was still and calm.

Four miles from the commencement of the descent the more open woodland of the sloping flanks turned into a kind of jungle, thick with vines and creepers and tree-ferns, even several varieties of palm. There were bellbirds everywhere, though try as she would, she couldn't see them; but their calls filled the air with the most delicate silvery chimes, thin and clear and elfin, utterly unbirdlike. And other birdsongs wove through the chimes, long carols from magpies, joyous trills from tiny fantails which fluttered only inches from her face and seemed to be welcoming her into their home.

That third hour of walking was very damp, the sun hardly showing through the canopy of leaves above, the track slippery from moss and mud and decaying forest detritus. When the first leech dropped on her and immediately attached its skinny slimy wriggling body to her hand, Missy's impulse was to screech and run in demented circles, especially after all her frantic efforts to dislodge it proved vain. But she made herself stand absolutely still and absolutely silent until the hair on her neck and arms subsided, then she gave herself a severe lecture; if these disgusting things lived in John Smith's forest, then she must cope with them in a way that would not brand her in his eyes as a silly woman. The leech had begun to swell up plumply, and, as she discovered when she began to feel areas of exposed skin on neck and face, had been joined by several equally vampirish brothers. Wretched things! They wouldn't let go! So she moved on in the hope that she would encounter fewer leeches moving than standing in one spot, a hope that was right. Replete, the first one to land detached itself without fuss and flopped to the ground, as did its brothers. She then learned that staunch the wounds as she would, they kept on bleeding away. What a sight she must look! Covered in blood. Lesson number one about dreams versus reality.

Shortly afterwards the sound of the river began to fill the distance, and Missy's courage started to bleed away as rapidly as her leech wounds; it took more resolution and strength to walk those last few hundred yards than to mount the whole expedition.

There it was, just around the next bend. A low small cabin built of wattle-and-daub, with a roof of wooden shingles and a lean-to off to one side that looked to be of more recent construction. However, the cabin had a sandstone chimney, and a thin blur of smoke smudged the perfect blue of the sky. He was home, then!

Since it was no part of her plan to pounce on him unaware, Missy stopped at the edge of the clearing and called his name several times in her loudest voice. Two horses grazing in a fenced-off yard lifted their heads to gaze at her curiously before going back to the endless business of feeding, but of John Smith there was no sign. He must be off somewhere, then. She sat down on a convenient tree stump to wait.

The wait wasn't long, for she arrived a little before one o'clock, and he came merrily whistling back to the cabin to get himself some lunch. Even after he entered the clearing he didn't see her; she was sitting in line with the horses, where he struck off towards the river flowing in noisy cascades behind the cabin.

'Mr Smith!' she called.

He stopped in his tracks, did not move for a moment, then turned. 'Oh, bloody hell!' he said.

When he reached her, he scowled at her horribly, not a scrap of welcome in his eyes.

'What are you doing here?'

Missy gulped in a big breath of much-needed air; it was now or never. 'Will you marry me, Mr Smith?' she asked, enunciating very distinctly.

His anger fled at once, replaced by unconcealed mirth. 'It's a long walk down, so you'd better come in and have a cup of tea, Miss Wright,' he said, eyes dancing. A finger flicked at the blood on her face. 'Leeches, eh? I'm surprised you lasted the distance.'

His hand went under her elbow and he walked her at a sedate pace across the clearing without saying another word, just muffling his laughter. The cabin had no verandah, unusual in that part of the world, and, as Missy saw when she entered its dimness, the floor was of packed earth, the fittings spartan. However, for a bachelor establishment it looked remarkably neat and clean, no dirty dishes, no untidiness. A new cast-iron cooking range filled half the chimney, an open fireplace the other half; there was a wooden bench for his washing-up dish, as well as a long rough-hewn table and two straight kitchen chairs. He had made his bed from timber slabs, piled what looked like at least three mattresses on top, and a feather quilt that ought to keep him warm in any weather. Some cow hide stretched across a chunky wooden frame served him as an easy-chair, and his clothing hung on wooden pegs hammered into the wall next to his bed. There were no curtains on the one window, which looked as if it had been recently glazed.

'But why have curtains?' Missy asked aloud.

'Eh?' In the act of lighting two kerosene lamps from a spill he had thrust into the stove, he looked at her.

'How splendid to live in a house that doesn't need any curtains,' said Missy.

He put one lamp on the table and the other on an orange crate beside his bed, then busied himself making tea.

'There's really enough light,' said Missy, 'without lamps.'

'You're sitting in front of the window, Miss Wright, and I want some light on your face.'

So Missy lapsed into silence, letting her eyes wander wherever they chose, from John Smith to his dwelling and back again. As usual he smelled clean, though dust and earth on his clothing and arms suggested that he had been doing something fairly strenuous

all morning, as did a long superficial graze on the back of his left hand and wrist.

He served the tea in enamel mugs and the biscuits still in their huge gaudy tin, but he did everything without apology and with no physical awkwardness. After he had served her and she had indicated she wished for nothing else, he carried his mug and a fistful of biscuits to the leather easy-chair, which he pulled round so he could sit facing her at close quarters.

'Why on earth, Miss Wright, would you want to marry me?'

'Because I love you!' said Missy, her tone astonished.

This answer threw him into confusion; as if suddenly he didn't wish her to see what might lie in his eyes, he removed his gaze from her person to the window behind her, frowning.

'That's ridiculous,' he said at last, chewing his lip.

'I would have said it was obvious.'

'You can't possibly love someone you don't even know, woman! It's ridiculous.'

'I know quite enough about you to love you,' she said earnestly. 'I know that you're very kind. You're strong on the inside. You're clean. You're different. And you – you have enough *poetry* in you to want to live here of all places.'

He blinked. 'Christ!' he exclaimed, and laughed. 'I must say that's the most interesting catalogue of virtues I've ever been privileged to hear. I like the clean bit best.'

'It's important,' said Missy gravely.

For a moment he looked as if amusement might get the better of him again, but with an effort he remained sober, and said, 'I'm afraid I can't marry you, Miss Wright.'

'Why?'

'Why? I'll tell you why,' he said, leaning forward in his chair. 'You are looking at a man who has found happiness for the first time in his life! If I were twenty, that would be a stupid statement, but I'm pushing fifty, Miss Wright, and that means I'm entitled to some happiness. I'm finally doing all the things I've always wanted to do and never had the time or the chance – and I'm *alone*! No wife, no relations, no dependents of any kind. Not even a dog. Just me. And I love it! To have to share it would spoil it. In fact, I'm going to put a bloody great gate across the top of my road and keep the whole world out. *Marriage*? Not in a fit!'

'It wouldn't be for very long,' said Missy quietly.

'A day would be too long, Miss Wright.'

'I understand how you feel, Mr Smith, and I do mean that most sincerely. I too have spent a confined life, I too have chafed against it. But I cannot imagine for a moment that your life has been as dull, as drab and uneventful as mine has always been. Oh, I don't wish to imply that I've been mistreated, or treated one iota worse than the other ladies of Missalonghi. We all live the same dull drab uneventful life. But I am tired of it, Mr Smith! I want to live a little before I die! Can you understand that?'

'Hell, who couldn't? But if you're in a proposing mood, why not put the hard word on some of the widowers or bachelors in Byron? There must be a few around somewhere.' His shell of hardness was setting with every word he said, and he was beginning to feel as if he might extricate himself from this most embarrassing situation without losing either his freedom or his self-respect.

'That would be a fate worse than Missalonghi, because it would be no different. I've chosen you because you're living exactly the kind of life I want to live – away from people, away from houses and smugness and gossip. Believe me, Mr Smith, I have no intention of cramping your style – on the contrary, I want you to free up mine! I won't be a millstone around your neck. In fact, I'll guarantee to leave you alone most of the time. And it wouldn't be forever, I promise you. A year. Just one little year!'

'So after a year of living the sort of life you're dying to live, you're going to pick up and tamely go back to the life you hate?' His tone was sceptical.

Missy drew up her meagre form with profound dignity. 'I only have a year to live, Mr Smith,' she said.

He looked desperately sorry for her, as if he now knew everything about her there was to know.

She pushed her advantage relentlessly. 'I understand very well your reluctance to share this paradise – if it were mine, I too would guard it jealously. But try to see my side, please! I am thirty-three years old, and I have never known any of the things most women my age either take for granted or wish they didn't have at all. I am an old maid! That is the most dreadful fate a woman can suffer, for it goes hand in hand with poverty and lack of beauty. If I had suffered one without the other, some man would have been prepared to marry me, but to suffer both is to be completely undesirable. Yet I *know* that if I can only get past these handicaps, I have a great deal to offer that most women don't, because they have no need to. You would enjoy all the advantages, Mr Smith, for I would be tied to you by the bonds of gratitude and thankfulness, as well as by love. I wish there was some way right at this moment whereby I could show you how little you'd lose by marrying me, and how much you'd gain you don't even know about. I have good sense, and no puffed-up notion of my own importance. And I would try with might and main to be the nicest of companions for you, as well as the most loving.'

He got up abruptly and went to stand looking out the door, his hands clasped behind his back. 'Women,' he said, 'are liars, cheats, connivers and fools. I wouldn't care if I never saw another woman as long as I lived. As for love – I don't *want* to be loved! I just want to be left alone!' This cry from the heart he seemed to think was enough, then, rethinking, he added harshly, 'How do I know you're telling me the truth?'

'Well, Mr Smith, you are not exactly at the top of the list of Byron's most eligible men! I have heard you described as everything from a jailbird to an eccentric, and it is common knowledge that you are not rich. Why therefore should I lie?' She opened her purse and fished out the neatly folded piece of paper she had appropriated from Dr Parkinson's desk, then got up from her chair and walked across to join him at the door. 'Here. Read this. You do know I'm ill, because you were there when I had my first bad turn. And when I met you the other day on my walk, I'm sure I told you I had to go to Sydney to see a heart specialist. Well, this is his report on my condition. I stole it, first of all because I don't want my mother and aunt to know I'm so sick. I don't want to become an object of worry for them, I don't want to be forced into bed and fussed over. So I told them I had a kinked spinal nerve, and if I can keep up the deception, that's what they're going to go on thinking is wrong with me. My second reason for stealing it concerns you. I knew I was going to ask you to marry me and I knew I'd need proof of my sincerity. There is no name on it except the doctor's, I know, but if you look at it carefully, you will see no patient's name has been erased from it, either.'

He took the paper, unfolded it, read it quickly and turned to face her. 'Aside from being awfully skinny, you look healthy enough to me,' he said doubtfully.

Missy did some fast thinking, and prayed he was no medical expert. 'Why, between my turns I am healthy enough! Mine is not the sort of heart trouble that saps the strength, it's more like – like – like having little strokes. The valves – stick – and – and when they do, the blood stops flowing. That I gather is what's going to kill me. I don't know any more than that – doctors never want to tell you anything. I suppose they find it hard enough to tell you you're going to die.' She heaved a sigh, and began to scale histrionic heights with the aplomb of an actress. 'I shall just go out like a light one day!' Her eyes lifted to his wistfully. 'I don't want to die at Missalonghi!' she cried pitifully. 'I want to die in the arms of the man I love!'

He was a born fighter, so he tried a different tack. 'How about a second opinion? Doctors can be wrong.'

'What for?' countered Missy. 'If I only have a year to live, I do not want to spend it traipsing from one doctor to another!' A big tear fell down her cheek, while others still swimming with telling effect threatened to follow its lead. 'Oh, Mr Smith, I want to spend my last year *happily*!'

He groaned the groan of a condemned man. 'For God's sake, woman, don't cry!'

'Why not?' sobbed Missy, scrabbling up her sleeve for her handkerchief. 'I think I have every right to cry!'

'Then cry, damn you!' he said, goaded beyond endurance, and marched out of the door.

Missy stood mopping her tears, eyes following him through them as he strode to the far side of the clearing and then disappeared from view. Head down, she returned to her chair and finished her cry with no more appreciative audience than a large blow-fly. After which, she didn't know what to do. Was he coming back? Was he hiding somewhere watching to see her leave before coming back?

Suddenly she felt very tired, utterly dispirited. All that, and no result. So much for Una's encouragement. So much for stolen reports. So much for her bright vision of emancipation. She sighed, and had never meant a sigh more, or sighed more. No use staying here. She wasn't wanted.

She let herself out of the cabin quietly, and made sure that she closed the door. It was gone two o'clock, and she had a nine-mile walk, all uphill, all difficult terrain; it would be late before she arrived back at Missalonghi.

'Yet I don't feel sorry I tried,' she said aloud. 'It was worth a try, I *know* it was.'

'Miss Wright!'

She turned, hope kindling and blazing.

'Hold on, I'll drive you home.'

'Thank you, I can walk,' she said, not stiffly or huffily, just in her old colourlessly polite manner.

By this he had reached her side, and put his hand beneath her elbow. 'No, it's too late and too hard a walk, especially for you. Sit here while I harness up.' And he deposited her on the same tree stump where she had sat waiting for him.

She really was too tired to argue, and perhaps too tired to face the walk, so she made no demur. When he was ready, he lifted her up into the cart as easily as if she had been a child.

'This only goes to prove what I've been telling myself lately,' he said as he turned the horses out of the clearing onto the track. 'I need a smaller vehicle, a sulky or a gig. It's a damned nuisance to have to use both horses and a big cart unless I've got a heavy load.'

'Yes, I'm sure you're right,' she said meaninglessly.

'Angry?'

Her face turned to his, its expression purely surprised. 'No! Why should I be?'

'Well, you didn't meet with much luck, did you?'

She laughed, not very heartily, yet still a genuine laugh. 'Poor Mr Smith, you don't understand at all.'

'Obviously I don't. What's the joke?'

'I had nothing to lose. Nothing!'

'Did you really think you might win?'

'I was sure I would win.'

'Why?'

'Because you're you.'

'And what does that mean?'

'Oh – just that you're so very kind. A decent person.'

'Thanks.'

After that little was said; the horses plodded reluctantly along the jungly track, obviously not understanding why they were proceeding away from home. But even when they came to the switchback up the landslide they plodded on without visible protest, which to the countrywise Missy indicated that they knew their master better than to baulk. Yet he was pleasant to them, and didn't ply the whip; he dominated them by the force of his will.

'I must say that it shows, your not being a Hurlingford,' he said abruptly as the journey neared its end.

'*Not* a Hurlingford? What makes you assume that?'

'Lots of things. Your name, for a start. Your appearance. The godforsaken position of your home, and the lack of money in it. Your nice nature.' He sounded as if he grudged this last admission.

'Not all Hurlingfords are rich, Mr Smith. As a matter of fact I am a Hurlingford, at least on the distaff side. My aunt and mother are the sisters of Maxwell and Herbert Hurlingford, and first cousins of Sir William's.'

He turned to stare at her while she explained this, then whistled. 'Well, that's a smack in the eye! A nest of genuine Hurlingfords all the way out at the end of Gordon Road, and scraping to make ends meet. What happened?'

So for the rest of the way home Missy regaled John Smith with an account of the perfidy of the first Sir William, and the compounded perfidy of his successors.

'Thank you,' he said at the end of it. 'You've answered a lot of questions for me, and given me quite a bit to think about.' He pulled his horses up outside the front gate of Missalonghi. 'Here you are, home again, and well before your mother would be worried.'

She jumped down without assistance. 'Thank you, dear Mr Smith. It's as I still maintain – you're a very kind man.'

In answer, he tipped his hat and flashed her a smile, then began turning his horses.

Octavia found Missy's note when she went to investigate Missy's whereabouts. There it sat, very white against the brown coverlet, with the single word MOTHER printed across its surface. Her heart thudded down into her boots; notes that said MOTHER never contained good news.

So when she heard Drusilla letting herself in through the front door, she scuttled into the hall with the note in her hand and her protuberant pale blue eyes all geared up to shed as many tears as the contents of the note dictated.

'Missy's gone, and she's left this note for you!'

Drusilla frowned, unalarmed. 'Gone?'

'*Gone*! She has taken all her clothes, and she has taken our carpetbag.'

The skin over Drusilla's cheeks began to prickle and stretch uncomfortably; she snatched the note from Octavia and read it aloud so Octavia could not misinterpret the contents.

'Dear Mother,' it said,

'Please forgive me for going off without a word, but I really think it is better that you do not know what I plan until I know whether or not it's going to work. I will probably be home tomorrow or the next day for a visit at least. Please do not worry. I am safe. Your loving daughter, Missy.'

Octavia's tears overflowed, but Drusilla did not weep. She folded the letter again and carried it into the kitchen, where she propped it very carefully on the shelf of the chimney.

'We must call in the police,' said Octavia tearfully.

'We will do no such thing,' contradicted Drusilla, and moved the kettle to the front of the stove. 'Oh, dear, I need a cup of tea badly!'

'But Missy might be in danger!'

'I very much doubt it. There's nothing in her note to indicate any kind of foolishness.' She sat down with a sigh. 'Octavia, *do* dry your eyes! The events of the last few days have taught me that Missy is a person to be reckoned with. I have no doubt that she is safe, and that, probably tomorrow, we will indeed see her again. In the meantime, we do not so much as mention to anybody that Missy has left home.'

'But she's out there somewhere without a soul to protect her from Men!'

'It may well be that Missy has decided she would rather not be protected from Men,' said Drusilla dryly. 'Now do as you're told, Octavia, stop crying and make us some tea. I have a lot to tell you that has nothing to do with Missy's disappearance.'

Curiosity overcame distress; Octavia poured a little hot water into the teapot and set it to stand by the stove. 'Oh, what?' she asked eagerly.

'Well, I gave Cornelia and Julia their money, and I bought myself a Singer sewing machine.'

'Drusilla!'

And so the two ladies left at Missalonghi drank their tea and discussed the events of the day more thoroughly, after which they went back to their routines, and eventually retired to their respective bedrooms.

'Dear God,' said Drusilla on her knees, 'please help and protect Missy, keep her from all harm and give her strength in all adversities. Amen.'

After which she climbed into her bed, the only double one, as befitted the only married lady. But it was some time before she managed to close her eyes.

The organ had saved Missy from detection when John Smith dropped her back at Missalonghi; no one heard his cart arrive or depart, and no one heard Missy as she crept around the side of the house and headed across the backyard towards the shed. It held no place capable of concealing her, but she managed to tuck the carpetbag down behind a sack of fodder, and then she left the shed for the shelter of the orchard until after her mother had milked the cow. Of course the cow knew her step and began to low pitifully to be milked, but before Buttercup became really agitated, out came Drusilla with the bucket.

Missy huddled down behind the fattest-trunked apple tree and closed her eyes and wished she did have terminal heart disease, preferably severe enough to ensure she would never see the morning.

Not until after full darkness had fallen did she stir; it was the penetrating Blue Mountains' cold spring air drove her from the orchard at last, into the relative warmth of the shed. Buttercup was lying with feet tucked under, placidly chewing cud, udder comfortably empty. So Missy put a clean sack down on the ground next to the cow, and curled up on the sack with her head and shoulders lying against Buttercup's warm rumbly side.

Of course she should have gathered up her courage and walked into the house the minute John Smith had gone, but when she tried to make her feet mount the front verandah steps, they just would not. How could you tell your mother that you'd proposed marriage to a near-stranger and been refused for your pains? Or failing that one, what convincing story could she have concocted? Missy was not a story spinner, she was only a story reader. Maybe in the morning she could confess, she told herself, gasping at the ache and sorrow of it; but how much worse would that be, with a night spent elsewhere than under the roof of Missalonghi to be accounted for? Who would ever believe she had spent it sleeping with a *cow*? Go inside at once, whispered her better self; but her worse self could not find the courage.

The tears began to gather and to fall, for indeed Missy was exhausted, not so much from her physical exertions as from the terrific burst of will that had sent her to see John Smith.

'Oh, Buttercup, what am I going to do?' she wept.

Buttercup merely huffed.

And shortly afterwards, Missy fell asleep.

The Missalonghi rooster woke her about an hour before dawn, screeching his clarion from the beam right above her head. She leaped up, confused, then subsided against her living pillow in a fresh agony of pain and bewilderment. She wasn't hungry, she wasn't thirsty. What to do? Oh, what to do?

But by dawn she had made up her mind what to do, and rose then to her feet with purpose in her movements. Pulling comb and brush from the carpetbag, she tidied herself as best she could, but at the end of her efforts was dismally aware she smelled strongly of cow.

No sound of stirring life came from Missalonghi as she crept past it, and faintly from out her mother's window came a series of little snores. Safe.

Down once more into John Smith's valley, not with the dreamy enchantment of yesterday, nor with the irrepressible happiness of yesterday, when nothing had seemed impossible and everything had seemed bound to end well. This time Missy marched with little hope but iron determination; he would not say her nay again, even if it meant she had to spend every night of the next year in her mother's shed with Buttercup for a bedmate, and every day marching down to the bottom of John Smith's valley to ask again. For ask again she would, and tomorrow if he said nay today, and the day after, and the day after that . . .

It was going on for ten o'clock when she came at last to the clearing and the cabin; there rose the same rippling blur from the chimney, but, as yesterday, no John Smith. Down on the tree stump she sat to wait.

Perhaps he too had passed beyond hunger; when noon came and went without a sign of him, Missy resigned herself to waiting the whole afternoon as well. Indeed, the sun had long gone behind the great walls above, and the light was fading rapidly, before he came home. More seriously than yesterday, but just as blind to Missy sitting on her stump.

'Mr Smith!'

'Bloody hell!'

He came across immediately to stand looking down at her, not angrily, but not pleasantly, either. 'What are you doing back here again?'

'Will you marry me, Mr Smith?'

This time he didn't put his hand beneath her elbow and walk her across to the cabin; he turned to face her fully as she rose to her feet, and looked down into her eyes.

'Is someone putting you up to this?' he asked.

'No.'

'Does it really mean that much to you?'

'It means my life, literally. I am not going home! I'm going to come here every day and ask again.'

'You're playing with fire, Miss Wright,' he said, lips thin and tight. 'Hasn't it occurred to you that a man might resort to violence if a woman refuses to leave him alone?'

She smiled up serenely, sublimely, seraphically. 'Some men, maybe. But not you, Mr Smith.'

'What do you really stand to gain? What if I did say I'd marry you? Is that the sort of husband you want, a man you've worn down until he doesn't know what else to do for peace than give in – or strangle you?' His voice dropped, became very hard. 'In this big wide world, Miss Wright, lives a malignant thing called *hate*. I beg of you, don't uncage it!'

'Will you marry me?' she asked.

He screwed up his mouth, blew air through his nose, and lifted his head to stare above hers at something she couldn't see. And said nothing for what seemed like a very long time. Then he shrugged, looked down at her. 'I admit I've thought a lot about you since yesterday, and even the heaviest work I could find didn't stop my thinking about you. And I started to wonder too if maybe I was being offered a way to atone, and if my luck might disappear because I ignored the offer.'

'A way to atone? Atone for what?'

'Just a figure of speech. Everyone has something to atone for, no one is free of guilt. In forcing yourself on me, you're creating a cause for atonement, don't you see that?'

'Yes.'

'But it makes no difference?'

'I'll take whatever comes to me gladly, Mr Smith, if I can take you along with it.'

'Very well, then. I'll marry you.'

All of Missy's pain and numbness flew away. 'Oh, thank you, Mr Smith! You won't regret it, I promise!'

He grunted. 'You're a child, Miss Wright, not a grown woman, and perhaps that's why I've given in rather than strangled you. I can't honestly believe there's woman's guile in you. Only don't ever give me reason to change that opinion.'

And now his hand went under her arm, the signal to walk.

'There's one thing I must ask, Mr Smith,' she said.

'What?'

'That we never refer to the fact that I'm going to die, nor let it influence our behaviour. I want to be free! And I cannot be free if I am to be perpetually reminded by word or deed that I'm going to die.'

'Agreed,' said John Smith.

Not wanting to push her luck, for she sensed she had gone about as far in that line as was prudent, Missy entered the cabin and went to sit quietly in one of the kitchen chairs, while John Smith swung round inside the door and stood staring out of it at the beginnings of a thin blue night's ground mist.

Silently she watched his back, which was long and broad and, at the moment, extremely eloquent. But after about five minutes she ventured to say, her voice very small and apologetic, 'What happens now, Mr Smith?'

He jumped as if he had forgotten she was there, and went to sit opposite her at the table. His face in the gloom was full of shadows, heavy, deadened, a little daunting. But when he spoke, it was cheerfully enough, as if he had decided there was no point in making himself more miserable than the situation called for. 'My name is John,' he said, and got up to light his two lamps, both of which he placed on the table so he could see her face. 'As to the main business, we get a licence, and we get married.'

'How long will it take?'

He shrugged. 'I don't know, if banns aren't called. A couple of days? Maybe even sooner, with a special licence. In the meantime, I'd better drive you home.'

'Oh, no! I'm staying here,' said Missy.

'If you stay here you're likely to start your honeymoon prematurely,' he said, hope blossoming. What a good idea! She might decide she didn't like it! After all, most women didn't. And he could be hard about it, not rape her exactly, just force her a little; a virgin of her age was bound to be easy to frighten. At which point he made the mistake of looking at her to see how she reacted. And there she was, poor little dying thing, just gazing at him with blinded foolish affection, like a puppy awash with love. John Smith's sleeping heart moved, felt a bitter and unaccustomed pain. For indeed she had haunted him all day, no matter how hard he worked to drive out her image and replace it by emptiness hacked out of physical labour. He had his secrets, some of them buried so deep he could tell himself in all truth that he had never suffered those secrets, that he was reborn in all the newness and nakedness of a life begun again. But all day things had nibbled and whispered and gnawed, and the utter pleasure he had found in his valley had vanished. Maybe he did have to atone; maybe that was why she had come. Only he honestly didn't have one thing to atone for so large, so depressing. He didn't. Oh no, he didn't, he didn't!

Maybe she wouldn't like it. Take her to bed, John Smith, show her what it's like in the wasteland of the body, fill her with yourself and with disgust for it. She's a woman.

But Missy liked it very well, and demonstrated a surprising aptitude for it. Another nail went thudding into John Smith's coffin, as he wryly admitted to himself about three hours after he and Missy had retired dinnerless to bed. Wonders never ceased. This ageing spinster virgin was made for it! Though dreadfully ignorant at first, she was neither shy nor shamed, and her affectionate responses warmed him, touched him, made it impossible for him to be cruel or unkind to her. The little baggage! None of your lying there passively with your legs open for her! And how much *life* there was in her, just waiting to be tapped. Suddenly the thought that the end of her life was imminent shocked him; it was one thing to pity someone he didn't know, quite another to face the same dilemma with someone he knew intimately. That was the trouble with beds. They turned strangers into intimates more quickly than ten years of polite teas in parlours.

Missy slept like a log and woke before John Smith did, probably because sleep eluded him long after it had claimed her. He had more to think about.

A faint light filtered through the window, so she eased herself carefully out of the bed and stood shivering until she donned the dressing gown out of her bag. How lovely it had been! More of a realist than she had suspected, she dismissed the initial unpleasantness of pain and remembered instead those big strong work-roughened hands stroking and soothing and comforting. Feelings and sensations, touches and kisses, heat and light – oh yes, it was lovely!

She moved as quietly as she could about the cabin, hotting up the stove and moving the kettle to a place where it would boil. But of course her activity woke him, and he got out of bed too, quite unconcerned at his nakedness; Missy was given an unparalleled opportunity to study the anatomical differences between men and women.

Even more delightful than this was his reaction to her presence. He walked straight across to her, folded her in his arms and stood rocking gently, still half-asleep and thus heavy against her, his beard scraping her neck.

'Good morning,' she whispered, her smiling lips pressing little kisses on his shoulder.

'Morning,' he mumbled, evidently liking her response.

Of course she was ravenous, having had virtually nothing to eat in two days. 'I'll get breakfast,' she said.

'Want a bath?' He sounded more awake, but made no attempt to move away from her.

He could smell Buttercup! Oh, poor man! Hunger fled yet again. 'Yes, please. But a lavatory too?'

'Get your shoes on.'

While she slid her feet into her boots, not bothering to lace them, he rummaged in a big chest and produced two towels, old and rough, but clean.

The clearing sparkled with frost and was still in heavy shade, but as Missy looked up, the great sandstone walls of the valley were already glowing red with the sunrise, and the sky was taking on the muted milky radiance of a pearl – or of Una's skin. Birds called and sang everywhere, never more prone to give voice than at dawn.

'The lavatory's a bit primitive,' he warned, showing her where he had dug a deep hole and placed some stone blocks around it for a seat, with newspaper tucked into a box to keep it dry; he had not enclosed it with roof or walls.

'It's the best-ventilated lavatory I've ever seen,' she said cheerfully.

He chuckled. 'Long job, or short?'

'Short, thank you.'

'Then I'll wait for you. Over there.' He pointed to the far side of the clearing.

When Missy joined him a minute later she was already shivering in anticipation of an icy plunge into the river; he looked like the kind of man who would relish freezing ablutions. Maybe, she thought, I'll be hoist with my own petard, and keel over stone dead from the shock.

But instead of steering her towards the river, John Smith drew her into the middle of a thicket of tree-ferns and wild clematis in feathery white flower. And there before her was the most beautiful bathroom in the entire world, a warm spring that trickled out of a cleft between two rocks at the top of a small stony incline, and fell, too thinly to be called a cascade, into a wide and mossy basin.

Missy had her robe off in a flash, and two seconds later was stepping down into a crystal-clear pool of blood-heat water, tendrils of steam rising languorously off it into the chilly air. It was about eighteen inches deep, and its bottom was clean smooth rock. No leeches, either!

'Go easy on the soap,' advised John Smith, pointing to where a fat cake of his expensive brand sat in a small niche alongside the pool. 'The water obviously gets away, because the level of the pool never rises any more than the spring stops flowing, but don't tempt fate.'

'Now I understand why you're so clean,' she said, thinking of Missalonghi baths, two inches of water in the bottom of the rusting tub, hot from a kettle and cold from a bucket. And that one miserably inadequate ration of water was used by all three ladies, with Missy, the shortest straw, last in line.

Quite unaware how alluring she looked, she smiled up at him and lifted out her arms until the small buff nipples of her slight breasts just rode clear of the water. 'Aren't you coming in too?' she asked in the tones of a professional temptress. 'There's plenty of room.'

He needed no further encouragement, and appeared to forget his strictures about the production of suds, so assiduous was he in making sure every part of her was thoroughly explored with his hand and the bar of soap; nor did she think that his thoroughness had much to do with Buttercup. She submitted with purring pleasure, but then insisted upon returning the service. And so bath-time occupied the best part of an hour.

However, over breakfast he got down to business. 'There must be a registry office in Katoomba, so we'll go on in and get a marriage licence,' he said.

'If I go only as far as Missalonghi with you and then walk on into Byron and catch the train, I imagine I'll get to Katoomba almost as quickly as you will in your cart,' said Missy. 'I must see Mother, I want to shop for food, and I have to take a book back to the library.'

He looked suddenly alarmed. 'You're not by any chance planning a big wedding, are you?'

She laughed. 'No! Just you and me will do very well. I left a note for Mother, though, so I want to make sure she's not too upset. And my dearest friend works in the library – would you mind if she came to our wedding?'

'Not if you want her there. Though I warn you, if I can persuade the powers that be, I'd like to get it over and done with today.'

'In Katoomba?'

'Yes.'

Married in brown! Wouldn't it? Missy sighed. 'All right, if you'll promise me something.'

'What?' he asked warily.

'When I die, will you bury me in a scarlet lace dress? Or if you can't find that, any colour but brown!'

He looked surprised. 'Don't you like brown? I've never seen you wear anything else.'

'I wear brown because I'm poor but respectable. Brown doesn't show the dirt, it never goes in or out of fashion, it never fades, and it's never cheap or common or trollopy.'

That made him laugh, but then he went back to business. 'Do you have a birth certificate?'

'Yes, in my bag.'

'What's your real name?'

Her reaction was extraordinary; she went red, shifted around on her chair, clenched her teeth. 'Can't you just use Missy? It's what I've always been called, honestly.'

'Sooner or later your real name is going to have to come out.' He grinned. 'Come on, make a clean breast of it! It can't be that bad, surely.'

'Missalonghi.'

He burst out laughing. 'You're pulling my leg!'

'I wish I were.'

'The same as your house?'

'Exactly the same. My father thought it was the most beautiful word in the world, and he loathed the Hurlingford habit of using Latin names. Mother wanted to call me Camilla, but he insisted on Missalonghi.'

'You poor little bitch!'

This time Missy's feet experienced no trouble mounting the steps to the front verandah of Missalonghi; she banged on the door as if she was a stranger.

Drusilla answered, and looked at her daughter as if she really was a stranger. Definitely there was nothing the matter with her! In fact, she looked better than in all her life.

'I know what you've been doing, my girl,' she said as she led the way down the hall to the kitchen. 'I wish you'd stuck to reading about it, but I daresay that's crying over spilt milk now, eh? Are you back for good?'

'No.'

Octavia came hobbling, and received a kiss on either cheek from the sparkling Missy.

'Are you all right?' she quavered, clutching at Missy's hands convulsively.

'Of course she's all right!' said Drusilla bracingly. '*Look* at her, for heaven's sake!'

Missy smiled at her mother lovingly; how odd, that only now the cord binding her to Missalonghi was broken did she understand the depth of her love for Drusilla. But maybe now she had opportunity to stand back and see Drusilla's worries, heartaches, difficulties.

'I thank you very much, Mother,' she said, 'for according me the dignity of assuming I know what I'm doing.'

'At going on thirty-four, Missy, if you don't know what you're doing, there's no hope for you. You tried it our way for long enough, and who's to say your way won't be better?'

'Very true. But what you're telling me now is a far cry from dictating the kind of books I might read, and the colour of my clothes.'

'You put up with it tamely enough.'

'Yes, I suppose I did.'

'You get the government you deserve, Missy, always.'

'If you can admit that, Mother, don't you think it's more than time you and the aunts and all the other manless Hurlingford women banded together to do something about the glaring injustices and inequalities in this family?'

'Ever since you told us how Billy has lied to us, Missy, I have been thinking along those lines, I assure you. And I have been talking to Julia and Cornelia too. But there is no law that compels a man – or a woman – to leave property equally divided between sons and daughters. In my book, the worst offenders of all have been Hurlingford women with money to leave – nothing goes to their daughters, not even a house on five acres! So I have always felt there was no chance for us, when our own female kind stand so solidly behind Hurlingford men. It is sad, but it is true.'

'You're speaking of the Hurlingford women who will lose a great deal if you win. I'm speaking of our fellow sufferers, and I know you can get them moving if you really try. You do have legal grounds to seek compensation for those unpaid dividends, and I think you should institute proceedings against Uncle Herbert to compel him to disclose the full details of his various investment schemes.' Missy shot a demure look at Drusilla from under her lashes. 'After all, Mother, you were the one who said it – you get the government you deserve.'

She walked from Missalonghi into Byron. What a beautiful, beautiful day! For the first time in her life she felt really well, the bursting out of one's skin sensation she had read about but never experienced; and for the first time in her life she was looking forward to living a long life. That is, until she remembered that the full measure of her happiness depended upon one John Smith, and John Smith only expected to put up with her for a year at most. She had lied and cheated and stolen to feel this happy, and she wasn't at all sorry for it. The Alicias of this world might snap their fingers and conjure up the men of their choice, but no use pretending a man like John Smith would have looked sideways at a Missy Wright, snap though she would. And yet she *knew* she could make John Smith the happiest man – if not in the world – at least in the town of Byron. She had better! Because when her year was up, he had to want her to live so badly he was prepared to forgive her the stealing and the cheating and the lying.

Time was getting on, and she had to make sure she caught the eleven o'clock train into Katoomba, where John Smith had promised to be waiting for her at the station. Groceries she could put off until tomorrow, but somehow she had a feeling Una could not be postponed. To the library it was, then.

A magnificent motorcar was purring sedately down the middle of Byron Street as Missy hurried along in her brown linen dress, inconspicuous as ever. Which was more than could be said for the motorcar, also brown; it had collected an admiring audience down both sides of the road, locals and visitors alike. Glancing at it in amusement, Missy decided the chauffeur had a definite edge over the two occupants of the tonneau when it came to haughty aloofness. The chauffeur she knew from hearsay; a handsome fellow with more love for cutting a fine figure than hard work, and a reputation for treating his many women badly. The occupants of the tonneau she knew from bitter experience; Alicia and Uncle Billy.

Alicia's eyes met hers. The next moment the sumptuous car had slewed sideways into the kerb, and Alicia and Uncle Billy were tumbling out well ahead of the startled chauffeur's attempt to open a door for them.

'What do you mean, Missy Wright, taking Aunt Cornelia's shares and selling them out from under our noses?' demanded Alicia without preamble, two bright red spots burning in her alabaster cheeks.

'Why shouldn't I?' asked Missy coolly.

'Because it's none of your damned interfering business!' barked Sir William, stiff with outrage.

'It's as much my business as it is yours, Uncle Billy. I knew where I could get Aunt Cornelia ten pounds a share, and what use were they to her when you'd led her to believe they were quite worthless? Aunt Cornelia badly needs an operation on her feet she couldn't afford because, Alicia, I gather you refused to give her either time off or a little extra money. So I sold her shares for a hundred pounds, and now she can have her operation. If you wish to terminate her employment, at least she has a sum in the bank to tide her over until she can find another position – I'm sure there are shops in Katoomba just dying to engage someone of her calibre. You might like to know that I have also sold Aunt Julia's shares, and Aunt Octavia's, and Mother's.'

'*What?*' squawked Sir William.

'All of them? You sold all of them?' faltered Alicia, the red spots in her cheeks draining away in a second.

'I most certainly did.' Missy stared at her cousin with a malice she had not known she possessed. 'Why, Alicia, don't tell me forty little shares in the great big Byron Bottle Company were enough to tip the balance!'

For a confused moment Alicia fancied Missy had grown horns and a tail. 'What's the matter with you?' she cried. 'You've got to be off your head! Soiling my dress, saying insulting things about me in front of my family, and now selling that family into ruin! You ought to be locked up!'

'I only wish what I did had resulted in your being locked up. Now if you'll both excuse me, I must dash. I have an appointment to be married.' And Missy walked away with her nose in the air.

'I think I'm going to faint,' announced Alicia, and suited action to words by flopping against Uncle Herbert's window, the one full of work clothes.

Sir William seized the opportunity to put his arms around her, head turned to call for assistance from his chauffeur; but somehow as they supported Alicia between them back to the car, it was the chauffeur's ungloved fingers that managed to ascertain the delicious size and shape of Alicia's nipples. By this time the crowd had swelled to include all of Uncle Herbert's sons and grandsons, so Sir William dumped Alicia unceremoniously on the seat and ordered the chauffeur to drive off immediately.

When her prospective father-in-law attempted to loosen her stays by lifting up her dress and groping inside her fine lawn drawers, Alicia revived in a hurry.

'Stop that, you lecherous old man!' she snapped, forgetting the need to be tactful, and leaned forward to press her cheeks between her palms. 'Oh, lord, I feel awful!'

'Would you like to go home now we don't have to drive out to Missalonghi?' asked Sir William, red-faced.

'Yes, I would.' She lay back against the seat and let the cool air fan her skin, and finally relaxed a little, and sighed. Thank heavens! She was beginning to feel better.

Right in front of her but on the other side of the glass that separated the tonneau from the open driving compartment, the chauffeur's proudly shaped head sat upon his strong smooth neck; what lovely ears he had for a man, small and set right against his skull. He was handsome, as dark as Missy, and as alien. It took a brawny man to heft her around as easily as he had, and his hands on her breasts – she felt her nipples pop up at the memory of them, and squirmed achingly on the seat. What was his name? Frank? Yes, Frank. Frank Pellagrino. He used to work at the bottling plant until he got the post as Uncle Billy's chauffeur.

A sidelong glance at Sir William revealed him sitting bolt upright, a very worried man.

'Do those forty shares make so much difference to us?'

'All the difference in the world, now we know Richard Hurlingford sold out a month ago.' Sir William sighed. 'And it explains why the mystery buyer thinks he has sufficient clout to call an extraordinary meeting tomorrow.'

'The little fool!' snarled Alicia. 'How could Missy be such a little fool?'

'I think we're the fools, Alicia. I for one never even noticed Missy Wright, but I see now that I should have. And been more attentive to all the ladies of Missalonghi. Did you take in how she looked this morning? As if she'd got to the cream ahead of every other cat in the district. And did she say she had an appointment to be married, or was that my imagination?'

Alicia snorted. 'Oh, she said it, but I suspect it was *her* imagination.' A more urgent grievance came to mind. 'Silly old Auntie Cornie!' she muttered savagely. 'Oh, how I wish I could have had the satisfaction this morning of sacking her when she came prattling about her shares and the time she was going to take off for her operation!'

'Well, why didn't you sack her?'

'Because I can't, that's why! My hat shop may well end up my only source of income, if things at the plant keep going from bad to worse. And I'll never find anyone else half so good to run the salon end of it, even if I paid them ten times what I pay Auntie Cornie. She's – indispensable.'

'You'd better pray she never realises it, or she'll ask for ten times what you currently pay her.' A tinge of satisfaction coloured his voice as he added, 'And then, my dear, if you can't afford it, you'll have to go into the shop as your own sales dame. You'd be even better at it than Cornie.'

'I can't do that!' gasped Alicia. 'It would *ruin* my social standing! It's one thing to be the creative genius behind a business of that nature, but quite another to have to peddle my wares in person.' She tugged at the lapels of her pale pink coat, her lovely face set into the lines of sullen discontent its construction made fatally easy. 'Oh, Uncle Billy, suddenly I feel as if I'm walking on ice, and it's going to crack any minute, and I'm going to go under!'

'We're in a pickle, it's true. But don't give up, we're not finished yet. Pounds to peanuts, when the mystery buyer turns up to his extraordinary meeting tomorrow, he'll turn out to be some self-made yokel easily manipulated by his betters. And for that sort of exercise, you will come in very handy.'

Alicia did not reply, merely flicked him a glance of mingled doubt and dislike; her eyes reverted to the back of the chauffeur's head, a far nicer prospect than Sir William's choleric countenance.

When Missy walked into the library she fully expected to find Una, even though it was not one of Una's days. And sure enough, there was Una.

'Oh, Missy, I'm so glad to see you!' she cried, jumping up. 'I have a surprise for you.'

'I have a few surprises for you too,' said Missy.

'Wait right there, I'll be back in two flicks of a dead lamb's tail.' Una vanished into the tea cubicle, and came out bearing a large white box and hatbox, each tied up with white ribbon. 'Happy anything, dearest Missy.'

They smiled at each other in complete understanding and great affection.

'It's a scarlet lace dress and hat,' said Missy.

'It's a scarlet lace dress and hat,' agreed Una.

'I shall wear it to my wedding.'

'John Smith! You've picked exactly the right man.'

'I had to resort to trickery and deception to get him.'

'If you couldn't get him any other way, why not?'

'I told him I was dying of heart trouble.'

'Aren't we all?'

'That,' said Missy, 'is splitting hairs. Can you come to my wedding?'

'I'd love to, but no.'

'Why?'

'It wouldn't be appropriate.'

'Because of your divorce? But we're not getting married in a church, so who can object?'

'It has nothing to do with divorce, darling. I don't think John Smith would appreciate a face from the past at his wedding.'

That made sense, therefore Missy left it alone. And there was nothing really left to say; her gratitude was quite beyond words, her need to go quickly was great. Una stood watching her painfully, as if with her she was taking something so precious the quality of Una's life would suffer ever afterwards – and that something was not so tangible as a scarlet lace dress and hat. On an impulse she didn't understand, Missy returned to the desk, leaned over it and put her arm about Una's shoulders, her lips against Una's cheek. So frail, so cold, so weightless!

'Goodbye, Una.'

'Goodbye, my best and dearest friend. Be happy!'

Missy made the train with a minute to spare, and saw John Smith on the platform in Katoomba before the train came to a standstill. Thank God for that. He hadn't changed his mind during his slow amble along the highway, then. And in fact when he saw her alight from her carriage, he even looked quite glad to see her!

'They'll issue us with a licence and marry us today,' he said, taking Missy's boxes from her.

'And I don't have to be married in brown,' said Missy, retrieving her boxes. 'If you'll excuse me, I'll pop into the platform toilet and change into my wedding dress.'

'*Wedding* dress?' He looked down at his grey flannel work shirt and his old moleskin trousers in comical dismay.

She laughed. 'Don't worry, it's not traditional. In fact, I guarantee that you're going to look a great deal more appropriate than I am.'

Her dress fitted perfectly. What an eye for size Una had! And what a wonderful colour! Her eyes swam with the strain of looking at it. Where on earth had Una managed to find a garment so elegant in style yet so wanton in colour?

The mirror on the wall seemed to own a touch of magic, for whoever it reflected, it lent a slight patina of beauty; adjusting her preposterous scarlet hat, Missy decided she looked very well. Her darkness was suddenly interesting, her thin body was suddenly merely slender as a young tree. Yes, very well! And certainly not spinsterish.

Once he recovered from the shock of that red, John Smith thought she looked very well too. 'Now this is my sort of wedding! I look like a hayseed, and you look like a madam.' He tucked her arm through his gleefully. 'Come on, woman, let's get the deed over before I change my mind.'

They strolled into Katoomba Street, the cynosure of all eyes, and actually quite pleased with the sensation they were creating.

'That was easy,' said Missy after the deed was done and they were sitting together in John Smith's cart. She held out her hand to see her ring. 'I am now Mrs John Smith. How nice it sounds!'

'I must say this time was a lot better than the last.'

'Was your first wedding a big affair, then?'

'It could have passed for a circus. Two hundred and fifty guests, the bride with a thirty-foot train that needed a whole regiment of runny-nosed little boys to lift it, twelve or fourteen bridesmaids, all of the men stuffed into tails, the archbishop of something presiding, a massed choir – God Jesus, at the time it was a nightmare! But compared to what followed, it was an idyll in paradise.' He looked sideways at her, one eyebrow raised. 'Do you want to hear this?'

'I think I'd better. They say the second wife always has to contend with the ghost of the first, and that it's a lot harder to fight a ghost than a living person.' She paused to gather her courage. 'Was she – dear to you?'

'She may have been when I married her, I honestly can't remember. I didn't know her, you see. I only knew of her. She must have meant to have me, because I'm sure I didn't do the proposing. I'm obviously the sort of bloke women propose to! Only I didn't mind your way of proposing, at least it was honest and above-board. But her – one minute she was all over me like a rash, the next minute she was acting as if I had the plague. Blowing hot and cold, they call it. I think women think it's expected of them, that if they don't do it, they're going to make life too easy for the bloke. Now that's where I like you very much, Mrs Smith. You don't blow hot and cold at all.'

'I'm too grateful,' said Missy humbly. 'Do go on! What happened after that?'

He shrugged. 'Oh, she decided she was entitled to make all the decisions, that what *she* wanted was all that mattered. Once she'd landed her fish, the fish didn't matter a bit. I was just there to prove she could catch a fish, to lend her respectability, to give her an escort here and there. She didn't exactly have lovers, she had what she called cicisbeos, pansified twerps with gardenias in their buttonholes and a better shine on their hair than on their patent leather shoes. If anyone was ever branded by the company she kept, my first wife certainly was – her women friends were as hard as nails and as tough as old boots, and her men friends were as soft as butter and as limp as last week's lettuce. She liked to mock me. In front of anyone, everyone. I was dull, I was stodgy. And she never kept our differences private, she'd get set on a quarrel no matter how public the place. In a nutshell, she held me in utter contempt.'

'And you? What light did you hold her in?'

'I *loathed* her.' Evidently he still did, for the feeling in his voice did not belong to an experience buried in the past.

'How long were you married?'

'About four or five years.'

'Were there any children?'

'Hell, no! She might have lost her figure. And of course that meant she was a great one for teasing, for kissing and cuddling, but to get my leg over her – it only happened when she got drunk, and afterwards she'd scream and howl and carry on in case anything came of it, then she'd pop out and visit the tame doctor they all patronised.'

'And she *died*?' asked Missy, scarcely able to credit that such a woman could have had so much consideration.

'We had a terrible fight one evening over – oh, I don't know, something small and idiotic that actually didn't matter a bit. We lived in a house that had a waterfrontage onto the Harbour, and apparently after I'd gone out she decided to go for a swim to cool her temper. They found her body a couple of weeks later, washed up on Balmoral Beach.'

'Oh, poor thing!'

He snorted. 'Poor thing, nothing! The police tried in every way they knew to pin it on me, but luckily the minute she'd done shouting at me, I went out, and I met a friend not twenty yards down the road. He'd been kicked out of bed too, so we walked to where he'd been going, the flat of a mutual friend – a bachelor, the wily bastard. There we stayed until past noon of the following day, getting drunker and drunker. And since the servants had seen her alive and well more than half an hour after my friend and I arrived at our mutual friend's flat, the police couldn't touch me. Anyway, after the body turned up the post mortem revealed that she'd died of simple drowning, with no evidence of foul play. Not that that stopped a lot of people in Sydney reckoning I did kill her – I just got a name for being too smart to get caught, and my friends for being bought to alibi me.'

'When did all this happen?'

'About twenty years ago.'

'A long time! What have you done with yourself since, that it's taken you so long to do what you've always wanted?'

'Well, I quit Australia as soon as the police let go. And I drifted round the world. Africa, the Klondike, China, Brazil, Texas. I had to live through almost twenty years of voluntary exile. Since I was born in London, I changed my name by deed-poll there, and when I did come back to Australia, I came as that bona-fide citizen of the world, John Smith, with all my money in gold and no past.'

'Why *Byron*?'

'Because of the valley. I knew it was coming up for sale, and I've always wanted to own a whole valley.'

Feeling she had probed enough, Missy changed the subject to the skulduggery going on at the Byron Bottle Company, and told her husband about the plight her mother and aunts were in because of it. John Smith listened most attentively, a smile playing round the corners of his mouth, and when she had ended her tale he put his arm around her, drew her across the seat against his side, and kept her there.

'Well, Mrs Smith, I really didn't want to marry you when you first brought the subject up, but I confess I'm growing more reconciled to it every time you open your mouth, not to mention your legs,' he said. 'You're a woman of sense, your heart's in the right place, and you're a Hurlingford of the Hurlingfords, which gives me a lot of power I didn't expect to have,' he said. 'Interesting, how things turn out.'

Missy rode the rest of the way home in blissful silence.

The next morning John Smith donned a suit, a collar, and a tie, all remarkably well cut and oddly smart.

'Whatever it is, it must be a lot more important than your wedding,' observed Missy without a trace of resentment.

'It is.'

'Are you going far afield?'

'Only to Byron.'

'Then if I'm quick about it, may I come as far as Mother's with you, please?'

'Good idea, wife! Wait there for me until some time late this afternoon, and you can introduce me to my in-laws when I pick you up. I'll probably have a lot to say to them.'

It's going to be all right, thought Missy as she rode in her bright red dress and hat alongside her unfamiliarly elegant husband up to the top of the ridge. I don't care if I got him by trickery and deceit. He likes me, he really does like me, and without even realising it himself, he's already moved over a little to fit me in alongside him. When my year is up, I'll be able to tell him the truth. Besides, if I'm lucky, I may well by then be the mother of his child. It hurt him badly when his first wife didn't want any, and now he's closer to fifty than to forty, so children will be even more important to him. He will be an excellent father, because he can laugh.

Before they set out for Byron he had taken her across the clearing and round its bend to where he intended to build his house. The waterfall, she discovered, fell so far that on a windy day it never reached the valley floor, spinning away instead into nothingness, and filling the air with clouds of rainbows. Yet there was a huge pool below it, wide and calm until it poured through a narrow defile and became the cascade-tortured river, a pool the colour of a turquoise or of Egyptian faience, opaque as milk, dense as syrup. The source of all this water, he showed her, was a cave below the cliffs, out of which issued a very large underground stream.

'There's an outcropping of limestone here,' he explained. 'That's why the pool is such a bizarre colour.'

'And this is really where we're going to live, looking at so much loveliness?'

'Where *I* will live, anyway. I doubt you'll be here to see it.' His face twisted. 'Houses don't get built in a day, Missy, especially when they're built single-handed. I don't want a horde of workmen down here, pissing in the pool and getting drunk on Saturdays and then telling any curious bystander what's going on in my valley.'

'I thought we had a bargain, not to mention my condition? Anyway, you won't be building single-handed, you'll have my hands as well,' said Missy cheerfully. 'I'm no stranger to hard work, and the cabin is so small it won't keep me busy. From what the doctor said, it makes no difference whether I lie in a bed or work like a navvy – one day it will happen, that's all.'

At which he took her in his arms and kissed her as if he enjoyed kissing her, and as if she was already a little precious to him. They finally set out for Byron somewhat later than originally intended, but neither of them minded.

Octavia and Drusilla were in the kitchen when Missy walked in unannounced. They stared at her in astonishment, trying to take in the full glory of that outlandish scarlet lace dress, not to mention the huge lopsided hat with its graceless plume of scarlet ostrich feathers.

She hadn't turned into a beauty overnight, but there was certainly an eye-catching quality about her, and she held herself too proudly to be mistaken for a trollop. In fact, she looked a lot more like a sophisticated visitor from London than one of the inhabitants of Caroline Lamb Place. There was also no doubting that the colour suited her down to the ground.

'Oh, Missy, you look lovely!' squeaked Octavia, sitting down in a hurry.

Missy kissed her, and kissed her mother. 'That's nice to know, Auntie, because I admit I feel lovely.' She grinned at them triumphantly. 'I came to tell you that I'm married,' she announced, waving her left hand under their noses.

'Who?' asked Drusilla, beaming.

'John Smith. We were married yesterday in Katoomba.'

Suddenly neither to Drusilla nor Octavia did it matter a scrap that the whole town of Byron called him a jailbird, or worse; he had rescued their Missy from the multiple horrors of spinsterhood, and he must therefore be loved for it with gratitude and respect and loyalty.

Octavia positively leaped up to put the kettle on, moving with more flexibility and ease than she had in years, though Drusilla didn't notice; she was too busy looking at her girl's convincingly massive wedding ring.

'Mrs John Smith,' she said experimentally. 'Why, bless my soul, Missy, it sounds quite distinguished!'

'Simplicity usually is distinguished.'

'Where is he? When is he coming to see us?' asked Octavia.

'He had some business or other in Byron, but he expects to be done later this afternoon, and he wants to meet you when he picks me up to take me home. I thought, Mother, that to fill in the day, you and I might walk into Byron. I have to buy groceries, and I want to go to Uncle Herbert's to choose some materials for me to make into dresses. Because I am done forever with brown! I won't even wear it to work in. I'm going to work in a man's shirt and man's trousers because they're a great deal more comfortable and sensible, and who's to see me?'

'Isn't it lucky that you bought a Singer sewing machine, Drusilla?' asked Octavia from the stove, too happy at the way things had turned out to worry about the trousers.

But Drusilla had something so important on her mind that neither Singer sewing machines nor trousers could loom larger. 'Can you afford it?' she asked anxiously. 'I can make for you for nothing, but the materials at Herbert's are so expensive, especially once one gets away from brown!'

'It seems I can indeed afford it. John told me last night that he was going to put a thousand pounds in the bank for me this morning. Because he said a wife shouldn't have to ask her husband for every little penny she needs, nor account for every little penny she spends. All he asked was that I didn't exceed the allowance he makes me – a thousand pounds every year! Can you imagine it? And the housekeeping is separate from that! He put a hundred pounds into an empty Bushell's coffee jar and says he'll keep it replenished, and doesn't want to see the dockets. Oh, Mother, I'm still breathless!'

'A thousand pounds!' Octavia and Drusilla stared at Missy in thunderstruck respect.

'Then he must be a rich man,' said Drusilla, and did some rapid mental gymnastics in which she saw herself finally able to cock a snook at Aurelia and Augusta and Antonia. Hah! Not only had Missy beaten Alicia to the altar, but now it began to look as if she might also have made the better bargain.

'I imagine he's comfortably off,' temporised Missy. 'I know his generosity to me suggests real wealth, but I suspect it's more that he's a truly generous man. Certainly I shall never, never embarrass him by overspending. However, I do need a few decent clothes – *not* brown! – a couple of winter dresses and a couple of summer ones is all. Oh, Mother, it's so beautiful down in the valley! I don't have any desire to lead a social life, I just want to be alone with my John.'

Drusilla looked suddenly troubled. 'Missy, there's so little we can give you for a wedding present. But I think, Octavia, that we could spare the Jersey heifer, don't you?'

'We can *certainly* spare the heifer,' said Octavia.

'Now that,' said Missy, 'is what I call a handsome wedding present! We would love the heifer.'

'We ought to send her to Percival's bull first,' said Octavia. 'She's due to come on any time now, so you won't have to wait

long for her, and with any luck she'll give you a calf next year too.'

Drusilla consulted the clock on the kitchen wall. 'If you want to go to Herbert's as well as to Maxwell's, Missy, I suggest we make a start. Then we might be able to fit in a bit of lunch with Julia in her tea room, and tell her the news. My word, she'll be surprised!'

Octavia twitched herself gently, and experienced no pain. 'I'm coming too,' she announced firmly. 'You're not going without me today of all days. If I have to crawl on hands and knees, I'm coming too.'

Thus in the late morning Drusilla strolled through the shopping centre with her daughter on one arm, and her sister on the other.

It was Octavia who spied Mrs Cecil Hurlingford on the opposite side of the road; Mrs Cecil was the wife of the Reverend Dr Cecil Hurlingford, Byron's Church of England minister, and everyone went in fear and trembling of her tongue. 'Dying of curiosity, aren't you, you old besom?' muttered Octavia through her teeth, smiling and bowing so frostily that Mrs Cecil thought the better of crossing the road to see what was what with the Missalonghi gaggle.

Then Drusilla completed the routing of Mrs Cecil by suddenly shouting with laughter and pointing one shaking finger in Mrs Cecil's direction. 'Oh, Octavia, Mrs Cecil hasn't recognised Missy! I do believe she thinks we've got one of the Caroline Lamb Place women in tow!'

All three of the ladies of Missalonghi dissolved into laughter, and Mrs Cecil Hurlingford tottered into Julia's tea room to get away from so much unseemly mirth, all apparently directed at *her*.

'What an uproar!' crowed Octavia.

'The bigger the better,' said Missy, entering Herbert Hurlingford's clothing emporium.

That whole experience was a terrific tonic, between Uncle Herbert's flabbergasted imitation of a codfish when Missy proceeded to buy men's shirts and trousers for herself, and James's tonguetied terror when she proceeded to buy lengths of lavender-blue taffeta, apricot silk, amber velvet, and cyclamen wool. Recovering somewhat after Missy left him to go to James, Herbert debated as to whether he should relieve his feelings by ordering the hussy from his premises; then when she paid for her purchases in gold, he changed his mind and humbly rang up the sale.

Staggering as Missy's visit was, he really only had half a mind to pay to it and her, for the other half was occupied in wondering what was going on up at the bottling plant, where the extraordinary meeting of shareholders was taking place. The shopkeeping Hurlingfords had despatched Maxwell as their representative, acknowledging that Maxwell had the best and bitterest tongue, and understanding that he would fight as hard for them as for himself. Business must go on as usual, after all, and if the bottling plant and its corollary activities like the baths and the hotel and the spas was going to go west, then the shops became more important than ever to their respective owners.

'You may deliver these to Missalonghi this afternoon, James,' said Missy grandly, and slapped a gold sovereign down on the counter. 'Here, this is for your trouble. And while you're about it, you can go into Uncle Maxwell's and pick up my grocery order as well. Come, Mother, Aunt Octavia! Let us go to Aunt Julia's for lunch.'

The three ladies of Missalonghi swept out of the shop more royally than they had swept in.

'Oh, this is such fun!' chuckled Octavia, whose walk was just about normal. 'I have never enjoyed myself so much!'

Missy was enjoying herself too, but less simply. It had been a shock to find the promised thousand pounds had actually been deposited for her, and even more of a shock to be treated with great civility by Quintus Hurlingford, the bank manager; John Smith had instructed him to pay Missy's withdrawals in gold, since the deposit had been in gold. A thousand pounds!

Well, she had her dress materials and her shirts and her trousers, and several pairs of pretty shoes into the bargain. She really didn't need anything else. If she kept a hundred pounds of that amazing thousand, it would be more than enough to last her until her allowance was replenished at this same time next year. After all, when had she ever owned more than a shilling or two? She would therefore use the bulk of her allowance to buy Mother and Aunt Octavia a little pony-and-trap. The pony wouldn't eat the place out the way a bigger horse would, they could manage its harnessing with ease, and never again would they have to walk anywhere, or humble their pride by begging that a conveyance be sent for them. Yes, they should go in style to Alicia's wedding in a smart pony-and-trap!

The hundred pounds Julia had realised from the sale of her

shares was already being spent; half the tea room was roped off, and two workmen were toiling at stripping and sanding.

Once she ceased apologising for the mess, Julia gathered her wits together sufficiently to absorb the full splendour of Missy's outfit. "It's a superb dress and hat, dear,' she said, 'but isn't the colour a little *lairy*?'

'Definitely lairy,' admitted Missy, without shame. 'But oh, Aunt Julia, I am so sick to death of brown, and can you name a colour further from brown than this? Besides, it suits me, don't you think?'

Yes, but does it suit my tea room? was the question Julia burned to ask, then decided it would be unpardonable to criticise her benefactress. And due to the renovations there weren't many patrons today; she would just have to hope no one would decide she had thrown open her doors to the likes of Caroline Lamb Place. Oh! That must have been what Mrs Cecil Hurlingford was gobbling about! Oh, dear! Oh, dear dear dear!

In the meantime she had ushered the ladies of Missalonghi to her very best table, and shortly thereafter served them an assortment of sandwiches and cakes, and a big pot of tea.

'I'm going to have a striped paper on the walls in cream and gold and crimson,' she said, sitting down to join her guests, 'and my chairs will be reupholstered in a matching but brighter brocade. I'm having the moulding on the ceiling picked out in gilt, canaries in gold cages, and pots of tall palms everywhere. Let Next Door' – her head tilting scornfully towards the wall she shared in common with the Olympus Café – 'compete with *that*!'

Drusilla's mouth was open to unburden herself of the news that Missy was married to John Smith and that John Smith was a rich man rather than a jailbird, when Cornelia Hurlingford erupted through the doors and descended upon them, her various scarves and ribbons trailing behind her like moulting feathers from a peacock's tail.

Cornelia and Julia lived together above the Weeping Willow Tea Room, which Julia did not own outright. She paid a large rent to her brother Herbert, who regularly assured her that one day she would have paid enough, between the rent and what her house and five acres had fetched, to buy the premises.

As well as sharing their living arrangements, the two maiden sisters also shared and relished every morsel of information their public occupations garnered, but mostly Cornelia, the less excitable of the two, could wait until Chez Chapeau Alicia closed its doors for the day; Alicia did not permit her to leave the shop while ever it was open. Obviously whatever she had to impart was urgent enough to run the risk of incurring Alicia's wrath, and so bursting was Cornelia with her news that Missy's scarlet outfit got no more than a cursory glance.

'Guess what?' she gasped, plumping herself down on a chair and forgetting she was supposed to be the formidably elegant and snooty sales dame of a formidably elegant and snooty one-off millinery establishment.

'What?' asked everyone, well aware of these various facts, and therefore prepared to be tremendously impressed.

'Alicia ran off with Billy's chauffeur this morning!'

'*What?*'

'She did, she did! She eloped! At *her* age! Oh, what a circus is going on at Aurelia's! Hysterics and tantrums all over the place! Little Willie nearly tore the house apart looking for Alicia because he refused to believe what her note to him said, and Billy was roaring like a gale because he had to go to some important meeting at the plant when what he really wanted to do was set the police onto his chauffeur! They carted Aurelia off to bed as stiff as a board, and had to send for Uncle Neville when she kept holding her breath until she passed out, and then Uncle Neville gave her such a wallop across the ears because he was cross at being called out for nothing, and he called her no better than a spoiled baby, so that set her off screaming, and she's still screaming! Oh, and Edmund is sitting on a chair just twitching, and Ted and Randolph are trying to pull him together so he can go to the meeting at the plant. But the worst of it is that Alicia and the chauffeur went off in Billy's brand new motorcar, for all the world as if they owned it!'

Cornelia ended her breathless recital with a bellow of laughter, Missy joined her, and one by one the others came in to ring a peal of glorious mirth over the events at Mon Repos. After that catharsis everyone felt absolutely tiptop, and settled to a quieter but no less enjoyable dissection of Missy's marriage and Alicia's elopement, not to mention lunch.

John Smith arrived at Missalonghi just before five o'clock, looking very pleased with himself. He shook his mother-in-law's hand with great affability, but refrained from kissing her, a piece of good sense she heartily approved of. The handshake he also offered Octavia disappointed her, but she had to admit, looking at him properly for the first time, that he was a fine figure of a man. Of course the suit aided her impression, as did the fresh haircut and neatly trimmed beard. Yes, Missy had nothing to be ashamed of in her choice of a life's partner, and to Octavia's way of thinking, his fifteen years of seniority made him just the right age for a husband.

He seemed a nice man on the inside too, for he made himself easily at home in the kitchen and sniffed at the scent of roast lamb appreciatively.

'I hope you and Missy will stay to dinner?' asked Drusilla.

'We'd love to,' he said.

'What about the road home? It isn't going to be too risky after dark?'

'Not at all. The horses know it blindfold.'

He leaned back in his chair and raised one eyebrow at his wife, who was sitting opposite and just beaming at him with a pride in him his first wife had certainly never owned. What fools men were! They always went after the pretty women, when their intelligence should tell them the homely ones were much better bets. However, she looked all right in that bright red getup, not beautiful, certainly not pretty, but interesting. In fact, she looked like the sort of woman most men would want to get to know because they weren't sure what went on inside. Attractive, bumpy nose and all. And as she sat there sparking with life, it was difficult to believe she could die at any moment. His heart twisted, an odd sensation. Tomorrow, tomorrow! Don't think about it until it happens! You are beginning to dwell on it, and you mustn't! Don't think of her death-sentence as a cosmic revenge on you!

Maybe if he could make her happy enough, it wouldn't happen at all. There were such things as miracles, he had seen one or two in his travels. Getting rid of his first wife undoubtedly fell into the category of a miracle.

'I want to talk to you ladies,' he said, dragging his eyes and his mind away from his present wife.

Three faces turned to him with interest. Drusilla and Octavia ceased fussing at the stove and sat down.

'There was a shareholder's meeting at the Byron Bottle Company today,' he said, 'and management of the company has changed hands. In fact, it passed into my hands.'

'*You*?' squeaked Missy.

'Yes.'

'Then you're the mystery buyer?'

'Yes.'

'But why? Uncle Billy said the mystery buyer had outlaid the kind of money for shares that no one could ever hope to get back! So why?'

He smiled, not attractively; for the first time since meeting him Missy saw a different John Smith, a powerful and flinty John Smith, a John Smith who might not know the meaning of the word mercy. It didn't frighten her and it didn't take her aback; rather, it pleased her. Here was no defeated refugee from life's insistent pressures, here was no weakling. On the outside he was so delightfully relaxed and easygoing, and there were people who might mistake that for weakness even after they knew him very well, perhaps intimately well. Like his first wife? Yes, she could understand how a wife might come to judge him as less than he actually was, if that wife was a rather stupid, self-centred kind of woman.

But he was answering her, so she paid attention to him.

'I had a bone to pick with the Hurlingfords. Present company excluded, of course. But by and large, I have found the Hurlingfords so damned smug, so sure that their quasi-noble free-settler English origins put them much higher than people like me who have the rattle of leg-irons on their mother's side and full Jew on their father's. I admit I set out to get the Hurlingfords, and didn't care how much it cost me to do it. Luckily I have enough money to buy out a dozen Byron Bottle Companies without ever feeling the pinch.'

'But you don't come from Byron,' said Missy, bewildered.

'True. However, my first wife was a Hurlingford.'

'Really! What was her name?' asked Drusilla, who was one of the clan experts on Hurlingford genealogy.

'Una.'

Fortunately Drusilla and Octavia were far too interested in what John Smith was saying, and John Smith himself was far too interested in saying it, to pay any attention to Missy.

She sat in stony stillness, unable to move the smallest part of her. Una. *Una*!

How could her mother and aunt sit there so unresponsive to that name, when they had met her and entertained her in this very house? Didn't they remember the biscuits, the documents?

'Una?' Drusilla was asking herself. 'Let me see now . . . . . Yes, she would have to be one of the Marcus Hurlingfords from Sydney, which would make Livilla Hurlingford her first cousin and her closest relative here in Byron. Humph! I never did meet her, but she died a long time ago, of course. A drowning accident, wasn't it?'

'Yes,' said John Smith.

Was that it, then? Was that why she glowed? Was that why every time Missy had needed her, she had been there? Was that why so many small incidents had happened so fortuitously in the library? The novels, all leading up to the one about the girl dying of heart trouble. The shares on the desk. The Power of Attorney forms. Una the conveniently handy Justice of the Peace. The impudence and the gay carelessness, so hugely attractive to one as repressed as Missy had been. The scarlet dress and hat *exactly* as it had flowered in Missy's imagination, and exactly the right size too. The curious significance she had managed to give all her words, so that they sank into Missy like water into parched soil, and germinated richly. Una. Oh, Una! Dear, radiant Una.

'But her married name definitely wasn't Smith,' Drusilla was saying. 'It was much more unusual, like Cardmom or Terebinth or Gooseflesh. He was a very rich man, as I recollect, which was the only reason the second Sir William approved the match. Yes, I see how they would have insulted you, if you were he.'

'I was he, and they did indeed insult me.'

'*We*,' said Drusilla, reaching out her hand to clasp his, 'are delighted to welcome you into this branch of the family, my dear John.'

The hard John Smith had gone, for the eyes resting on his mother-in-law were soft, amused in a gentle way. 'Thank you. I've changed my name, of course, and I'd prefer you didn't speak of all this ancient history.'

'It will go no further than Missalonghi,' said Drusilla, and sighed, assuming he had changed his name to sever all the painful memories. The sordid ramifications Missy knew of from John Smith himself were obviously not a part of Hurlingford history in Byron.

'Poor thing, drowning like that,' said Octavia, shaking her head. 'It must have hit you hard, John. Still, I'm very glad things have turned out the way they have, the bottling plant and all.

And isn't it interesting that you've gone and married another Hurlingford?'

'It was a great help today,' said John Smith calmly.

'There are Hurlingfords and Hurlingfords, like any other family,' said Drusilla with truth. 'Una may not have turned out the right sort of wife for you, so perhaps it's better she died so young. Where Missy – *I* think she will make you happy.'

He grinned and reached his arm across the table to take hold of Missy's cold clammy hand. 'Yes, I think she will too.' He managed to kiss the trembling fingers in spite of their distance from where he sat, then he released the hand and gave all his attention to Drusilla and Octavia.

'Anyway, now I'm in control of the Byron Bottle Company and its auxiliary industries, I want to make some much-needed changes. Naturally I shall sit as chairman of the board of directors and Missy will be my vice-chairman, but I also require eight other directors. Now I need a group of busy, interested individuals who will be as concerned about the town and people of Byron as about the bottling plant itself. Today I received the necessary votes to enable me to restructure the board any way I want, and I want to do something so different that when I announced my intentions, I acquired a few more shares! Sir William, Edmund Marshall, the brothers Maxwell and Herbert Hurlingford, and some dozen others sold out to me when the meeting concluded. Their spleen got the better of their judgement, which only confirms what I've suspected for a very long time – they're fools. The Byron Bottle Company is going to get bigger and better! It's going to become more civic-minded, and it's going to diversify its interests.'

He laughed, shrugged. 'Well, no point in dwelling on the likes of Sir William Hurlingford, is there! I want *women* on my board, and I want to start with you two ladies and the Misses Julia and Cornelia Hurlingford. All of you have coped magnificently with your hardships, and you certainly don't lack courage. It may be a radical departure to staff a board of directors with women, but in my opinion most boards already consist of women – *old* women.'

He lifted that magical eyebrow at Drusilla and Octavia, who were listening to him in spellbound silence. 'So? Are you interested in my offer? Naturally you'll be paid directors' fees. The previous board paid each of its members five thousand pounds per annum, though, I warn you, I shall cut that figure to two thousand pounds.'

'But we don't know what to do!' cried Octavia.

'Most boards don't, so that's no handicap. The chairman is John Smith, remember, and John Smith will teach you every rope. Each of you will have a specific area to deal with, and I know you'll look at hoary problems with fresh eyes and new problems with the kind of unorthodoxy a usual board can't match.'

He looked at Drusilla sternly. 'I'm waiting on your answer, Mother. Are you going to join my board, or not?'

Drusilla shut her gaping mouth with an audible snap. 'Oh, indeed I am! And so are the others, I'll see to that.'

'Good. Then the first item of business you have to deal with is who we're going to appoint to the remaining four board places. Women, mind!'

'I must be dreaming,' said Octavia.

'Not at all,' said Drusilla, at her most majestic. 'This is real, sister. The ladies of Missalonghi have come into their own at last.'

'What a day!' sighed Octavia.

What a day, indeed. The last of it was going on outside the open back door, which faced west. So did Missy's chair. She could see the great fanning ribbons of high cloud dyed as scarlet as her dress, and the apple-green sky between them, and the mass of blossom on the fruit trees in the orchard, drifts of white and pink gone pinker in that lovely waning sun. But her mind and her eyes, normally so receptive to the natural beauty of the world, were not preoccupied with that glory. For Una was standing in the doorway, smiling at her. Una. Oh, Una!

'Don't ever tell him, Missy. Let him believe his love and care cured you.' Una chuckled gleefully. 'He's a darling man, darling, but he has a terrible temper! It's not in your nature to provoke it, but whatever you do, don't tempt fate by telling him about your heart trouble. No man likes to be the dupe of a woman, and he's already had a fair taste of that. So mark what I say – don't ever, ever tell him.'

'You're leaving,' said Missy desolately.

'With knobs on I'm leaving, darling! I've done what I was sent to do, and now I'm going to take a well-deserved rest on the softest, fattest, pinkest, *champagniest* cloud I can find.'

'I can't do it without you, Una!'

'Nonsense, darling, of course you can. Just be good, and especially be good in bed, and you can't go wrong. That is, as long as you heed my warning – *don't ever tell him the truth*!'

That exquisite radiance welling from within Una had fused with the last of the sun; she stood a moment longer in the doorway with the light pouring through her and out of her, then she was gone.

'Missy! Missy! Missy! Are you all right? Are you in pain? Missy! For God's sake, answer me!'

John Smith was standing over her, chafing her hands, a look of desperate horror in his eyes.

She managed to smile up at him. 'I'm quite all right, John, truly. It's been the day. Too much happiness!'

'You'd better get used to too much happiness, my little love, because I swear I shall drown you in it,' he said, and caught his breath. 'You're my second chance, Missalonghi Smith.'

A chill breeze puffed in through the open door, and just before Drusilla reached to shut it out, it whispered for Missy's ears alone, 'Never tell him! Oh, please, *never* tell him!'

Tim

1

Harry Markham and his crew arrived on the job at exactly seven o'clock that Friday morning, Harry and his foreman Jim Irvine sitting inside the pickup cabin and Harry's three men in the open back of the truck, perched wherever they could find a level space for their behinds. The house they were renovating lay on Sydney's North Shore in the suburb of Artarmon, just behind the spreading desolation of the brick pits. It was not a big job, even for a small-time builder like Harry; merely covering the red brick bungalow with stucco and adding a sleepout to the back veranda, the kind of job Harry welcomed from time to time because it filled in the gaps between larger contracts.

The weekend promised heat and endless sun, if Friday morning was any indication; the men piled out of the pickup grumbling among themselves, plunged into the gloomy tree-shielded aisle of the side passage and shed their clothes without a twinge of self-consciousness or shame.

Changed into their work-shorts, they came round the back corner of the house just as the Old Girl was shuffling down the backyard in her faded pink chenille bathrobe, circa 1950, carefully carrying a gaudily flowered china chamber pot in both hands, her head a twinkling mass of tin butterfly hair wavers, also circa 1950. No new-fangled rollers for Mrs Emily Parker, thank you very much. The yard slipped gradually into the maw of a gravelly clay canyon which had once been the source of a considerable number of Sydney's bricks; now it served as a convenient place for the Old Girl to empty her chamber pot every morning, for she clung doggedly to the habits of her rural origins and insisted on her potty at night.

As the contents of the pot flew in a solid-looking arc of pale amber towards the bottom of the brick pit, she turned her head and eyed the nearly naked men sourly.

'G'day, Miz Parker!' Harry called. 'Oughta finish this today, I reckon!'

'And about bloody time, too, you lazy lot of bots!' the old Girl snarled as she came slopping up the yard again, quite unembarrassed. 'The things I have to put up with on account of youse! Miss Horton complained to me last night that her prize pink geranyimums is all covered with cement dust, and her maidenhair fern got squashed flat when some useless coot buzzed a brick over her fence yestiddy.'

'If Miss Horton's that prune-faced old spinster next door,' Mick Devine muttered to Bill Naismith, 'then I bet her bloody maidenhair didn't get squashed by a brick only yestiddy, it up and died years ago from no fertiliser!'

Still complaining loudly, the Old Girl disappeared inside with her empty chamber pot; a few seconds later the men heard the energetic sounds of Mrs Emily Parker cleaning her chamber pot in the back veranda toilet, followed by the swoosh of the toilet cistern discharging and a sound of ringing china as the pot was hung on its diurnal hook above the more orthodox repository of human wastes.

'Jesus Henry, I bet the bloody grass is green down in that brick pit,' Harry said to a grinning crew.

'It's a bloody wonder she ain't flooded it out long before now,' Bill sniggered.

'Well, if youse asks me, she ain't the full quid,' Mick said. 'In this day and age and with two proper bogs in her house, she's still peeing into a guzunda.'

'A guzunda?' Tim Melville echoed.

'Yeah, sport, a guzunda. A guzunda is the thing that guzunda the bed every night and that you always put your flaming foot in when you get up in a hurry,' Harry explained. He looked at his watch. 'The Readymix Concrete truck ought to be here any tick, I reckon. Tim, you get out the front and wait for it. Take the big wheelbarrow off the truck and start ferrying the mud back to us as soon as the blighter shows, okay?'

Tim Melville smiled, nodded, and trotted off.

Mick Devine, absently watching him go and still pondering on the vagaries of Old Girls, started to laugh. 'Oh, struth! I just thought of a beaut! Listen, you blokes, at smoke-oh this morning you just follow my lead, and maybe we'll teach Tim a thing or two about guzundas and such-like.'

2

Mary Horton screwed her long, very thick hair into its habitual bun on the back of her neck, thrust two more pins into it and eyed her reflection in the mirror without joy or sorrow, or indeed much interest. The mirror was a good one, and gave back her image without flattery or distortion; had her eyes been engaged in a more personal inspection they would have seen a short, rather stocky woman of early middle age, with white hair as colourless as crystal pulled cruelly away from a square but regular-featured face. She wore no make-up, deeming it a waste of time and money to pay homage to vanity. The eyes themselves were dark brown and snappingly alert, no-nonsense eyes which echoed the decisive, slightly hard planes of her face. Her body was clad in what her fellow workers had long ago decided was her equivalent of army uniform or nun's habit; a crisp white shirt buttoned high at her throat, over which the top half of a severely cut grey linen suit slipped smoothly. Her hemline was decently below her knees, the skirt cut generously enough to avoid its riding up when she sat down, her legs were sheathed in sensibly thick support hose, and on her feet she wore black lace-up shoes with solid block heels.

The shoes were polished until they twinkled, not a speck or a spot marred the white surface of her shirt, no crease sullied the perfection of the linen suit. To be at all times absolutely impeccable was an obsession with Mary Horton; her young assistant at the office swore that she had seen Miss Horton remove her clothes carefully and put them on a hanger before she used the lavatory so they would not become creased or disarranged.

Satisfied that she measured up to her inflexible standards, Mary Horton nudged a black straw hat onto the upper margin of her bun, stuck a hatpin through it in one movement, drew on her black kid gloves and pulled her huge handbag to the edge of the dressing table. She opened the bag and methodically checked to see that it contained keys, money, handkerchief, spare Kotex pad, pen and notebook, appointment diary, identification and credit cards, driver's licence, parking lot gate card, safety pins, straight pins, needle and thread box, scissors, nail file, two spare shirt buttons, screwdriver, pliers, wirecutters, flashlight, steel tape measure in centimetres and inches, box of .38 cartridges, and police service revolver.

She was a crack shot. It was a part of her duties to do Constable Steel & Mining's banking, and since the time she had neatly winged a felon as he scuttled away with Constable Steel & Mining's payroll under his arm, there was not a criminal in Sydney with sufficient intestinal fortitude to tackle Miss Horton on her way from the bank. She had yielded her briefcase so imperturbably, with such composure and lack of protest, that the thief had thought himself perfectly safe; then as he turned to run she opened her handbag, took out the pistol, levelled it, aimed it and fired it. Sergeant Hopkins of the NSW Police pistol range maintained she was faster on the draw than Sammy Davis, Junior.

Thrown on her own resources at the age of fourteen, she had shared a room at the YWCA with five other girls, and worked as a salesclerk in David Jones until she completed a night secretarial course. At fifteen she had commenced work in the general typists' pool at Constable Steel & Mining, so poor that she wore the same scrupulously laundered skirt and blouse every day and darned her cotton stockings until they contained more darns than original fabric.

Within five years her efficiency, unobtrusive quietness, and remarkable intelligence took her from the general office to the post of private secretary for Archibald Johnson, the managing director, but during her first ten years with the firm she continued to live at the Y, darn her stockings over and over again and save much more than she spent.

When she was twenty-five years old she approached Archie Johnson for advice on investing her savings, and by the time she was thirty she had made many, many times her initial outlay. Consequently, at the age of forty-three she owned a house in Artarmon, a quiet middle-class suburb, drove a very conservative but very expensive British Bentley upholstered in genuine leather and panelled in genuine walnut, owned a beach cottage on twenty acres of land north of Sydney, and had her suits made by the man who tailored for the wife of the Governor General of Australia.

She was very well satisfied with herself and her life; she enjoyed the small luxuries which only money permitted, kept almost totally to herself at work and at home, had no friends save five thousand books which lined the walls of her den and several hundred LPs devoted almost entirely to Bach, Brahms, Beethoven, and Handel. She loved gardening and cleaning house, never watched television or went to the movies, and had never wanted or had a boyfriend.

When Mary Horton let herself out of her front door she stood on the stoop for a moment, screwing up her eyes against the glare and checking the state of her front garden. The grass needed mowing badly; where was that dratted man whom she paid to barber it every Thursday fortnight? He had not come for a month, and the closely cropped green velvet surface was becoming tussocky. Most annoying, she thought, really most annoying.

There was a curious thrumming in the air, half a sound and half a sensation, a sort of faintly heard *boom, boom, boom* that seeped into the bones and told the experienced Sydneysider that today was going to be a very hot day, up over the century. The twin West Australian flowering gums on either side of her front gate fluttered their blue, sickled leaves limply downward in sighing protest against the hammer of the heat, and Japanese beetles clicked and rattled busily among the suffocating masses of yellow flowers on the cassia bushes. A bank of magnificent red double oleanders flanked the stone-flagged pathway leading from the front door to the garage; Mary Horton set her lips together tightly and began to walk along it.

Then the duel began, the struggle which recurred every morning and evening of summer. As she drew level with the first beautiful, blooming bush, it began to shriek and caterwaul in an incredible volume of shrilling sound which rang in her ears until it set her head reeling.

Down went the handbag, off came the gloves; Mary Horton marched to the neat green coils of the garden hose, turned its faucet full on and began to drench her oleanders. Gradually the noise dwindled away as the bushes became saturated, until there was only a single basso profundo 'breek!' emanating from the bush nearest to the house. Mary shook her fist at it vindictively.

'I'll get you yet, you old twirp!' she said through clenched teeth.

'Breeeeeek!' answered the cicada choirmaster derisively.

On went the gloves, up came the handbag; Mary proceeded to the garage in peace and quiet.

From her driveway it was possible to see the mess that had

once been Mrs Emily Parker's pretty red brick bungalow next door. Mary eyed the havoc disapprovingly as she hefted up the door of her garage and glanced idly towards the sidewalk.

Walton Street's sidewalks were lovely; they consisted of a narrow concrete path and a beautifully kept, very wide stretch of lawn from path to curb. Every thirty feet down each side of the street there grew a huge oleander tree, one white, one pink, one red, one pink, in successive quartets that were the pride of Walton Street's residents and one of the chief reasons why Walton Street was generally a prizewinner in the annual *Herald* garden competition.

A massive concrete carrier was parked with its idly revolving drum slapping against one of Emily Parker's sidewalk oleanders, and a chute was discharging gluey grey gallons of concrete on to the grass. It dripped from the sad, petrified branches of the tree, it ran and oozed sluggishly into pools where the lawn was uneven, it slopped onto the paved path. Mary's mouth was a thin white line of vexation. What on earth had possessed Emily Parker to poultice the red brick sides of her house with this disgusting substance? There was no accounting for taste, or rather the lack of it, she reflected.

A young man was standing bare-headed in the sun, dispassionately watching the desecration of Walton Street; from where she stood some twenty feet away Mary Horton gazed at him, dumbfounded.

Had he lived two and a half thousand years before, Phidias and Praxiteles would have used him as model for the greatest Apollos of all time; instead of standing with such superb lack of self-consciousness in the backwater of a Sydney street to suffer the oblivion of utter mortality, he would have lived forever in the cool, smoothly satin curves of pale marble, and his stone eyes would have looked indifferently over the awed heads of generations upon generations of men.

But here he stood, amid a slushy concrete mess on Walton Street, obviously a member of Harry Markham's building crew, for he wore the builder's uniform of khaki shorts with legs rolled up until the lower curve of the buttocks was just visible, the waistline of the shorts slipped down until they rode his hips. Aside from the shorts and a pair of thick woollen socks turned down over the tops of heavy, clumping workman's boots, he wore nothing; not shirt or coat or hat.

Momentarily turned side-on to her, he glistened in the sun like living, melted gold, legs so beautifully shaped that she fancied he was a long-distance runner; indeed, that was the cast of his whole physique, long and slender and graceful, the planes of his chest as he swung towards her tapering gradually from wide shoulders to exquisitely narrow hips.

And the face – oh, the face! It was flawless. The nose was short and straight, the cheekbones high and pronounced, the mouth tenderly curved. Where his cheek sloped in towards the corner of his mouth on the left side he bore a tiny crease, and that minute furrow saddened him, lent him an air of lost, childlike innocence. His hair, brows, and lashes were the colour of ripe wheat, magnificent with the sun pouring down on them, and his wide eyes were as intensely, vividly blue as a cornflower.

When he noticed her watching him he smiled at her happily, and the smile snatched Mary Horton's breath from her body in an uncontrolled gasp. She had never gasped so in all her life; horrified to find herself spellbound by his extraordinary beauty, she made a sudden mad dash for the haven of her car.

The memory of him stayed with her all through the crawling drive into North Sydney's commercial centre, where Constable Steel & Mining had its forty-storey office building. Try as she would to concentrate on the traffic and the coming events of the day, Mary could not banish him from her mind. If he had been effeminate, if his face had been merely pretty or he had exuded some indefinable aura of brutishness, she could have forgotten him as easily as long self-discipline had trained her to forget anything unwelcome or upsetting. Oh, God, how beautiful he was, how completely, appallingly beautiful! Then she remembered Emily Parker saying the builders would be finished today; driving on doggedly, everything in the quivering, shimmering mist of heat around her seemed to dim a little.

3

With Mary Horton gone and the garden hose rendered impotent, the cicada choirmaster in his oleander bush emitted a deep, resonating 'breeek!' and was immediately answered by the diva soprano two bushes over. One by one they came in, tenors, contraltos, baritones, and sopranos, until the beating sun charged their little iridescent green bodies with such a singing power of sound that to attempt a conversation within feet of the bushes was useless. The deafening chorus spread, over the tops of the clattery denizens of the cassias to the flowering gums, across the fence to the oleanders along Walton Street's sidewalks, and into the row of camphor laurels between Mary Horton's and Emily Parker's back gardens.

The toiling builders hardly noticed the cicadas until they had to shout to each other, scooping trowel-loads of concrete from the big heap Tim Melville kept replenishing and throwing them – *slurp!* – against the chipped red brick sides of the Old Girl's bungalow. The sleepout was finished, all save a final coat of stucco; bare backs bending and straightening in the swing and rhythm of hard labour, the builders flowed steadily up and around the house, bones basking in the wonderful warmth of summer, sweat drying before it had a chance to bead on their silky brown skins. Bill Naismith slapped wet concrete on the bricks, Mick Devine smoothed the splashes into a continuous sheet of coarse-grained, greenish plaster, and behind him Jim Irvine slithered along a rickety scaffold, sweeping his shaping trowel back and forth in easy curves that imparted a swirling series of arcs to the surface. Harry Markham, eyes everywhere, glanced at his watch and shouted for Tim.

'Oy, mate, go inside and ask the Old Girl if you can put the billy on, will you?' Harry yelled when he gained Tim's attention.

Tim parked his wheelbarrow in the side passage, gathered the gallon-capacity tin billycan and the box of supplies into his arms, and kicked a query of admission on the back door.

Mrs Parker appeared a moment later, a shadowy lump behind the veiling darkness of the fly-screening.

'Oh, it's you, is it, love?' she asked, opening the door. 'Come in, come in! I suppose you want me to boil a kettle for them 'orrible warts outside, do yer?' she went on, lighting a cigarette and leering appreciatively at him as he stood blinking in the gloom, sun-blinded.

'Yes, please, Mrs Parker,' Tim said politely, smiling.

'Well, all right then, I suppose I don't have much choice, do I, not if I want me house finished before the weekend? Sit yourself down while the kettle boils, love.'

She moved around the kitchen sloppily, her salt-and-pepper hair crimped into an impossible battery of waves, her uncorseted figure swathed in a cotton housedress of purple and yellow pansies.

'Want a bikkie, love?' she asked, extending the cookie jar. 'I got some real grouse choccy ones in there.'

'Yes, please, Mrs Parker,' Tim smiled, pawing in the jar until his hand closed on a very chocolatey cookie.

He sat silently on the chair while the Old Girl took his can of supplies from him and spooned a good quarter of a pound of loose tea into the billycan. When the kettle boiled she half-filled the billycan, then put the kettle on to boil again while Tim set out battered enamel mugs on the kitchen table and stood a bottle of milk and a jar of sugar alongside them.

'Here, pet, wipe yer hands on the tea towel like a good bloke, will yer?' the Old Girl asked as Tim left a brown smear of chocolate on the table edge.

She went to the back door, stuck her head outside and bawled, 'Smoke-oh!' at the top of her voice.

Tim poured himself a mug of coal-black, milkless tea, then added so much sugar to it that it slopped over the top of the mug onto the table and set the Old Girl clucking again.

'Christ, you're a grub!' she grinned at him forgivingly. 'I wouldn't put up with it from them other bots, but you can't help it, can you, love?'

Tim smiled at her warmly, picked up his cup and carried it outside as the other men began to come into the kitchen.

They ate at the back of the house, where it began to curve around the newly erected sleepout. It was a shady spot, far enough from the garbage cans to be comparatively free of flies, and they had each arranged a small, flat-topped cairn of bricks to sit on while they ate. The camphor laurels between Miss Horton's backyard and Mrs Parker's leaned over them thickly, with a shade dense enough to make resting there a pleasure after working in the baking sun. Each man sat down with his mug of tea in one hand and his brown paper bag of food in the other, stretching his legs out with a sigh and snorting the flies away.

Since they started work at seven and finished at three, this morning break occurred at nine, followed by lunch at eleven-thirty. Traditionally the nine o'clock pause was referred to as 'smoke-oh,' and occupied about half an hour. Engaged in heavy manual labour, they ate with enormous appetite, though they had little to show for it on their spare, muscular frames. A breakfast of hot porridge, fried chops or sausages with two or three fried eggs, several cups of tea, and slices of toast started each man's day off around five-thirty; during smoke-oh they consumed home-made sandwiches and slabs of cake, and for lunch the same, only twice as much. There was no afternoon break; at three they were gone, working shorts thrust into their oddly medical-looking little brown bags, once more clad in open-necked shirts and thin cotton trousers as they headed for the pub. Each day led inexorably to this, its culmination and high point; within the buzzing, latrine-like interior of a pub they could relax with a foot on the bar rail and a brimming fifteen-ounce schooner of beer in one fist, yarning with workmates and pub cronies and flirting sterilely with the hard-faced barmaids. Homecoming was total anticlimax after this, a half-surly submission to the cramping pettiness of women and offspring.

There was a rather tense, expectant air about the men this morning as they sat down to enjoy their smoke-oh. Mick Devine and his boon companion Bill Naismith sat side by side against the high paling fence, mugs at their feet and food spread out in their laps; Harry Markham and Jim Irvine faced them, with Tim Melville nearest to the back door of the Old Girl's house, so he could fetch and carry when the others demanded. As junior member of the team, his was the position of menial and general dogsbody; on Harry's books his official title was 'Builder's Labourer,' and he had been with Harry for ten of his twenty-five years without promotion.

'Hey, Tim, what youse got on yer sandwiches this morning?' Mick asked, winking heavily at the others.

'Gee, Mick, the same as always, jam,' Tim answered, holding up untidily hacked white bread with thick amber jam oozing out its edges.

'What sorta jam?' Mick persisted, eyeing his own sandwich unenthusiastically.

'Apricot, I think.'

'Wanta swap? I got sausages on mine.'

Tim's face lit up. 'Sausages! Oh, I love sausage sandwiches! I'll swap!'

The exchange was made; Mick bit clumsily into the apricot jam sandwich while Tim, oblivious of the grinning regard of the others, disposed of Mick's sausage sandwich in a few bites. He had the last wedge poised to eat when Mick, shoulders shaking with suppressed laughter, reached out a hand and grasped his wrist.

The blue eyes lifted to Mick's face in a helpless, childish question, fear lurking in them; his sad mouth dropped slackly open.

'What's the matter, Mick?' he asked.

'That bloody sausage sandwich didn't even touch the sides, mate. How did it taste, or didn't you keep it in yer mouth long enough to find out, eh?'

The tiny crease to the left side of Tim's mouth quivered into being again as he closed his mouth and looked at Mick in apprehensive wonder.

'It was all right, Mick,' he said slowly. 'It tasted a bit different, but it was all right.'

Mick roared, and in a moment they were all writhing in paroxysms of laughter, tears running down their faces, hands slapping at aching sides, gasping for breath.

'Oh, Christ, Tim, you're the dizzy limit! Harry thinks you're worth at least sixty cents in the quid, but I said you weren't worth more than ten, and after this effort I reckon I'm right. You couldn't possibly be worth more than ten cents in the quid, mate!'

'What's the matter?' Tim asked, bewildered. 'What did I do? I know I'm not the full quid, Mick, honest I do!'

'If yer sandwich didn't taste like sausage, Tim, what did it taste like?' Mick grinned.

'Well, I dunno . . .' Tim's golden brows knit in fierce concentration. 'I dunno! It just tasted different, like.'

'Why don't youse open that last bit and take a real good look, mate?'

Tim's square, beautifully shaped hands fumbled with the two fragments of bread and pulled them apart. The last piece of sausage was squashed out of shape, its edges slippery and sticky-looking.

'Smell it!' Mick ordered, glancing around the helpless circle and wiping the tears out of his eyes with the back of his hand.

Tim brought it to his nose; the nostrils twitched and flared, then he put the bread down again and sat looking at them in puzzled wonder. 'I dunno what it is,' he said pathetically.

'It's a *turd*, you great ding!' Mick answered disgustedly. 'Christ, are you dim! You still don't know what it is, even after taking a whiff of it?'

'A turd?' Tim echoed, staring at Mick. 'What's a turd, Mick?'

Everyone collapsed in a fresh storm of laughter, while Tim sat with the small remnant of sandwich between his fingers, watching and waiting patiently until someone recovered sufficiently to answer his question.

'A turd, Tim me boy, is a big fat piece of *shit*!' Mick howled.

Tim shivered and gulped, flung the bread away in horror and sat wringing his hands together, shrinking into himself. They all moved away from his vicinity hastily, thinking he might vomit, but he did not; he just sat staring at them, grief-stricken.

It had happened again. He had made everyone laugh by doing something silly, but he didn't know what it was, why it was so funny. His father would have said he ought to be a 'wakeup,' whatever that meant, but he hadn't been a wakeup, he had happily eaten a sausage sandwich that hadn't been a sausage sandwich. A piece of shit, they said it was, but how could he know what a piece of shit tasted like, when he had never eaten it before? What was so funny? He wished he knew; he hungered to know, to share in their laughter and understand. That was always the greatest sorrow, that he could never seem to understand.

His wide blue eyes filled with tears, his face twisted up in anguish and he began to cry like a small child, bellowing noisily, still wringing his hands together and shrinking away from them.

'Jesus bloody Christ, what a lot of bastards you dirty buggers are!' the Old Girl roared, erupting from her back door like a harpy, yellow and purple pansies swirling about her. She came across to Tim and took his hands, pulling him to his feet as she glared around at the sobering men. 'Come on, love, you come inside with me a little minute while I give you something nice to take the nasty taste away,' she soothed, patting his hands and stroking his hair. 'As for you lot,' she hissed, sticking her face up to Mick so viciously that he backed away, 'I hope you all fall down a manhole arse-first onto a nice iron spike! You oughta be horse-whipped for doing something like this, you great myopic gits! You'd better see this job is finished today, Harry Markham, or it won't be finished at all! I never want to see you lot again!'

Clucking and soothing, she led Tim inside and left the men standing staring at each other.

Mick shrugged. 'Bloody women!' he said. 'I never met a woman yet what had a sense of humour. Come on, let's get this job finished today, I'm sick of it too.'

Mrs Parker led Tim into the kitchen and sat him on a chair.

'You poor flaming little coot,' she said, moving to the refrigerator. 'I dunno why men think it's so bloody funny to bait dimwits and dogs. Listen to 'em out there, yahaing and yawhawing, real funny! I'd like to bake 'em a dirty great chocolate cake and flavour it with shit, since they think it's so bloody funny! You, you poor little bugger, didn't even throw it up again, but they'd be spewing for an hour, the walloping great heroes!' She turned to look at him, softening because he still wept, the big tears spilling down his cheeks as he hiccoughed and snuffled miserably. 'Oh, here, stop it!' she said, pulling a tissue out of a box and taking his chin in her hand. 'Blow yer nose, booby!'

He did as he was told, then suffered her ungentle ministrations as she tidied up his face.

'Christ, what a waste!' she said, half to herself, looking at his face, then she threw the tissue into the kitchen tidy and shrugged. 'Oh, well, that's the way it goes, I suppose. Can't have everything, even the biggest and best of us, eh, love?' She patted his cheek with one ropey old hand. 'Now what do you like best, love, ice cream with choccy syrup all over it, or a big bit of jam pud with cold banana custard all over it?'

He stopped sniffling long enough to smile radiantly. 'Oh, jam pud, please, Mrs Parker! I love jam pud and cold banana custard, it's my favourite!'

She sat opposite him at the kitchen table while he shovelled the pudding into his mouth in huge spoonfuls, chiding him for eating too fast and telling him to mind his manners.

'Chew with yer mouth closed, love, it's 'orrible looking at someone slopping their food around in an open mouth. And take yer elbows off the table, like a good boy.'

4

Mary Horton put her car in the garage at six-thirty that evening, so tired that she could hardly walk the few feet to her front door without her knees trembling. She had pushed herself furiously all day long, and succeeded in deadening all sensations save weariness. Mrs Parker's house was evidently finished; the red brick exterior had entirely gone, replaced by wet, green-grey stucco. The phone began to ring as she closed the front door, and she ran to answer it.

'Miss Horton, that you?' rasped her neighbour's voice. 'It's Emily Parker here, pet. Listen, can you do something for me?'

'Certainly.'

'I've got to go out now, me son's just rung from Central and I've got to go and pick him up there. The builders finished this arvo, but there's still a lot of their stuff in the backyard, and Harry said he was coming back to clean it up. Just keep an eye on things for me, will youse?'

'Certainly, Mrs Parker.'

'Ta, love! Hooroo, see youse tomorrow.'

Mary sighed in exasperation. All she wanted was to sit down in her easy chair by the picture window, put her feet up with her before-dinner sherry and read the *Sydney Morning Herald*, as was her nightly custom. She went through to the living room and opened her liquor cabinet tiredly. Her glassware was all Waterford hobnail, exquisitely graceful, and she took one of the long-stemmed sherry glasses from its place on a polished shelf. Her preference was for a medium-sweet sherry, which she mixed herself by pouring half a glass of dry Amontillado and topping it up with a very sweet sherry. The ritual completed, she carried the glass through to the kitchen, and then out onto her back terrace.

Her house was better designed than Mrs Parker's; instead of a back veranda she had a high, wide patio of sandstone flags, which fell away on three sides as a terraced rock garden to the lawn fifteen feet below. It was very pretty and in the heat of summer very cool, for an overhead trellis covered one side of it completely with a roof of grapevine and wistaria. In summer she could sit beneath the thick green canopy, shielded from the sun; in winter she could sit under bare gnarled branches and let the sun warm her; in spring the lilac clusters of wistaria made it stunningly beautiful, and in late summer and autumn the trellis hung heavy with great bunches of table grapes, red and white and purple.

She walked soundlessly across the flagstones in her neat black shoes, for she was a cat-footed kind of person and liked to approach people silently so she could see them before they saw her. It was sometimes very useful to catch people off guard.

At the far edge of the patio was a balustrade of white-painted wrought iron in a grape pattern, just two or three feet of it on either side of a flight of steps leading down to the sweeping stretch of lawn below. Noiseless as always, she stood with her glass balanced on the top of the balustrade and looked towards Mrs Parker's backyard.

The sun was dying down to the horizon of the western sky, which she faced, and had she been the kind of person whom beauty moved, she would have been awe-struck at the prospect before her. Between her back terrace and the Blue Mountains twenty miles away there was nothing higher; even the hills of Ryde did not obstruct her outlook but rather enhanced it, lending it a mid-distance perspective. It had been well over the hundred during the afternoon and even now was close to that, so there were no clouds in the sky to score a splendid end to the day. But the light itself was beautiful, deep yellow and faintly bronzing, tinting the greenest things more green and everything else amber. Mary shaded a hand over her eyes and scanned Mrs Parker's backyard.

The young man of the morning was sweeping a cloudy heap of cement dust towards a pile of trash and builder's remains, golden head bent absorbed over the simple task, as if he liked to give everything, even this, all his attention. He was still half-naked, still as beautiful, perhaps even more beautiful in the last limpid light than he had been in the first prickling sharpness of day. Drink forgotten, Mary stood in lost loneliness watching him, not aware of herself, not conscious that she was possessed by an emotion alien to her whole being, neither guilty nor confounded. She simply watched him.

The sweeping finished, he lifted his head and saw her, waved a cheery hand in her direction, then disappeared. Mary jumped, heart in mouth, and before she could stop herself she had crossed to the row of camphor laurels between the two back gardens and was slipping through a space in the paling fence.

He had evidently completed whatever he had been set to do, for he had his workman's bag in his hand and was pulling his street clothes out of it.

'Hullo,' he said, smiling at her without a shadow of self-awareness, as if he had no idea of his own beauty or of its inevitable impact on others.

'Hullo,' Mary replied, not smiling; something wet touched her hand, and she glanced down to see her sherry slopping over the rim of the forgotten glass.

'You're spilling your drink,' he observed.

'Yes, isn't that idiotic of me?' she ventured, trying to fix her features into a pleasant mask.

He had no answer for that, but stood watching her in his bright, interested way, and smiling.

'Would you like to earn a little extra money?' Mary inquired eventually, staring at him searchingly.

He looked puzzled. 'Eh?'

She flushed, her dark eyes surveying him a little ironically. 'My grass needs cutting badly and my man hasn't been in a month, I doubt if I'll ever see him again. I'm very proud of my garden and I hate to see it like this, but it's extremely difficult to get someone to cut the grass. So I thought, seeing you here working overtime on a Friday, that you might be in need of a little extra money. Would you be able to come tomorrow and cut my grass? I have a tractor mower, so it's really more a question of time than effort.'

'Eh?' he repeated, still smiling, but not quite so broadly.

She twitched her shoulders impatiently. 'Oh, for heaven's sake! If you don't want the work, say so! I merely want to know if you'd like to come and cut my grass tomorrow. I'll pay you more than Mr Markham does.'

He walked across to the gap in the paling fence and peered through into her yard curiously, then nodded. 'Yes, it does need cutting, doesn't it? I can cut it for you.'

She slipped back through to her own side of the fence and

turned to face him. 'Thank you. I appreciate it, and I assure you I'll make it well worth your while. Just come to the back door tomorrow morning and I'll give you your instructions.'

'All right, Missus,' he answered gravely.

'Don't you want to know my name?' she asked.

'I suppose so,' he smiled.

His veneer of permanent amusement flicked her on the raw, and she flushed again. 'My name is Miss Horton!' she snapped. 'What's your name, young man?'

'Tim Melville.'

'Then I'll see you tomorrow morning, Mr Melville. Goodbye, and thank you.'

'Bye bye,' he said, smiling.

When she turned at the top of her patio steps to look back into Mrs Parker's yard, he had gone. Her sherry had gone too, the last of it spilled when she absently turned the glass upside down in her hurry to escape that innocent blue gaze.

5

The Seaside Hotel was a very popular drinking place among the citizens of Randwick. They came to it from all parts of the big, sprawling suburb, from Randwick proper and Coogee and Clovelly and even Maroubra. It served an excellent brand of beer, beautifully chilled, and there was plenty of room to spread, but whatever the reason for its popularity, there was not a moment of its opening life that was not busy and cheerful with the noises of contented beer drinkers. Several storeys high, it had walls of pure white stucco, and between them and its Alhambra-like row of arches across the front, it looked something like a massive hacienda. Perched two hundred feet above the ocean that lay in front of it and not half a mile away, it commanded a magnificent view of Coogee Beach, one of the smaller surfing beaches in the eastern suburbs. Most of the drinkers stood outside the public bar on the long red veranda, which was plunged into deep shade from three in the afternoon. On a hot evening it was a perfect spot to drink, for the sun set behind the hill at the back of the pub, and the sea breeze puffed in off the luminous blue Pacific without a thing to hinder it.

Ron Melville was standing on the veranda with his two best drinking mates, his eyes alternating between his watch and the beach far below. Tim was late; it was nearly eight o'clock and he ought to have been there by six-thirty at the outside. Ron was more annoyed than worried, for long experience had taught him that worrying over Tim was a good way to train for an early heart attack.

The short Sydney twilight was at its peak, and the Norfolk Island pines bordering the sandstone beach promenade had turned from dark green to black. The tide was coming in and the surf was getting up into a roar, spreading itself in a spent sheet of bubbles far up the sloping white sand, and the shadows were slipping further and further out across the water. The buses came down the hill alongside the beach park, and the bus stop was on the corner far below; Ron watched a bus squeal to a halt at the stop and passed his eyes over the disembarking passengers, looking for Tim's unmistakable yellow head. It was there, so Ron turned away immediately.

'There's Tim on that bus, so I think I'll go in and get him a beer. Another round?' he asked casually.

By the time he emerged again the street lights were turned on, and Tim was standing smiling at Ron's mates.

'Hullo, Pop,' he said to Ron, smiling.

'G'day, mate, where've you been?' his father demanded sourly.

'I had to finish up a job. Harry didn't want to come back on Monday.'

'Well, we can do with the overtime.'

'I got another job, too,' Tim said importantly as he took the glass of beer from his father and downed it in one long gulp. 'That was great! Can I have another one, Pop?'

'In a minute. What other job?'

'Oh, that! The lady next door wants me to cut her grass tomorrow.'

'Next door to who?'

'Next door to where we were today.'

Curly Campbell sniggered. 'Did youse ask her where she wanted her grass cut, Tim? Inside or outside?'

'Shut up, Curly, you drongo!' Ron snarled irritably. 'You know Tim don't understand that sort of talk!'

'Her grass is too long and it needs cutting,' Tim explained.

'Did you say you'd do it, Tim?' Ron asked.

'Yes, tomorrow morning. She said she was going to pay me, so I thought you wouldn't mind.'

Ron stared at his son's exquisite face cynically. If the lady in question had any ideas, five minutes with Tim would squelch them. Nothing cooled their ardour faster than discovering Tim wasn't the full quid, or, if that didn't turn them off, they soon found out that trying to seduce Tim was a lost cause, since he had no concept of what women were for or about. Ron had trained his son to flee the moment a woman got too excited or tried some sexy little come-on; Tim was very susceptible to a suggestion of fear, and he could be taught to fear anything.

'Can I have another beer, Pop?' Tim asked again.

'Righto, son. Go and ask Florrie for a schooner. I reckon you've earned it.'

Curly Campbell and Dave O'Brien watched his tall, slender form disappear under the arches.

'I've known youse for twenty bloody years, Ron,' Curly said, 'and I still haven't worked out who Tim gets his looks from.'

Ron grinned. 'I dunno either, mate. Tim's a throwback to someone we've never heard of, I reckon.'

The Melvilles, *père et fils*, left the Seaside a little before nine and walked briskly down past Coogee Oval to the row of brightly lit milk bars, fun parlours, and wine shops at the far end of the beach park. Ron herded his son past them quickly as they cut from Arden Street across to Surf Street, making sure that the hungry glances Tim evoked in the lolling tarts and trollops had no chance to develop.

The Melville house was in Surf Street but not in the posh section on top of the hill, where Nobby Clark the jockey lived. They walked up the one-in-three pitch of the incredibly steep hill easily, neither of them so much as breathing heavily, for they both worked in the building trade and were in superb physical condition. Halfway down the other side of the hill in the hollow which lay between the ritzy top and the far hump of Clovelly Road they turned into the side gate of a very ordinary brick semi-detached house.

The female Melvilles had long since eaten, but as Ron and Tim let themselves in the back door Esme Melville came out of the living room and met them in the kitchen.

'Your dinner's ruined,' she said, without much indignation.

'Go on, Es, you always say that,' Ron grinned, sitting down at the kitchen table, where his place and Tim's still lay undisturbed. 'What's to eat?'

'As if you care when you're full of beer,' Esme retorted. 'It's Friday, mug! What do youse always eat on Friday, eh? I got fish and chips from the Dago's as usual.'

'Oh, goody! Fish and chips!' Tim exclaimed, beaming. 'Gee, Mum, I love fish and chips!'

His mother looked at him tenderly, ruffling his thick hair in the only kind of caress she ever gave him. 'It wouldn't matter what I gave you, love, you'd still think it was your favourite. Here youse are.'

She slapped heaped plates of greasy, batter-coated fish and soft, very un-crisp French fries in front of her men and went back to the living room, where the television set was in the middle of the umpteenth re-run of *Coronation Street*. That glimpse of English working-class life was fascinating, and she loved it; she would sit there thinking of her nice big house and garden and the fine weather and the tennis and the beach, pitying the inhabitants of Coronation Street from the bottom of her heart. If you had to be working-class, Aussie working-class was the only one to be.

Tim didn't tell his mother and father about eating the turd sandwich, because he had forgotten all about it; when he finished his fish and chips he and his father left their empty plates on the table and entered the living room.

'Come on, Es, it's time for the cricket summary,' Ron said, switching channels.

His wife sighed. 'I wish you'd stay out a bit longer, then I might get to see a Joan Crawford picture or something instead of sport, sport, sport!'

'Well, if Tim gets a bit more part-time work, love, I'll buy youse your own TV set,' Ron rejoined, kicking his shoes off and stretching himself out full-length on the sofa. 'Where's Dawnie?'

'Out with some fella, I suppose.'

'What one this time?'

'How the hell do I know, love? I never worry about her, she's too smart to get into trouble.'

Ron looked at his son. 'Ain't it the dizzy limit, Es, the way life turns out? We got the best looking boy in Sydney and he's about fourpence in the quid, then we go and get Dawnie. There's him, can only sign his name and count to ten, and Dawnie so clever she can win university gold medals without even studying.'

Esme picked up her knitting, looking at Ron sadly. He felt it, poor old Ron, but in his own way he'd been real good to Tim, watched out for him without treading on him or treating him like a baby. Didn't he let the boy drink with him, hadn't he insisted Tim should earn his own bread like any normal boy? It was just as well, because they weren't as young as they used to be. Ron was almost seventy and she was only six months behind him. That was why Tim had been born simple, the doctors told her. He was twenty-five now, and he was the first-born. Well over forty, she and Ron were when he was born; the doctors said it was something to do with her ovaries being tired and out of practice. Then a year later Dawnie was born, perfectly normal, which was how it went, the doctors said. The first one was usually the hardest hit when a woman began having children at over forty years of age.

She let her eyes dwell on Tim as he sat in his own special chair by the far wall, closer to the TV than any of the other chairs: like a small child, he liked to be in the middle of the picture. There he sat, the loveliest, sweetest boy, eyes shining as he applauded a cricketing run; she sighed, wondering for the millionth time what would become of him after she and Ron were dead. Dawnie would have to see to him, of course. She was devotedly fond of her brother, but in the normal way of things she would get tired of studying one day and decide to marry instead, and then would her husband want someone like Tim around? Esme doubted it very much. Who wanted a grown-up five-year-old kid if he wasn't their own flesh and blood?

6

Saturday was just as fine and hot as Friday had been, so Tim set off for Artarmon at six in the morning wearing a short-sleeved sports shirt and tailored shorts with knee socks. His mother always looked out what clothes he was to wear, cooked his breakfast and packed his daytime food, made sure his bag contained a clean pair of work shorts and that he had enough money to see him through any possible difficulty.

When Tim knocked on Mary Horton's door it was just seven, and she was sound asleep. She stumbled, bare-footed, through the house, wrapping a dark grey robe around her sensible white cotton pyjamas, pushing the few stray wisps of hair away from her face impatiently.

'My goodness, do you always arrive at seven in the morning?' she muttered, blinking the sleep out of her eyes.

'That's when I'm supposed to start work,' he replied, smiling.

'Well, since you're here I'd better show you what to do,' Mary decided, leading him down the patio steps and across the lawn to a little fern-house.

The ferns disguised the fact that it was actually a repository for gardening equipment, tools, and fertilisers. A small, urban-looking tractor was parked neatly inside the door, covered with a waterproof cloth in case the roof ever leaked, which of course it didn't, since it belonged to Mary Horton.

'Here's the tractor, and it's got the mower already attached. Can you operate it?'

Tim took the cover off and stroked the tractor's shiny surface lovingly. 'Oh, it's a beaut!'

Mary suppressed her impatience. 'Beaut or not, can you work it, Mr Melville?'

'Oh, yes! Pop says I'm awfully good with machinery.'

'Isn't that nice?' she remarked waspishly. 'Is there anything else you're likely to need, Mr Melville?'

The blue eyes regarded her with puzzled wonder. 'Why do you keep calling me Mr Melville?' he asked. 'Mr Melville is my father! I'm just Tim.'

'Heavens!' she thought, 'he's a child!,' but she said, 'Well, I'll leave you to it. If you need anything, just knock on the back door.'

'Righto, Missus!' he said cheerfully, smiling.

'I'm not a Missus!' she snapped. 'My name is Horton, *Miss* Horton!'

'Righto, Miss Horton,' he amended happily, not at all disconcerted.

By the time she returned inside she was wide awake, and had abandoned any thought of snatching two or three more hours in bed. In a moment he would start the tractor, and that would be the end of it. The house was centrally air conditioned, so was cool and dry no matter what the humidity and temperature outside were, but as she got herself some toast and tea Mary decided that it would be very pleasant to eat on the terrace, where she could keep an eye on her new gardener.

When she carried her little tray out she was fully dressed in her weekend at-home uniform of a plain dark grey cotton dress, as creaseless and perfect as everything about her always was. Her hair, which she wore in a long braid for sleeping, was dragged into its daytime bun. Mary never wore slippers or sandals, even when she was at her beach cottage near Gosford; the moment she got out of bed she dressed, which meant support stockings and stout black shoes.

The mower had been purring smoothly from the backyard for twenty minutes when she sat down at a white-painted wrought-iron table by the balustrade and poured herself a cup of tea. Tim was working down at the far end where the yard tipped over into the brick pit, and he was going about it as slowly and methodically as he had seemed to work for Harry Markham, getting down from the tractor as he completed a strip to make sure the next one would overlap it. She sat munching toast and sipping tea, her eyes never leaving his distant figure. Since she was not given to self-analysis or even to mild introspection, it did not occur to her to wonder why she watched him so fixedly; it was enough to realise that he fascinated her. Not for one moment did she think of her fascination as attraction.

'G'day there, Miss Horton!' came the raucous voice of Mrs

Parker, and the next moment the Old Girl flopped her violently coloured body into the spare chair.

'Good morning, Mrs Parker. Would you care for a cup of tea?' Mary said, rather coldly.

'Ta, love, that sounds real nice. No, don't get up, I can find another cup meself.'

'No, please don't. I have to freshen up the tea anyway.'

When she returned to the patio with a new pot of tea and some more toast Mrs Parker was sitting with her chin in her hand, watching Tim.

'That was a good idea, getting Tim to mow yer lawn. I noticed yer usual bloke hasn't been for a while. That's where I'm lucky. One of me sons always comes over to mow me lawn, but you've got no one, eh?'

'Well, I did as you asked yesterday and checked to see that everything was all right regarding the builders and their mess. That was when I met Tim, who seemed to have been left to clean up on his own. He was quite grateful for the offer of a little extra money, I think.'

Mrs Parker disregarded the last part of Mary's statement. 'If that ain't typical of them rotten buggers!' she snarled. 'Not content to make the poor little blighter's life a misery during the day, but scooted off to the pub and left him to do their dirty work! They had the hide to tell me they was all coming back to clean up! I've a good mind to knock a couple of hundred quid off of Mr Harry Markham's bill!'

Mary put down her teacup and stared at Mrs Parker, puzzled. 'What makes you so indignant, Mrs Parker?'

The yellow and purple pansies swathing Mrs Parker's ample bosom heaved. 'Well, wouldn't you be? Oh, I forgot, I didn't see youse last night to tell youse what those miserable bastards did to the poor little bloke, did I? Sometimes I swear I could kill every man that was ever born! They don't seem to have a skerick of sympathy or understanding for the underdog, unless of course he's a drunk or a no-hoper like themselves. But someone like Tim, what does a decent day's work and keeps his end up, they don't feel any pity for him at all. He's their butt, their whipping boy, and the poor little coot's too dill-brained to realise it! He can't help it if he was born simple, now can he? A terrible shame, though, ain't it? Fancy a boy what looks like him not being the full quid! I could cry! Well, anyway, wait until I tell you what they did to him yestiddy morning at smoke-oh . . .'

Mrs Parker's nasal, common voice whined on as she told Mary her horrible little story, but Mary only half-listened, her eyes riveted on the bent golden head at the bottom of her yard.

Last night before she had gone to bed she had culled the shelves of her library, searching for a face that looked like his. Botticelli? she wondered, and finding some of his reproductions in a book she dismissed the artist contemptuously. Those faces were too soft, too feminine, too subtly cunning and feline. In the end she had given up the search, quite unsatisfied. Only in the ancient Greek and Roman statues had she found some hint of Tim, perhaps because his kind of beauty was better illustrated in stone than on canvas. He was a three-dimensional creature. And she had wished bitterly that in her ungifted hands there had resided the skill to immortalise him.

She was conscious of a terrible, crushing disappointment, a desire to weep: Mrs Parker's presence had faded to the back of her thoughts. It was a kind of ironic anticlimax to discover now that Tim's tragic mouth and wistful, wondering eyes led inward to a nothing, that his spark had been snuffed out of existence long before there could possibly have been tragedy or loss. He was no better than a dog or a cat, which one kept because it was good to look upon and blindly, lovingly faithful. But it could not think, it could never answer intelligently and draw out a shivering response in another questing mind. All the beast did was sit there, smiling and loving. As did Tim, Tim the simpleton. Tricked into eating excrement, he had not vomited it as any thinking being must; he had cried instead, as a dog would have howled, and been cajoled back into smiling again by the prospect of something good to eat.

Childless, loveless, destitute of any humanising influence, Mary Horton had no emotional yardstick whereby to measure this new, frightening concept of a mindless Tim. As retarded emotionally as he was intellectually, she did not know that Tim could be loved because of his stunted mental growth, let alone in spite of it. She had thought of him the way Socrates must have thought of Alcibiades, the aging, unlovely philosopher confronted with a youth of surpassing physical and intellectual beauty. She had imagined herself introducing him to Beethoven and Proust, expanding his careless young mind until it encompassed music and literature and art, until he was as beautiful within as he was without. But he was a simpleton, a poor, silly half-wit.

They had a pungently evocative way of expressing it, smacking of the earthy callousness so typical of the Australian; they translated intelligence into money, and expressed the one in terms of the other. He who was poorly equipped mentally was 'not the full quid'; a value was set upon his intellectual powers, expressed in parts of the dollar or in the vernacular, *quid*. He might be worth as much as ninety cents or as little as nine cents, and still be not the full quid.

Mrs Parker was not aware that she held only a small part of Mary's attention, and chattered on happily about the insensitivity of the average male, drank several cups of tea, and answered her own queries when Mary did not. At length she heaved herself to her feet and took her leave.

'Cheery-bye, pet, and thanks for the cuppa tea. If you don't have anything he'd fancy in yer fridge, send him across to me and I'll feed him.'

Mary nodded absently. Her visitor disappeared down the steps, while she returned to her contemplation of Tim. Glancing at her watch she saw the time was creeping on towards nine, and remembered that these outdoor workmen liked their morning tea around nine. She went inside and made a fresh pot, thawed a frozen chocolate cake and covered it with freshly whipped cream.

'Tim!' she called, putting down her tray on the table under the vines; the sun was stealing across the ridge of the roof, and the table by the steps was getting too hot for comfort.

He looked up, waved to her and stopped the tractor immediately to hear what she was saying.

'Tim, come and have a cup of tea!'

His face lit up with puppyish eagerness; he bounded off the tractor and up the yard, dived into the little fern-house, reappeared with a brown paper bag, and took the back steps two at a time.

'Gee, thanks for calling me, Miss Horton, I wasn't caught up with the time,' he said happily, sitting down in the chair she indicated and waiting docilely until she told him he might begin.

'Can you tell the time, Tim?' she asked gently, amazed that she could ask gently.

'Oh, no, not really. I sort of know when it's time to go home, that's when the big hand's at the top and the little hand is three thingies behind it. Three o'clock. But I don't have a watch of my own, because Pop says I'd lose it. I don't worry. Someone always tells me the time, like when it's time to make the tea for smoke-oh or break for lunch or go home. I'm not the full quid, but everyone knows I'm not, so it doesn't matter.'

'No, I suppose it doesn't,' she answered sadly. 'Eat up, Tim, the cake's all for you.'

'Oh, goody! I love choccy cake, especially with lots of cream on it like this one! Thanks, Miss Horton!'

'How do you like your tea, Tim?'

'No milk and lots of sugar.'

'Lots of sugar? How much is that?'

He looked up at her, frowning, cream all over his face. 'Gosh, I can't remember. I just sort of fill it up until it spills into the saucer, then I know it's all right.'

'Did you ever go to school, Tim?' she probed, beginning to be interested in him again.

'For a little while. But I couldn't learn, so they didn't make me keep on going. I stayed home and looked after Mum.'

'But you do grasp what's said to you, and you did cope with the tractor all by yourself.'

'Some things are real easy, but reading and writing's awful hard, Miss Horton.'

Much surprised at herself, she patted his head as she stood stirring his tea. 'Well, Tim, it doesn't matter.'

'That's what Mum says.'

He finished all the cake, then remembered he had a sandwich from home and ate that as well, washing the repast down with three big cups of tea.

'Struth, Miss Horton, that was super!' he sighed, smiling at her blissfully.

'My name is Mary, and it's much easier to say Mary than Miss Horton, don't you think? Why don't you call me Mary?'

He looked at her doubtfully. 'Are you sure it's all right? Pop says I mustn't call old people anything but Mister or Missus or Miss.'

'Sometimes it's permissible, as between friends.'

'Eh?'

She tried again, mentally expunging all polysyllables from her vocabulary. 'I'm not really all that old, Tim, it's just this white hair of mine that makes me seem so old. I don't think your Pop would mind if you called me Mary.'

'Doesn't your hair mean you're old, Mary? I always thought it did! Pop's hair is white and so is Mum's, and I know they're old.'

'He's twenty-five,' she thought, 'so his Pop and Mum are probably only slightly older than I am,' but she said, 'Well, I'm younger than they are, so I'm not quite old yet.'

He got to his feet. 'It's time for me to go back to work. You've got an awful lot of lawn, Mary. I hope I finish it in time.'

'Well, if you don't, there are plenty of other days. You can come some other time and finish it, if you'd like to.'

He considered the problem gravely. 'I think I'd like to come back, as long as Pop says I can.' He smiled at her. 'I like you, Mary, I like you better than Mick and Harry and Jim and Bill and Curly and Dave. I like you better than anyone except Pop and Mum and my Dawnie. You're pretty, you've got such lovely white hair.'

Mary struggled with a hundred indefinable emotions rushing in on her from all sides, and managed to smile. 'Why, thank you, Tim, that's very nice of you.'

'Oh, think nothing of it,' he said nonchalantly, and hopped down the stairs with his hands flapping at each side of his head and his behind poking out. 'That was my special imitation of a rabbit!' he called from the lawn.

'It was very good, Tim, I knew you were a rabbit the minute you started hopping,' she replied. She gathered up the tea things and carried them inside.

She found it terribly hard to alter her conversation to a toddler level, for Mary Horton had never had anything to do with children since she ceased being a child herself, and she had never really been young anyway. But she was perceptive enough to sense that Tim could be easily hurt, that she had to mind what she said to him, control her temper and her exasperation, that if she let him feel the sting of her tongue he would divine the tenor of the statement if not the actual words. Remembering how she had snapped at him the previous day when he had been, as she thought at the time, deliberately obtuse, she was mortified. Poor Tim, so utterly unaware of the nuances and undercurrents of adult conversation, and so completely vulnerable. He liked her; he thought she was pretty because she had white hair, as did his mother and father.

How could his mouth be so sad, when he knew so little and functioned on such a limited scale?

She got her car out and went down to the supermarket to shop before lunch, since she had nothing in the house that would appeal to him. The chocolate cake was her emergency entertaining fund, the cream a fortuitous mistake on her milkman's part. Tim had brought his lunch with him, she knew, but perhaps he hadn't enough, or could be charmed by the production of something like hamburgers or hot dogs, children's party fare.

'Have you ever been fishing, Tim?' she asked him over lunch.

'Oh, yes, I love fishing,' he replied, beginning on his third hot dog. 'Pop takes me fishing sometimes, when he isn't too busy.'

'How often is he busy?'

'Well, he goes to the races and the cricket and the football and things like that. I don't go with him because I get sick in crowds, the noise and all the people make my head ache and my tummy go all queer.'

'I must take you fishing sometime, then,' she said, and left it at that.

By the middle of the afternoon he had finished the backyard and came to ask about the front. She looked at her watch.

'I don't think we'll bother about the front today, Tim, it's nearly time for you to go home. Why don't you come back next Saturday and do the front for me then, if your Pop will let you?'

He nodded happily. 'All right, Mary.'

'Go and fetch your bag from the fern-house, Tim. You can change in my bathroom, then you'll be able to see if you have everything on properly.'

The interior of her house, so chaste and austere, fascinated him. He roamed about the grey-toned living room in his bare feet, digging his toes into the deep wool carpet with an expression of near-ecstasy on his face, and stroking the pearl-grey crushed velvet upholstery.

'Gosh, Mary, I love your house!' he enthused. 'It all feels so soft and sort of cool!'

'Come and see my library,' she said, wanting to show him her pride and joy so badly that she took him by the hand.

But the library did not impress him in the least; it made him frightened and inclined to be tearful. 'All those books!' he shuddered, and would not stay even when he saw that his reaction had disappointed her.

It took her several minutes to coax him out of his odd dread of the library, and she took care not to repeat the mistake by showing him anything else intellectual.

Once recovered from his initial delight and confusion, he evinced a critical faculty, and took her to task for not having any colour in the house.

'It feels so lovely, Mary, but it's all the same colour!' he protested. 'Why isn't there any red? I love red!'

'Can you tell me which colour this is?' she asked, holding up a red silk bookmark.

'It's red, of course,' he answered scornfully.

'Then I'll see what I can do,' she promised.

She gave him an envelope with thirty dollars in it, a much higher wage than any labourer could command in Sydney. 'My address and telephone number are written on a piece of paper inside,' she instructed him, 'and I want you to give it to your father when you get home, so that he'll know where I am and how to get in touch with me. Now don't forget to give it to him, will you?'

He gazed at her, hurt. 'I never forget anything when I'm told properly,' he said.

'I'm sorry, Tim, I didn't mean to hurt you,' said Mary Horton, who had never cared whether what she said hurt anyone. Not that she habitually said hurtful things; but Mary Horton avoided saying hurtful things from motives of tact, diplomacy, and good manners, not because she wanted to avoid giving another being pain.

She waved him goodbye from her front stoop, after he had refused to let her drive him to the railway station. Once he had gone a few yards down the street she walked to the front gate and leaned over it to watch him until he disappeared around the corner.

To anyone else in the street watching, he would have seemed an amazingly handsome young man striding along the road at the height of his health and looks, the world his to command. It was like some divine jest, she thought, the kind of joke the Greek immortals had loved to play on their creation, man, when he got conceited or forgot what was owed to them. The gargantuan laughter Tim Melville must provoke!

7

Ron was at the Seaside as usual, but early for a Saturday. He had loaded up his portable ice chest with beer and gone off to the cricket match clad in shorts, thong sandals, and a shirt left open all the way down to let in the breeze. But Curly and Dave had not shown up, and somehow the pleasure of lying on the grassy hill in the Sydney cricket ground sleeping in the sun was not the same alone. He stuck it for a couple of hours, but the cricket proceeded at its normal snaily pace and the horses he had backed at Warwick Farm had both come in last, so at about three he had packed up his beer chest and radio, and headed for the Seaside with the unerring instinct of a bloodhound. It would never have occurred to him to go home; Es played tennis with the girls on Saturday afternoons, their local Hit and Giggle Club as he called it, and the house would be deserted with Tim working; Dawnie was off somewhere with one of her Quiz Kid boyfriends.

When Tim turned up a little after four Ron was very pleased to see him, and bought him a schooner of Old.

'How'd it go, mate?' he asked his son as they leaned their backs up against a pillar and stared across the sea.

'The grouse, Pop! Mary's a real nice lady.'

'Mary?' Ron peered into Tim's face, startled and concerned.

'Miss Horton. She told me to call her Mary. I was a bit worried, but she said it was all right. It's all right, isn't it, Pop?' he queried anxiously, sensing something unusual in his father's reaction.

'I dunno, mate. What's this Miss Mary Horton like?'

'She's lovely, Pop. She gave me a whole heap of beaut things to eat and showed me all over her house. It's air conditioned, Pop! Her furniture's real nice, so's her carpet, but everything's grey, so I asked her why she didn't have anything red around, and she said she'd see what she could do about it.'

'Did she touch you, mate?'

Tim stared at Ron blankly. 'Touch me? Gee, I dunno! I suppose she did. She took me by the hand when she was showing me her books.' He pulled a face. 'I didn't like her books, there were too many of them.'

'Is she pretty, mate?'

'Oh, gee, yes! She's got the most lovely white hair, Pop, just like yours and Mum's, only whiter. That's why I didn't know whether it was all right for me to call her Mary, because you and Mum always tell me it isn't polite to call old people by their first name.'

Ron relaxed. 'Oh!' He slapped his son playfully on the arm. 'Struth, you had me worried for a minute there, I tell you. She's an old girl, right?'

'Yes.'

'Did she pay you like she promised?'

'Yes, it's here in an envelope. Her name and address is inside. She said I was to give it to you in case you wanted to talk to her. Why would you want to talk to her, Pop? I don't see why you'd want to talk to her.'

Ron took the proffered envelope. 'I don't want to talk to her, mate. Did youse finish the job?'

'No, she had too much lawn. If it's all right with you, she wants me to do the front garden next Saturday.'

There were three crisp, new ten-dollar bills in the envelope; Ron stared at them and at the clear, heavy overtones of authority and education in Mary Horton's handwriting. Silly young girls or lonely housewives didn't have handwriting like that, he decided. Thirty quid for a day's gardening! He put the notes in his own wallet and patted Tim on the back.

'You done good, mate, and you can go back next Saturday and finish her lawn if you want to. In fact, for what she pays you can work for her any time she wants.'

'Gee, Pop, thanks!' He wiggled his empty glass from side to side suggestively. 'Can I have another beer?'

'Why can't you ever learn to drink it slowly, Tim?'

Tim's face fell into misery. 'Oh, gee, I forgot again! I really did mean to drink it slowly, Pop, but it tasted so good I went and forgot.'

Ron regretted his momentary exasperation immediately. 'No matter, mate, don't let it worry you. Go and ask Florrie for a schooner of Old.'

The beer, extremely potent as Australian beer was, seemed to have no effect on Tim. Some dimwits went crazy if they even smelled grog, Ron puzzled, but Tim could drink his old man under the table and then carry him all the way home, he felt it so little.

'Who is this Mary Horton?' Es asked that night, after Tim had been packed off to bed.

'Some old geezer out at Artarmon.'

'Tim's very taken with her, isn't he?'

Ron thought of the thirty quid in his wallet and stared at his wife blandly. 'I suppose so. She's nice to him, and doing her garden on a Saturday will keep him out of mischief.'

'Free you to skip around the pubs and racetracks with the blokes, you mean,' Es interpreted with the skill of many years.

'Jesus bloody Christ, Es, what a rotten thing to say to a man!'

'Hah!' she snorted, putting down her knitting. 'The truth hurts, don't it? Did she pay him, eh?'

'A few quid.'

'Which you pocketed, of course.'

'Well, it wasn't that much. What do you expect for mowing a bloody lawn by machine, you suspicious old twit? No fortune, and that's for bloody sure!'

'As long as I get me housekeeping, I don't give a sweet bugger how much she paid him, mate!' She got up, stretching. 'Want a cuppa tea, love?'

'Oh, ta, that'd be real nice. Where's Dawnie?'

'How the hell should I know? She's twenty-four and her own flaming mistress.'

'As long as she's not someone else's flaming mistress!'

Es shrugged. 'Kids don't think the way we did, love, and there's no getting around it. Besides, are you game to ask Dawnie where she's been and if she's shagging with some bloke?'

Ron followed Es into the kitchen, fondly patting her on the bottom. 'Cripes, no! She'd look down that long bloody nose of hers and come out with a string of words I didn't understand, and a man would end up feeling pretty flaming silly.'

'I wish God had rationed out the brains a bit more fairly between our kids, Ron, love,' Es sighed as she put the kettle on to boil. 'If He'd split them down the middle they'd both be all right.'

'No use crying over spilt milk, old girl. Got any cake?'

'Fruit or seed?'

'Seed, love.'

They sat down on either side of the kitchen table and polished off half a seed cake and six cups of tea between them.

8

Self-discipline carried Mary Horton through the week at Constable Steel & Mining as if Tim Melville had not even entered her life. She doffed her clothes before using the lavatory as usual, ran Archie Johnson as well as ever and chewed out a total of seventeen typists, office boys, and clerks. But at home each night she found her books unenticing and spent the time in the kitchen instead, reading recipe books and experimenting with cakes, sauces, and puddings. Judicious pumping of Emily Parker had given her a better idea of Tim's taste in goodies; she wanted to have a varied selection for him when Saturday came.

During one lunch hour she went to a north Sydney interior decorator and bought a very expensive ruby glass coffee table, then found an ottoman in matching ruby crushed velvet. The touch of deep, vibrant colour disturbed her at first, but after she got used to it she had to admit that it improved her glacial living room. The bare, pearl-grey walls suddenly looked warmer, and she found herself wondering if Tim, like so many naturals, had an instinctive eye for art. Perhaps one day she could take him around the galleries with her, and see what his eye discovered.

She went to bed very late on Friday night, expecting a phone call any minute from Tim's father to say he didn't want his son hiring himself out as a gardener on precious weekends. But the call never came, and promptly at seven the next morning she was roused from a deep sleep by the sound of Tim's knock. This time she brought him inside immediately, and asked him if he wanted a cup of tea while she dressed.

'No thanks, I'm all right,' he replied, blue eyes shining.

'Then you can use the little toilet off the laundry to change in while I get dressed. I want to show you how to do the front garden.'

She returned to the kitchen a short time later, cat-footed as always. He did not hear her come in, so she stood silently in the doorway watching him, struck anew by the absoluteness of his beauty. How terrible, how unjust it was, she thought, that such a wonderful shell should house such an unworthy occupant; then she was ashamed. Perhaps that was the *raison d'être* of his beauty, that his progress towards sin and dishonour had been arrested in the innocence of early childhood. Had he matured normally he might have looked quite different, truly a Botticelli then, smugly smiling, with a knowing look lurking behind those clear blue eyes. Tim was not a member of the adult human race at all, except on the sketchiest of premises.

'Come along, Tim, let me show you what's to be done out front,' she said at last, breaking the spell.

The cicadas were shrieking and screaming from every bush and tree; Mary put her hands over her ears, grimaced at Tim and then went to her only weapon, the hose.

'This is the worst year for cicadas I can ever remember,' she said when the din had subsided somewhat and the heavy oleanders dripped steadily onto the path.

'Breeeek!' gurgled the basso profundo choirmaster, after all the others had ceased.

'There he goes, the old twirp!' Mary went over to the oleander nearest her front door, parting its soggy branches and peering futilely into the cathedral-like recesses of its interior. 'I can never find him,' she explained, squatting on her haunches and turning her head to smile at Tim, who stood behind her.

'Do you want him?' Tim asked seriously.

'I most certainly do! He starts the whole lot of them off; without him they seem to be dumb.'

'I'll get him for you.'

He slipped his bare torso in among the leaves and branches easily, disappearing from sight above the waist. He was not wearing boots or socks this morning, since there was no concrete to blister and crack his skin, and wet humus from the grass clung to his legs.

'Breeeeek!' boomed the cicada, drying off enough to begin testing.

'Gotcha!' shouted Tim, scrambling out again with his right hand closed around something.

Mary had never actually seen more of a cicada than its cast-off brown armour in the grass and thus edged up a little fearfully, for like most women she was frightened of spiders and beetles and crawly, cold-blooded things.

'There he is, look at him!' Tim said proudly, opening his fingers gingerly until the cicada was fully exposed, tethered only by Tim's left index finger and thumb on his wing tips.

'Ugh!' Mary shuddered, backing away without really looking.

'Oh, don't be afraid of him, Mary,' Tim begged, smiling up at her and stroking the cicada softly. 'Look, isn't he lovely, all green and pretty like a butterfly?'

The golden head was bent over the cicada; Mary stared down at them both in sudden, blinding pity. Tim seemed to have some kind of rapport with the creature, for it lay on his palm without panic or fear, and it was indeed beautiful, once one forgot its Martian antennae and lobsterish carapace. It had a fat, bright green body about two inches long, tinted with a powdering of real gold, and its eyes glittered and sparkled like two big topazes. Over its back the delicate, transparent wings were folded still, veined like a leaf with bright yellow gold and shimmering with every colour of the rainbow. And above it crouched Tim, just as alien and just as beautiful, as alive and gleaming.

'You don't really want me to kill him, do you?' Tim pleaded, gazing up at her in sudden sadness.

'No,' she replied, turning away. 'Put him back in his bush, Tim.'

By lunchtime he had finished the front lawn. Mary gave him two hamburgers and a heaping pile of chips, then filled his empty corners with a hot steamed jam pudding smothered in hot banana custard.

'I think I'm finished, Mary,' Tim said as he drank his third cup of tea. 'Gee, but I'm sorry it wasn't a longer job, though.' The wide eyes surveyed her mistily. 'I like you, Mary,' he began. 'I like you better than Mick or Harry or Jim or Bill or Curly or Dave, I like you better than anyone except Pop and Mum and my Dawnie.'

She patted his hand and smiled at him lovingly. 'It's very sweet of you to say that, Tim, but I don't really think it's true, you haven't known me long enough.'

'There's no more grass to mow,' he sighed, ignoring her refusal to accept the compliment.

'Grass grows again, Tim.'

'Eh?' That little interrogative sound was his signal to go slow, that something had been done or said beyond his understanding.

'Can you weed garden beds as well as you can mow a lawn?'

'I reckon I can. I do it for Pop all the time.'

'Then would you like to come every Saturday and look after my garden altogether, mow the grass when it needs it, plant seedlings and weed the flower beds, spray the bushes and trim the pathways and put down fertiliser?'

He grasped her hand and shook it, smiling broadly. 'Oh, Mary, I do like you! I'll come every Saturday and I'll look after your garden, I promise I'll look after your garden!'

There were thirty dollars in his envelope when he left that afternoon.

9

Tim had been coming for five weeks before Mary Horton phoned his father late on Thursday night.

Ron answered the phone himself. 'Yeah?' he asked it.

'Good evening, Mr Melville. This is Mary Horton, Tim's Saturday friend.'

Ron pricked up his ears immediately, beckoning Es to join him for a listen. 'Oh, nice to hear from you, Miss Horton. How's Tim doing, all right?'

'He's a pleasure to have around, Mr Melville. I do enjoy his company.'

Ron chuckled self-consciously. 'From the tales he brings home, I gather he's eating youse out of house and home, Miss Horton.'

'No, not at all. It's a pleasure to see him eat, Mr Melville.'

There was an awkward pause, until Ron broke it to say, 'What's the matter, Miss Horton? Tim not wanted this week?'

'Well, he is and he isn't, Mr Melville. The fact of the matter is, I have to go up to Gosford this weekend to see how my summer cottage is getting on. I've neglected it sadly so far, concentrated on the garden at home. Anyway, I was wondering if you'd object to my taking Tim with me, to help me? I could do with some help, and Tim is terrific. It's very quiet out where I am, and I give you my word he wouldn't be subjected to strangers or undue stress or anything like that. He told me he loved to fish, and the cottage is situated right in the middle of the best fishing for miles around, so I thought perhaps – perhaps he might enjoy it. He seems to like coming to me, and I certainly like his company.'

Ron squiggled his eyebrows at Es, who nodded vigorously and took the receiver.

'Hullo, Miss Horton, this is Tim's mother here . . . Yes, I'm very well, thank you, how are you? . . . Oh, that's nice to hear . . . Miss Horton, it's very thoughtful of you to think of inviting Tim to go with you this weekend . . . Yes, he is a bit lonely, it's hard for a poor chap like him, you know . . . I really can't see any reason why Tim couldn't go with you, I think the change would do him good . . . Yes, he does like you an awful lot . . . Let me hand you back to my husband, Miss Horton, and thank you very, very much.'

'Miss Horton?' Ron asked, snatching the receiver from his wife. 'Well, you heard the Old Woman, it's all right with her, and if it's all right with her it had better be all right with me, ha-ha-ha! Yeah, right you are! Okay, I'll see he packs a bag and gets to your place by seven on this Satiddy morning . . . Right, Miss Horton, thank you very, very much . . . Bye bye now, and ta again.'

Mary had planned the sixty-mile trip as a picnic, and had jammed the back of the car with provisions, diversions, and comforts she thought the summer cottage might lack. Tim arrived promptly at seven on Saturday morning. The day was fine and clear, the second weekend in a row that it had not threatened rain, and Mary shepherded Tim out to the garage immediately.

'Hop in, Tim, and make yourself comfortable. Are you all right?'

'All right,' he answered.

'My house is not in Gosford itself,' she said as the car headed out along the Pacific highway in the direction of Newcastle. 'Living and working in the city, I didn't want to have a holiday cottage right in the middle of another crowd of people, so I bought a property quite a way out, on the Hawkesbury near Broken Bay. We have to go into Gosford because the only road to my place starts there, you see.

'My word, how Gosford has grown! I remember it when it used to consist of a pub, a garage, two men, and a dog; now it's jammed with commuters and vacationers, there must be sixty thousand of them at least, it seems . . .'

She trailed off nervously, glancing sidelong at him in sudden embarrassment. There she was, trying to make conversation with him as though he was somewhat like the person she imagined his mother might be. In his turn he was trying to be an interested auditor, snatching his fascinated glance away from the passing landscape every so often to fix his bright, loving eyes on her profile.

'Poor Tim,' she sighed. 'Don't take any notice of me, just relax and look out the window.'

For a long time after that there was silence. Tim was obviously enjoying the journey, turned side on with his nose almost against the window, not missing a thing, and it made her wonder just how much variety there was in his life, how often he was lifted out of what must be a very humdrum existence.

'Does your father have a car, Tim?'

He didn't bother to turn and face her this time, but continued to look out the window. 'No, he says it's a waste of time and money in the city. He says it's much healthier to walk, and much less trouble to catch the bus when you need to ride in something.'

'Does anyone ever take you out for a drive?'

'Not very often. I get carsick.'

She turned her head to stare at him, alarmed. 'How do you feel now? Do you feel sick?'

'No, I feel good. This car doesn't bump me up and down like most cars, and anyway, I'm in the front not the back, so it doesn't bump as much, does it?'

'Very good, Tim! That's quite right. If you should feel sick you'll tell me in plenty of time, though, won't you? It isn't very nice if you make a mess in the car.'

'I promise I'll tell you, Mary, because you never yell at me or get cranky.'

She laughed. 'Now, Tim! Don't be martyrish! I'm quite sure no one yells at you or gets cranky with you very often, and only then if you deserve it.'

'Well, yes,' he grinned. 'But Mum gets real mad if I'm sick all over everything.'

'I don't blame her in the least. I'd get real mad too, so you must be sure to tell me if you ever feel sick, and then hang on until you get outside. All right?'

'All right, Mary.'

After a little while Mary cleared her throat and spoke again. 'Have you ever been out of the city, Tim?'

He shook his head.

'Why not?'

'I dunno. I don't think there was anything Mum and Pop wanted to see outside the city.'

'And Dawnie?'

'My Dawnie goes all over the place, she's even been to England.' He made it sound as though England were just around the corner.

'What about holidays, when you were a little boy?'

'We always stayed at home. Mum and Pop don't like the bush, they only like the city.'

'Well, Tim, I come down to my cottage very often, and you can always come too. Perhaps later on I can take you to the desert or the Great Barrier Reef for a real holiday.'

But he wasn't paying any attention to her, for they were coming down to the Hawkesbury River, and the view was magnificent.

'Oh, isn't it *lovely*?' he exclaimed, wriggling on the seat and gripping his hands together convulsively the way he always did when he was moved or upset.

Mary was oblivious of everything except a sudden pain, a pain so new and alien that she had no real idea why she should feel it. The poor, sad fellow! Somehow events had conspired to stunt his every avenue of expansion and mental growth. His parents cared for him very much, but their lives were narrow and their horizons restricted to the Sydney skyline. In all justice she could not find it in her heart to blame them for not realising that Tim could never hope to get as much out of their kind of life as they did themselves. It had simply never occurred to them to wonder whether he was truly happy or not, because he *was* happy. But could he perhaps be happier still? What would he be like if he were freed from the chain of their routine, permitted to stretch his legs a little?

It was so difficult to draw all the threads of her feeling for him together: one moment she thought of him as a small child, the next moment his physical magnificence would remind her that he was a man grown. And it was so hard for her to feel at all, when it was so long since she had done more than merely exist. She possessed no built-in emotional gauge whereby she could distinguish pity from love, anger from protectiveness. She and Tim were like a weirdly juxtaposed Svengali and Trilby: the mindless it was that mesmerised the mind.

Since first seeing Tim all those weeks ago she had confined herself to action, had kept herself mentally out and about, doing things. She had never allowed herself to sit in the quiet withdrawal of private contemplation, for by nature she was not given to probing how and why and what she felt. Even now she would not do it, would not pull herself far enough away from the centre of her pain to come to grips with the cause of it.

The cottage had no neighbours closer than two miles, for the area was not yet 'developed.' The only road was atrocious, no more than an earthen track through the eucalyptus forest; when it rained mud made it impassable and when it didn't rain the dust rose in vast, billowing clouds that settled on the vegetation nearest to the road, petrifying it into spindling brown skeletons. The ruts, ridges, and potholes in the road itself imperiled the stoutest car so severely that there were few people willing to risk the inconvenience and discomfort for the sake of isolation.

Mary's property was quite large for the area, some twenty acres; she had bought it with an eye towards the future, knowing that the cancerous encroachment of the city would eventually lead to development and fantastic profits. Until such time, it suited her love of solitude very well.

A track diving into the trees indicated the beginning of Mary's land; she swung the car off the road and put it over the track, which continued for about a half a mile through the beautiful, aromatic bush, virgin and unspoiled. At the end of the track lay a big clearing which opened on its far side into a tiny beach; beyond it, still salty and tidal here, the Hawkesbury River twisted and turned its wide way through the towering sandstone landscape. Mary's beach was no more than a hundred yards long, and was flanked at each end by soaring yellow cliffs.

The cottage was unpretentious, a square little frame structure with a corrugated iron roof and a wide, open veranda running all the way around it. Mary kept it painted because she could not abide disorder or neglect, but the drab brownish colour she had chosen did not improve the appearance of the house. Two huge galvanised iron water tanks stood on high towers at one end of the rear of the house, which faced the track. Trees had been planted at intervals in the clearing, and were at last growing large enough to take some of the bareness away. She had made no attempt at a garden and the grass grew long, but in spite of everything the place had a certain indefinable charm about it.

Mary had spent a considerable amount of money on the cottage since buying the property fifteen years before. The massive water tanks, to have enough fresh water for modern plumbing; electricity, to avoid lanterns and fuel fires. Mary saw no allure in open fires, candlelight, or outhouses; they meant extra work and inconvenience.

From the approaching car the house showed to worst advantage, but Tim was enthralled. Mary pried him out of his seat with some difficulty, and coaxed him through the back door.

'This is your room, Tim,' she said, showing him a plain but big bedroom with white walls and furniture; it looked rather like a nun's cell. 'I thought perhaps if you like coming here you might think about what colour you'd like your room painted, and what kind of furniture you'd like in it. We could shop for it one day in the city.'

He could not reply, too excited and overcome with the whole experience to assimilate this fresh delight. She helped him unpack his suitcase and put his few things in the empty drawers and cupboards, then she took him by the hand and led him out to the living room.

Only here had she made major changes in the actual construction of the house, which had once possessed a dark, poorly lit living room extending the entire length of the front veranda. She had pulled the outer wall away piecemeal and replaced it with floor-to-ceiling sliding glass doors all the way along, so that when the weather was good there was nothing between the living room and the open air.

The view from this room was breath-taking. The grass sloped downward to the bright yellow sand of the sunny, immaculate little beach, the blue water of the Hawkesbury lapped gently along its border, and on the far side of the wide river wonderful cliffs, splendidly crowned with forest, rose to meet the clear, high sky. The only sounds of man to intrude were those coming from the river; the put-put of outboard motors, the chug of excursion ferries, the roar of speedboats towing water skiers. But the birds screeched and carolled from every tree, the cicadas deafened, the wind moaned softly as it filtered through the sighing branches.

Mary had never shared her retreat with anyone before, but on many occasions she had rehearsed the imaginary conversation she and her first guests would have. They would exclaim and marvel over the view, pass endless comments on everything. But Tim said nothing; she had no idea how much assessment and comparison he could make. That he thought it 'lovely' was apparent, but he thought everything was 'lovely' that didn't make him unhappy. Was Tim capable of gradations of happiness? Did he enjoy some things more than others?

When she had done her own unpacking and stocked the kitchen, she got him his lunch. He said very little as the meal progressed, chewing steadily through all the food she put in front of him.

Unless he was starving or upset, his table manners were impeccable.

'Do you swim?' she asked him after he had helped her wash the dirty dishes.

His face lit up. 'Yes, oh, yes!'

'Then why don't you change into your swimming trunks while I finish up here, then we'll go down onto the beach. All right?'

He disappeared immediately, returning so quickly that she had to make him wait while she tidied up the last few odds and ends around the kitchen. Carrying two canvas deck chairs, an umbrella, towels, and various other bits of beach paraphernalia, they staggered laden down to the sand.

She had settled herself into her deck chair and opened her book before she realised that he was still standing looking at her, puzzled and apparently distressed.

She closed her book. 'What's the matter, Tim? What is it?'

He fluttered his hands helplessly. 'I thought you said we were going swimming!'

'Not we, Tim,' she corrected gently. 'I want you to swim to your heart's content, but I never go into the water myself.'

He kneeled beside her chair and put both his hands on her arm, very upset. 'But then it isn't the same, Mary! I don't want to go swimming all by myself!' Tears sparkled on his long fair lashes, like water beading on crystal. 'Please, oh, *please* don't make me go in all by myself!'

She reached out to touch him, then drew her hand away quickly. 'But I don't have a swimsuit with me, Tim! I couldn't go in even if I wanted to.'

He shook his head back and forth, growing more and more agitated. 'I don't think you like being with me, I don't think you like me! You're always dressed up as if you're going into town, you never wear shorts or slacks or no stockings the way Mum does!'

'Oh, Tim, what am I going to do with you? Just because I'm always dressed up doesn't mean I don't like being with you! I don't feel comfortable unless I'm all dressed up, it's as simple as that. I just don't like wearing shorts or slacks or no stockings.'

But he didn't believe her, and turned his head away. 'If you were having fun you'd wear the sort of clothes Mum does when she's having fun,' he persisted stubbornly.

There was a long silence, incorporating, though Mary didn't

realise it, their first duel of wills. In the end she sighed and put her book down. 'Well, I'll go inside and see what I can find, only you must promise me faithfully that you won't play tricks on me in the water, duck me under or disappear on me. I can't swim, which means you'll have to look after me all the time I'm in the water. Do you promise?'

He was all smiles again. 'I promise, I promise! But don't be long, Mary, please don't be long!'

Though it galled her tidy soul to do so, Mary eventually put on a fresh set of her customary white cotton underwear, and over it one of her grey linen button-down-the-front weekend dresses which she hacked into briefer form with a pair of scissors. She cut the skirt off at mid-thigh, ripped the sleeves out and lopped the neck away until her collar bones were exposed. The cutting was naturally neat, but there was no time to turn a hem or put on facings, which irritated her and put her out of humour.

Walking down to the beach she felt horribly naked, with her fish-belly white legs and arms and the support of girdle and stockings absent. The feeling had little to do with Tim; even when she was totally alone for days, she always put on every layer of clothes.

Tim, an uncritical audience now that he had got his own way, danced up and down gleefully. 'Oh, that's much better, Mary! Now we can both go in swimming! Come on, come on!'

Mary waded into the water with shuddering distaste. As fastidious as the most disdainful of cats, it was all she could do to make herself continue wading out deeper, when what she wanted to do was turn tail and run back to her comfortable, dry deck chair. Displaying the important maturity of a very young male placed in sole charge of a treasure, Tim would not let her go out beyond the point where the water reached her waist. He hovered all around her like a sticky little fly, anxious and confused. It was no use; he could sense that she hated it, and she knew she was spoiling his day. So she suppressed a strong shudder of revulsion and dunked herself down to the neck with a gasp of shock at the coldness, and an involuntary laugh.

The laugh was all he was waiting to hear; he began to frolic around her like a porpoise, as at ease and at home in the water as any fish. Forcing herself to smile and slapping the palms of her hands on the surface of the water in what she hoped was a good imitation of someone thoroughly enjoying a dip, Mary blundered about after him.

The water was exquisitely clear and clean, her disarticulated feet wobbled like sickly white blancmange on the sandy bottom whenever she looked down, and the sun rested on the back of her neck like a warm and friendly hand. After a while she began to enjoy the feel of the mildly stinging saltiness; it stimulated and exhilarated, and to submerge to the shoulders in delicious, weightless coolness with the full strength of the sun rendered suddenly impotent was truly marvellous. The vulnerability of her lack of clothes faded, and she began to luxuriate in feeling her body so free of restriction.

She did not lose quite all her good sense, however, and after twenty minutes or so she called Tim to her side. 'I must go out now, Tim, because I'm not used to the sun. See how white I am, and how brown you are? Well, one of these days I'll be as brown as you, but I have to do it very slowly, because the sun burns white skins like mine and it could make me very sick. Please don't think I'm not having fun, because I am, but I really must get into the shade now.'

He accepted this calmly. 'I know, because when I was a little boy I got so sunburned one day I had to go to the hospital. It hurt so much that I cried all day and all night and all day and all night. I don't want you to cry all day and all night, Mary.'

'I tell you what I'll do, Tim, I'll sit under the shade of my umbrella and watch you. I promise I won't read, I'll just watch you. Is that all right?'

'All right, all right, all right!' he sang, playing at being a submarine but nobly refraining from torpedoing her.

Making sure she was entirely shielded by the umbrella, Mary spread her dripping body along the deck chair and mopped her face. The bun at the back of her neck was trickling water down her spine in a most annoying way, so she took the pins out and shook her hair over the back of the chair to dry. She had to admit that she felt wonderful, almost as if the salt water possessed medicinal value. Her skin tingled, her muscles were slack and her limbs heavy . . .

. . . She was paying one of her infrequent visits to the beauty parlour, and the hairdresser was rhythmically brushing her hair, one-two-three, one-two-three, tugging at her scalp each time the brush engaged and drawing the tug out deliciously as the brush travelled down the length of her hair. Smiling with pleasure, she opened her eyes to find she was not in a beauty parlour at all, but lying in a deck chair on the beach, and that the sun was slipping down so low behind the trees that shadows had blanketed the sand completely.

Tim was standing behind her with his head bent over her face, playing with her hair. Panic overwhelmed her; she sprang away from his touch in inexplicable terror, snatching at her loose hair and scrabbling frantically in the pocket of her cut-down dress for the pins. A safe distance away and more fully awake, she turned to look at him, eyes dilated in fright and heart thumping.

He still stood in the same spot, gazing at her out of those incredible eyes with the peculiarly helpless, agonised expression she only saw when he knew he had done wrong but did not understand what it was he had done wrong. He wanted to atone, he wanted so badly to understand what sort of sin he had unknowingly committed; at such times he seemed to feel his exclusion most acutely, she thought, like the dog which does not know why its master kicked it. Utterly at a loss, he stood wringing his hands together, mouth slack.

Her arms went out to him in a gesture of remorse and pity. 'Oh, my dear! My dear, I didn't mean it! I was asleep and you frightened me, that's all! Don't look at me so! I wouldn't hurt you for all the world, Tim, truly! Oh, please don't look at me like that!'

He avoided her hands, holding himself just out of her reach because he wasn't sure if she meant it or not, if she wasn't just trying to soothe him.

'It was so beautiful,' he explained timidly. 'I just wanted to touch it, Mary.'

She stared at him, astonished. Had he said 'beautiful'? Yes, he had! And said it as if he really knew what the word meant, as if he understood that it was different from 'lovely' or 'nice' or 'super' or 'grouse' or 'beaut' in degree, these being the only adjectives of praise she had heard him use. Tim was learning! He was picking up a little of what she said, and interpreting it correctly.

She laughed at him tenderly and went right up to him, taking his reluctant hands and gripping them strongly. 'Bless you, Tim, I like you better than anyone else I know! Don't be annoyed with me, I didn't mean to hurt you, really I didn't.'

His smile came out like the sun, the pain faded from his eyes.

'I like you too, Mary, I like you better than anyone except Pop and Mum and my Dawnie.' He paused thoughtfully. 'I think I like you better than my Dawnie, actually.'

There he went again! He had said 'actually,' just the way she did herself! Of course, to a large extent it was simply parroting, but not entirely; there was a suggestion of sureness about his usage.

'Come on, Tim, let's go inside before it gets chilly. When the evening breeze comes up the river it cools things down awfully fast, even at the height of summer. What would you like for your supper?'

After the supper had been eaten and the dishes washed and put away, Mary made Tim sit in her one comfortable armchair, then looked through her records.

'Do you like music, Tim?'

'Sometimes,' he answered cautiously, craning his neck to see her as she stood behind him.

What would appeal to him? The cottage was actually better equipped with the kind of music he might like than the house in Artarmon, for she had brought all her old, outgrown tastes here. Ravel's *Bolero*, Gounod's *Ave Maria*, Handel's *Largo*, the march from *Aïda*, Sullivan's *Lost Chord*, the *Swedish Rhapsody*, Sibelius' *Finlandia*, melodies from Gilbert and Sullivan, Elgar's *Pomp and Circumstance* march: they were all there with dozens of other selections equally rich in mood and melody. Try him on stuff like this, she thought; he doesn't care if it's hackneyed, so see how it goes.

Overwhelmed, he sat entranced and all but physically inserted himself into the music. Mary had been doing some reading on mental retardation, and remembered as she sat watching him that many retarded people had a passion for music of a fairly high order and complexity. Seeing that vivid, eager face reflecting every mood change, her heart ached for him. How beautiful he was, how very beautiful!

Towards midnight the wind coming up the river from the sea grew cooler still, gusting in through the open glass doors so vigorously that Mary closed them. Tim had gone to bed about ten, worn out with all the excitement and the long afternoon of swimming. It occurred to her that he might be cold, so she rummaged in the hall closet and unearthed an eiderdown to put over him. A tiny kerosene lantern was burning dimly beside his bed; he had confided to her, rather hesitantly, that he was afraid of the dark, and did she have a little light he could keep near him? Treading noiselessly across the bare white floor with the eiderdown hugged close in her arms in case it brushed against something and made a sound, Mary approached the narrow bed.

He was lying all curled up, probably because he had grown cold, his arms wrapped across his chest, knees almost touching his chest. The blankets had half slipped off the bed, baring his back to the open window.

Mary looked down at him, hands twisting within the cuddly folds of the eiderdown, mouth open. The sleeping face was so much at peace, the crystal lashes fanned down across the lean planes of his cheeks, the wonderful golden mass of his hair curling around his perfectly shaped skull. His lips were slightly turned up, the sad little crease to their left side lending the smile a Pierrot quality, and his chest rose and fell so quietly that for a moment she fancied him dead.

How long she remained staring down at him she never knew, but at length she shivered and drew away, unfolding the eiderdown. She did not attempt to pull the blankets up around him, contenting herself with straightening them on the bed and tucking them in, then dropping the eiderdown over his shoulders and twitching it into place. He sighed and moved, nuzzling into the warmth, but in a moment he had slipped back again into the world of his dreams. What did a mentally retarded young man dream about, she wondered: did he venture forth as limited in his nocturnal wanderings as he was during his waking life, or did the miracle happen which freed him from all his chains? There was no way to know.

After she left his room Mary found the house unbearable. Shutting the glass doors silently, she crossed the veranda and descended the steps to the path which led down to the beach. The trees were tossing restlessly in the grip of the wind, a mopoke was calling, 'more pork! more pork!,' sitting with his round owl's eyes blinking from the blurred darkness of a low branch that drooped over the path. Mary glanced at the bird without really seeing him, and the next moment ran into something soft and clinging. As it stuck to her face she gasped in fright, then realised it was a spider's web. She felt all over herself cautiously, dreading the thought that the web's owner might be roaming on her somewhere, but her hand encountered nothing more than her dress.

The beach fringes were littered with dead branches; Mary gathered them in her arms until she had enough to build a fire, then she stacked them in the middle of the sand near a convenient rock and put a match to the twigs at their base. The cold sea breeze at night was the East Coast's saving grace, but it was hard on the human body, sweltering all day and then chilling to the bone at night. She could have gone back to the house for a sweater, but there was something very friendly about a fire, and Mary needed comfort desperately. When the flames were spitting and spurting she sat herself on the rock and spread her hands out to warm.

Rocking leisurely back and forth upside down by its tail from a nearby tree, a possum stared at her intently from wise round eyes, its sweet face apprehensive. What an odd creature she was, squatting before the glaring thing he knew only as a danger, with the light throwing bizarre shadows in ever-changing patterns across her. Then he yawned, plucked a loquat from the branch above him and munched it loudly. She was nothing to fear, just a hunched-up woman with a face drawn in pain, not young or pretty or enticing.

It had been a long time since pain had been a part of her life, Mary reflected, chin in hand; she had to go all the way back to a little girl in an orphanage dormitory, sniffling herself to sleep. How lonely it had been then, so lonely there had been times when she had wished for the friendly ignorance of death. People said a child's mind could not comprehend or long for death, but Mary Horton knew differently. There was no memory of a home, of loving arms, of being wanted; her desolation had been one of pure, unrecognised loss, for she could not hunger after something she did not know existed. She had thought her unhappiness was rooted in her unattractiveness, the hurt that came when her adored Sister Thomas passed her by, as usual, for a child who was prettier and more appealing.

But if her genes had not endowed her with personal allure, they had carried the codes of strength; Mary had disciplined herself as she grew up, until by the time she was fourteen and the moment came to leave the orphanage, she had learned to subjugate and crush unhappiness. After that she had ceased to feel on a human, emotional level, contenting herself with the pleasure she got out of doing her job well and watching her savings grow. It had not been an empty pleasure exactly, but it had not softened or warmed her either. No, life had not been empty or lacking in stimuli, but it had been utterly devoid of love.

Never experiencing the stirrings of a maternal drive or the urge to seek a mate, Mary was not capable of gauging the quality of her love for Tim. Indeed, she did not even know whether what she felt for Tim could rightly be called love. He had simply become the pivot of her life. In every waking moment she was conscious of Tim's existence, he sprang to her mind a thousand times a day, and if she thought, 'Tim,' she found herself smiling or she felt something that could only be called pain. It was almost as if he lived within her mind as an entity quite distinct from his real being.

When she sat in her dimly lit living room listening to the haunting searching of some violin she mentally reached for an unknown, still withholding some reserves of feeling, but when she sat in her dimly lit living room looking at Tim there was nothing left to seek, everything she had ever yearned after was embodied in him. If she had expected anything of him in the few hours between first seeing him and coming to realise that he was mentally undeveloped, once she had discovered the truth she had ceased to expect anything more from him than the mere fact of his existence. He enthralled her; that was the only word she could think of which halfway fitted.

All the hungers and yearnings of her woman's years had been ruthlessly suppressed; they had never gained a hold on her, for she had always been careful to avoid any situation which might encourage them to flower. If she found a man attractive she studiously ignored him, if a child began to laugh its way into her heart she made sure she never saw the child again. She avoided the physical side of her nature as she would the plague, shut it up in some dark and sleeping corner of her mind and refused to admit it existed. *Keep out of trouble*, the orphanage nuns had told her, and Mary Horton had kept out of trouble.

In the very beginning Tim's beauty and helplessness had disarmed her: Mary found herself impaled on the pin of twenty-nine solitary years. It was as if he genuinely needed her, as if he could see something in her to which even she herself was blinded. No one had ever preferred her above all others, until Tim. What was it about her dry, matter-of-fact personality that Tim found so fascinating? The responsibility was a terrible thing, so hard to deal with for one quite unversed in the emotions. He had a mother, so it was not that which he sought; and he was too much the child and she too much an old maid for it to be a sexual thing. There must have been many, many people in his life who had been cruel to him, but there must also have been many, many people who were kind, even loving. No one with Tim's appearance and nature would ever go short of love. Why, then, did he prefer her?

The fire was dying. Mary went to seek more wood, then decided not to build it up again. She sat awhile longer, staring at the twinkling lights among the coals, her eyes unfocused. A worm popped its head out of the sand and looked at her; the heat of the fire was seeping slowly through the ground and forcing hundreds of its minute denizens to flee or fry. Unaware of the havoc her source of warmth was causing, Mary doused the embers with sand instead of water; safe enough as a fire hazard precaution, but no cooler for the sand and its inhabitants.

10

Mary continued to take Tim to Gosford with her all through the summer. By the time April was coming in and autumn with it, Tim's mother and father were well acquainted with her, but only over the phone. She had never invited Ron and Es Melville to Artarmon, and they had not liked to ask her to visit them. It did not occur to any of the four to wonder if each held the same impression of Mary Horton.

'I intend taking a holiday on the Great Barrier Reef this winter, perhaps in July or August, and I would very much like to take Tim with me, if it's all right with you,' she said to Ron Melville one Sunday evening.

'Cripes, Miss Horton, you're too good to Tim now! He can go with you, yes, but only on condition that he pays his own way.'

'If you'd rather it was that way, Mr Melville, then certainly, but I assure you I'd be only too delighted to have Tim along simply as my guest.'

'That's very, very nice of you, Miss Horton, but I do think Tim would be best off paying his own way. We can afford it. We could have taken him ourselves any time if we'd thought of it, but somehow Es and I never seem to get any further from Sydney than Avalon or Wattamolla.'

'I quite understand, Mr Melville. Goodbye.'

Ron hung up the receiver, shoved his thumbs through his trouser belt and sauntered into the living room, whistling.

'Hey, Es, Miss Horton wants to take Tim to the Great Barrier Reef with her in July or August,' Ron announced as he stretched himself comfortably on the sofa with his feet higher than his head.

'Very nice of her,' Es said.

A few minutes later the clip-clop of high heels sounded under the window, followed by the snap of the back door closing. A young woman walked into the room, nodded to them and sat down with a sigh, kicking her shoes off. She was both like Tim and not like him; the height and the fair hair were there, but she lacked the absolute perfection of his bone structure and her eyes were brown.

'I think I just saw the elusive Miss Horton,' she mumbled through a yawn, pulling an ottoman close enough to put her feet on.

Es put down her knitting. 'What's the old girl like?'

'I couldn't see much detail, but she's sort of stubby and has a head of silver hair with a bun on the back of her neck, typical old maid. Sixty-five-ish, I'd say, though I couldn't really see her face. What a car, mates! A big black Bentley something like the sort of car old Queen Lizzie rides in. Phew! Wall to wall money, I'd reckon.'

'I don't know about that, love, but I suppose she must be quite well off to own all that property.'

'Rather! I wonder what she sees in Tim? Sometimes it worries me . . . He's so awfully taken with her.'

'Oh, Dawnie, I think it's nice,' Es said. 'You're getting too clucky about Tim and Miss Horton.'

'What do you mean, I'm getting too clucky?' Dawnie demanded sharply. 'Darn it all, he's my brother! I don't like this new friendship of his, and that's that. What do we really know about Miss Mary Horton?'

'We know all we really have to know, Dawnie,' Es said gently. 'She's good for Tim.'

'But he's so wrapped in her, Mum! It's Mary this and Mary that until sometimes I could strangle him!'

'Oh, come on, Dawnie, don't be such a nark! You sound like green eyes to me!' Es snorted.

Ron frowned at Dawnie. 'Who were you out with tonight, sport?' he asked, changing the subject.

Her mood dropped away as her lively, extremely intelligent eyes laughed at him. 'The managing director of some big international drug firm. I'm thinking of going into industry.'

'My bloody foot! I reckon industry's thinking of going into you! How can you keep so many blokes on a string, Dawnie? What on earth do they see in youse?'

'How should I know?' She yawned, then listened. 'And here comes Tim.'

A moment later he entered, tired and happy.

'G'day there, mate!' his father said cheerfully. 'Have a good weekend?'

'Extra good, Pop. We're making a flower garden all around the house, and we're building a brick barbecue on the beach for cookouts.'

'Sounds like you're making a real picture-book place out of it, don't it, Es?'

But Es did not reply; she sat up straight suddenly, clutching Ron's arm. 'Hey, Ron, how could Miss Horton talk to you on the phone one minute and be outside dropping Tim off the next?'

'Stone the flaming crows! Tim, did Miss Horton phone us a few minutes ago, just before she dropped you?'

'Yes, Pop. She's got a phone in her car.'

'Blimey Charlie! That sounds a bit like putting on the dog to me, mate.'

'She has to have a phone in her car!' Tim answered indignantly. 'She told me her boss Mr Johnson needs to talk to her in a hurry sometimes.'

'And why couldn't she have come inside for a minute to talk to us in person if she was almost outside the house?' Dawnie sneered.

Tim's brow wrinkled. 'I dunno, Dawnie. I think she must be a little bit shy, just like you say I am.'

Ron stared at him, puzzled, but said nothing until after Tim had gone to bed. Then he swung his feet off the sofa and sat where he could see his wife and daughter comfortably.

'Is it my imagination, girls, or is Tim improving a bit? It struck me the other day that he's using fancier words than he used to, less down to earth, like.'

Es nodded. 'Yes, I've noticed it.'

'So have I, Pop. Apparently Miss Horton spends some of her time with Tim teaching.'

'Hooray and good luck to her!' Es said. 'I never had the patience and nor did the teachers at school, but I always reckoned Tim has it in him to learn.'

'Oh, come off it, Mum!' Dawnie snapped. 'Next thing you'll be expecting us to call her Saint Mary!' She got up abruptly. 'Since you can't find anything better to talk about than that woman's influence over Tim, I'm going to bed!'

Ron and Es were left staring after her, startled and perturbed.

'You know, Ron, I think Dawnie's a wee bit jealous of Miss Horton,' Es said at last.

'But why on earth should she be jealous?'

'Oh, I dunno, love. Women are real possessive sometimes. I have a feeling Dawnie's peeved because Tim don't hang around her so much these days.'

'But she oughta be glad! She always used to moan about Tim getting under her feet, and besides, the older she gets the more she leads her own life.'

'But she's human, pet, she don't see it like that. You know, dog in the manger.'

'Well, she's going to have to let go a bit, that's all. I'm real glad Tim's got Miss Horton instead of mooning around here waiting for Dawnie to come home.'

The following day Ron met his son at the Seaside as usual and walked home with him through the closing darkness, for the days were getting short.

When they came in the back door Es was waiting for them, a peculiar expression on her face. She had a flat, colourful little book in her hand, and waved it at Tim wildly.

'Tim, love, is this yours?' she squeaked, eyes alight.

Tim glanced at the book and smiled, as if at a pleasure remembered. 'Yes, Mum. Mary gave it to me.'

Ron took the book, turned it over and looked at the title. '*The Kitten Who Thought He Was a Mouse*,' he read out slowly.

'Mary's teaching me to read,' Tim explained, wondering what all the fuss was about.

'And can you read any of it yet?'

'A bit. It's awfully hard, but not as hard as writing. But Mary doesn't mind when I forget.'

'She's teaching youse to write, mate?' Ron asked, hardly able to believe it.

'Yes. She writes a word for me, and I copy it down so it looks just like hers. I can't write a word of my own yet.' He sighed. 'It's much harder than reading.'

Dawnie came home just then, seething with suppressed excitement, words bubbling on her lips, but for the first time in her life she found herself taking an intellectual back seat to Tim; her parents did not even bother to ask her what she was so excited about, they simply went 'Ssssh!' and drew her into the semicircle around Tim.

He read a page in the middle of the book without having to search around too much for a word or a letter, and when he was done they shouted and cheered, clapped him on the back and ruffled his hair. Sticking his chest out like a pouter pigeon, he strutted through to his room holding the little book reverently between his hands, and smiling; in all his life he had never known a moment more supreme. He had pleased them, really pleased them, made them proud of him the way they were proud of Dawnie.

Just after Tim had gone to bed Es raised her head from her endless knitting. 'How about a cuppa tea, pet?' she asked Ron.

'That sounds like a real good idea, old girl. Come on, Dawnie, come out to the kitchen with us like a good kid, eh? You've been awful quiet all night.'

'There's a bit of nice dark fruitcake with orange juice icing on it, or a cream sponge I bought at the Jungo this arvo,' Es announced, putting cups and saucers on the kitchen table.

'Cream sponge,' Ron and Dawnie chorused.

There was a delicious nip in the air, for it was the end of April and the worst of the heat was over. Ron got up and closed the back door, then chased an enormous moth with a rolled-up newspaper until he caught it thudding vainly against the light fixture. It fell to the ground amid a faint shower of gold powder from its wings; he picked it up, still fluttering madly, carried it into the bathroom and flushed it down the lavatory.

'Thanks, Pop,' Dawnie said, relaxing again. 'Jeez, I hate those bloody things, flipping and flopping in my face. I'm always scared they'll get into my hairdo or something.'

He grinned. 'You women! Frightened of anything that flies, creeps, or crawls.' He picked up a huge wedge of cake and jammed most of it into his mouth. 'What's the matter, Dawnie love?' he mumbled indistinctly, licking the cream from around his nose.

'Nothing, nothing!' she parried brightly, sectioning her cake and delicately conveying a small piece to her mouth on the tines of a baby fork.

'Come on, sport, you can't fool your old man!' he said more clearly. 'Spit it out, now! What's moping you, eh?'

Dawnie put her fork down, frowning, then lifted her large, light-filled eyes to his face. They softened, looking at him, for she was genuinely attached to him. 'If you must know the gory details, I'm ashamed of myself. I had a piece of news of my own to tell you when I came in tonight, and when I found Tim the centre of attention I got a bit peeved. You know, that's disgusting. The poor little bloke! He's taken a back seat to me all his life, and tonight, when he had something to show us that made us proud of him, I got shirty because he'd stolen my thunder.'

Es reached out and patted her arm. 'Don't fret about it, love. Tim didn't realise anything was wrong and that's the main thing, isn't it, eh? You're a good girl, Dawnie, your heart's in the right place.'

Dawnie smiled; suddenly she was very like Tim and it was easy to see why she had so many boyfriends. 'Ta, old girl! What a comfort you are, love. You can always find something nice to say, or something to take the sting out.'

Ron grinned. 'Except when she's lacing into me. Nasty old bat you are, Es!'

'What else can a drunken old sod like you expect?'

They all laughed. Es poured the tea, milk in the bottom of each cup and then a brew of tea on top of it that was as black and strong as coffee dregs. The resulting drink was dark brown in colour and opaque because of the milk; they all sugared their cups liberally and drank the steaming liquid straight down. Only when seconds were poured did they resume their talk.

'What was it you wanted to tell us, Dawnie?' her mother asked.

'I'm going to get married.'

There was a startled silence, broken by Ron's cup landing noisily in its saucer.

'That's a bombshell!' he said. 'Gord struth and little apples, what a bombshell! I never thought you'd go and get married, Dawnie. Cripes, the house'll be empty without youse!'

Es looked at her daughter gently. 'Well, love, I knew you'd up and tie the knot one of these days, and if it's what you want, I'm glad for you, real glad. Who's the bloke?'

'Mick Harrington-Smythe, my boss.'

They stared at her blankly.

'But isn't he the bloke you never got on with because he reckoned women belonged in the kitchen, not in the research lab?'

'That's him, that's my Mick!' Dawnie replied cheerfully, and grinned. 'I suppose he decided marrying me was the only way he'd get me out of the research lab and back into the kitchen where I belong.'

'A bit hard to get on with, isn't he?' Ron queried.

'Sometimes, but not if you know how to handle him. His worst fault is that he's a snob. You know the sort I mean – school at King's, home in Point Piper, ancestors who came out with the First Fleet – only they weren't convicts, of course, or if they were the family's not owning up to it now. But I'll wean him away from all that after a while.'

'How come he's marrying the likes of you, then?' Es asked acidly. 'We dunno what our ancestors were, except most likely they were thieves and cutthroats, and Surf Street Coogee isn't exactly the poshest address in Sydney, nor is Randwick High the poshest girls' school.'

Dawnie sighed. 'Oh, Mum, don't worry about it! The important thing is that he wants to marry me, and he knows exactly where, what, and who I come from.'

'We can't afford a big expensive wedding for you, love,' Es said sadly.

'I have a bit of money saved myself, so I can pay for whatever sort of wedding his parents want. Personally I hope they'll decide on a quiet one, but if they want a big, splashy affair they'll get a big, splashy affair.'

'Youse'll be ashamed of us,' Es quavered, tears in her eyes.

Dawnie laughed, stretching her hands out until the slender muscles rippled under her beautiful brown skin. 'Not on your life, mates! Why on earth should I be ashamed of you? You gave me the best and happiest life a girl could ever have asked for, you brought me up free of all the hangups, neuroses, and problems everyone else my age seems to have. In fact, you did a darned sight better job bringing me up than Mick's parents did him, let me tell you! He likes me and my family or he lumps us, that's all there is to it. It must be the attraction of opposites,' she went on more thoughtfully, 'because we really don't have a thing in common except brains. Anyway, he's thirty-five and he's had his pick of all the blue-bloods Sydney's had to offer in the last fifteen years, but he ended up picking good old common, garden-alley Dawnie Melville.'

'A point in his favour, I reckon,' Ron said heavily. He sighed. 'I don't suppose he'll ever want to meet Tim and me for a beer or two at the Seaside. A scotch and water in some pansy lounge is more the style of that sort of bloke.'

'At the moment it is, but he doesn't know what he's missing. You just wait! At the end of a year I'll have him meeting you at the Seaside.'

Es got up abruptly. 'Leave everything, I'll clear it up in the morning. I'm going to bed, I'm tired.'

'Poor old Dawnie, she's in for a miserable time being married to a prawn like that,' Es said to Ron as they climbed into their comfortable old bed.

'It don't pay to step out of your class, Es,' Ron replied sternly. 'I wish she'd had less brains, then she would have married some ordinary bloke from around the next corner and settled down in a fibro Housing Commission house in Blacktown. But Dawnie don't like ordinary blokes.'

'Well, I hope it turns out all right, but I can't see that happening unless she breaks her ties with us, Ron. She's not going to like it, but I think we must gradually edge our way out of her life after she's married. Let her carve a spot for herself in their world, because that's the world she'll have to raise his kids in, ain't it?'

'You're dead right, old girl.' He stared at the ceiling, blinking hard. 'Tim's the one will miss her. Poor old bloke, he won't understand.'

'No, but he's like a little kid, Ron, his memory's short. You know how he is, poor little coot. He'll miss her the way a little kid does at first, but then he'll sort of forget her. Just as well he's got Miss Horton, I reckon. I daresay she won't be around forever either, but I hope she'll be around long enough to tide him over Dawnie's marrying.' She patted his arm. 'Life never works out the way you hope, does it? I'd sort of thought at one time that Dawnie wouldn't marry at all, that she and Tim would end up their days sharing this old house together after we're gone. She's so terribly fond of him. But I'm glad she's taking the plunge, Ron. Like I told her lots of times, we don't expect her to sacrifice her life for Tim. It wouldn't be right. And yet . . . I still think she's a wee bit jealous of Miss Horton. This engagement's so sudden. Tim finds himself a friend, Dawnie's nose is pushed out of joint a bit because Miss Horton's taken the time to teach him how to read and Dawnie never did, and the next thing, boomp! she goes and gets engaged.'

Ron reached over and switched out the light. 'But why this one, Es? I never even thought she liked him.'

'Oh, but he's a lot older than she is, and she's real flattered because he picked her after all those Lady Mucks he could have had. Probably she's a bit scared of him too, a bit bluffed by his background and the fact that he's her boss. You can have all the brains in the world and still not be any wiser than the silliest coot in Callan Park.'

Ron wriggled down until his head found its natural dent in the pillow. 'Well, love, there's nothing we can do about it, is there? She's over twenty-one, and she never took much notice of us, anyway. The only reason she's stayed out of trouble is that she's so bloody smart, horse-sense smart, like.' He kissed her on the mouth. 'Night-night, love. I'm tired, aren't you? All this flaming excitement.'

'Too right,' she yawned. 'Night-night, love.'

11

When Tim arrived at Mary's house in Artarmon the following Saturday he was quiet and a little withdrawn. Mary did not question his mood, but put him in the Bentley and got on the road immediately. They had to stop at a nursery in Hornsby to pick up a lot of plants and shrubs Mary had ordered during the week, and the business of getting them all in the car occupied Tim so much that she told him to stay in the back seat when they started out again, so he could watch the plants and make sure none of them fell over or stained the leather upholstery.

At the cottage she left him to unload the plants and went through to his room with his case to unpack it, though these days he kept a small wardrobe there permanently. The room was changed; no longer bare and white, it sported a thick orange carpet, pale yellow walls, crome yellow drapes, and Danish modern furniture. His suitcase disposed of, she moved on to her own room and tidied herself up before returning to the car to see how Tim was doing.

Something was wrong with him, he was not himself at all. Frowning, she watched him closely as he finished taking the last of the plants out of the trunk. She did not think his problem was a physical one, for his skin was its usual healthy gold and his eyes were clear and bright. Apparently whatever plagued him was a happening in his personal sphere, though she doubted that it had anything to do with her, unless of course his parents had said something about her which had upset or puzzled him. But surely not! Only the other night she had spoken at length with Ron Melville, and he had been brimming over with enthusiasm about Tim's progress in reading and calculating.

'You're so bloody good for him, Miss Horton,' Ron had told her. 'Whatever you do, don't give him up as a bad job. I wish he'd known you years ago, I really do.'

They had a silent lunch and went out to the garden with Tim's problem, whatever it was, still unmentioned. He would tell her in his own good time; perhaps it was better if she acted as though nothing was the matter, if she went ahead and made him help her plant all the new acquisitions. Last weekend they had had such fun over the garden, wrangling about whether they should have a bed entirely of stocks, or whether they ought to mix larkspurs and snapdragons in with them. He had not known the names of any of the flowers, so she had taken out her books and shown him pictures of them; he had learned about them with delight, and walked around muttering their names over and over to himself.

They worked silently all afternoon, until the shadows lengthened and the sea breeze came gusting up the lofty river canyon to warn of the coming night.

'Let's build a fire in the barbecue and cook on the beach,' Mary suggested desperately. 'We can go for a swim while the fire's getting itself to the right stage for cooking, and then we can build another fire on the sand to get dry over and warm us while we eat. How does that sound, Tim?'

He tried to smile. 'It sounds lovely, Mary.'

By this time Mary had learned to love the water and could even swim a few strokes, enough at least to be able to venture out where Tim liked to frolic. She had bought a black grosgrain swimsuit with a fairly long, full skirt on it for modesty's sake; Tim thought it was gorgeous. Her skin had darkened now that she exposed herself to the sun, and she looked better for it, younger and healthier.

Tim was not his usual high-spirited self in the water; he swam about quietly, forgetting to divebomb and torpedo her, and when she suggested they should go out onto the beach he followed her at once. Normally getting him out of the water was a battle royal, for he would stay in until midnight if she let him.

She had tiny baby lamb chops and big fat sausages to toast over the fire, two of his favourites, but he picked half-heartedly at a chop for a while without reducing its size very much, then pushed the plate away with a sigh, shaking his head wearily.

'I'm not hungry, Mary,' he said sadly.

They sat side by side on a towel in front of the second fire, warming themselves comfortably in the teeth of the wintry wind. The sun had set, and the world was in that half-dark stage when everything was bled of its vividness but was not yet dimmed to black or white or grey. Above them in the clear vast sky the evening star glittered against an apple-green horizon, and a few more high magnitude stars struggled to overcome the light, appearing for a moment and then disappearing. Birds twittered and screamed everywhere, bedding down for the night in querulous fussiness, and the bush was full of mysterious squeaks and rustles.

Mary never used to notice such things, had been quite indifferent to the world around her except when it intruded itself, but now she found that she was intensely aware of the surrounding sphere, the sky and the land and the water, its animals and plants, all so wonderful and beautiful. Tim had taught her that, from the moment when he had shown her the cicada choirmaster in her oleander tree. He was always coming to display some little natural treasure he had found, a spider or a wild orchid or some tiny furry animal, and she had learned not to jump away in revulsion but to see them as he did for what they were, perfect, as much a functional part of the planet earth as she was herself if not more so, for sometimes what he brought her was rare.

Worried and upset, Mary wriggled around on the towel until she sat looking at his profile, etched against the pearly rim of the sky. The cheek towards her was faintly outlined, the eye sunk invisible into a darkened socket, the mouth at its saddest. Then he moved slightly, and what light there was left collected itself into a sparkling row of tiny droplets on his lashes, glistening all the way down his cheek.

'Oh, Tim!' she cried, her hands going out to him. 'Don't weep, my darling boy, don't weep! What is it, what's the matter? Can't you tell me, when we're such very good friends?'

She remembered Ron telling her that he used to cry a lot, and like a small child in noisy, hiccoughing bellows, but that of late he had stopped crying so. On the rare occasions these days when he was moved to tears, he cried more like an adult, Ron said, quietly and into himself. Just the way he was weeping now, she thought, wondering how often he had wept today without her noticing, when she had not been there or when she had been too busy to see.

Too upset to question the wisdom of her own conduct, she put her hand on his arm and stroked it softly, trying to soothe him as best she could. He turned towards her at once, and before she could jerk away he put his head down against her chest, drawing himself in against her like a small animal in need of a place to hide, his hands clutching at her sides. Her arms seemed to find a natural resting place across his back, and she dropped her head until her cheek rested on his hair.

'Don't cry, Tim,' she whispered, smoothing his hair back and kissing his brow.

She sat back on her heels cradling him, all else forgotten save the reality of being able to give him comfort. He needed her, he had turned to her and hidden his face as if he thought her empowered to shield him from the world. Nothing could ever have prepared her for this; she had not dreamed life could give her a moment so infinitely sweet, so bounded with pain. His back under her hand was cool and slippery, like satin; the unshaven cheek resting just above her breasts scratched her skin like fine sandpaper.

Awkwardly and hesitantly at first, she gathered him closer, hugging one arm gently but strongly around his back, her other arm protectively about his head, its fingers buried in his thick, faintly salty hair. The forty-three empty, loveless years of her life were cancelled out of existence, payment extracted in this one small flake of time. With this at their end they did not matter, and if there were forty-three more just as empty still to be endured, they could never matter either. Not now.

After a while he ceased weeping and lay absolutely motionless within her arms, only the slight rise and fall of his breathing under her hand telling her that he lived. Nor did she move; the thought of moving terrified her, for instinct told her that once either of them shifted even the smallest bit, he would withdraw or she would have to draw away herself. She pressed her mouth further into his hair and closed her eyes, profoundly happy.

He gave a deep, sobbing sigh and moved a little to get more comfortable, but to Mary it was the signal that her moment was over; gently she eased herself slightly away from him, so that he still lay within her arms but could lift his head to look at her. Her hand in his hair tugged at it until he was forced to raise his face, and the breath caught in her throat. In the faint light his beauty had a fey quality about it, he was an Oberon or a Morpheus, unreal, other-worldly. The moon had got into his eyes and sheeted them with a glaze of blued silver; they stared at her blindly, as though he saw her from the other side of a filmy curtain. Perhaps indeed he did, for what he saw in her no one else ever had, she reflected.

'Tim, won't you tell me what's making you so unhappy?'

'It's my Dawnie, Mary. She's going away soon and we won't see her very often. I don't want my Dawnie to go away, I want her to keep on living with us!'

'I see.' She looked down into the unblinking, moonstone eyes. 'Is she getting married, Tim? Is that why she's going away?'

'Yes, but I don't want her to get married and go away!' he cried defiantly.

'Tim, as you go on through the years you'll find that life is made up of meetings, knowings, and partings. Sometimes we love the people we meet, sometimes we don't like the people we meet, but knowing them is the most important thing about living, it's what keeps us human beings. You see, for many years I refused to admit this, and I wasn't a very good human being. Then I met you, and knowing you has sort of changed my life, I've become a better human being.

'Ah, but the partings, Tim! They're the hardest, the most bitter to accept, especially if we loved. Parting means it can never be the same afterward; something has gone out of our lives, a bit of us is missing and can never be found or put back again. But there are many partings, Tim, because they're as much a component of living as meeting and knowing. What you have to do is remember knowing your Dawnie, not spend your time grieving because you have to part from her, because the parting can't be avoided, it has to come. If you remember knowing her rather than grieve at losing her, it won't hurt so much.

'And that's far too long and complex and you didn't understand a word of it, did you, love?'

'I think I understood a bit of it, Mary,' he answered seriously.

She laughed, dispelling the last of the moment, and thus inched him out of her arms. Standing upright again, she reached down her hands and pulled him to his feet.

'Mary, what you said, does that mean one day I'll have to see you go away, too?'

'Not unless you want me to go away, or unless I die.'

The fires were quenched, thin tendrils of steam curling up between the grains of sand, and the beach was suddenly very cold. Mary shivered, hugging herself.

'Come, let's go back to the house, Tim, where it's warm and light.'

He detained her, staring into her face with a passionate eagerness normally quite foreign to him. 'Mary, I've always wanted to know, but no one will ever tell me! What's die, and dying, and dead? Are they all the same thing?'

'They all relate to the same thing, yes.' She took his hand in hers and pressed its palm against his own chest, just over the left nipple. 'Can you feel your heart there beating, Tim? Can you feel that thump-thump, thump-thump, thump-thump under your hand, always there, never stopping for a moment?'

He nodded, fascinated. 'Yes, I can! I really can!'

'Well, while it beats, thump-thump, thump-thump, you can see and hear, walk around, laugh and cry, eat and drink and wake up in the morning, feel the sun and the wind.

'When I talk about living that's what I mean, the seeing and hearing and walking around, the laughing and crying. But you've seen things get old, wear out, break apart? A wheelbarrow or a concrete mixer, perhaps? Well, we, all of us with beating hearts under our ribs – and that's everyone, Tim, everyone! – we get old and tired, and wear out too. Eventually we begin to break apart and that beating thing you can feel stops, like a clock that's not been wound. It happens to all of us, when our time comes. Some of us wear out faster than others, some of us get accidentally stopped, if we're in a plane crash or something like that. No one of us knows when we'll stop, it isn't something we can control or foretell. It just happens one day, when we're all worn out and too tired to keep going.

'When our hearts stop, Tim, we stop. We don't see or hear ever again, we don't walk around, we don't eat, we can't laugh or cry. We're dead, Tim, we are no more, we've stopped and we have to be put away where we can lie and sleep undisturbed, under the ground forever.

'It happens to us all, and it's nothing to be frightened of, it can't hurt us. It's just like going to sleep and never waking up again, and nothing ever hurts us while we're asleep, does it? It's nice to be asleep, whether it's in a bed or under the ground. What we have to do is enjoy living while we're living, and then not be frightened to die when the time comes for us to stop.'

'Then I might die just as easily as you, Mary!' he said intensely, his face close to hers.

'Yes, you might, but I'm old and you're young, so if we go on as people usually do, I should stop before you. I'm more worn out than you are, you see.'

He was on the verge of tears again. 'No, no, no! I don't want you to die before I do, I don't want it like that!'

She took his hands in hers, chafing them urgently. 'There, there, Tim, don't be unhappy! What did I just tell you? Living is to be enjoyed for every moment we're still alive! Dying is in the future, it isn't to be worried about or even thought about!

'Dying is the final parting, Tim, the hardest one of all to bear, because the parting is forever. But all of us come to it, so it's something we can't close our eyes to and pretend it doesn't exist.

'If we're grown-up and sensible, if we're good strong people, we understand dying, we know about it but we don't let it worry us. Now I know you're grown-up and sensible, I know you're a good strong person, so I want you to promise me you won't worry about dying, that you won't be frightened of it happening to me, or to you. And I want you to promise that you'll try to be a man about partings, that you won't make poor Dawnie unhappy by being unhappy yourself. Dawnie is alive too, she has as much right to find her own way of enjoying living as you do, and you mustn't make it hard for her by letting her see how upset you are.'

She took his chin in her hand and looked into the clouded eyes. 'Now I know you're good and strong and kind, Tim, so I want you to be all of those things about your Dawnie, and about all the things that will happen to make you sad, because you mustn't be sad a minute longer than you can help. Promise?'

He nodded gravely. 'I promise, Mary.'

'Then let's go back to the house. I'm cold.'

Mary turned on the big space-heater in the living room to warm it up, and put on some music she knew would make him light-heartedly happy. The treatment worked, and he was soon laughing and talking as if nothing had ever happened to threaten his world. He demanded a reading lesson, which she gave him gladly, then declined another form of amusement, curling up on the floor at her feet instead and sitting with his head resting against the arm of her chair.

'Mary?' he asked after a long while, and just before she opened her mouth to tell him it was time to go to bed.

'Yes?'

He twisted around so that he could see her face. 'When I cried and you hugged me, what's that called?'

She smiled, patting his shoulder. 'I don't know that it's called anything very much. Comforting, I suppose. Yes, I think it's called comforting. Why?'

'I liked it. Mum used to do it sometimes a real long time ago when I was just a little shaver, but then she told me I was too big and never did it again. Why didn't you think I was too big?'

One hand went up to shield her eyes and stayed there a moment before she dropped it onto her lap and clenched it tightly around her other hand. 'I suppose I didn't think of you as big at all, I thought of you as a little shaver. But I don't think how big you are is very important, I think how big your trouble is is much more important. You might be a big man now, but your trouble was much bigger, wasn't it? Did it help, to be comforted?'

He turned away, satisfied. 'Oh, yes, it helped a lot. It was real nice. I'd like to be comforted every day.'

She laughed. 'You might like to be comforted every day, but it isn't going to happen. When something is done too often it loses its attraction, don't you think? If you were comforted every day whether you needed it or not, you'd soon get a wee bit tired of it. It wouldn't be nearly as nice any more.'

'But I need comforting all the time, Mary, I need to be comforted every day!'

'Pooh! Fiddle! You're a conniver, my friend, that's what you are! Now I think it's bedtime, don't you?'

He climbed to his feet. 'Night-night, Mary. I like you, I like you better than anyone except Pop and Mum, and I like you the same as I like Pop and Mum.'

'Oh, Tim! What about poor Dawnie?'

'Oh, I like my Dawnie too, but I like you better than I like her, I like you better than anyone except Pop and Mum. I'm going to call you my Mary, but I'm not going to call Dawnie my Dawnie any more.'

'Tim, don't be unforgiving! Oh, that's so cruel and thoughtless! Please don't make Dawnie feel that I've taken her place in your affections. It would make her very unhappy.'

'But I like you, Mary, I like you better than I like Dawnie! I can't help it, I just do!'

'I like you too, Tim, and really better than anyone else in the whole world, because I don't have a Pop and a Mum.'

12

It transpired that Dawnie wanted to marry Michael Harrington-Smythe at the end of May, which left little time for preparations. Learning the background of their son's bride-to-be, Mick's parents were just as anxious as Dawnie's to reduce the size of the wedding to a bare minimum.

The two sets of parents plus the engaged pair met on neutral ground to plan the wedding, neutral ground being a private room at the Wentworth Hotel, where the reception was to be held. Everyone was uncomfortable. Distressed in collar and tie and Sunday corsets, Ron and Es sat on the edges of their chairs and refused to be drawn into polite conversation, while Mick's parents, to whom collar and tie and corsets were an everyday occurrence, chatted in bored voices which held a slight suggestion of plum-in-mouth. Mick and Dawnie tried desperately to lessen the stiffness, without much success.

'Dawn will naturally be married in a long white gown and have at least one attendant,' Mrs Harrington-Smythe said challengingly.

Es looked stupid; she had forgotten that Dawnie's real name was Dawn, and found it disagreeable to be reminded that the Melville family had chosen a low-class diminutive. 'Um,' she answered, which Mrs Harrington-Smythe took to mean acquiescence.

'The men in the wedding party had better wear dark suits and plain blue satin ties,' Mrs Harrington-Smythe continued. 'Since it's a small, private wedding, morning dress or white tie and tails would be most unsuitable.'

'Um,' said Es, her hand fumbling underneath the table until it found Ron's and clutched thankfully.

'I'll give you a full list of those the groom's side will want invited, Mrs Melville.'

And so it went, until Mrs Harrington-Smythe remarked, 'I

believe Dawn has an older brother, Mrs Melville, but Michael hasn't given me any idea of what part he's to play in the wedding. Naturally you realise he can't be best man, since Michael's own friend Hilary Arbuckle-Heath is filling that role, and I really can't see what other function is available for him in such a small wedding party. Unless, of course, Dawn chooses to change her mind and have a second attendant.'

'That's all right, Ma'am,' Ron said heavily, squeezing Es's hand. 'Tim don't expect to be in the wedding party. In fact, we were thinking of letting him go to Miss Mary Horton's for the day.'

Dawnie gasped. 'Oh, Pop, you can't do that! Tim's my only brother, I want him to see me married!'

'But Dawnie love, you know Tim don't like crowds!' her father protested. 'Think what an uproar there'd be if he vomited all over the place! Sweet balls of Christ, wouldn't that be just lovely? No, I think it would be better all around if Tim just went to Miss Horton's.'

Dawnie's eyes glittered with tears. 'Anyone would think you were ashamed of him, Pop! I'm not ashamed of him, I want everyone to meet him and love him as much as I do!'

'Dawnie love, I think your old man's right about Tim,' Es contributed. 'You know how he hates crowds, and even if he wasn't sick everywhere he wouldn't be very happy if he had to sit still all through a wedding ceremony.'

The Harrington-Smythes were looking at each other, absolutely bewildered. 'I thought he was older than Dawn,' Mrs Harrington-Smythe said. 'I'm sorry, I didn't realise he was only a child.'

'Well, he isn't a child!' Dawnie flared, red spots staining her cheeks. 'He's a year older than me but he's mentally retarded, that's what they're trying to conceal from everyone!'

There was an appalled silence; Mr Harrington-Smythe drummed his fingers on the table, and Mick looked at Dawnie in surprise.

'You didn't tell me Tim was retarded,' he said to her.

'No, I didn't, because it just never occurred to me that it was important! I've had Tim there all my life, and he's a part of my life, a very important part of my life! I never remember that he's retarded when I'm talking about him, that's all!'

'Don't be angry, Dawn,' Mick pleaded. 'It really isn't important, you're quite right about that. I was simply a little surprised.'

'Well, I am angry! I'm not trying to hide the fact that my only sibling is mentally retarded, it's my mother and father who've apparently taken it upon themselves to do that! Pop, how could you?'

Ron looked embarrassed. 'Well, Dawnie, it isn't that we was trying to hide it exactly, it's that we thought it would be less of a business for you if he didn't come. Tim don't like crowds, you know that. Everyone always stares at him so much that it makes him go all funny.'

'Oh, dear, is he very bad to look at?' Mrs Harrington-Smythe asked, a slight doubt in her eyes as they rested on Dawnie. Perhaps it ran in the family? What an idiot Michael was, to choose a low-class girl like this after all the perfectly marvellous girls he had ignored! Of course, they said she was extraordinarily brilliant, but brilliance was no substitute for good breeding, it could never outweigh vulgarity, and the whole wretched family was vulgar, vulgar, vulgar! The girl had absolutely no polish, no idea of how to comport herself in decent company.

'Tim is the finest-looking man I've ever seen,' Dawnie replied fiercely. 'People stare at him in admiration, not in disgust, but he doesn't know the difference! All he knows is that they're looking at him, and he doesn't like the sensation.'

'Oh, he is lovely to look at,' Es offered. 'Like a Greek god, Miss Horton says.'

'Miss Horton?' Mick asked, hoping to change the subject.

'Miss Horton is the lady Tim gardens for on weekends.'

'Oh, really? Tim is a gardener, then?'

'No, he's not a bloody gardener!' Dawnie snapped, nettled at the tone. 'He works as a builder's labourer during the week, and he earns a little extra money on the weekends by gardening for this wealthy old lady.'

Dawnie's explanation only made matters worse; the Harrington-Smythes were shifting on their chairs and trying not to look at each other or the Melvilles.

'Tim has an IQ of about 75,' Dawnie said, more quietly. 'As such he's not supposed to be employable, but my parents were wonderful about him, right from the start. They realised they wouldn't be here to support him all of his life, so they brought him up to be as self-sufficient and independent as possible under the circumstances. From the day he was fifteen Tim's earned his own living as an unskilled labourer, which is the only kind of work he's fit for. I might add that he's still working for the man who took him when he was fifteen, which may help you understand what a valuable and well-liked employee he is.

'Pop has paid on an insurance policy for him since he first knew Tim was retarded, so he'll never have to worry financially, he'll always have enough to live on. Since I started working I've helped increase the size of the premiums, and some of Tim's wages go into it, too. Tim is the richest member of the family, ha-ha!

'Until recently he couldn't read or write or do any sort of arithmetic, but Mum and Pop taught him the really important things, like how to get about the city from job to job and place to place without having to have someone always with him. They taught him to count money though he can't count anything else, which is strange: you'd think he would associate what he can do with money with other kinds of counting, but he can't. One of the weird little jokes the retarded mind plays, that is. But he can buy himself a ticket for the bus or the train, he can buy himself food and clothes. He isn't a burden to us now any more than he ever has been. I'm very fond of my brother and I'm very devoted to him. A kinder, sweeter, more lovable person doesn't exist. And, Mick,' she added, turning to her fiancé, 'when Tim's all alone and needs a home, I'm taking him in. If it doesn't suit you, then it's too bloody bad! You'd better call the whole thing off right now.'

'My dear, dear Dawn,' Mick said imperturbably, 'I fully intend to marry you, if you have ten mentally retarded and utterly moronic brothers.'

The answer did not please her, but she was too upset to analyse why it did not please her, and later on forgot all about it.

'It don't run in the family,' Es explained, a little pathetically. 'It was me ovaries, the doctors said. I was over forty when I married Ron, and I'd never had any kids before that. So Tim was born not the full quid, you see. Dawnie was fine because me ovaries had got going by then. It was only the first one, Tim, what got affected by them. But it's like Dawnie says, a nicer little bloke than Tim just don't exist.'

'I see,' said Mr Harrington-Smythe, not knowing what else to say. 'Well, I'm sure it isn't up to anyone but Mr and Mrs Melville to decide whether their son should attend the wedding.'

'And we decided,' Es said firmly. 'Tim don't like crowds, so

Tim don't go. Miss Horton will be glad to take him for the weekend.'

Dawnie burst into tears and rushed to the powder room, where her mother found her a few minutes later.

'Don't cry, love,' Es soothed, patting her shoulders.

'But everything's going wrong, Mum! You and Pop don't like the Harrington-Smythes, they don't like you either, and I don't know what Mick thinks any more! Oh, it's going to be awful!'

'Stuff and fiddle! Ron and me come from a different world to the Harrington-Smythes, that's all. They don't normally mix with the likes of us, so how can you expect them to know what to do when they find themselves having to mix with the likes of us? And the same goes the other way, love. The Harrington-Smythes aren't the sort of people I play tennis with on Tuesdays and Thursdays and Saturdays, or the sort Ron meets at the Seaside and the Leagues Club.

'You're a big girl, Dawnie, and a real brainy girl. You ought to know we couldn't ever be friends. Why, we don't even laugh at the same things! But we aren't enemies either, not with our kids getting married to each other. We just won't meet either side of this wedding, except maybe for christenings and suchlike. And that's how it should be. Why should we have to pee in each other's pockets just because our kids got married, eh? Now you're clever enough to understand that, aren't you?'

Dawnie dried her eyes. 'Yes, I suppose so. But, oh, Mum, I wanted everything to be so perfect!'

'Of course you did, love, but life ain't like that, not ever. It was you picked Mick and him you, not us or the Harrington-Smythes. If it had been left to us, we'd never have matched you with Mick, and nor would the pewie Harrington-Smythes. Double-barrelled name, indeed! Bloody putting on the dog, if you ask me. But we're all making the best of it, love, so don't go creating a big fuss over poor Tim, for heaven's sake. Tim don't enter into this and it ain't right of you to make him enter it. Leave poor Tim to his own life, and don't go pushing him down the Harrington-Smythes' throats. They don't know him the way we do, so how can you expect them to understand?'

'Bless you, Mum, I don't know what I'd do without you! I'm supposed to be the clever Melville, but sometimes I get the funny feeling that it's really you and Pop who are the clever ones. How did you get so wise?'

'I didn't, love, and nor did your old man. Life makes us wise, the longer we live it. When you've got kids as old as you are now, you'll be doing the dazzling, and I'll be shoving up daisies.'

In the end Ron telephoned Mary Horton and asked her to resolve the question of whether Tim should be allowed to go to the wedding. Though they had never met and he was aware that Miss Horton belonged more in the Harrington-Smythe circle than the Melville, Ron somehow felt at home with her; she would both understand his dilemma and offer a reasonable solution for it.

'It's a bad business, Miss Horton,' he said, breathing noisily into the receiver. 'The Harrington-Smythes aren't too pleased with their precious son's choice of a wife, and I can't honestly say I blame them. They're afraid she won't fit in, and if it wasn't that Dawnie's so bloody smart I'd be afraid on that score, too. As it is, I think she'll learn a lot faster than they can teach, and no one will ever have the chance to be embarrassed because of anything she says or does.'

'I don't know Dawnie personally, Mr Melville, but from what I've heard, I'm sure you're right,' Mary responded sympathetically. 'I wouldn't worry about her.'

'Oh, I ain't!' he answered. 'Dawnie's got the iron in her, she'll be apples. It's Tim that's getting me down.'

'Tim? Why?'

'Well, he's different, like. He's never going to grow up properly, and he don't know when he makes a mistake, he can't learn from making it. What's going to happen to the poor little bugger after we're gone?'

'I think you've done a splendid job with Tim,' Mary said, her throat unaccountably tight. 'You've brought him up to be remarkably independent and self-sufficient.'

'Oh, I know all that already!' Ron replied, a little impatiently. 'If it was just a question of him looking after himself I wouldn't be worried, but it ain't, you know. Tim needs his Mum and Pop for love and peace of mind, because he ain't growed up enough to find someone to replace us, a wife and family of his own, I mean, which is what a man normally does.'

'But he'll have you for many years to come, Mr Melville! You're young yet, you and your wife.'

'That's where you're wrong, Miss Horton, Es and me ain't young at all. We was born six months apart, and we had our seventieth birthday this year.'

'Oh!' There was a blank silence for a moment, then Mary's voice came again, rather uncertainly. 'I hadn't realised you and Mrs Melville were as old as that.'

'Well, we are. I tell you, Miss Horton, with Dawnie marrying a bloke who definitely won't want his wife's mentally retarded brother hanging around, Es and me is nearly mental ourselves worrying about Tim. Sometimes at night I hear poor old Es crying, and I know she's crying about Tim. He won't outlive us long, youse know. When he finds out he's all alone, he'll up and die of a broken heart, you wait and see.'

'People don't die of broken hearts, Mr Melville,' Mary said gently, out of the ignorance of her emotionally impoverished existence.

'Bullshit they don't!' Ron exploded. 'Oh, I beg your pardon, Miss Horton! I know I shouldn't swear like that, but don't you ever believe people don't die of broken hearts! I've seen it happen, and more than once, too. Tim will, he'll just fade away. You need the will to live as much as the health to live, love. And when there's no one to care about him, Tim will die; he'll just sit there crying and forgetting to eat until he dies.'

'Well, as long as I'm here I'll see there's someone to care for him,' Mary offered tentatively.

'But you're not young either, Miss Horton! It was Dawnie I was hoping for, but not any longer . . .' He sighed. 'Oh, well, no use crying over spilt milk, is there?'

It was on the tip of Mary's tongue to assure him she wasn't seventy, but before she could speak Ron began again.

'What I really rang to ask you was about Tim going to the wedding. I'd like to have him come but I know he'll be miserable, sitting still all through the ceremony and then the reception. Dawnie was very upset when I said I didn't think Tim ought to go, but I still don't think he ought to go. What I was wondering was, would you mind if Tim stayed with you that weekend?'

'Of course not, Mr Melville! But it seems a great shame that Tim can't be in the house to see Dawnie getting ready, and that he can't see her married . . . I tell you what, why don't you bring him to the church to see her married, and I'll pick him up outside right afterward, so he doesn't have to go to the reception?'

'Hey, that's a great idea, Miss Horton! Crikey, why didn't I think of that? It would solve all our worries, wouldn't it?'

'Yes, I think it would. Give me a call when you have all the details about time and place and et cetera, and I give you my word I'll look after Tim after the ceremony.'

'Miss Horton, you're the grouse, you really are!'

13

Tim found the wedding preparations exciting. Dawnie was especially considerate and tender during the week preceding what in her heart she termed her desertion, and devoted all her time to her family.

On the morning of the wedding, a Saturday, he was enthralled with the bustle and panic that seemed threatening to overwhelm them any moment, and wandered about getting under everyone's feet, full of helpful suggestions. They had bought him a new, dark blue suit with flared trousers and a waisted, slightly skirted coat, à la Cardin, and he was thrilled with it. He put it on the moment he got up and strutted about in it preening himself and trying to catch glimpses of his reflection in the mirrors.

When he saw Dawnie dressed he was awed.

'Oh, Dawnie, you look just like a fairy princess!' he breathed, staring at her with blue eyes wide.

She caught him to her in a violent hug, winking away tears. 'Oh, Tim, if I ever have a son I hope he'll be as nice as you,' she whispered, kissing his cheek.

He was delighted, not with the reference to her son, which he didn't understand, but with the hug. 'You comforted me!' he carolled gleefully. 'You comforted me, Dawnie! I like being comforted, it's the nicest thing I know!'

'Now, Tim, go out to the front gate and watch for the cars like a good boy,' Es instructed, wondering whether she would ever think straight again, and trying to ignore the silly little pain in her side she had felt sometimes of late.

Dawnie was handed into the leading limousine with her father, the lone maid of honour got into the second one, and Es herded Tim into the third with her.

'Now sit still, Tim, and try to be a good boy,' she admonished, settling herself onto the luxuriously padded back seat with a sigh.

'You look lovely, Mum,' Tim said, more used to the feel of

an expensive car than his mother, and taking it completely for granted.

'Thanks, love, I wish I felt lovely,' Es replied.

She had tried not to overdress, sensing that Dawnie's grand in-laws would not be impressed with the usual garb of mothers of the bride in the Melville circle. So, with a sigh of regret she had abandoned her delicious dream of a mauve guipure lace dress, coat, shoes, and hat with a corsage of lilies dyed to match; she chose instead a dress and coat of subdued pale blue silk shantung with no corsage to speak of, just two modest white roses.

The church was crowded when she and Tim found their pew in the front on the bride's side; all the way down the aisle Es was conscious of the stares people gave Tim from the groom's side, gaping, she told herself, just as if they were low-class nothings. Mrs and Mr Harrington-Smythe were looking at him as though they could scarcely believe their eyes, while every female under ninety fell madly in love with him. Es was devoutly glad he was not going to the reception.

He behaved beautifully during the ceremony, which was not a long one. Afterward, while the photographer's camera flashed and the usual congratulations were under way, Es and Ron quietly led Tim out to the wall near the front gate of the church, and made him sit on it.

'Now you wait here for Mary like a good boy, and don't you dare wander away, do you hear?' Es said firmly.

He nodded. 'All right, Mum, I'll wait here. Can I turn around and watch Dawnie come down the steps, though?'

'Of course you can. Just don't wander away, and if anyone comes over to try and talk to you, answer them politely and then don't say anything at all. Now Pop and me have to go back to the church, because they want us for the photographs, heaven help them. We'll see you again tomorrow night when Miss Horton brings you home.'

The bridal party and the wedding guests had been gone ten minutes when Mary Horton drove down the street. She was vexed with herself, for she had got lost in the maze of small streets around Darling Point, thinking St Marks was a different church closer to New South Head Road.

Tim was still sitting on the low stone wall in front, with the autumn sun filtering through the leafy trees in soft gold bars that danced with dust. He seemed so lost, so alone and lonely, staring helplessly at the road and obviously wondering what had happened to her. The new suit fitted him perfectly but it made him seem a stranger, very handsome and sophisticated. Only the pose was Tim, obedient and quiet, like a well-behaved small boy. Or like a dog, she thought; like a dog he would sit there until he died of starvation rather than move on in order to survive, because his loved ones had told him to sit there and not move.

Ron's words on the phone about Tim dying of a broken heart still plagued her; obviously Ron believed she was in his own age group, getting on towards seventy, but she had not disillusioned him, curiously reluctant to air her true age. And why did I do that? she asked herself; it was needless and silly.

Could anyone really die of a broken heart? Women did, in those old romantic tales so much out of fashion at the moment; she had always assumed the heroine's demise to be as much a figment of the writer's fevered imagination as the rest of the lurid plot. But perhaps it truly was so; what would she do herself were Tim to depart from her life forever, taken away by irate parents or, God forbid, by death? How grey and empty life would be if it held no Tim, how futile and useless it would be to continue in a world without Tim. He had become the nucleus of her entire existence, a fact which several people had noticed.

Mrs Emily Parker had invited herself over not long before, as, she explained, 'I don't never get to see youse at the weekends no more, do I?'

Mary had muttered something about being very busy.

'Ha ha ha!' Mrs Parker leered. 'Busy is right, eh?' She winked at Mary and poked her in the ribs good-naturedly. 'I must say you've taken quite a fancy to young Tim, Miss Horton. Them old busybodies up and down the street have their tongues wagging something scandalous.'

'I did take quite a fancy to young Tim,' Mary replied calmly, beginning to regain her equilibrium. 'He's such a nice fellow, so anxious to please, and so lonely. At first I gave him the gardening because I gathered he could do with the money, then as I got to know him I began to like him for himself, even if he isn't the full quid, as everyone calls it. He's sincere, warm, and utterly lacking in deceit. It's so refreshing to encounter someone with absolutely no ulterior motives, isn't it?' She stared at Mrs Parker blandly.

Mrs Parker stared back, outwitted. 'Um, ah, I suppose so. And you being on your own the way you are, it's real company for youse, ain't it?'

'Most certainly! Tim and I have a lot of fun together. We garden and listen to music, swim and picnic, lots of things. He has simple tastes, and he's teaching me to appreciate simplicity. I'm not a very easy person to get on with, but somehow Tim just suits me. He brings out the best in me.'

For all her nosiness, the Old Girl was kind-hearted and generally uncritical. She patted Mary on the arm encouragingly. 'Well, I'm real glad for you, duckie, I think it's nice you've found someone to keep you company, you being so alone and all. I'll soon put you right with them nasty old biddies up and down the street. I told them you wasn't the sort to buy yourself a boyfriend.

'Now how about a cuppa tea, eh? I want to hear all about young Tim, how he's getting along.'

But Mary didn't move for a moment, her face curiously expressionless. Then she looked at Mrs Parker in wonder. 'Is that what they thought?' she asked sadly. 'Is that really what they thought? How absolutely disgusting, how despicable of them! It isn't myself I care about that much, but Tim! Oh, God, how sickening!'

Mary's boss Archie Johnson was another one who had noticed the change in Mary, though he was not aware of the reason for it. They were eating a hasty lunch together in the staff cafeteria one day when Archie broached the matter.

'You know, Mary, it's none of my business and I'm quite prepared to be put in my place, but have you branched out a bit lately or something?'

She had stared at him, bewildered and caught off her guard. 'I beg your pardon, sir?'

'Oh, come off it, Mary! And don't call me "sir" or "Mr Johnson"! We're on lunch break.'

She put her knife and fork down and looked at him calmly. He and she had worked together for more years than either of them cared to count, but their relationship had always been severely restricted to business, and she still had trouble unbending sufficiently during their infrequent but obligatory social encounters.

'If you mean have I changed lately, Archie, why don't you say so? I won't be offended.'

'Well, that is what I mean. You've changed. Oh, you're still a terrible old bitch and you still frighten the living daylights out of the junior typists, but you've changed. By God, how you've changed! Even the other inhabitants of our little world have noticed it. For one thing you look better than you used to, as if you've been out in the sun instead of living under a rock like a slug. And I actually heard you laugh the other day, when that idiot Celeste was clowning around.'

She smiled faintly. 'Well, Archie, I think it can best be summarised by saying that I've finally joined the human race. Isn't that a lovely phrase? As solid and respectable a cliché as one could possibly hope for.'

'What on earth made an old maid like you join the human race after all these years? Got a boyfriend?'

'Of sorts, though not what I'm sure everyone is thinking. Sometimes, my dear Archie, there are things which can benefit an old maid much more than mere sexual gratification.'

'Oh, I agree! It's being loved that works the miracles. Mary, it's that wonderful feeling of being wanted and needed and esteemed. The sexual business is just the icing on the cake.'

'How very perspicacious of you! It's no wonder we've worked together so well for so many years. You've got lots more sense and sensitivity than the average businessman, Archie.'

'Great steaming impossibilities, Mary, but you've changed! And for the better, I might add. If you continue improving I might even ask you out to dinner.'

'By all means! I'd love to see Tricia again.'

'Who said Tricia was invited?' he grinned. 'But I might have known you hadn't changed that much! Seriously, I think Tricia would love to see the change in you for herself, so why don't you come to dinner one evening?'

'I'd love to come. Tell Tricia to call me and I'll put it in the book.'

'All right, now, enough evasion! What's the source of your new lease on life, dear?'

'I suppose you would have to say, a child, except that he's a very special kind of child.'

'A child!' He sat back, immensely pleased. 'I might have guessed it would be a child. A sea-green incorruptible like you would soften far faster under a child's influence than a man's.'

'It isn't as simple as that,' she answered slowly, amazed that she could be so relaxed and free of self-consciousness; she had never felt so comfortable with Archie before. 'His name is Tim Melville and he's twenty-five years old, but he's a child for all that. He's mentally retarded.'

'Holy man-eating toads!' Archie exclaimed, staring at her; he was addicted to coining unusual, if benign, expletives. 'How on earth did you get into that?'

'It just crept up on me, I suppose. It's hard to be defensive with someone who doesn't understand what defensiveness is, and it's even harder to hurt the feelings of someone who doesn't understand why they're being hurt.'

'Yes, it is.'

'Well, I take him to Gosford with me at weekends, and I hope to take him to the Great Barrier Reef this winter for a holiday. He genuinely seems to prefer my company to anyone else's, except his parents. They're fine people.'

'And why shouldn't he prefer your company, you old fire-eater? Swash me buckles, look at the time! I'll tell Tricia to arrange a date for dinner, then I want to hear all about it. In the meantime, old war-horse, back to the grind. Did you hear from McNaughton about the Dindanga exploration concession?'

She had been glad in a way that both Mrs Parker and Archie had accepted her friendship with Tim so casually, had been so pleased for her. The promised dinner date with Archie and his equally volatile wife had not yet happened, but she found herself looking forward to the meeting for the first time in twenty years.

When Tim saw the Bentley cruising down the street his face lit up with joy, and he jumped off the low stone wall immediately.

'Oh, Mary, I'm so glad to see you!' he exclaimed, wriggling into the front seat. 'I thought you'd forgotten.'

She took his hand and held it to her cheek for a moment, so filled with pity and remorse over being late that she forgot she had resolved never to touch him. 'Tim, I wouldn't ever do that to you. I lost my way. I got St Marks all confused in my mind with another church and lost my way, that's it. Now sit there and be happy, because I've just decided to go to Gosford.'

'Oh, goody! I thought we'd have to stay at Artarmon because it's so late.'

'No, why shouldn't we go anyway? There's plenty of time for a swim when we get there unless the water's too cold, and we can certainly cook our supper on the beach no matter how chilly it is.'

She glanced sidelong at him, savouring the contrast between his smiling happiness now and the despairing solitude of a few minutes before. 'How did the wedding go?'

'It was beautiful,' he answered seriously. 'Dawnie looked like a fairy princess, and Mum looked like a fairy godmother. She had a lovely light blue dress on, and Dawnie had a long white dress on with lots of frills and a big bunch of flowers in her hand and a long white veil on her head, like a cloud.'

'It sounds marvellous. Was everyone happy?'

'I think so,' he said dubiously, 'but Mum cried and so did Pop, only he said it was the wind made his eyes water, then he got mad at me when I said there wasn't any wind in the church. Mum said she was crying because she was so happy about Dawnie. I didn't know people cried when they were happy, Mary. I don't cry when I'm happy, I only cry when I'm sad. Why should you cry if you're happy?'

She smiled, suddenly so happy herself that she was close to tears. 'I don't know, Tim, except that sometimes it does happen that way. But when you're so happy you cry it feels different, it feels very nice.'

'Oh, I wish I could get so happy that I cried, then! Why don't I get so happy that I cry, Mary?'

'Well, you have to be quite old, I think. One of these days it might happen to you too, when you're old and grey enough.'

Perfectly satisfied now that he had been reassured, he sat back and watched the passing view, something he never seemed to tire of. He had all the insatiable curiosity of the very young, and the capacity to do the same thing over and over again without becoming bored. Each time they went to Gosford he acted as if it was the first time, as stunned with the scenery and the parade of life, as delighted to see the cottage at the end of the track, agog to discover what might have grown a little bit larger or burst into flower or withered away.

That night when Tim went to bed Mary did something she had never done before; she came into his room and tucked the blankets around him, then kissed his forehead.

'Goodnight, Tim dear, sleep well,' she said.

'Night-night, Mary, I will,' he answered drowsily; he was always half-asleep the minute his head touched the pillow.

Then, as she was closing his door softly, his voice came again: 'Mary?'

'Yes, Tim, what is it?' She turned around and came back to the bed.

'Mary, you won't ever go away and get married like my Dawnie, will you?'

She sighed. 'No, Tim, I promise I won't do that. As long as you're happy I'm here, I'll be here. Now go to sleep and don't worry about it.'

14

In the end Mary could not get away from her job to take Tim on the promised vacation. Constable Steel & Mining bought a mineral-laden piece of territory in the far northwest of the continent, and instead of going to the Great Barrier Reef with Tim, Mary found herself accompanying her boss on an inspection tour. The trip was supposed to be for a week, but ended up lasting over a month.

Usually she enjoyed these infrequent jaunts; Archie was good company and his mode of travel tended to be very luxurious. This time, however, they went to an area which lacked roads, townships, and people. The last stage of the journey had to be made by helicopter, since there was no way to get into the area from the ground, and the party camped in an unseasonal rain, perpetually wet, plagued by heat, flies, mud, and an outbreak of dysentery.

Most of all, Mary missed Tim. There was no way to send him a letter, and the radio telephone was restricted to business and emergency calls. Sitting in her dripping tent trying to scrape some of the gluey black mud from her legs and clothes, with a dense cloud of insects flocking around the solitary kerosene lamp and her face swollen from dozens of mosquito bites, Mary longed for home and Tim. Archie's exuberance at the results of the ore assay were hard to bear, and it took all her customary composure to seem even civilly enthusiastic.

'There were twelve of us in the party,' Archie told Tricia when they were safely back in Sydney again.

'Only twelve?' Mary asked incredulously, winking at Archie's wife. 'There were times when I'd have sworn there were at least fifty!'

'Listen, you bloody awful old bag, shut up and let me tell the story! Here we are just back from the worst month I've ever spent, and you're stealing my thunder already! I didn't have to ask you to spend your first night back in civilisation under my roof, but I did, so the least you can do is sit there nice and quiet and prim the way you used to be, while I tell my wife what happened!'

'Give him another whisky, Tricia, before he has an apoplectic seizure. I swear that's the reason he's so crotchety on his first night back. For the last two weeks, ever since he licked the last drop off the last bottle of scotch we had with us, he's been unbearable.'

'Well, how would you be, love?' Archie appealed to his wife. 'Permanently soaked to the skin, bitten alive by a complete spectrum of the insect world, plastered with mud, and with nothing female closer than a thousand miles except for this awful old bag? And how would you like it having nothing to eat but canned stew and then the booze running out? Sweet Bartlett pears, what a bog of a place! I would have given half the flaming ore content we found for one single big steak and a Glen Grant to wash it down!'

'You don't need to tell me,' Mary laughed, turning to Tricia impulsively. 'He nearly drove me mad! You know what he's like when he can't have his rich foods and his twelve-year scotch and his Havana cigars.'

'No, I don't know what he's like when he can't have his little comforts, dear, but thirty years of being married to him makes me shudder at the very thought of what you must have had to put up with.'

'I assure you I didn't put up with it for long,' Mary answered, sipping her sherry luxuriously. 'I took myself off for a walk after a couple of days of listening to him moaning, and shot some birds I found wallowing in a swamp so we'd at least have a change from that eternal stew.'

'What happened to the supplies, Archie?' Tricia asked curiously. 'It's most unlike you not to pop in a few little tidbits in case of emergencies.'

'Blame our glamorous outback guide. Roughly half of us were from headquarters here in Sydney, but the surveyors I picked up in Wyndham along with said guide, Mr Jim Bloody Barton. He thought he'd show us what sterling stuff real bushmen are made of, so after assuring me that he'd take care of the supplies, he stocked up with what he usually eats himself – stew, stew, and more stew!'

'Don't be too hard on the poor man, Archie,' Mary remonstrated. 'After all, we were outsiders and he was in his element. If he came to the city, wouldn't you make it your business to dazzle him with all our urban frivolities?'

'What utter codswallop, Mary! It was you took all the starch out of him, not me!' He turned to his wife. 'I just wish you could have seen her walking back into camp, love! There she was, strolling along in that ghastly British old maid uniform of hers, covered up to her belly button in stinking black mud and lumping about a dozen bloody great dead birds behind her. She'd tied their necks together with a bit of string and she was dragging them on the ground behind her, using the string like a tow-rope. I thought our glamorous Jim Barton was going to have a stroke, he was so mad!'

'He was, wasn't he?' Mary agreed complacently.

'Well, he hadn't wanted to bring Mary along in the first place, being a confirmed misogynist; reckoned she'd slow us down, be nothing but a dead weight and a bloody nuisance and a few other things. And there she was bringing us culinary salvation, just when he was sure he'd begun to show us what soft stuff we city slickers were made of. Hah! Leave it to my Mary to put him in his place! What a doughty old bird you are, love!'

'What sort of birds were they?' Tricia asked, trying to keep a straight face.

'Lord, I don't know!' Mary answered. 'Just birds, big gangly tropical ones. They were fat, which was all I was interested in.'

'But they might have been poisonous!'

Mary burst out laughing. 'What rot! To the best of my knowledge, very little out of what we call living matter is actually poisonous, and if you run the odds through a big computer, you'll find chance is on your side most of the time.'

'Barton the Bushman tried that one, too, come to think of it,' Archie grinned reminiscently. 'Mary chopped the birds up with some of the gravy out of a few cans of stew, and some sort of leaves she'd picked off a bush because she thought they smelled good. Barton the Bushman took off straight up in the air, reckoned they could be poisonous, but Mary just looked at him with that nerve-rattling stare of hers and told him that in her opinion our noses were originally designed to tell us whether things were edible or not, and her nose told her the leaves were perfectly all right. Of course they were, that goes without saying. She then proceeded to give him a long lecture on *Clostridium botulinum*, whatever that might be, which apparently grows in canned stew and is ten times as toxic as anything you can pick off a bush. Lord, did I laugh!'

'Were they happy with your cooking, Mary?' Tricia asked.

'It tasted like nectar and ambrosia rolled in one,' Archie enthused before Mary could speak. 'Holy galloping stingrays, what a meal! We gorged ourselves, while Mary sat there picking daintily at a wing with not a hair out of place and nary a smile. I tell you, Mary, you must be a local legend in Wyndham about now, with all those surveyors talking about you. You sure took the wind out of Barton the Bushman's sails!'

Tricia was helpless with laughter. 'Mary, I ought to be madly jealous of you, but thank God I don't have to be! What other wife not only doesn't need to experience the slightest twinge of jealousy because of her husband's secretary, but can also rely on her bringing him safely home from whatever mess he's landed himself in?'

'It's easier to bring him home in the long run, Tricia,' Mary said solemnly. 'If there's one thing I hate, it's the thought of breaking in a new boss.'

Tricia jumped up quickly, reaching for the sherry. 'Have another glass, Mary, please do! I never thought I'd hear myself say I was thoroughly enjoying your company, but I don't know when I've had so much fun!' She stopped, her hand going to her mouth ruefully. 'Oh, Lord! That sounded awful, didn't it? I didn't mean it that way, I meant that you've changed, come out of yourself, that's all!'

'You're only making things worse, love,' Archie said gleefully. 'Poor Mary!'

'Don't "Poor Mary!" me, Archie Johnson! I know quite well what Tricia means, and I couldn't agree with her more.'

15

When Tim knocked on the back door the first Saturday after Mary arrived back in Sydney, she went a little reluctantly to let him in. How would it be, seeing him again after this first separation? She pulled the door open in a hurry, words springing to her lips, but they never found voice; a great lump had blocked her throat, and she could not seem to clear it away to speak. He was standing on the doorstep smiling at her, love and welcome shining in his beautiful blue eyes. She reached out and took his hands in hers speechlessly, her fingers closing around them hard, the tears running down her face. This time it was he who put his arms around her and pressed her head against his chest, one hand stroking her hair.

'Don't cry, Mary,' he crooned, rubbing his palm clumsily across her head. 'I'm comforting you so you don't have to cry. There there, there there!'

But in a moment she drew away, groping for her handkerchief. 'I'll be all right, Tim, don't be upset,' she whispered, finding it and drying her eyes. She smiled at him and touched his cheek caressingly, unable to resist the temptation. 'I missed you so much that I cried from happiness at seeing you again, that's all.'

'I'm awfully glad to see you, too, but I didn't cry. Cripes, Mary, I missed you! Mum says I've been naughty ever since you went away.'

'Have you had your breakfast?' she asked, fighting to regain her composure.

'Not yet.'

'Then come and sit down while I make you something.' She looked at him hungrily, hardly able to believe that he was really there, that he had not forgotten her. 'Oh, Tim, it's so good to see you!'

He sat down at the table, his eyes never leaving her for a second as she moved about the kitchen. 'I felt sort of sick all the time you were away, Mary. It was real funny! I didn't feel like eating much, and the TV made my head ache. Even the Seaside wasn't much good, the beer didn't taste the same. Pop said I was a bloody nuisance because I wouldn't keep still or stay in one place.'

'Well, you're missing Dawnie too, you know. It must have been very lonely for you, not having Dawnie and not having me either.'

'Dawnie?' He said the name slowly, as if pondering its significance. 'Gee, I dunno! I think I sort of forgot Dawnie. It was you I didn't forget. I thought of you all the time, all the time!'

'Well, I'm back now, so it's all over and done with,' she said cheerfully. 'What shall we do this weekend? How about going up to the cottage, even though it's too cold to swim?'

His face lit up with joy. 'Oh, Mary, that sounds just great! Let's go to Gosford right now!'

She turned to look at him, smiling at him so very tenderly that Archie Johnson would not have known her. 'Not until you've had some breakfast, my young friend. You've got thin since I've been away, so we have to feed you up again.'

Chewing the last morsel of his second chop, Tim stared at her in frowning wonder.

'What's the matter?' she asked, watching him closely.

'I dunno . . . I felt funny just now, when I was comforting you . . .' He was finding it difficult to express himself, seeking words beyond his vocabulary. 'It was real funny,' he concluded lamely, unable to think of another way to put it, and aware that he had not succeeded in transmitting what he meant.

'Perhaps you felt all grown-up like your Pop, do you think? It's really a very grown-up sort of thing to do, comforting.'

The frown of frustration cleared away immediately, and he smiled. 'That's it, Mary! I felt all grown-up.'

'Have you finished? Then let's get our things together and start, because it gets dark very early these days and we want to get as much work done in the garden as we can.'

Winter in the area around Sydney hardly deserved the name, except to its thin-blooded residents. The eucalyptus forest retained its leaves, the sun shone warmly all the daylight hours, things continued to bud and blossom, life did not enter into the curiously stilled, sleeping suspension that it did in colder climes.

Mary's cottage garden was a mass of flowers: stocks and dahlias and wallflowers; the perfume saturated the air for a hundred yards around. Her lawn was much improved, and greener in the winter than at any other time. She had had the cottage painted white with a black trim, and the iron roof had been resilvered.

Driving into the little clearing where it lay, she could not help but admire it. Such a difference between how it looked now and how it had looked six months ago! She turned to Tim.

'Do you know, Tim, you're an excellent critic? See how much prettier it is, all because you said you didn't like it brown, and because you made me go to work on the garden? You were quite right, and it all looks so much nicer than it used to. It's a real pleasure to arrive these days. We must think of more things to do to keep the improvement going.'

He glowed at the unexpected praise. 'I like helping you, Mary, because you always make me feel as though I'm the full quid. You take notice of what I say. It sort of makes me think I'm just like Pop, all grown up into a man.'

She turned off the engine and looked at him gently. 'But you are all grown up into a man, Tim. I can't think of you any other way. Why shouldn't I take notice of what you say? Your suggestions and criticisms have been quite right, and so very helpful. It doesn't matter what anyone says about you, Tim, I will always think of you as being absolutely the full quid.'

He threw back his head and laughed, then twisted to show her eyes sparkling with unshed tears. 'Oh, Mary, I'm so happy I almost cried! See? I almost cried!'

She sprang out of the car. 'Come on, lazy-bones, get cracking now, no displays of maudlin sentimentality! We've had far too much of that sort of thing this morning! Off with your good clothes and into your gardening gear, we've got a lot of work to do before lunchtime.'

16

One evening not long after she returned from Archie Johnson's expedition, Mary read an article in the *Sydney Morning Herald* entitled 'Teacher of the Year.' It dealt with the remarkable success of a young schoolteacher in working with mentally retarded children, and it stimulated her to read more widely on the subject than she had. As she had seen things on the local library's shelves about mental retardation she had taken them out and pored over them, but until reading the newspaper article it had not occurred to her to delve more deeply.

The going was hard; she was forced to read with a medical dictionary at her elbow, though to a layman it was singularly unhelpful in elucidating the meaning of long, technical terms like *Porencephaly* and *Lipidosis* and *Phenylketonuria* and *Hepatolenticular Degeneration*. Indeed, many of the terms were so specialised even the medical dictionary did not list them. She waded miserably through a morass of such words, growing less and less sure of her ground, and less and less informed. In the end she went and saw the young teacher of the newspaper article, one John Martinson.

'I was an ordinary primary schoolteacher until I went to England and got accidentally drafted into a school for mentally retarded kids,' John Martinson said as he led her into the school. 'It fascinated me from the very beginning, but I didn't have any formal training in the techniques and theories, so I just had to teach them the way I would any normal kids. These are the mildly retarded children I'm referring to, of course; there are many who are totally ineducable. Anyway, I was staggered at how much they learned, how much they responded to being treated like ordinary kids. It was terribly hard work, naturally, and I had to develop a massive storehouse of patience, but I persevered with them, I wouldn't give in, and I wouldn't let them give in either. And I began to study. I went back to school myself, I did research and went all over the place looking at other people's methods. It's been a very satisfying career.'

The deep-set, dark blue eyes surveyed her keenly all the time he talked, but without curiosity; he seemed to accept her presence as a phenomenon she would explain herself in her own good time.

'So you think mildly retarded people can learn,' Mary said thoughtfully.

'There's no doubt of it. Too many uninformed people treat the mildly retarded child as more retarded than he really is, because in the long run it's easier to adopt this line than spend the staggering amount of time necessary to coax a normal response out of him.'

'Perhaps a lot of people feel they haven't got the special qualities needed,' Mary offered, thinking of Tim's parents.

'Perhaps. These kids long for approval, praise, and inclusion in normal family life, but so often they're left sitting on some outer perimeter, loved but half-ignored. Love isn't the whole answer to anything; it's an integral part of everything, but it has to be joined to patience, understanding, wisdom, and foresight when dealing with someone as complex as the mentally retarded child.'

'And you try to fuse love to all these other things?'

'Yes. We have our failures, of course, quite a few of them, but we have a larger proportion of successes than most schools of this kind. Often it's well-nigh impossible to evaluate a child accurately, either neurologically or psychologically. You have to understand that first and foremost this child is organically impaired, no matter what degree of psychological overlay may also be present. Something upstairs in the brain isn't working just as it should.'

He shrugged his shoulders and laughed at himself. 'I am sorry, Miss Horton! I haven't given you time to get a word in edgeways, have I? It's a bad habit of mine to talk the leg off my visitors without having the vaguest idea why they've come to see me.'

Mary cleared her throat. 'Well, Mr Martinson, it isn't a personal problem really, it's more an interested onlooker's curiosity which prompted me to get in touch with you. I'm very well acquainted with a young man of twenty-five who is mildly retarded, and I want to find out more about his situation. I tried reading, but I didn't understand the technical jargon very well.'

'I know. Authoritative tomes there are aplenty, but good basic books for the layman are hard to come by.'

'The thing is, since I commenced taking an interest in him, which is over the past nine months or so, he's shown signs of improving. It took a long time, but I've even taught him to read a tiny bit, and do very simple sums. His parents have noticed the change, and are quite delighted. However, I don't know how much progress I ought to expect, how hard I ought to push him.'

He patted her arm and put his hand beneath her elbow to signal her that it was time they moved on. 'I'm going to take you on a tour of our classrooms, and I want you to look at all the children very closely. Try to find one who strikes you as similar to your own young man in behaviour and attitude. We don't permit visitors to disturb our classes, so you'll find we do all our observing through one-way windows. Come with me now, and see what you think of our children.'

Mary had never really taken much notice of the scant few retarded children she had encountered during her life, for like most people she was acutely uncomfortable when caught staring. It amazed her now to discover how varied they were in physical make-up, let alone mental capacity; they ranged from children who looked quite normal to some so terribly malformed it was an effort not to turn the eyes away.

'I used to teach a class of mental giants once,' John Martinson said a little dreamily as he stood beside her. 'Not one kid in the class who rated below 150 on the old IQ scale. But do you know, I get more satisfaction out of spending a month teaching one of these kids to tie his own shoelaces? They never jade or grow bored with achieving, I suppose because they have to work so hard to achieve. The harder anything is to attain, the more one prizes it, and why should that be any the less true for a retarded human being?'

After the tour John Martinson conducted her to his little office and offered her coffee.

'Well, did you see anyone who reminded you of Tim?' he asked.

'Several.' She described them. 'There are times when I want to weep for Tim, I pity him so much,' she said. 'He's so aware of his shortcomings, you see! It's dreadful to have to listen to the poor fellow apologising because he's "not the full quid" as he terms it. "I know I'm not the full quid, Mary," he'll say, and just to hear him breaks my heart.'

'He sounds educable, though. Does he work?'

'Yes, as a builder's labourer. I suppose his workmates are kind enough to him in their way, but they're also very thoughtlessly cruel. They get a terrific kick out of playing practical jokes on him, like the time they tricked him into eating excrement. He cried that day, not because he'd been victimised but because he couldn't understand the joke. He wanted to be in on the joke!' Her face twisted, and she had to stop.

John Martinson nodded encouragement and sympathy. 'Oh, it's a pretty common sort of pattern,' he said. 'What of his mother and father, how do they treat him?'

'Very well, all considered.' She explained the circumstances of Tim's life to him, surprised at her own fluency. 'But they worry about him,' she ended sadly, 'especially about what will happen to him after they pass away. His father says he'll die of a broken heart. I didn't believe it at first, but as time goes on I'm beginning to see that it's very likely.'

'Oh, I agree, very likely. There are many such cases, you know. People like your Tim need a loving home a lot more than we normal people, because they can't learn to adjust to life without it if once they've known it. It's a very difficult world for them, this one of ours.' He considered her gravely. 'I take it, from your choice among our children who remind you of Tim, that he's quite normal to look at?'

'Normal to look at?' She sighed. 'If only he was! No, Tim's not normal to look at. Undoubtedly he's the most spectacular young man I've ever seen – like a Greek god, for want of a more original simile.'

'Oh!' John Martinson dropped his eyes from her to his folded hands for a moment, then sighed. 'Well, Miss Horton, I'll give you the titles of some books I think you'll have no trouble understanding. You'll find they'll help you.'

He rose and walked with her to the front hall, bending his head down to her courteously. 'I hope you'll bring Tim to see me one of these days. I'd very much like to meet him. Perhaps you'd better call me first, though, because I think it would be better for him if you came to my home rather than the school.'

Mary held out her hand. 'I'd like that. Goodbye, Mr Martinson, and thank you so much for your kindness.'

She went away thoughtful and saddened, conscious that the most insoluble problems are those which by their very nature can have no space within them for dreams.

17

Spring in Sydney was not the brilliant, burgeoning explosion of new growth and awakening it was in the Northern Hemisphere. All but a few kinds of imported deciduous trees retained their leaves throughout the brief, balmy winter, and there was always something flowering in Sydney gardens the year round. The greatest change was in the air, a sparkling softness that somehow filled the heart with renewed hope and joy.

Mary's cottage would have been the showplace of the district, could anyone have seen it. She and Tim had worked hard on the garden all through the winter, even going so far as to buy fully grown trees and having them planted by a specialist. So when October came there were flowers everywhere, massed in huge beds alongside the veranda and circling every tree. Iceland poppies, carnations, asters, pansies, phlox, sweet peas, tulips, wistaria, daffodils, hyacinths, azaleas, gladioli; flowers of every colour, size, and shape splashed their crowded heads in sheets of beauty everywhere, and the wind carried their perfumes through the wild forest and out across the river.

Four exquisitely sad weeping cherries drooped their loaded pink branches down over pink hyacinths and tulips growing in the grass beneath them, and six flowering almonds creaked under a weight of white blossom, the grass around them smothered with lily of the valley and daffodils.

The first weekend that everything was fully out in flower, Tim went wild with delight. He capered from cherries to almonds, marvelling at Mary's shrewdness in choosing only pink bulbs to surround the cherries and white and yellow for the almonds, exclaiming at how they looked as if they grew wild out of the grass. Mary watched him, smiling in spite of all her resolutions to be serious no matter how he reacted. His joy was so transparent, so tender and experimental; Paris wandering the springtime slopes of Mount Ida before returning to the drudgery of an urban Troy.

It was indeed a beautiful garden, Mary thought, her eyes following Tim as he danced about, but how did he see it, how different did it appear in his eyes, that it awed and delighted him so? Insects and even some higher animals were supposed to see a different world through differently constructed eyes, see colours and shapes a human being could not; what shade was infrared, what hue was ultraviolet? Perhaps Tim, too, saw things beyond her ken; perhaps among all the other tangled circuits in his brain he saw a different spectrum and heard a different frequency band. Did he hear the music of the spheres, could he see the shape of the spirit and the colour of the moon? If there was only some way to tell! But his world was forever barred, she could not enter it and he could not tell her what it was like.

'Tim,' she said that night, as they sat in the darkened living room with the glass doors open to the perfume-saturated wind, 'Tim, what do you feel now, at this moment? What do the flowers smell like, how do you see my face?'

He withdrew himself reluctantly from the music they were playing, turning his dream-clouded eyes upon her mistily, smiling in the gentle, almost vacant way he had. Her heart seemed to quiver and dissolve under that look, something unidentifiable welled up in her, so surrounded by sadness that she had to wink away tears.

He was frowning as he puzzled over the questions, and when he answered it was slowly, hesitantly. 'Feel? Feel? Cripes, I dunno! Sort of happy, good. I feel good, that's it!'

'And what do the flowers smell like?'

He smiled at her, thinking she was joking. 'Why, they smell like flowers, of course!'

'And my face?'

'Your face is beautiful, like Mum's and Dawnie's. It looks like Saint Teresa in my holy picture.'

She sighed. 'That's a lovely thing to say, Tim. I'm sure I never thought of myself as having a face like Saint Teresa.'

'Well, it is,' he assured her. 'She's on the wall at the end of my bed at home, Mum put her up there because I like her, I like her. She looks at me every night and every morning as though she thinks I'm the full quid, and you look at me like that, too, Mary.' He shivered, gripped by a kind of painful joy. 'I like you, Mary, I like you better than Dawnie, I like you as much as I like Pop and Mum.' The beautifully shaped hands moved, and said more in their moving than his poor, limited speech ever could. 'But it's sort of different, Mary, different from Pop and Mum. Sometimes I like them better than you, and sometimes I like you better than them.'

She got up abruptly and went to the doors. 'I'm going outside for a little walk, Tim, but I want you to stay here like a good fellow and listen to the music. I'll be back soon.'

He nodded and turned back to the record player, watching it fixedly, as though to do so helped him hear the music.

The scent of the garden was unbearable, and passing through the daffodils like a shadow she made her way down to the beach. There was a rock in the sand at the far end, just tall enough to serve as a back rest, but when Mary dropped to her knees in the sand she turned to face it, put her arms upon it and buried her face against them. Her shoulders drew together and her body twisted in a spasm of devastating grief, so desolate and despairing that for a moment a part of her held back from participating, horrified. But the grief could not be suppressed or denied any longer; she wept and moaned in pain.

They were like a moth and a bright, burning light, she and Tim; she the moth, endowed with senses and the dignity of life, he the light, filling her entire world with a brilliant, searing fire. He did not know how desperately she buffeted herself against the walls of his isolation, he could never comprehend the depth and urgency of her desire to immolate herself on the flame of his fascination. Fighting the uselessness of her hunger and knowing it was beyond him to appease it, she ground her teeth in rage and pain and wept inconsolably.

What must have been hours later she felt his hand on her shoulder.

'Mary, are you all right?' His voice was filled with fear. 'Are you sick? Oh, Mary, please say you're all right, please say you're all right!'

She forced her shaking arms down to her sides. 'I'm all right, Tim,' she answered wearily, lowering her head so that he could not see her face, even though it was very dark. 'I just felt a bit sick, and came out for a breath of air. I didn't want to worry you, that's all.'

'Do you still feel sick?' He squatted on his haunches beside her and tried to peer into her face, stroking her shoulder clumsily. 'Were you sick?'

She shook her head, inching away from his hand. 'No, I'm all right now, Tim, really I am. It passed off.' One hand on the rock for leverage, she tried to get to her feet but could not, cramped and defeated. 'Oh, Tim, I'm so old and tired,' she whispered. 'I'm so old and tired.'

He stood up and stared at her anxiously, fidgeting nervously. 'Mum was sick once and I remember Pop made me carry her to bed. I'll carry you to bed, Mary.'

He bent and gathered her up effortlessly, shifting her weight within his arms until one was crooked under her knees and the other cradled her back. Too exhausted to protest, she let him carry her up the path, but when he stepped onto the veranda she turned her face into his shoulder, not wanting him to see it. He paused, blinking in the light, and put his cheek against her head lovingly.

'You're so small, Mary,' he said, rubbing his face back and forth across her hair. 'You're all soft and warm, like a kitten.' Then he sighed and crossed the living room.

He could not find the light switch in her bedroom, and when he would have groped for it she stopped him, her hand pressing gently at his throat.

'Don't worry about the light, Tim, you can see to put me on the bed. I just want to lie down in the dark for a while, then I'll be fine.'

He laid her on the bed carefully, looming above her in the darkness, and she sensed his worried indecision.

'Tim, you know I wouldn't tell you a lie, don't you?'

He nodded. 'Yes, I know that.'

'Then you'll believe me when I tell you that there's no need to worry about me, that I'm all right now. Haven't you ever felt a bit sick after you've eaten something that didn't agree with you?'

'Yes, I did once, after I'd eaten some candied fruit,' he answered gravely.

'Then you understand how I felt, don't you? Now I want you to stop worrying about me and go to bed, and sleep, sleep! I feel much better and all I need is to sleep, too, but I can't sleep if I think you're upset or worried. Now promise me that you'll go straight to bed and be happy.'

'I will, Mary.' He sounded relieved.

'Goodnight, Tim, and thank you very much for helping me like that. It's so nice to be looked after, and you look after me very well. I don't ever need to worry about myself while I've got you, do I?'

'I'll always look after you, Mary.' He stooped and kissed her forehead, the way she sometimes did with him when he was in bed. 'Night-night, Mary.'

18

When Esme Melville let herself in the back door after her Thursday afternoon tennis match it was all she could do to walk the few yards more to the living room and a comfortable chair. Her legs were shaking; it had been a tremendous strain to get home without letting anyone see how distressed she was. She felt so nauseated that after a few moments in the chair she got up and went to the bathroom. Even kneeling with her head over the lavatory bowl didn't relieve the sickness; somehow she could not vomit, the pain under her left shoulder blade made the effort of retching unbearable. She hung there for several minutes panting, then dragged herself by stages to her feet, grasping at the bathroom cupboard and the shower door. It shocked her to realise that the frightened face in the wall mirror was her own, all muddy grey and beaded with sweat. The sight of it terrified her more than anything ever had, and she took her eyes away from the mirror immediately. She managed to stagger back to the living room and flopped into the chair, gasping, her hands flapping about helplessly.

Then the pain took her and tore at her like some huge, maddened beast; she leaned forward, her arms folded across her chest, their fists digging into her armpits. Small, moaning whimpers escaped her each time the knifelike agony worked itself up to a crescendo, and she could think no further than the pain. After an eternity it lessened; she leaned back in the chair, spent and shaking in every limb. Something seemed to be sitting on her chest, forcing all the air out of her lungs and making it impossible to suck in more. She was wet everywhere; the white tennis dress was soaked with sweat, her face with tears, the chair seat with urine she had voided during the worst of her rigours. Sobbing and choking through purpled lips, she sat there praying that Ron would think to come home before going to the Seaside. The phone in the hall was light-years away, absolutely beyond her.

It was seven that evening before Ron and Tim let themselves in the back door of the house in Surf Street. All was oddly quiet and undisturbed; no places had been laid on the dining room table, and there was no friendly smell of food.

'Hullo, where's Mum?' Ron asked cheerily as he and Tim stepped into the kitchen. 'Es, love, where are youse?' he called, then shrugged. 'Must have decided on a couple of extra sets at the Hit and Giggle Club,' he said.

Tim went on into the living room while Ron switched on the kitchen and dining room lights. There was a terrified scream from the interior of the house; Ron dropped the kettle he was holding and dashed with pounding heart to the living room. Tim was standing wringing his hands together and weeping, staring at Esme as she lay in the chair, curiously still, her arms folded and her hands knotted into fists in her sides.

'Oh, God!'

The tears sprang to Ron's eyes as he went to the chair and bent over his wife, reaching out a shaking hand to touch her skin. It was warm; hardly able to believe it, he discovered that her chest was rising and falling slowly. He got to his feet at once.

'Now, Tim, don't cry,' he said through chattering teeth. 'I'm going to ring Dr Perkins and Dawnie, then I'll come right back. You stay here, and if Mum does anything, you yell. All right, mate?'

Dr Perkins was at home, eating supper; he told Ron that he would call an ambulance and meet them at Prince of Wales Hospital casualty room. Wiping away the tears with the back of his hand, Ron dialled Dawnie's number.

Mick answered, his voice betraying his impatience; it was their dinner hour, and he hated to be disturbed then.

'Listen, Mick, it's Ron here,' Ron said, enunciating carefully. 'Now don't go frightening Dawnie, but it's her Mum. I think she's had a heart attack, only I'm not sure. We're getting her to Prince of Wales casualty immediately, so there's no point in coming here. It would be best for you and Dawnie to meet us at the hospital as soon as you possibly can.'

'I'm terribly sorry, Ron,' Mick mumbled. 'Of course Dawn and I will come immediately. Try not to worry.'

When Ron came back to the living room, Tim was still standing watching his mother and weeping desolately; she had not moved.

Ron put his arm around his son's shoulders and hugged him, not knowing what else to do.

'Jeez, don't cry, Tim me boy,' he muttered. 'Mum's all right, the ambulance is coming and we're going to get her to the hospital. They'll fix her up in no time. You've got to be a good bloke and be calm, for Mum's sake. She won't like it if she wakes up and sees you standing there howling like a great big booby, will she?'

Snuffling and hiccoughing, Tim tried to stop crying while his father approached Esme's chair and knelt down, taking her doubled fists in his hands and forcing them into her lap.

'Es!' he called, his face old and lined. 'Es, love, can you hear me? It's Ron, love, it's Ron!'

She was grey in the face and shrunken, but her eyes opened. They flooded with light as they saw him kneeling there, and she returned his clasp gratefully.

'Ron . . . Jeez, I'm glad you come home . . . Where's Tim?'

'He's here, love. Don't worry about Tim, now, and don't go getting all upset. The ambulance is coming and we're going to get you into POW right away. How do you feel?'

'Like something the . . . cat dragged in . . . Oh, Christ, Ron . . . the pain . . . it's awful . . . I wet meself . . . The chair's sopping . . .'

'Don't worry about the bloody furniture, Es, it'll dry out. What's the odd leak between friends, eh?' He tried to smile, but his face twisted. For all his control, he began to weep. 'Oh, Es, don't let nothing happen to youse, love! Oh, God, what will I do without youse? Hang on, Es, hang on until we get you to hospital!'

'I'll . . . hang on . . . Can't . . . leave Tim . . . all alone now . . . Can't . . . leave Tim . . . alone . . .'

Five minutes after Ron called Dr Perkins the ambulance was outside. Ron directed the ambulance men around to the back door, for there were twenty steps up to the front door and none to the back. They were big, quietly cheerful men, highly trained professionals in the field of emergency medicine; as aware of their skill as other Sydneysiders, Ron felt no qualms over Dr Perkins' decision to meet them at the hospital. They checked Es's condition swiftly and lifted her onto the stretcher. Ron and Tim followed their navy blue uniforms out the back door, feeling useless and unwanted.

Ron put Tim in the front with one of the ambulance men and rode in the back with the other. They seemed to know immediately that Tim was not the full quid, for the one who was driving settled Tim in the adjoining seat with a cheery word that seemed to have more effect on him than anything Ron could have said.

They did not put the siren on; the one travelling in the back with Ron slipped a plastic airway into Es's mouth and connected her to his oxygen supply, then draped himself along the stretcher with his hand on her pulse.

'Why don't you put the siren on?' Ron asked, looking about wildly, the oxygen and airway frightening him.

Wide, reassuringly steady eyes gazed back at him; the ambulance man patted him on the back. 'Now take it easy, mate,' he said calmly. 'We only put the siren on going to an emergency case, very rarely when there's someone inside. It terrifies the patient, does more harm than good, you know. She's okay, and at this time of night we'll get there just as soon without a siren. Only a couple of miles.'

The ambulance threaded its way deftly through the thin traffic, drawing in to the brilliantly lit casualty room at the Prince of Wales Hospital five minutes after leaving Surf Street. Just as the sleek big car came to a halt, Es opened her eyes and coughed out the airway. The ambulance man assessed her rapidly, then decided to leave it out unless she went into another spasm. Maybe she wanted to say something, and that was important; it was better to let a patient find her own level, less distressing.

'Ron . . .'

'I'm here, love. You're at the hospital, we'll soon have you fixed up now.'

'I dunno . . . Ron . . .'

'Yes, love?' The tears were running down his face again.

'It's Tim . . . What we . . . always worried about . . . What's . . . going . . . to happen to . . . Tim . . . when I'm not . . . here? . . . Ron . . .'

'I'm here, love.'

'Look after . . . Tim . . . Do the . . . right . . . thing . . . for . . . Tim . . . Poor Tim . . . Poor . . . Tim . . .'

It was the last thing she ever said. While Ron and Tim were still milling futilely around casualty entrance, the emergency staff had whisked the stretcher away out of sight. The Melville men stood watching the white doors flap to a stop, then were directed firmly but gently to the waiting area. Someone came not long afterwards and brought them tea with some sweet biscuits, smilingly refusing to give them any news.

Dawnie and her husband arrived half an hour later. Dawnie was beginning to be very pregnant, her husband plainly anxious for her. She waddled to her father's side and sat between him and Tim on the bench, weeping.

'Now, now, love, don't cry,' Ron comforted. 'The old girl will be all right, we got her here okay. They've taken her off somewhere, and when there's any news they'll tell us. You just sit down and stop crying. Think of the baby, love, you mustn't get into a taking at this stage.'

'What happened?' Mick asked, lighting a cigarette and trying not to stare at Tim.

'I dunno. When Tim and I come home she was lying unconscious in a chair in the living room. I dunno how long she'd been there. Christ, why didn't I go straight home from work, why did I go to the Seaside? I could of gone home for once!'

Dawnie blew her nose. 'Pop, don't blame yourself. You know you always come home at the same time during the week, how were you to know today she'd need you? You know she didn't mind your habits! She liked to see you enjoy your little drop after work, and besides, it gave her the chance to lead her own life. Many's the time I've heard her say it was such a break for her knowing you wouldn't be home from the Seaside before seven, because she could play her tennis until six and still have a meal ready for you and Tim when you came in.'

'I oughta knowed she was getting on and not too well, I oughta seen it for meself.'

'Pop, there's no point in recrimination! What's done is done. Mum wouldn't have wanted her life or yours any other way, and you know it. Don't waste time fretting over things you can't undo, love, think of her and Tim instead.'

'Oh, Christ, I am!' His tone was despairing.

They turned to look at Tim, sitting quietly on the seat with his hands clenched together, his shoulders hunched in the withdrawn pose he always assumed when grief-stricken. He had stopped weeping, his eyes fixed on something they could not see. Dawnie wriggled closer to her brother.

'Tim!' she said softly, her small square hand stroking his arm.

He flinched, then seemed to become aware of her. The blue

eyes transferred their gaze from infinity to her face, and he stared at her sadly.

'Dawnie!' he said, as if wondering what she was doing there.

'I'm here, Tim. Now don't worry about Mum, she's going to be all right, I promise.'

He shook his head. 'Mary says you should never make promises you can't keep.'

Dawnie's face stiffened dangerously, and she turned her attention back to Ron, ignoring Tim completely.

The night was very old when Dr Perkins came into the waiting room, his face drawn and fatigued. They all rose at once, like condemned men as the judge pulls on his cap.

'Ron, may I see you outside?' he asked quietly.

The corridor was deserted, the spotlights dotted down the centre of the high ceiling flooding the tiled floor crudely. Dr Perkins put his arm about Ron's shoulders.

'She's gone, mate.'

There seemed to be a terrible, dragging weight in Ron's chest; he looked into the elderly doctor's face pitifully.

'You don't mean it!'

'There was nothing we could do. She'd had a massive heart attack, and then she had another one a few minutes after she got here. Her heart stopped. We tried to get it going again, but it was useless, useless. I suspect she must have had trouble before today, and this sudden cold spell of weather plus the tennis didn't help.'

'She never told me she was sick, I didn't know. But that's Es, never complains.' Ron had good control now, he could manage. 'Oh, Doctor, I dunno what to do! There's Tim and Dawnie in there, thinking she's all right!'

'Do you want me to tell them, Ron?'

Ron shook his head. 'No, I'll do it. Just give me a minute. Can I see her?'

'Yes. But keep Tim and Dawnie away.'

'Then take me to her now, Doctor, before I tell them.'

They had wheeled Es out of the intensive care unit and put her in a small side room reserved for such occasions. All the evidence of her medical treatment was gone, the tubes and cables; a sheet was drawn up over her head. It struck Ron like a mammoth fist as he stood in the doorway, looking at the utterly quiet form outlined beneath the drape. That was Es there, under the sheet, and she could never move again; it was all over for her, the sun and laughter, the tears and the rain. No more, no more. Her portion of life's feast was ended, here like this in a dimly lit room with a snowy white cloth to cover her. No fanfare, no warning. No chance to prepare, not even the time for a proper goodbye. Just finished, over, done with. He approached the bed, suddenly conscious of a sickly sweet smell of jonquils stealing from a huge vase on a nearby table. Never afterwards could he bear the smell of jonquils.

Dr Perkins stood on the far side of the narrow bed and twitched the sheet back quickly, then turned his head away; could one ever grow used to the grief in another's face, could one ever learn to accept death?

They had closed her eyes and folded her hands across her breast; Ron looked at her for a long moment, then leaned over to kiss her lips. But it was not like kissing Es. Those bleached, cold lips brought nothing to him of Es. Sighing, he turned away.

In the waiting room, three pairs of eyes riveted themselves on his face when he came in. He stood looking at them, squaring his shoulders.

'She's gone,' he said.

Dawnie cried out and let herself be taken into Mick's arms; Tim just sat staring at his father like a lost and bewildered child. Ron came over and took his son's hand very tenderly.

'Let's go for a little walk, mate,' he said.

They left the waiting room and the corridor behind them, heading for the open air. Outside it was growing light, and the eastern rim of the world was pearly with the first flush of rose and gold. The little dawn wind puffed itself in their faces softly and sighed away again.

'Tim, there's no use letting you think Mum's ever going to come back,' Ron said wearily. 'Mum died a little while ago. She's gone, mate, gone. She can't never come back no more, she's gone away from us to a better life, no more pain or sadness. We're going to have to learn to get along without her, and it's going to be awful, awful hard . . . But she wanted us to carry on without her, it was the last thing she said, to carry on and not to miss her too much. We will at first, but after a while, when we're used to it, it won't be quite so bad.'

'Can't I see her before she goes, Pop?' Tim asked desolately.

His father shook his head, swallowing painfully. 'No, mate. You can't see her ever again. But you mustn't blame her for that, it wasn't the way she wanted it, to go off so suddenly with never a chance to say goodbye. Sometimes things get out of our control, things happen too fast for us to catch up with them, and then it's too late. Mum died like that, too soon, too soon . . . Her time had come and there was nothing she could do to push it away, you see, mate.'

'Is she really and truly dead, Pop?'

'Yes, she's really and truly dead, Tim.'

Tim lifted his head to the cloudless sky; a seagull screeched and wheeled far above them, dipping towards the alien earth and then soaring in search of its watery home.

'Mary told me what dead was, Pop. I know what it is. Mum's gone to sleep, she's gone to sleep in the ground under a blanket of grass and she's going to rest there until we all go too, isn't she?'

'That's about the size of it, mate.'

When they came back to the casualty room, Dr Perkins was waiting for them. He sent Tim in to be with Dawnie and Mick, but detained Ron.

'Ron, there are arrangements to be made.'

Ron quivered. 'Oh, God! Doctor, what do I do? I don't have the faintest idea!'

Dr Perkins told him about undertakers, and offered to call one particular man for Ron.

'He's good and kind, Ron,' the doctor explained. 'He won't charge you more than you can afford and he handles it all very quietly, with a minimum of fuss and glorification. She'll have to be buried tomorrow, you know, because the day after is Sunday and they should be buried within forty-eight hours. It's the hot climate. Don't embalm her, what's the point of it? Just let her alone. I'll tell Mortimer you're an old family of mine, and he'll take care of everything. Now why don't you call a taxi and take your family home?'

When they let themselves into the deserted house Dawnie seemed to come to life a little, and busied herself making breakfast. Ron went through to the phone and called Mary Horton. She answered at once, which relieved him; he had dreaded finding her muddled with sleep.

'Miss Horton, it's Ron Melville here. Listen, I know it's an awful lot to ask, but I'm desperate. My wife died this morning, it was very sudden . . . Yes, thanks very much, Miss Horton . . . Yes, I am sort of numb . . . Yes, I'll try to get some rest . . . What

I rang you about was Tim . . . yes, he knows, I couldn't see the sense in keeping it from him, he had to know sometime, and why not now? . . . Thanks, Miss Horton, I'm real glad you think I done the right thing in telling him. I'm awful grateful to you, too, for explaining dying to him . . . Well, it was a terrific help, it really was . . . No, it wasn't nearly as hard making him understand as I thought it would be. I thought it would take me all day to get it through to him, but he took it like a regular little trump . . . Yes, he's all right, he's accepting it very well, no tears or tantrums. He was the one who found her, terrible. Miss Horton, I know you work all week, but I know you're real fond of Tim, so I'm going to get up my courage to ask if you could come out and see me today, real soon, and maybe take Tim off with you until Sunday. She's being buried tomorrow, can't be buried the day after because it's Sunday. I don't want him at the funeral . . . All right, Miss Horton, I'll be here and so will Tim . . . Thanks very, very much, I do appreciate it . . . Yes, I'll try, Miss Horton. See you soon. Bye bye now, and thanks again.'

Dawnie took Tim out into the garden while Ron talked to Mr Mortimer the undertaker, who was indeed all that Dr Perkins had promised. A death in an Australian working-class family was neither an expensive nor a long-drawn-out affair, and rigid laws made exploitation of the bereaved difficult. Uncomplicated, earthy people, they felt no compulsion to make up a lifetime of real or imagined guilts to a corpse; no opulent coffins, wakes, or putting the body on display. It was all conducted quickly and quietly, so much so that often friends and neighbours would have known little about it except for the gossip grapevine.

Shortly after the undertaker left, Mary Horton parked her Bentley in the street outside the Melville house and mounted the steps to the front door. Word had got around the vicinity during the early morning, and many front windows showed telltale rifts in their curtains as Mary disappeared onto the front veranda to wait for an answer to her knock.

Dawnie's husband, Mick, opened the door, and stared at Mary in bewilderment. For a moment he thought she was someone professionally connected with the undertaker, and said, 'Oh, you've just missed Mr Mortimer, he left about five minutes ago.'

Mary looked at him appraisingly. 'You must be Dawn's husband. I'm Mary Horton, and I've come to fetch Tim. But please, would you quietly let Mr Melville know I'm here first, don't mention my arrival to Tim? I'll wait here.'

Mick shut the door and trod down the long hallway, his thoughts in confusion. From what the Melvilles said he had gathered Miss Horton was an old lady, but though the woman on the front veranda had white hair, she was far from old. Ron was trying to interest Tim in a television programme; Mick wriggled his brows mutely towards the front door, and Ron got up at once, closing the door between the hallway and the living room as he went out.

'Dawn, Miss Horton's here,' Mick whispered as he sat down beside her.

She looked at him curiously. 'So?'

'She's not old, Dawn! Why do you speak of her as if she's Ron's age? I could hardly believe my eyes when I opened the front door! She can't be more than forty-five, if she's that old!'

'What on earth's the matter with you, Mick? Of course she's old! I admit I didn't get a good look at her that night I saw her outside in her car, but it was close enough to tell she was old. And her hair's whiter than Pop's!'

'People can go white at twenty, you know that. I tell you she's a relatively young woman!'

Dawnie sat in silence for a moment, then shook her head, smiling wryly. 'The sly old bezom! So that was her game!'

'What was her game?'

'Tim, of course! She's sleeping with him!'

Mick whistled. 'Of course! But wouldn't your parents have suspected something like that? They watch him so carefully, Dawn.'

'Mum wouldn't hear a word against her precious Miss Horton, and Pop's been like the cat that swallowed the canary ever since Tim began bringing home the extra money Miss Mary Horton pays him for doing her garden. Hah! Doing her garden, indeed!'

Mick shot a quick glance towards Tim. 'Keep your voice down, Dawn!'

'Oh, I could kill Pop for turning a blind eye!' Dawnie said through clenched teeth. 'All along I've thought there was something suspicious about that woman, but Pop wouldn't hear a word of it. Okay, I can understand Mum not suspecting, but Pop should have listened to me! Too busy thinking of all that extra money coming in!'

Ron in his turn gaped at Mary Horton, shocked out of his numbness for a moment. 'Are *you* Miss Horton?' he croaked, voice cracking from the long hours and the strain.

'Yes, I'm Mary Horton. Did you think I was an old lady too, Mr Melville?'

'Yes, I did.' He recollected himself sufficiently to hold the door fully open. 'Won't you come in, Miss Horton? I hope you don't mind stepping into the front bedroom for a minute before I take you through to Tim.'

'Of course not.' She followed Ron into the bedroom, ill at ease; this looked like the master bedroom, and she wondered how Ron would hold up under the stress of talking to her in the place where he and his wife had lain each night for years. But he scarcely seemed to be aware of his surroundings; he could not take his eyes from her face. She was nothing like the person he had imagined, and yet she was exactly like the person he had imagined. Her face was young and unlined, she could not be more than forty-five, if that. But it was not a rapacious, intensely feminine face, it was a kind, slightly stern face with a touch of suffering about it, in the fierce brown eyes and the determined mouth. Her hair was very white, like crystal. In spite of the shock of discovering she was much younger than he had thought, Ron trusted that face and the person who owned it. A severely handsome sort of exterior, he decided, a fitting exterior for Mary Horton, whom he always thought of as one of the kindest, most generous, and understanding people ever to enter his life.

'Mr Melville, I'm at a loss for words. I'm so very sorry for this, for you and Tim and Dawnie . . .'

'I know, Miss Horton. Please don't try, I understand. It's a terrible blow, but we'll weather it. I'm only sorry Es never met you. We just never seemed to get around to it, did we?'

'No, we didn't, and I'm sorry for that, too. How is poor Tim?'

'A bit dazed, like. He don't quite know what's happening, except that Mum's dead. I'm awful sorry to have to bring youse into this, but I just don't know what else to do. I can't let Tim come to the funeral, and he shouldn't be left on his own while the rest of us go.'

'I quite agree. I'm so glad you thought to call me, Mr Melville, and you can rest assured I'll take good care of Tim for you. I was wondering if this Sunday night coming I could drive you and Tim up to my cottage and have you stay there for a while, to get over it in different surroundings. I'll keep Tim in Sydney today, tomorrow, and Sunday, then on Sunday evening I'll come back here and collect you, then drive you both up to my cottage. Would that be all right?'

Ron's face twisted for a moment, then composed itself. 'That's real considerate of you, Miss Horton, and for Tim's sake I'll take youse up on it, too. His boss and my boss won't mind if we take a week off.'

'Then it's all settled. Dawnie would be better off with her husband, don't you think? It will take a load off her mind to know that you and Tim aren't sitting here in the house all alone.'

'That's right, it will take a load off her mind. She's just about eight months gone with the baby.'

'Oh, I didn't know!' Mary wet her lips and tried not to look at the old double bed against the far wall. 'Shall we go and say hullo to Tim now?'

It was a curious little group in the living room. Mick and Dawnie sat huddled together on the sofa and Tim sat in his special chair, hunched over and leaning forward, his unseeing eyes fixed on the television set. Mary stood in the hall doorway quietly, watching him; he had his lost look about him, defenceless and bewildered.

'Hullo, Tim,' she said.

He leaped to his feet, half overjoyed and half too saddened to feel joy, then stood with his face twitching and his hands going out to her. She went to him and took them, smiling at him tenderly.

'I've come to take you to my house for a little while, Tim,' she said softly.

He snatched his hands away sharply, flushing; for the first time since knowing him Mary saw him uncomfortable and quite conscious of his actions. Involuntarily his eyes had gone to Dawnie, seen her outrage and revulsion, and something in him was developed and mature enough to sense that Dawnie thought he had done something unpardonable, that she condemned him for holding this beloved woman's hands. His own hands fluttered to his sides, lonely and empty again, and he stood looking at his sister pleadingly. She compressed her lips and sidled to her feet like a fizzing cat, eyes flashing angrily from Tim to Mary.

Mary walked forward with her hand extended. 'Hullo, Dawnie, I'm Mary Horton,' she said pleasantly.

Dawnie ignored the hand. 'What are you doing here?' she spat.

Mary pretended not to notice her tone. 'I've come for Tim,' she explained.

'Oh, I'll just bet you have!' Dawnie sneered. 'Look at you! My mother not cold and here you are with your tongue hanging out for poor, stupid Tim! What do you mean, tricking us into thinking you were old? A fine lot of fools you've made us out to be, and in front of my husband at that!'

'Oh, for Christ's sake, Dawnie, pipe down!' Ron interrupted desperately.

Dawnie turned on him furiously. 'I'll pipe down when I've said what I intend to say, you greedy old bastard! Selling your own dill-brained son every weekend for a few measly dollars! Did it feel good, guzzling your extra beer in the Seaside every day? Did you ever stop to think of the disgrace? Look at her, trying to brazen it out as though her interest in Tim was pure and spiritual and completely altruistic! Well, *Miss* Mary Horton,' she hissed, whipping round to face Mary again, 'I'm a wakeup to your little game! Tricking us all into thinking you were at least ninety! I wonder how many people up and down Surf Street are laughing their heads off right now because they just got a good long daylight look at Tim's weekend hostess? You've made us the laughingstock of the whole district, you frustrated old cow! If you had to have a man, why the hell couldn't you have bought yourself a gigolo instead of preying on a mental weakling like my poor, silly brother? You're a disgusting, loathsome, wicked woman! Why don't you get your ugly carcass out of here and leave us alone?'

Mary stood in the centre of the living room with her hands limply by her sides, two bright patches of colour flaring in her cheeks. The tears trickled down her face in mute protest at the appalling accusation; she was so shocked and devastated by it that she could do nothing to justify herself; she had neither the energy nor the will to fight back. Ron had begun to shake, clenching his hands together so tightly that his knuckles showed as bloodless splotches. Tim had gone to his chair and collapsed on it, his upturned face swivelling from the accuser to the accused. He was confused, anguished, and strangely ashamed, but the reason for it was quite beyond him; he could not fathom it. It seemed as though Dawnie thought it was wrong for him to be friends with Mary, but why was it wrong, how could it be wrong? What had Mary done? It didn't seem fair for Dawnie to scream at Mary like that, but he didn't know what to do about it because he didn't understand what it was all about. And why did he want to run away and hide himself in some dark corner, as he had the time he stole Mum's tennis club cake?

Ron shivered, trying to control his anger. 'Dawnie, I don't never want to hear you saying things like that ever again, do you hear? What in God's name is the matter with you, girl? A real decent woman like Miss Horton! Struth and little apples, she don't have to stand here and listen to scut like this! You've disgraced me, you've disgraced Tim, and you've disgraced your poor dead mother, and at a time like this! Oh, God, Dawnie, what makes you say things like that?'

'I say them because I think they're true,' Dawnie retorted, huddling herself on the sofa within Mick's arm. 'You've let her filthy money make you blind and deaf!'

Mary passed a trembling hand across her face, wiping away the tears. She looked directly at Dawnie and her husband. 'You're very, very wrong, my dear,' she managed to say. 'I understand how shocked and upset you are by all that's happened in the last few hours, and I'm sure you don't really think any of the things you're saying.' She drew a shuddering breath. 'I didn't deliberately conceal my age, it just never seemed that important, because I never thought for one moment that anyone would interpret Tim's and my relationship on such a basic plane. I'm very deeply attached to Tim, but not in the way you're implying. It isn't very complimentary to me; I'm old enough to be Tim's and your mother, you know. And you're quite right, too: if I wanted a man I could afford to go out and buy a gold-plated gigolo. Why indeed should I employ Tim on such a project? Can you in all honesty say that you've seen any evidence of sexual awakening in Tim since he's known me? If it had occurred, you would have seen it immediately: Tim's far too transparent a creature to conceal anything as deep-reaching as that. I've enjoyed Tim so much in, if you'll pardon my hackneyed choice of words, such a pure and innocent way. Tim *is* pure and innocent, it's part of his allure. I wouldn't change that in him if I had ten thousand carnal demons gnawing at my flesh incessantly. And now you've spoiled it, spoiled it for us both, because if Tim can't understand, he can at the very least sense change. It was in its way so perfect, and I use the past tense deliberately. It can never be so again. You've made me conscious of something I hadn't considered, and you've made

Tim feel uncomfortable when he extends normal affection to me.'

Mick cleared his throat. 'But surely, Miss Horton, you must have had some inkling of what other people were bound to think. I find it hard to believe that you, a mature and responsible woman, could go on month after month spending all your free time with a young and extremely good-looking man without so much as a passing thought as to what other people must be thinking?'

'So that's it!' Ron roared, dragging Mick off the couch and holding him by his lapels. 'I might have known my girl Dawnie didn't think of all that muck-raking bullshit without some help from you! You certainly are a fast worker, mate! Between answering the door to Miss Horton and her coming into this room ten minutes later you managed to plant your filthy suggestions in my daughter's mind so bloody well that she's shamed and disgraced us all! You cocktail drinking shirt-lifter! Christ, why couldn't Dawnie have married a dinkum bloke instead of a simpering, stuck-up pansy like you? I oughta kick your teeth in, you miserable, rotten, fucking *arsehole*!'

'Pop!' Dawnie gasped, grabbing at her waistline. 'Oh, Pop!' She burst into tears, drumming her heels on the floor.

Then Tim moved, so suddenly that it took the rest of them several seconds to realise what had happened. Ron and Mick were separated, Mick put back on the sofa and Dawnie and Ron thrust into chairs, all without a word. Tim turned his back on Mick and touched his father lightly on the shoulder.

'Pop, don't let him get your goat,' he said earnestly. 'I don't like him either, but Mum said we had to treat him real well, even if we don't like him. Dawnie belongs to him now, that's what Mum said.'

Mary began to laugh in shivering, gasping gusts; Tim went to her side and put his arm about her.

'Are you laughing or crying, Mary?' he asked, peering into her face. 'Don't take any notice of Dawnie or Mick, they're upset. Why can't we go now? Can't I pack my case?'

Ron was staring at his son in amazement and dawning respect. 'You go and pack your case, mate, you go and pack it right this minute. Mary will come and help you in half a tick. And you know something, mate? You're the grouse, the real, dinkum good oil!'

Tim's beautiful eyes shone, his smile flashed out for the first time since they had come home to discover Es. 'I like you too, Pop,' he grinned, and went to pack his case.

After he had gone there was a strained silence; Dawnie sat looking everywhere but at Mary Horton, and Mary continued to stand in the middle of the floor, not knowing what she ought best to do.

'I reckon you owe Miss Horton an apology, Dawnie,' Ron said, staring his daughter down.

She stiffened, her fingers curling into claws. 'I'm buggered if I'll apologise!' she spat. 'After what's been done to us here I reckon Mick and I are the ones owed an apology! Manhandling my husband like that!'

Ron gazed at her sorrowfully. 'I'm real glad your Mum's not here,' he said. 'She always said you'd change, that we'd have to get out of your life, but I know bloody well she never thought you'd go all twitty like this. You're too big for your boots, my girl, and you could take a few lessons in manners from Miss Horton here, not to mention your flaming snotty husband!'

'Oh, please!' Mary exclaimed wretchedly. 'I'm terribly sorry I've caused all this unpleasantness. If I'd known what would happen I assure you I would never have come. Please don't quarrel on my account, I'd hate to think I caused a permanent breach in Tim's family. If it wasn't that I think Tim needs me now, I'd willingly get out of all your lives – including his – and I give you my word that as soon as Tim is over his mother's loss I'll do just that. I'll never see him again or cause any of you further pain and embarrassment.'

Ron got up from the chair Tim had thrust him into, his hand extended. 'Tommyrot! It's just as well this all came out, it would have eventually. As far as me and Mum are concerned, Tim's the only one who matters, and Tim will always needs youse, Miss Horton. The last thing Mum said was poor Tim, do the right thing for Tim, poor Tim, poor Tim. Well, I'm going to do just that, Miss Horton, and if that pair of gits over on the couch can't see it my way, then it's too bloody bad for them. I gotta honour Mum's wishes, because she ain't here any more.' His voice broke, but he lifted his chin towards the ceiling, swallowed several times and managed to continue. 'Mum and I wasn't always polite to each other, you know, but we thought a lot of each other for all that. We had some bloody good years, and I'm going to remember them with a smile and a lift of me beer glass. He wouldn't understand' – a jerk of his head towards the sofa – 'but Mum would be real disappointed if I didn't give her the old toast in beer every day at the Seaside.'

It was with difficulty that Mary restrained her impulse to go to the gallant old man and comfort him physically, but she knew how much his control meant to him, so she kept her arms by her sides and tried to tell him with her tear-dimmed eyes and lopsided smile that she understood very well.

19

Tim sat silently in the car all the way to Artarmon. He had not slept in her Sydney house very often, and the room he always occupied there did not have the same sense of belonging about it as his room at the cottage did. He did not seem to know what to do when she prepared to leave him to change his clothes and rest; he stood in the middle of the floor fiddling with his hands, looking at her pleadingly. Never proof against that particular expression, Mary sighed and came to his side.

'Why don't you change into your pyjamas and try to sleep for a little while, Tim?' she asked.

'But it's not night time, it's the middle of the day!' he protested, the pain and fear he was suffering revealing themselves in his voice.

'That's nothing to worry about, love,' she replied, her throat aching. 'I think you'd manage to sleep if I closed all the blinds and made the room dark.'

'I feel sick,' he said, gulping ominously.

'Oh, poor old Tim!' she responded instantly, remembering how he dreaded being chided for making a mess. 'Come on, I'll hold your forehead for you.'

He began to vomit just as they reached the bathroom entrance. She held his brow in the palm of her hand, crooning softly and stroking his back while he writhed and gagged wretchedly.

'Finished?' she asked softly, and when he nodded she sat him on her padded bathroom chair and ran warm water into the bath. 'You've made rather a mess of yourself, haven't you? I think you ought to just get out of those clothes and hop into a nice bath, don't you? You'll feel much better the minute you're soaking.' She wrung out a washcloth and cleaned the worst of it from his face and hands, slipped his shirt off and folded it in on itself carefully, then used it as a rag to wipe the splattered floor. He watched her apathetically, white and trembling.

'I'm soh-soh-sorry, Mary,' he gasped. 'I made a meh-meh-mess and you'll be mah-mah-mad at me.'

She smiled up at him from where she was kneeling on the tiles. 'Never, Tim, never! You couldn't help it, and you tried so hard to get to the bathroom in time, didn't you? That's all that matters, dear heart.'

His pallor and weakness alarmed her; he did not seem to be recovering as quickly as he should, so she was not surprised when he fell on his knees in front of the lavatory and began to retch again.

'I think that's definitely it,' she said when he was quiet once more. 'Now how about that bath?'

'I'm so tired, Mary,' he whispered, clinging to the sides of the chair seat.

She dared not leave him; the chair was straight-backed and armless, and if he fainted he would never stay on it. The best place for him was the lukewarm bath, where he could stretch out supine and warm himself through to his bones. Shutting Dawnie's bitter words out of her mind and praying that he would never mention it at home, she got him out of his clothes and helped him into the bath with one arm firmly around his waist and his arm about her shoulders. He sank into the water with a grateful sigh; relieved, she saw his colour begin to return, and while he relaxed she finished cleaning the floor and the lavatory. The sickish smell was horribly pervasive, so she opened the door and the window to the windy autumn air. Only then did she turn back to the bath and look at him.

He was sitting like a child, hunched forward and smiling faintly as he watched the tendrils of steam smoking off the surface of the water, his thick gold hair curling damply. So beautiful, so beautiful! Treat him like a child, she told herself as she picked up a bar of soap; treat him like the child he is, don't look at him and see him as a man. Yet even as she said it, her eyes fixed on the full length of his body in the clear water, for he had lain back again suddenly with a murmur of almost voluptuous content. Nudity in a book was, after all, a far cry from Tim's reality; in books it had never possessed the power to move or excite her. She forced herself to look away, but involuntarily her gaze crept back, furtively, until she discovered he had closed his eyes, then in a kind of wondering but disciplined greed, not so much a carnal hunger as a tangled and confused one.

Some change in him made her glance towards his face, to find that he watched her wearily but curiously; the blood felt so hot beneath her skin that she half waited for him to comment, but he did not. With a crablike motion she sat on the edge of the bath and rubbed the soap into his chest and back, her slippery fingers sliding over the flawless skin which was like oiled silk, casually straying every so often to his wrist to check his radial pulse. But he did seem better, if still listless, and he actually laughed when she threw water over his head and made him bend far forward to wash his hair. She did not let him linger, but made him stand up the moment he was washed thoroughly, then she let the water out of the tub and turned on the shower. It amused her to see his naïve pleasure in the huge towel she handed him when he stepped on to the floor, but she managed to listen gravely while he assured her he had never seen such an enormous towel before and what fun it was to be completely wrapped up like a baby.

'That was beaut, Mary,' he confided, lying in bed with the covers drawn up to his chin. 'I think Mum used to bathe me when I was a little shaver, but I don't remember it. I like being bathed, it's much nicer than bathing myself.'

'Then I'm glad,' she smiled. 'Now I want you to roll over on your side and go to sleep for a little while, all right?'

'All right.' He laughed. 'I can't say night-night, Mary, because it's the middle of the day.'

'How do you feel now, Tim?' she asked, drawing the blinds and plunging the room into semi-darkness.

'I feel all right, but I'm awfully tired.'

'Then sleep, love. When you wake up you can come and find me, I'll be here.'

The weekend passed fairly uneventfully; Tim was quiet, still not himself physically, but Mary saw little to indicate that he was as yet actively missing his mother. On Sunday afternoon she made him sit in the front of the big Bentley, and drove back to Surf Street to pick up Ron. He was waiting on the front veranda, and when he saw the car draw up he ran down the steps two at a time, suitcase in hand. How old he is, Mary thought, twisting around to open the back door. In spite of his neat, wiry physique and his boyish way of moving, not a young man at all. The sight of him worried her; all she could think of was Tim left utterly alone, bereft of both mother and father. After Dawnie's outburst on Friday there seemed little likelihood that she could or would compensate; her husband had gained the ascendancy. A good thing for Dawnie perhaps, but it boded ill for her erstwhile family. And how on earth could she, Mary Horton, possibly take in Tim if anything happened to Ron? It seemed that everyone thought the worst now, so what would they think and do if Tim came to live with her permanently? The very thought appalled her. Only Ron, Archie Johnson, old Emily Parker next door, and Tim himself thought the relationship was a good thing. She shrank from even imagining what Dawnie would say, and what she might do. Certainly there would be a scandal, maybe a lawsuit as well; but whatever happened, Tim must be shielded from harm and ridicule. It didn't really matter what became of her, or Dawnie, or their lives. Tim was the only one who mattered.

In spite of his shock and grief, Ron was amused at Tim's behaviour on the trip to Gosford, how he glued his nose to the window and stared raptly at the passing scene, fascinated. Mary caught him looking at his son when her eyes went to the rear-vision mirror, and she smiled.

'It never palls, Mr Melville. Isn't that a wonderful thing, to know that he enjoys every trip as much as the first one?'

Ron nodded. 'Too right, Miss Horton! I never realised that he enjoyed travelling so much. From what I remember of the few times we tried to take him out in a car, he hurked over everything. What a mess! And terribly embarrassing, because the car wasn't ours. If I'd known he would grow out of it, I would have bought a car and taken him round a bit. Makes me mad I didn't try later on, seeing him now.'

'Well, Mr Melville, I wouldn't be upset about it. Tim is always happy if everything is going well. This is just a different sort of happiness for him, that's all.'

Ron did not answer; his eyes filled with tears, and he had to turn his head away to gaze out of his own window.

After she settled them into the cottage, Mary prepared to return to Sydney. Ron looked up, dismayed.

'Crikey, Miss Horton, are youse going? I thought you was going to stay here with us.'

She shook her head. 'Unfortunately, I can't. I have to be at work tomorrow; my boss has a week of very important meetings and I must be there to support him. I think you'll find everything you might need. Tim knows where things are, and he'll help you if you have any problems in the kitchen or around the house. I want you to make yourselves absolutely at home, do exactly what you like when you like. There's all sorts of food, you won't run short. If you find you have to go into Gosford, the number of the local taxi service is in the telephone notepad, and I insist that you charge it to me.'

Ron stood up, for she was drawing on her gloves, ready to go. He shook her hand warmly and smiled.

'Why don't youse call me Ron, Miss Horton? Then I can call youse Mary. It seems a bit silly to go on calling each other Mister and Miss.'

She laughed, her hand resting on his shoulder caressingly for a moment. 'Yes, I agree, Ron. Let's make it Ron and Mary from now on.'

'We'll see youse when, Mary?' Ron asked, not knowing whether as a guest he ought to see her off her own premises or just return to his easy chair.

'Friday night sometime, but don't wait supper for me. I may have to stay in town and eat dinner with my boss.'

It was Tim who saw her to the car; surprised, Ron watched his son thrust himself between them rather like a dog bristling with annoyance because it has been forgotten. He took the hint and sat down again with his newspaper, while Tim followed Mary outside.

'I wish you didn't have to go back, Mary,' he said, staring down at her with a look in his eyes she had never seen there before, and could not identify.

She smiled, patting his arm. 'I have to go, Tim, I really do. But that means I have to rely on you to look after your Pop, because he doesn't know his way round the house or grounds, whereas you do. Be good to him, won't you?'

He nodded. His hands, slack by his sides, moved and clenched in on themselves. 'I'll look after him, Mary, I promise I'll look after him.'

He stood watching the track until the car had gone into the trees, then turned and went back into the house.

20

Mary's week was quite as hard as she had expected. Of the several meetings the Board of Constable Steel & Mining held during the year, this was the most important one. Three representatives of the parent firm in the United States flew in from New York to attend it. There were the usual secretarial problems related to unsatisfactory hotels, unavailable foods, bored wives, lagging schedules, and the like; when Friday night came Mary's sigh of relief was as heartfelt as Archie Johnson's. They sat in his office on the top floor of Constable Tower with their feet up, staring dazedly out at the spinning panorama of lights spreading away in all directions to the starstruck horizon.

'Christ on a bicycle, Mary, am I glad that's over and done with!' Archie exclaimed, pushing away his empty plate. 'That was a jolly good idea of yours to have a Chinese meal sent up, it really was.'

'I thought you might like it.' She wiggled her toes luxuriously. 'My feet feel like size fourteens, and I've been dying to take my shoes off all day. I thought Mrs Hiram P. Schwartz would never find her passport in time for the plane, and I had ghastly visions of having to put up with her for the weekend.'

Archie grinned. His impeccable secretary's shoes were lying higgledy-piggledy on the far side of the room, and she had almost disappeared into the maw of an enormous chair, her stockinged feet propped up on an ottoman.

'You know, Mary, you ought to have adopted a mentally retarded kid years ago. Sacred blue-arsed flies, what a difference it's made in you! I've never been able to do without you, but I confess it's a great deal more fun to work with you these days. I never thought I'd live to see the day when I'd have to admit I actually enjoyed your company, you nasty old twit, but I do, I really do! To think that all through the years it's been there inside you the whole time, and you never let it out once. That, my dear, is a bloody shame.'

She sighed, half smiling. 'Perhaps. But you know, Archie, nothing ever happens out of its due time. Had I met Tim years ago I would never have become interested in him. Some of us take half our lives to awaken.'

He lit a cigar and puffed at it contentedly. 'We've been so busy I haven't had a chance to ask you exactly what happened last Friday. His mother died?'

'Yes. It was dreadful.' She shivered. 'I took Tim and his father Ron up to my cottage last Sunday, and left them there. I'm going up to join them tonight. I do hope they're all right, but I suppose if they'd had any problems I would have heard from them. Tim hasn't realised yet what's happened, I think. Oh, he knows his mother's dead and he knows what that means, but the concrete reality of her going hadn't begun to work on him, he hadn't begun to miss her before I left. Ron says he'll get over it very quickly, and I hope he does. I feel very sorry for Ron. His daughter made quite a scene when I went out to pick up Tim on Friday.'

'Oh?'

'Yes.' Mary got up and went to the bar. 'Would you like a brandy or something?'

'After Chinese food? No, thanks. I'll have a cup of tea, please.' He watched her move around behind the bar to the little stove and sink. 'What sort of a scene?'

Her head was bent over the kettle. 'It's a little embarrassing to talk about it. An ugly scene, let's leave it at that. She – oh, it doesn't matter!' The cups rattled.

'She what? Come on, now, Mary, spit it out!'

The eyes looking at him were bright with defiance and wounded pride. 'She implied that Tim was my lover.'

'Great sausages of shit!' He threw back his head and laughed. 'Way off base, way off base! I would have told her that if she'd asked me.' He heaved himself out of his chair and came to lean on the bar. 'Don't let it upset you, Mary. What a wart the girl must be!'

'No, she isn't a wart. She married a wart, that's all, and he's doing his best to wartify her. I don't honestly think that what she said was anything more than a parroting of what her husband had been whispering in her ear. She's very fond of Tim, and intensely protective.' Her head went down below the level of the bar top, and the next words were muffled. 'You see, they all thought I was much older than I really am, so when I appeared to collect Tim they all got rather a shock.'

'How did they get that impression?'

'Tim told them I had white hair, and because I had white hair Tim assumed I was old, really old. So he told them I was very old.'

'But hadn't you ever met them before the mother died? It isn't like you to sneak around back alleys, Mary! Why didn't you correct their misapprehension?'

She flushed painfully. 'I honestly don't know why I didn't ever introduce myself personally to Tim's parents. If I did have any fears that they'd stop the friendship if they found out my true age, I assure you those fears were quite unconscious. I knew Tim was perfectly safe with me. I enjoyed hearing about Tim's family from him, and I think I was sort of postponing meeting them because they wouldn't be at all like the people Tim talked of.'

He reached over the counter and patted her shoulder. 'Well, not to worry. Go on, you were saying Tim's sister is very fond of him?'

'Yes. Tim was as fond of her as she was of him until she got married, when he rather grew away from her a little. He seemed to feel she had deserted him, though I tried to reason with him. From all he said about her, I had gathered she was a sane, sensible, warm-hearted sort of girl. Very brilliant. Isn't that strange?'

'I don't know. Is it? What did you do?'

Down went the head again. 'I was devastated. I think I cried. Fancy me crying!' She looked up, trying to smile. 'Boggles the imagination, doesn't it?' Then she sighed, her face pensive and sorrowful. 'But I've done my share of crying lately, Archie, I've done my share of crying.'

'It does rather boggle the imagination, but I believe you. Still, we should all cry occasionally. I've even cried myself,' he admitted grandly.

She laughed, relaxing. 'You are, in your own language, a bot, Archie.'

He watched her pour the tea, something akin to pity in his eyes. It must have been a terrible blow to her pride, he thought, to have this rare, treasured thing reduced to such an elemental level. For to her the very thought of a physical component debased it;

she had a monkish outlook on life, and was it any wonder? Such a strange, sequestered, isolated life she had led! We are what we are, he thought, and we can be no more than what circumstances have made us.

'Ta, dear,' he said, taking his tea. Sitting in his chair once more staring out the window, he spoke again. 'I'd like to meet Tim some time if I may, Mary.'

There was a long silence behind him, then her voice came, very quietly. 'One of these days.' She made it sound very far away.

21

It was after midnight when Mary parked the Bentley outside the cottage. The lights were still on in the living room, and Tim came bounding out to open the car door. He was trembling with joy at sight of her, and almost lifted her off the ground in a suffocating hug. It was the first time his emotions at seeing her had overridden the training of years, and it told her more than anything else could have done how miserable he had been all week, how much he must have missed his mother.

'Oh, Mary, I'm so glad to see you!'

She disengaged herself. 'My goodness, Tim, you don't know your own strength! I thought you'd be in bed by now.'

'Not before you came. I had to stay up until you came. Oh, Mary, I'm so glad to see you! I like you, I like you!'

'And I like you, and I'm very glad to see you, too. Where's your Pop?'

'Inside. I wouldn't let him come out, I wanted to see you first all by myself.' He danced along beside her, but she sensed that somehow a little of his delight was quenched, that she had failed him. If only she knew how! 'I don't like it here without you, Mary,' he went on, 'I only like it when you're here too.'

He calmed down by the time they entered the house, and Mary went to greet Ron, her hand outstretched.

'How are you?' she asked gently.

'I'm all right, Mary. It's good to see youse.'

'It's good to be here.'

'Did youse eat yet?'

'Yes, I did, but I'm going to make a cup of tea all the same. Would you like some?'

'Ta, I would.'

Mary turned back to Tim, who was standing some distance away from them. He was wearing his lost look. How have I failed him? she asked herself again. What have I done to make him look like that, what did I neglect to do?

'What's the matter, Tim?' she asked, going to him.

He shook his head. 'Nothing.'

'Are you sure?'

'Yes, it's nothing.'

'I'm afraid it's bedtime, my friend.'

He nodded desolately. 'I know.' At the door he looked back, a mute appeal in his eyes. 'Will you come and tuck me up, please?'

'I wouldn't miss it for the world, so hurry, hurry! I'll be in to see you in five minutes.'

When he had gone she looked at Ron. 'How has it been?'

'Good and bad. He cried a lot for his mother. It's not easy, because he don't cry the way he used to, all outward. These days he just sits there with the tears rolling down his face, and you can't tempt him out of them by waving something good under his nose.'

'Come to the kitchen with me. It must have been very hard for you, and I'm terribly sorry I couldn't manage to be here to take some of the load off your shoulders.' She filled the kettle, then looked at her watch anxiously. 'I must go and say goodnight to Tim. I'll be back soon.'

Tim was already in bed, looking towards the door fixedly. She came over to him, fussed with the covers until they were wedged tightly underneath his chin, and tucked them firmly around him. Then she bent and kissed his forehead. He struggled with the blankets until he got his arms free and put them about her neck, pulling her down so that she was forced to sit on the edge of the bed.

'Oh, Mary, I wish you'd been here,' he said, the words muffled against the side of her face.

'I wish I'd been here, too. But it's all right now, Tim, I'm here now, and you know I'll always be here with you as much as I can. I like being here with you better than anything else in the whole world. You missed your Mum, didn't you?'

The arms about her neck tightened. 'Yes. Oh, Mary, it's awful hard to remember that she isn't ever coming back! I forget and then I remember again, and I want her to come back real bad and I know she can't come back, and it's all muddled up. But I wish she could come back, I do so much wish she could come back!'

'I know, I know . . . But it will be easier in a little while, dear heart. You won't always feel it so badly, it will fade. She'll get further and further away from you and you'll grow used to it, it won't hurt so much any more.'

'But I get a pain when I cry, Mary! It hurts an awful lot, and it won't go away!'

'Yes, I know. I get it too. It's as if they'd cut a whole big chunk out of your chest, isn't it?'

'That's right, that's exactly what it's like!' He passed his hands clumsily across her back. 'Oh, Mary, I'm so glad you're here! You always know what everything is like, you can tell me and then I feel better. It was awful without you!'

The muscles of the leg wedged against the side of the bed went into agonising spasm, and Mary withdrew her head from his clasp. 'I'm here now, Tim, and I'll be here all weekend. Then we'll all go back to Sydney together, I won't leave you here alone. Now I want you to roll over on your side and go to sleep for me, because we have a lot to do in the garden tomorrow.'

He turned obediently. 'Night-night, Mary. I like you, I like you better than anyone except Pop now.'

Ron had made the tea, and sliced up a block of seed cake. They sat in the kitchen, one on either side of the table facing each other. Though she had not met Ron until after Esme died, Mary knew instinctively that he had aged and shrunk in upon himself during this last week. The hand holding the cup to his mouth trembled, and all the life was leached out of his face. There was a hint of transparency about him, a spiritual attenuation that had crept into his flesh. She put out a hand and placed it over his.

'How hard it must have been for you, concealing your own grief and yet having to watch Tim's. Oh, Ron, I wish there was something I could do! Why do people have to die?'

He shook his head. 'I dunno. That's the hardest question in the world, ain't it? I've never found an answer that satisfied me. Cruel of God to give us loved ones, make us in His image so that we can love them, then take them away. He oughta thought out a better way of doing it, don't you reckon? I know we're none of us angels and we must seem sort of like worms to Him, but most of us do our best, most of us aren't all that bad. Why should we have to suffer like this? It's hard, Mary, it's awful, awful hard.'

The hand under hers went up to shield his eyes, and he wept. Mary sat there helplessly, her heart aching for him. If only there was something she could do! How terrible it was, to have to sit and watch another's grief and be so utterly powerless to lighten it. He wept for a long time, in spasms that seemed to eat away at his very soul, so deep and alone they were. When he could weep no more he dried his eyes and blew his nose.

'Could you drink another cup of tea?' Mary asked.

For a ghostly moment it was Tim's smile that hovered on his lips. 'Ta, I could.' He sighed. 'I never thought it would be like this, Mary. Maybe it's that I'm old, I dunno. I never thought her going would leave such a great big empty space. Even Tim don't seem to matter quite so much any more, only her, only losing her. It ain't the same without the old girl there bitching and snarling about me staying too late at the Seaside, guzzling beer, as she used to put it. We had a real good life together, Es and me. That's the trouble, you grow towards each other as the years go on, until you're sort of like a pair of old boots, warm and comfortable. Then all of a sudden it's gone! I feel like half of me was gone too, sort of like a bloke feels after he loses an arm or a leg, youse know what I mean. He still thinks it's there, and he gets a terrible shock when he goes after an itch and finds there's nothing left to scratch. I keep thinking of things I oughta tell her, or have to stop meself saying out loud that she'd enjoy this joke, we'll have a good laugh about it. It's so hard, Mary, and I dunno that it's even worth trying.'

'Yes, I think I understand,' Mary said slowly. 'A spiritual amputee . . .'

He put his cup down. 'Mary, if anything should happen to me, will you look after Tim?'

She didn't expostulate with him, she didn't attempt to tell him he was being morbid or silly, she just nodded and said, 'Yes, of course I will. Don't worry about Tim.'

22

In the long, sad winter which followed his mother's death, Tim changed. It was like seeing an animal mourn; he wandered from place to place looking for something that wasn't there, his eyes lighting restlessly on some inanimate object and then flicking away disappointed and bewildered, as if he always expected the impossible to occur, and was beyond understanding why it did not. Even Harry Markham and his crew could get nowhere with him, Ron told Mary despairingly; he went to work every day without fail, but the thoughtlessly malicious practical jokes of other days fell on stony ground: he endured the crew's tormenting brand of humour as patiently as he endured everything else. It was as if he had withdrawn from the real world, Mary thought, gone into a sphere that was his alone, and forever barred against intruders.

She and Ron had endless, unavailing conferences about him, sitting long into the rainy nights with the wind howling in the trees around the cottage, while Tim took himself off somewhere on his own or went to bed. Since Esme's death Mary had insisted Ron come to the cottage every weekend, for it was more than her heart could bear to drive off with Tim on Friday nights and leave the old man sitting beside his empty fireplace all alone.

There was a dull, dragging weight of sadness on them. For Mary it could not be the same, having to share her hours with Tim; for Ron nothing mattered very much except the barrenness of his days; for Tim, no one knew. It was Mary's first close contact with grief, and she had never imagined anything like it. The most frustrating part of it was her helplessness, her inability to put things right; nothing she could say or do made a particle of difference. She had to bear with the long silences, the furtive creeping away to indulge in bouts of fruitless tears, the pain.

She had come to care for Ron, too, because he was Tim's father, because he was so alone, because he never complained, and as time went on he occupied her thoughts more and more. With the coldest season drawing towards its close she noticed an increasing fragility about him; sometimes when they were sitting in the weak but warming sun together and he held his hand to the light, she fancied that the veined, blotchy extremity let the light shine straight through it until she could see the silhouette of his bones. He trembled so, and his once firm footsteps would hesitate when there was no obstacle in their path. No matter how she tried to feed him, he lost weight steadily. He was dissolving in front of her very eyes.

The trouble pulled at her like an invisible force; she seemed to spend her days walking a featureless plain without landmark or direction, and only working with Archie Johnson had any reality. At Constable Steel & Mining she could be herself, lift her mind from Ron and Tim and plunge it into something concrete. It was the only steadying influence in her life. She had come to dread Fridays and welcome Mondays; Ron and Tim had become a nightmarish incubus chained about her neck, for she did not know what to do to avert the disasters she sensed were coming.

One Saturday morning early in spring she was sitting on the front veranda of the cottage looking towards the beach, where Tim was standing just at the water's edge staring out across the wide river. What did he see? Was he looking for his mother, or was he looking for the answers she had failed to give him? It was her failure with Tim which worried Mary more than anything else, for she sensed that she herself was one of the main reasons for his odd withdrawal. Ever since the night she had returned to the cottage after that week Ron and Tim had spent there alone, Mary was aware that Tim thought she had failed him. But talking to him was like talking to a brick wall, he seemed not to want to hear her. She had tried more times than she could count, approached the subject by casting out what used to be infallible lures, but he ignored them, almost spurning her. Yet it was such an intangible thing; he was his normal polite self, he worked willingly in the garden and about the house, he voiced no discontent. He had just gone away.

Ron came out on to the veranda with a tray of morning tea, and set it on a table near her chair. His eyes followed hers to the still, sentry-like figure on the beach, and he sighed.

'Have a cuppa, Mary. You didn't eat anything for brekkie, love.

I baked a real nice seed cake yestiddy, so why don't you have a bit now with your tea, eh?'

She dragged her thoughts away from Tim and smiled. 'My word, Ron, you've developed into quite a cook these last few months.'

He bit his lip to still its sudden quivering. 'Es used to love seed cake, it was her favourite. I was reading in the *Herald* that in America they eat bread with seeds in it, but they don't put seeds in cakes. Barmy! I can't think of anything worse than caraway seeds in bread, but in a nice, sweet yellow cake they're the grouse.'

'Customs vary, Ron. They'd probably say exactly the opposite if they ever read in their papers that Australians never put caraway seeds in bread but eat them in cake instead. Though, to be honest, if you go to one of the continental bakeries in Sydney you can buy seeded rye bread these days.'

'I wouldn't put anything past them bloody new Australian wogs,' he said with the old Australian's innate contempt for the new European immigrants. 'Anyway, it don't matter. Have a bit of the cake, Mary, go on.'

Half her slice of cake eaten, Mary put her plate down. 'Ron, what's the matter with him?'

'Gord struth and little apples, Mary, we've squeezed the last juice out of that subject weeks ago!' he snapped, then turned to press her arm contritely. 'I'm sorry, love, I didn't mean to bite your head off like that. I know you're only worried about him, I know that's the only reason you keep on asking. I dunno, love, I just dunno. I never ever thought he'd take on so after his Mum died, I never thought it'd last half so long. It's enough to break your heart, ain't it?'

'It's breaking mine. I don't know what to do, but I've got to do something, and soon! He's going farther and farther away from us, Ron, and if we can't pull him back we'll lose him forever!'

He came and sat on the arm of her chair, pulling her head against his meagre chest and cradling it there. 'I wish I knew what to do, Mary love, but I don't. The worst thing is that I can't make meself care the way I used to, it's sort of as if Tim's not me son any more, as if I can't be bothered. That sounds awful, but I've got me reasons. Wait here.'

He let her go abruptly and disappeared into the house, emerging a moment later with a flat portfolio of papers under his arm. He threw it on to the table beside the tea tray. Mary looked up at him, puzzled and upset. Ron got another chair and pulled it over until it faced hers, then he sat down and stared directly into her eyes, his own glittering queerly.

'That's all the papers about Tim,' he said. 'Inside there is me will, all the bank books and insurance policies and annuities. Everything to make sure Tim's financially secure for the rest of his life.' He looked behind him towards the beach, and Mary could no longer see his face.

'I'm dying, Mary,' he went on slowly. 'I don't want to live, and I can't seem to make meself live any more. I'm running down like a clockwork monkey – you know the ones, they beat a little drum and march up and down and then it all goes into slow motion and then it all stops, the feet stop marching and the drum stops beating. Well, that's me. Running down, and there's nothing I can do about it.

'And oh, Mary, I'm glad! If I'd been a young man I wouldn't have felt her going like this, but age makes a big difference. She's left a great big hole I can't fill with anything, even Tim. All I want is to be lying there with her, under the ground. I keep thinking she must be awful cold and lonely. She couldn't be anything else, not after sharing her sleep with me all those years.' His face was still turned away from her towards the beach. 'I can't stand the thought of her so cold and lonely, I can't bear it. There ain't nothing left with her gone, and I can't even make meself care about Tim. That's why I went to me lawyer this week and got him to make everything all right.

'I'm not leaving youse anything but trouble, I suppose, but somehow right from the beginning I always felt that you was terrible fond of Tim, that you wouldn't mind the trouble. It's selfish, but I can't help it. I'm leaving Tim to you, Mary, and there's all his papers. You take them. I've given you a power of attorney in Tim's financial affairs for as long as you live. I don't think Dawnie will make any big trouble for youse, because Mick doesn't want Tim around, but just in case I've left a couple of letters in there, one for Dawnie and one for that shirt-lifting bugger Mick. I gave me notice at work, told the boss I was retiring. I'm just going to stay at home and wait, except that I'd still like to come up with Tim on weekends if you don't mind. It won't be too long now, anyway.'

'Oh, Ron, oh, Ron!' Mary found herself weeping; the slender

shape on the beach melted in a shimmer of tears, and she reached out her hands to Tim's father.

They rose and clung together hard, each the victim of a different kind of pain. After a while Mary discovered that he comforted her more than she could ever comfort him, that it was exquisitely peaceful and healing to stand there within his arms and feel his tenderness and compassion, his intensely male protectiveness. She held him more tightly, her face pushing into the sagging folds of his skinny neck, and closed her eyes.

Suddenly something alien intruded: a shiver of dread passed down her spine, and she opened her eyes with a start of fear. Tim was standing several feet away staring at them, and for the first time in all the long months of their friendship, she saw him angry. He was shaking with rage; it flared in his eyes and turned them as dark as sapphires, it spasmed his muscles into tremor after furious tremor. Terrified, she let her arms fall and stepped back from Ron so abruptly that he staggered and had to grasp at the roof post. Turning, he saw Tim; they stared at each other for perhaps a minute without speaking, then Tim twisted away and ran down the path to the beach.

'What's the matter with him?' Ron whispered, aghast. He made a movement to follow his son, but Mary pulled him back, clawing at him.

'No, no!'

'But I gotta see what's the matter with him, Mary! What did he do? What made youse jump like that and look so frightened of him? Let me go!'

'No, Ron, please! Let me go after him, you stay here, please! Oh, Ron, don't ask me why, just let me find him by myself!'

He yielded reluctantly, stepping away from the edge of the veranda. 'Well, all right, love. You're good with him, and maybe he needs a woman's touch more than a man's. If Mum was alive I'd send her, so why not you?'

There was no sign of him on the beach as Mary sped down the path; she stopped on the fringe of the sand and shaded her eyes to peer up and down the whole length of the bay, but he was not there. She turned into the trees, heading for a little clearing where she knew of late he liked to go to be alone. And he was there; gasping with relief, Mary sagged against a tree trunk and watched him silently. His terrible misery and grief struck her like a blow from some gargantuan hammer; every long, achingly beautiful line of him spoke of inarticulate suffering, the pure outline of his profile was knotted into pain. It was impossible to stand aloof, but she came up to him so quietly that he was not aware of her presence until she touched him on the arm. He flinched away as if her fingers burned and her hand fell to her side, useless.

'Tim, what is it? What have I done?'

'Nothing, nothing!'

'Don't keep it from me, Tim! What have I done?'

'Nothing!' He almost screamed the word.

'But I have! Oh, Tim, I've known for months that I've failed you somehow, but I don't know what I did wrong! Tell me, tell me!'

'Go away!'

'No, I won't go away! I won't go away until you tell me what's the matter! It's been worrying your Pop and me out of our minds, and back there on the veranda you looked at us both as if you hated us. Hated us, Tim!' She came round to face him and put her hands on his upper arms, her fingers digging into his skin.

'Don't *touch* me!' He wrenched away and turned his back on her.

'Why, Tim? What have I done that I can't touch you?'

'Nothing!'

'I don't believe you! Tim, I never thought you'd lie to me, but you are lying to me! Please tell me what's the matter, oh, please!'

'I can't!' he whispered despairingly.

'But you can, of course you can! You've always been able to tell me everything! Oh, Tim, don't turn away from me and shut me out any more! You're pulling me into little pieces, I'm so beside myself with worry and fear for you that I don't know what to do!' She began to weep, and wiped the tears away with the palm of her hand.

'I can't, I can't! I don't *know*! I feel so many things that I can't think out, I don't know what they mean!'

He spun round to face her, goaded and harried beyond patience, and she backed away; a stranger glared at her, there was nothing familiar in him to reach for.

'I only know you don't like me any more, that's all! You like Pop better than me now, you don't like me any more! You haven't liked me since you met Pop, and I knew it would happen, I knew it would happen! How could you like me more than him when he's the full quid and I'm not? *I* like him better than me!'

She put out her hands. 'Oh, Tim! Oh, Tim! How could you think that? It's not true! I like you as much as I always did, I haven't stopped liking you for one little wee minute! How could I ever stop liking you?'

'You did when you met Pop!'

'No, no! It's not true, Tim! Please believe me, it's just not true! I like your Pop, but I could never like him as much as I like you, never! If you must know, most of the reason I like your Pop is because he is your Pop; he made you.' She tried to keep her voice calm, hoping it would calm him.

'You're the one who's lying, Mary! I can feel things! I always thought you thought I was all grown up, but now I know you don't, not now, not now I've seen you and Pop! You don't like me any more, it's Pop you like now! You don't mind if *Pop* hugs you! I've seen you, hugging and comforting him all the time! You won't let *me* hug you and you won't comfort *me*! All you do with me is tuck me into bed, and I want you to hug me and comfort me, but you won't! But you do it to Pop!

'What's wrong with me, why don't you like me any more? Why did you change after Pop started coming with us? Why am I always left out? I can tell you don't like me, I can tell it's Pop you like!'

Mary stood absolutely still, yearning to respond to that despairing, lonely plea for love, but too aghast at its suddenness. He was jealous! He was furiously, possessively jealous! He regarded his own father as a rival for her affections, and it was not entirely the jealousy of a child. There was a man in it: primitive, possessive, sexual man. The glib words of reassurance would not come; she could find nothing to say.

They stood staring at each other, stiff and with hackles raised, then Mary found that her legs were trembling so much they scarcely supported her. She groped for a nearby hillock and sat down without taking her eyes from his face.

'Tim,' she said hesitantly, trying to choose her words with extreme delicacy, 'Tim, you know I've never lied to you. Never! I couldn't lie to you, I like you far too much. What I'm going to tell you now is something I couldn't tell a little child, I could only say it to a man grown. You've assured me that you're all grown up, so now you have to take all the hard, painful things which go along with being a man. I can't properly explain why I let your Pop hug me and won't let you, but it isn't because you're a little child to me, it's because he's an old man. You've got it the wrong way round, don't you see?

'Tim, you have to be ready to take another shock like your Mum's death, and you have to be strong. You have to be grown up enough to keep what I tell you an absolute secret, especially from your Pop. He must never know I told you.

'Do you remember a long time ago I explained to you what happened to people when they died, why they died, that they just got too old and tired to keep going, that they ran down like a forgotten clock until their hearts stopped beating? Well, sometimes a thing happens which makes the wearing out go much faster, and it's happened to your Pop. When your Mum died he began to run down faster and faster, he got more and more tired with each day he had to live without her.'

He was still standing over her, trembling as he listened, but she did not know whether this was an aftermath of his rage or a reaction to what she was telling him. She laboured on doggedly.

'I know you miss your Mum dreadfully, Tim, but you don't miss her the way he does, because you're young and he's old. Pop wants to die, he wants to lie under the ground next to your Mum sleeping, just the way they did each night when she was alive. He wants to be with her again. They belong together, you see, he can't get along without her. Just now, when you found me comforting him on the veranda, he had just told me that he knew he was going to die. He doesn't want to go on walking and talking any more because he's old and he can't learn to live without her. And that's why I was holding him. I was saddened and I cried for him; actually it was Pop who was comforting me, not the other way around. You mistook it entirely.'

An abrupt movement from him made her look up, and she lifted her hand in command.

'No, don't cry, Tim! Come on now, you've got to be very brave and strong, you can't let him see that you've been crying. I know I've given a lot of time to your Pop that you think rightly belonged to you, but he has so little time left, and you have all your life ahead of you! Is it wrong of me to want to give him a wee bit of happiness to lighten what days he has left? Give him those days, Tim, don't be selfish! He's so alone! He misses your Mum terribly, dear heart, he misses her the way I'd miss you if you died. He's walking around in a half-lit world.'

Tim had never learned to school his features to impassivity; the emotions chased each other across his face as he stood staring at her, and it was all too plain that he understood enough. Making Tim comprehend was largely a matter of familiarity, and he had known her a long time now, he had little trouble with the words and phrases she used. The nuances were beyond him, but the truth was not.

She sighed wearily. 'I haven't found it very easy either all these months, with two of you to look after instead of only you. There have been many, many times when I've longed to have you to myself again. But when I've caught myself wishing that I've been ashamed of myself, Tim. You see, we can't always have things the way we want. Life is so seldom ideal, and we just have to learn to put up with it. During this time we have to think of Pop first. You know what a good, kind man Pop is, and if you're fair to him you'll admit he's never treated you like a baby, has he? He's let you go out into the world on your own, make your own mistakes, he loves to share his time at the Seaside with you, he's been the best and truest mate you've ever had; he's taken the place of the mates your own age you've never had the chance to find. And yet he's led his own life, too, but not because he's selfish; he's always had you and Mum and Dawnie there in his mind, all sort of warm and comforting, rounding out his life. You're very lucky, Tim, to have a father like Ron, so don't you think we ought to try and give him back a little bit of what he's given you so ungrudgingly all these years?

'From now on, Tim, I want you to be very good to your father, and very good to me. You mustn't worry him by going off by yourself the way you've been doing, and you mustn't ever let him know I told you what the matter is. Whenever Pop is around I want you to sing and talk and laugh as if you're happy, really happy.

'I know it's hard for you to understand, but I'll sit here and go over it with you until you get it all straight.'

Like rain and wind and sun the grief and joy mingled in his eyes, then they dulled and he burrowed his head into her lap. She sat and stroked his hair and talked to him softly, tracing the outline of his neck and ear tenderly with the tip of her finger, round and round and round.

When he lifted his head at last he looked at her, trying to smile and failing. Then his expression changed, the lost look came into his face and the bewildered eyes retreated behind their veil of sad exclusion. Along the left side of his mouth the little crease became very pronounced; he was the tragic clown of every comedy, he was the unwanted lover, he was the cuckoo in the lark's nest.

'Oh, Tim, don't look at me so!' she pleaded.

'At work they call me Dim Tim,' he said, 'but if I try really hard, I can think a little bit. Ever since Mum went away I've been trying to think of something to show you how much I like you, because I thought you liked Pop better than me. Mary, I don't know what you do to me, I only feel it and I can't tell you because I don't know the words. I never can find the words . . . But in the movies I see on TV the man hugs the girl and then he kisses her, and then she knows how much he likes her. Oh, Mary, I like you! I liked you even when I thought you didn't like me any more, I like you, I like you!'

He snatched at her shoulders and pulled her to her feet, his hold inexpertly strong as he put his arms about her back; her head came up, seeking air. Not knowing how to find her mouth, he pressed his cheek against hers until he fumbled to her lips. Completely taken off guard, for his last words and his action had been too swift and startling for immediate comprehension, Mary fought frantically to free herself. Then somehow it no longer mattered, there was only the feel of that beautiful young body and anxiously experimenting mouth. As inexperienced as he but intellectually much better prepared, Mary felt his need for help and reassurance. She could not fail him in this too, she could not bring herself to crush his pride, humiliate him by rejecting him. His hold slackened enough for her to free her hands; they went immediately to his head, smoothing his brows and closing his open eyes, exploring the silkiness of his lashes and the hollowed curves of his cheeks. He kissed her the way he imagined it was done, his lips pressed firmly shut, and it dissatisfied him; she pulled away from him for a moment and pushed her thumb against his lower lip caressingly, slightly opening his mouth, then her hands went up to his hair and drew his head down. He was not dissatisfied this time, and his shivering delight transmitted itself to her.

She had held him in her arms before, but as child, never as man, and the shock of discovering the man in him awed her. To lose herself in his arms, to feel his mouth, permit her hands to follow the planes of his neck down to the smooth muscular chest, was to discover in herself a need for this, an agonised pleasure in feeling his hands on her body. He found the cloth-shielded contours of her breasts without guidance, then his hand slipped under the collar of her dress and curved around her bare shoulder.

'Mary! Tim! Mary! Tim! Where are you, can you hear me? It's Ron! Answer me!'

She wrenched away from him and took his hand, dragging him after her into the shelter of the trees. They ran until Ron's voice had long faded behind them, then stopped. Mary's heart was pounding so hard she could scarcely catch her breath, and for a moment she thought she was going to faint. Panting and gasping, she clung to Tim's arm until she felt better, then moved away from him a little self-consciously.

'You're looking at a stupid old fool,' she said then, turning to face him.

He was smiling at her in the old, totally loving way, but there was a difference now, an added fascination and wonder, as if in his eyes she had gained an entire dimension. It sobered her as nothing else could have done; she put her hand to her head, trying to think. How had it happened? How was she going to deal with it, how could she put them back on the old footing without hurting him?

'Tim, we shouldn't have done that,' she said slowly.

'Why?' His face was alight with happiness. 'Oh, Mary, I didn't know that was how it felt! I liked it, I liked it much better than hugging you or being comforted!'

She shook her head vehemently. 'It doesn't matter, Tim! We shouldn't have done it. There are some things people aren't allowed to do, and that's one of them. It's too bad we liked it, because it can't happen again, it must never happen again, not because I didn't like it as much as you did, but because it isn't allowed. You've got to believe me, Tim, it just isn't allowed! I'm responsible for you, I have to look after you the way your Mum and Pop would want, and that means we can't kiss, we just can't.'

'But why, Mary? What's wrong with it? I liked it!' All the light had died out of his face.

'In itself, Tim, there's nothing wrong. But between you and me it's forbidden, it's a sin. Do you know what a sin is?'

'Of course I do! That's when you do something God doesn't like.'

'Well, God doesn't like us to kiss.'

'But why should God mind? Oh, Mary, I've never felt like that before! It was the closest I've ever felt to the full quid! Why should God mind it? It isn't fair that God should mind, it just isn't fair!'

She sighed. 'No, Tim, it isn't fair. But sometimes it's hard for us to understand God's purposes. There are a lot of rather silly things you have to do without properly understanding why, isn't that so?'

'Yes, I suppose so,' he replied sulkily.

'Well, when it comes to understanding God's purposes none of us are the full quid – you're not the full quid and I'm not the full quid and your Pop's not the full quid, the Prime Minister of Australia isn't the full quid, and nor is the Queen. Tim, you've got to believe me!' she pleaded. 'You've got to believe me, because if you won't we can't be friends any more; we'll have to stop seeing each other. It isn't possible for us to hug and kiss, it's a sin in the eyes of God. You're only a young man and you're not the full quid, where I'm getting old and I'm absolutely the full quid. I'm old enough to be your mother, Tim!'

'But what does that have to do with it?'

'God doesn't like us to hug and kiss when there's such a big difference in our ages and mentalities, Tim, that's all. I like you, I like you better than anyone else in the whole world, but I can't hug and kiss you. It isn't allowed. If you try to kiss me again, God will make me stop seeing you, and I don't want to stop seeing you.'

He pondered on it sadly, then sighed in defeat. 'Well, Mary, I did like it an awful lot, but I'd rather keep on seeing you than kiss you and then not see you.'

She clapped her hands together delightedly. 'Oh, Tim, I'm so proud of you! That was spoken like a man, a real, full-quidded man. I'm so very proud of you.'

He laughed shakily. 'I still think it isn't fair, but I like it when you're proud of me.'

'Are you happier now that you know everything?'

'Much happier!' He sat down under a tree and patted the ground beside him. 'Sit down, Mary. I promise I won't kiss you.'

She crouched beside him and took his hand, spreading the fingers apart lovingly. 'This is as much as we can do when we touch, Tim. I know you won't kiss me, I'm not at all worried that you'll break your promise. You have to promise me something else, too.'

'What?' His free hand plucked at the few dusty blades of grass under his thigh.

'What happened, I mean the kiss, it has to be our little secret. We must never tell anyone about it, Tim.'

'All right,' he answered docilely. He was reverting to the child again, accepting his role with the peculiar sweetness and desire to please that were so much his alone. After a while he turned his head to look at her, and the wide blue eyes were so filled with love that Mary caught her breath, angry and soured. He was so right; it wasn't fair, it just wasn't fair.

'Mary, what you told me about Pop, how he wants to be asleep with Mum under the ground. I know what you mean. If you died I'd want to die too, I wouldn't like to keep walking and talking and laughing and crying, honest. I'd like to be with you, under the ground asleep. I won't like it if Pop isn't here, but I know why he wants to go.'

She raised his hand to her cheek and held it there. 'It's always easier to understand things when you can put yourself in the same position, isn't it? Listen, I can hear Pop calling us. Do you think you can talk to him without crying?'

He nodded tranquilly. 'Oh, yes, I'll be all right. I like Pop an awful lot, next to you I like him best, but he sort of belongs to Mum, doesn't he? I belong to you, so I'm not worried nearly as much now. I belong to you now. Just belonging isn't a sin, is it, Mary?'

She shook her head. 'No, Tim, it isn't a sin.'

Ron's voice was drawing closer; Mary hallooed to let him know where they were, and got up to wait.

'Mary?'

'Yes?'

He was still sprawled on the ground, looking up at her in dawning comprehension. 'I just thought of something! Do you remember the day after Mum died, when you came to our house to fetch me?'

'Yes, I most certainly do.'

'Well, Dawnie said some horrible, nasty things to you, and I didn't know what she was so upset about. I tried and tried, but I didn't know what she was so upset about. When she was yelling at you I felt all queer, because I thought she thought we'd done something awful. Now I think I know! Did she think it was us kissing?'

'Something like that, Tim.'

'Oh!' He thought about it for a moment. 'Then I do believe you, Mary, I do believe we aren't allowed to kiss. I've never seen Dawnie like that before, and ever since then she's been real unfriendly to Pop and me. She had a big fight with Pop about me coming to stay with you a few weeks after that, and now she doesn't come to see us any more. So I do believe it's a sin, it must be a sin for Dawnie to carry on like that. But why did she think you'd let us kiss all the time? She ought to know you better than that, Mary. You'd never let us do anything wrong.'

'Yes, she ought to know it, I agree, but sometimes people get too upset to think straight, and after all she doesn't know me nearly as well as you and Pop do.'

He stared at her, strangely wise. 'But Pop took your side, and he didn't know you at all then either.'

Ron came through the trees, puffing. 'Everything all right, Mary love?'

She smiled, winking at Tim. 'Yes, Ron, perfectly all right. Tim and I had a talk, and straightened it all out. No big problem, I promise you, just a misunderstanding.'

23

But everything was not all right; the sleeping dogs had been wakened. Mary had good reason to be thankful that Ron was failing, for if he had been in his normal state of health and mind, he would have seen the change in Tim at once. As it was, the cheerful good humour which had come back to the relationship was enough to satisfy him, and he looked no further. Only Mary realised that Tim was suffering. She would look up to find his hungry, angry eyes on her a dozen times a day, and when she caught him looking so he would go out of the room immediately, guilty and confused.

Why must things change? she asked herself; why can't something perfect stay perfect? Because we're all human beings, her reasoning self would answer, because we're so complex and flawed, because once a thing occurs to us it must recur, and in recurring it alters the form and essence of what has gone before. There was no way back to the first phase of their friendship, therefore only two alternatives remained; to go forward, or to stay still. But neither alternative seemed possible or workable. Had Tim been mentally normal she would have tried, but to go into the matter again would only have confused him, made him even unhappier. It's stalemate, she thought, then shook her head in worried exasperation; too explosive to be a stalemate. Impasse, then.

At first she thought of talking to Archie Johnson, but rejected the idea. He was a brilliant and sympathetic man, but he would never understand all the nuances of the situation. Emily Parker? She was a nice old girl, and from its beginning she had followed Mary's relationship with Tim, keenly interested, but something in Mary shrank from exposing her dilemma to that florid embodiment of matriarchal suburbia. In the end she phoned John Martinson, the teacher of retarded children. He remembered her immediately.

'I've often wondered what happened to you,' he said. 'How is everything, Miss Horton?'

'Not very good, Mr Martinson. I need to talk to someone desperately, and you're the only person I can think of. I'm terribly sorry to inflict you with my problems, but I just don't know what to do, and I need qualified help. I was wondering if I could bring Tim to see you.'

'Of course you can. How about after supper tomorrow night at my house?'

Mary took the address, then rang the Melville residence.

'It's Mary here, Ron.'

'Oh, g'day there, love. What's the matter?'

'Nothing, really. I was wondering if I might take Tim out to see someone tomorrow night after supper.'

'I don't see why not. Who is it?'

'A teacher of retarded children, a wonderful man. I thought he might be able to assess Tim, give us some idea of what sort of pace we ought to force in his formal learning.'

'Anything you like, Mary. See youse tomorrow night.'

'Fine. By the way, I'd appreciate it if you didn't tell Tim too much about it, I want him to meet this man quite unprepared.'

'Sure thing. Hooroo, love.'

John Martinson lived near his school, which was in the satellite town of Penrith, just at the foot of the Blue Mountains. Tim, used to heading north, enjoyed the drive out of Sydney in another direction; the Post Road flavour of the Great Western Highway kept his nose glued to the window, counting the brilliantly lit car salesrooms, all-night hamburger joints, and drive-in movie lots.

The Martinson house was big but very unpretentious, built of fibrous board painted pale pink, and it rang with the shrill laughter of children.

'Why don't you come through to the back veranda?' John Martinson asked Mary when he answered the door. 'I've made it into my study, and we won't be disturbed there.'

They were introduced to his wife and three oldest children briefly, and went straight through to the back of the house.

John Martinson's eyes rested on Tim curiously, and with keen admiration. He produced two quart bottles of beer and shared them with Tim while he talked, sitting easily in a big chair to one side of his work table. For half an hour Mary said nothing while the two men conversed comfortably over the beer. Tim liked the teacher and he relaxed at once, chattering about the cottage and its garden and his work with Harry Markham, quite unaware that he was being drawn out by an expert.

'Do you like TV Westerns, Tim?' John Martinson asked him at last.

'Oh, yes, I love them!'

'Well, I have some business to discuss with Miss Horton for a while, and I don't think you'll find it very much fun to stay here and listen to us. Why don't I take you inside to see my kids? There's a real beaut Western starting on TV in a few minutes.'

Tim went happily, and as her host came back into the study Mary could hear Tim laughing somewhere inside.

'He'll be all right, Miss Horton. My family is very used to people like Tim.'

'I'm not worried.'

'What's it all about, Miss Horton? May I call you Mary?'

'Yes, of course.'

'Good! Call me John. By the way, I quite see what you meant when you told me Tim was spectacular. I don't think I've ever seen a better looking man, even in the movies.' He laughed, peering down at his own too-thin body. 'He makes me feel like a ninety-pound weakling.'

'I thought you were going to say what a shame it is that someone so good-looking should be mentally retarded.'

He seemed surprised. 'Why should I think that? Not one of us is born without something beautiful and something undesirable within us. I admit that Tim's body and features are magnificent, but don't you think that a great deal of that absolutely stunning beauty comes from the soul?'

'Yes,' Mary said gratefully; he understood, she had been right to choose him.

'He's a dear fellow, I could tell that immediately. One of the sweet ones . . . Do you want me to have him assessed by the experts?'

'No, that isn't why I came to see you at all. I came because circumstances have placed me in what seems to be a total quandary, and I really don't know what to do for the best. It's awful, because no matter what I decide, Tim has to get hurt, perhaps badly.'

The dark blue eyes never deviated from her face. 'It doesn't sound good. What happened?'

'Well, it all started when his mother died nine months ago. I don't know if I told you, but she was seventy years old. Ron, Tim's father, is the same age.'

'I see, or at least I think I do. Tim's missing her?'

'No, not really. It's Tim's father who is missing her, so much so that I don't expect him to live much longer. He's a fine old man, but all the light seemed to go out of his life when his wife died. I can see him fading away before my very eyes. He knows; he told me he knew the other day.'

'And when he dies Tim's all alone.'

'Yes.'

'Does Tim have any idea of this?'

'Yes, I had to tell him. He took it very well.'

'Has he any sort of financial security?'

'Plenty. The family put almost everything they had into making sure Tim would never want for money.'

'And where do you come into it, Mary?'

'Ron – Tim's father – asked me if I'd take Tim when he was gone, and I said yes.'

'Do you realise what you're in for?'

'Oh, yes. But there are unforeseen complications.' She glanced down at her hands. 'How can I take him, John?'

'You mean what will people say?'

'Partly, although if it was only that I'd be prepared to take the consequences. I can't adopt him, he's well over the majority age, but Ron has given me a complete power of attorney in Tim's affairs, and anyway, I have plenty of money myself; I don't need Tim's.'

'What is it, then?'

'Tim's always been very attached to me, I don't know why. It was strange . . . Right from the beginning he liked me, as if he saw something in me that I can't even see myself. It's very nearly two years since I met him . . . In those early days it was simple. We were friends, such good friends. Then when his mother died I went to see the family, and Tim's sister Dawnie, who is a very clever girl and devoted to Tim, levelled some dreadful and quite untrue accusations at me. She implied that I was Tim's mistress, that I was trading on Tim's mental weakness to exploit and corrupt him.'

'I see. It was a shock, wasn't it?'

'Yes. I was horrified, because none of it was true. Tim was

present when she said all this, but luckily he didn't understand what she meant. However, she spoiled it for me and thus for him. I was shamed. Tim's father was there, too, but he took my side. Isn't that odd? He refused to believe a word of what she said, so it shouldn't have made any overt difference in my friendship with Tim. But it did make a difference, perhaps unconscious, perhaps conscious too, I don't know. I found it harder to relax with Tim, and besides, I felt so sorry for Ron that I brought him along to the cottage with us at weekends.

'This went on for six months, almost, during which time Tim changed. He grew silent and withdrawn, he wouldn't communicate with either of us. We were terribly worried. Then one morning there was a terrific scene between Tim and me, it all came out into the open. Tim was jealous of his father, he thought Ron had replaced him in my affections. That was why I had to tell him his father was dying.'

'And?' John Martinson prompted when she hesitated; he was leaning forward, watching her fixedly.

Strangely, the sheer quality of his interest gave her courage to continue.

'Tim was absolutely overjoyed when he realised that my feelings towards him hadn't changed, that I still liked him. Like is his special little word; he'll say he loves cake or TV Westerns or jam pudding, but if he's talking of people he's fond of, he always says like, never love. Odd, isn't it? His mind is so pure and direct that he took the literal interpretation of like and love; he listened to people say they loved food or a good time, but he noticed that when they talked of another human being, they said like. So he says the same thing, sure he's right. Perhaps at that he is.'

Her hands were shaking; she stilled them by clasping them together in her lap. 'Apparently during this period when he thought I liked Ron better than I liked him, he was so perturbed that he sat down and worked out a way of proving to me that his own liking for me was genuine and undying. Television gave him his answer; he reasoned it out for himself that when a man liked a woman he showed her by kissing her. No doubt he also noticed that in movies such an action usually results in a happy ending.' She shivered slightly. 'I'm really to blame. Had I been more on the *qui vive* I might have averted it, but I was too obtuse to see it in time. Fool!

'We had a really dreadful scene, during which he accused me

of liking Ron more than I liked him, and so on. I had to explain to him why I was paying so much attention to Ron, that Ron was dying. As you can imagine, he was shattered. Neither of us was our emotional self, we were upset and very tense. When the shock of learning about his father wore off a bit, it dawned on him that I still like him better than Ron. He sort of leaped to his feet and grabbed me so fast that I didn't realise what he was doing until it was far too late.'

She stared at John Martinson pleadingly. 'I didn't know what to do for the best, but somehow I couldn't bring myself to humiliate him by repulsing him.'

'I understand that very well, Mary,' he said gently. 'So you responded, I take it?'

She had flushed in embarrassment, but she managed to speak calmly. 'Yes. At the time it seemed the best thing to do, that it was more important to make sure he suffered no rejection than it was to push him away. Besides, I – I was in too deep myself, I couldn't seem to help it. He kissed me, and luckily I didn't have to contend with anything more serious than that, because we heard Ron calling us and it gave me an excellent excuse to break away from him.'

'How did Tim react to the kiss?'

'Not quite as I imagined. He liked it too much, it excited him. From then on I could tell he was seeing me differently, that he wanted more of this new sensation. I explained to him that it was bad, that it was forbidden, that although it could happen between lots of people it couldn't happen between us, and superficially he understood. He really did grasp the fact that it was forbidden, and he cooperated splendidly. It's never happened again, nor will it in the future.'

A sudden scream of laughter came from the house; Mary jumped in fright, momentarily losing her train of thought. Plucking at the clasp of her handbag, she sat voiceless and white-faced.

'Go on,' he said. 'It's never happened again, nor will it in the future.'

'I suppose for Tim it must be like opening a door into a whole new world and then discovering that you can't enter. Yet all the time you know this, the door is still open and the new world is green and beautiful. I feel so sorry for him, and so helpless to heal him. I'm the cause of his misery. He won't do it again, but neither can he forget the time it happened. Ron had kept him absolutely ignorant about matters of a physical nature, and never having heard of it, let alone known of it, he didn't miss it. Now he's had a small taste, and it's gnawing at him without mercy.'

'Of course.' He sighed. 'That was inevitable, Mary.'

She looked past his head and fixed her eyes on a tiny spider crawling down the wall, unable to meet his gaze. 'Naturally I couldn't tell Ron what had happened, and yet at the same time everything is changed. How can I take him when Ron dies? If Ron knew he'd never ask it of me, I'm sure. I *can't* take him now, it would drive me mad! At the moment I manage, I can keep Tim occupied and happy two days a week, especially with Ron there. But how can either of us contend with living in the same house together all the time? Oh, John, I just don't know what to do! If I thought there was any chance Tim might forget it would be different, I'd find the strength somehow. But I know he won't forget, and when I catch him looking at me, I . . . Tim isn't one of those unretentive simpletons, you see; he has the ability to absorb and cement memories if they make a big enough impression or he repeats them enough. Every time he looks at me he remembers, and he isn't clever enough to hide it. He's angry and hurt and very resentful, and though he understands it can't happen again, he'll never really understand why.'

'Have you thought of a solution, Mary?'

'Not really. Is there some sort of hostel perhaps, where people like Tim who are adults physically but still children in mind could stay when they're all alone and have no family? If he lived in a place like that I could have him on weekends. I could manage that.'

'Anything else occur to you?'

'Not seeing him again. But how can I do that, John? It wouldn't help him to hand him over to Dawnie – or is that simply selfishness on my part? Do I really mean as much to him as I think, or is it only self-delusion? I suppose it's possible that he might forget me once he's installed in Dawnie's house, but I keep seeing her and her husband living their lives with Tim as an afterthought. She has more important responsibilities, she can't devote herself to him the way I can!'

'There is another answer, you know.'

'There is?' She leaned forward eagerly. 'Oh, if you only knew how much I've yearned to hear you say something like that!'

'Why don't you marry Tim?'

Mary gaped at him, so dumbfounded that it took her a few seconds to say 'You're joking!' The chair was suddenly too hard and confining; she got up and paced the length of the room once, then came back to face him. 'You're joking?' she repeated pitifully, turning it into a question.

A pipe lay on the work table; he picked it up and began to fill it, tamping the tobacco down slowly and very carefully, as though by doing so he could concentrate on remaining calm. 'No, I'm not joking, Mary. It's the only logical answer.'

'*Logical answer?* Heavens above, John! It's no answer at all! How can I possibly marry a mentally retarded boy young enough to be my son? It's criminal!'

'Utter twaddle!' He sucked on the pipe furiously, teeth biting down on the stem. 'Be sensible, woman! What else is there to do but marry him? I can understand why you didn't think of it for yourself, but now that the idea has been put into your mind there's no excuse for throwing it aside! To do so would be criminal, if you like the word. Marry him, Mary Horton, marry him!'

'Under no circumstances!' She was stiff with anger.

'What's the matter, frightened of what other people will say?'

'You know I'm not! I can't possibly marry Tim! The very idea is straight out of cloudcuckooland!'

'Stuff and nonsense! Of course you can marry him.'

'No, I can't! I'm old enough to be his mother, I'm a sour, ugly old maid, no fit partner for Tim!'

He got up, went over to her, took her shoulders, and shook her until she was dizzy. 'Now you listen to me, Miss Mary Horton! If you're no fit partner for him, he's no fit partner for you, either! What is this, noble self-sacrifice? I can't abide nobility, all it does is make everyone unhappy. I said you ought to marry him, and I mean it! Do you want to know why?'

'Oh, by all means!'

'Because you can't live without each other, that's why! Good lord, woman, it sticks out a mile how besotted you are for him, and he for you! It's no platonic friendship, and it never was! What would happen if you chose the second of your two alternatives and stopped seeing him? Tim wouldn't survive his father more than six months, you know that, and you'd probably live out a full span of years like a shadow of your former self, in a world so grey and full of tears that you'd wish you were dead a thousand times in each and every endless day. As for your first alternative, there isn't any such place because what places there are have waiting lists literally years long. Tim would never live long enough to make it in the door. Is that what you want – to kill Tim?'

'No, no!' She groped for a handkerchief.

'Listen to me! You've got to stop thinking of yourself as a sour, ugly old maid, even if that's what you really are. I defy anyone to explain what one person sees in another, and as for you, you shouldn't even dare to query it. Whatever you think you are, Tim thinks you're something quite different and much more desirable. You said you didn't know what on earth he saw in you, that whatever it was you couldn't even see it yourself. Be grateful for that! Why toss it away in an excess of self-sacrifice and pride? It's such useless, pointless self-sacrifice!

'Do you think he'll change, grow tired of you? Be your age! This isn't an exquisitely beautiful, sophisticated man of the world, this is a poor, silly creature as simple and faithful as a dog! Oh, you don't like my saying things like that, eh? Well, right at this moment there's no room for euphemism or illusion, Mary Horton; there's only room for the truth, as plain and unvarnished as the truth can get. I'm not interested in why Tim should have fixed his affections on you, I'm only interested in the fact that he has. He loves you, it's as simple as that. He loves you! As improbable, impractical, inexplicable as it may be, he loves you. I don't know why any more than you do, but it is a concrete fact. And what on earth is the matter with you, that you can even contemplate throwing his love away?'

'You don't understand!' Mary wept, her head in her hands, her fingers wreaking havoc upon the orderly strands of her hair.

'Oh, I understand better than you think,' he said, more gently. 'Tim loves you, with every corner of his being he loves you. For some reason, out of all the people he's ever known, he fixed his affection on you, and with you it will stay. He's not going to grow bored or jaded with you, he's not going to throw you over for a younger, prettier woman in ten years' time, he isn't after your money any more than his father is. You're certainly nothing to write home about now, so it's not as though you've got any beauty to lose, is it? Besides, he has more than enough beauty for the two of you.'

She lifted her head and tried to smile. 'You're nothing if not honest.'

'I am because I have to be. But that's only the half of it, isn't it? Don't tell me you've never admitted to yourself that you love him every bit as much as he loves you?'

'Oh, I've admitted it,' she answered wryly.

'When? Recently?'

'A long time ago, before his mother died. He told me one night that I looked like his picture of Saint Terese, and for some reason his saying that knocked the wind out of my sails. I'd loved him from the first moment of seeing him, but it was then I admitted it to myself.'

'And are you likely to grow tired of him?'

'Grow tired of Tim? No, oh, no!'

'Then why can't you marry him?'

'Because I'm old enough to be his mother, and because he's so beautiful.'

'It isn't good enough, Mary. All that appearance business is crap, and I'm not even going to be bothered arguing with you about it. As to the age objection, I think it's worth discussing. You're *not* his mother, Mary! You don't feel like his mother and he doesn't think of you as his mother. This isn't an ordinary situation, you know; this isn't two people fully grown in mind and body but with a disparity in age casting doubt on the genuineness of the emotional ties between them. You and Tim are unique in the annals of man. I don't mean that a spinster in her middle forties has never married a man young enough to be her son before, even perhaps a mentally retarded one, I mean that you're a completely odd couple from every standpoint and you may as well accept your uniqueness. Nothing holds you together except your love for each other, does it? There's the difference in age, in beauty, in brain, in wealth, in status, in background, in temperament – I could go on and on, couldn't I? The emotional ties between you and Tim are genuine, genuine enough to have transcended all of these innate differences. I don't think anyone on earth including you yourself will ever be able to discover the reason why you fit together. You just do. So marry him, Mary Horton, marry him! You'll have to endure an awful lot of sniggers, levelled fingers, and conjecture, but it doesn't really matter, does it? You've had a fair bit of that all along, I'd say. Why not give the old biddies something really worthwhile to talk about? *Marry him!*'

'It's – it's indecent, it's almost obscene!'

'I'm sure that's what everyone will say.'

Her chin went up. 'I don't care what other people say, I'm only concerned with its effect on Tim, how people will treat him if he marries me.'

John Martinson shrugged. 'He'll survive speculation a lot better than separation, I assure you.'

Her hands lay clenched in her lap, and he put his own over them strongly, eyes glittering.

'Think about this one, Mary. Why shouldn't Tim marry? What's so special about Tim? You can protest all you like that you think of him as a man, but I disagree. The only times you've thought of him as a man, you've almost died of horror, haven't you? That's because you've made the mistake everyone makes with mentally retarded people. In your mind Tim is fixed as a child. But he's *not* a child, Mary! Like normal people, retards are subject to the growth and change which comes with maturation; within the limited scope of their psychic development, they cease to be children. Tim is a grown man, with all the physical attributes of a grown man and a perfectly normal hormonal metabolism. If he'd been injured in the leg he'd walk with a limp, but because his injury is to the brain he limps mentally, and that kind of handicap doesn't prevent him being a man any more than a maimed leg would.

'Why should Tim have to go through life deprived of the opportunity to satisfy one of the most driving needs his body and his spirit know? Why should he be denied his manhood? Why should he be sheltered and shielded from his body? Oh, Mary, he's already deprived of so much! *So much!* Why deprive him of yet more? Isn't he, a man, entitled to his manhood? Honour the man in him, Mary Horton! Marry him!'

'Yes, I see.' She sat silently for a while, thinking. Then she lifted her head. 'All right, then, if you think it's the best thing under the circumstances, I'll marry him.'

'Good girl!' His face softened. 'You'll both get more out of it than you think, you know.'

She frowned. 'But it's so fraught with difficulties!'

'His father?'

'I think not. No, I imagine Ron will be pleased, though he may well be the only one. But Tim and I, we're equally inexperienced in this, and I'm not sure I'm competent to deal with all the problems involved.'

'You're worrying unnecessarily. The trouble is you're a thinker, you try to contend with things that have a habit of solving themselves when the time comes. Where Tim's needs are concerned you're very well attuned, I'd say.'

Suppressing her urge to squirm, Mary managed to appear composed. 'I shouldn't have children, should I?'

'No, you shouldn't. Not that Tim's deficiencies are hereditary, it doesn't seem there's much chance of that. But you're getting into an age group where it's possible that you won't live to see any offspring through to their maturity, and Tim's condition precludes him from fulfilling your role should anything happen to you. Besides which, you're more than old enough to repeat his mother's misfortune, and if you did that it would be life's greatest irony. Statistically speaking, if you start having children past the thirty-five mark your chances of having a normal child go right down, and the farther you are past thirty-five when you begin, the lower your chances get.'

'I know.'

'Do you think you'll regret not having children? Is it likely to colour your life with disappointment?'

'No! How could it? I never expected to get married, or yearned to get married. Tim is more than enough for me.'

'It won't be easy.'

'I know.'

John put down his pipe and sighed. 'Well, Mary, I do wish you all the luck and happiness in the world. It's up to you now.'

She rose, gathering her bag and gloves together. 'And I thank you very much, John. You've put me deeper than ever in your debt, and I give you my word that I'll work to help your cause in whatever way I can.'

'You owe me nothing. The pleasure I'll get from just knowing Tim is happy is more than enough reward for me. Just come and see me from time to time.'

Instead of simply dropping Tim off in Surf Street, Mary came in with him. Ron was sitting in the living room with the television blaring a late-night sports roundup.

'G'day there, Mary! I didn't expect you'd come in this late.'

She sat down on the sofa while Tim busied himself putting her bag and gloves in a safe place. 'I wanted to have a talk with you, Ron. It's rather important, and I'd like to get it over and done with while I've still got the courage.'

'Right you are, love! How about a cuppa tea and a bit of fresh cream sponge?'

'That sounds nice.' She looked up at Tim, smiling. 'Do you have to work tomorrow, Tim?'

He nodded.

'I don't want to push you off, then, but I think it's bedtime for you, Charlie. Your Pop and I have something to talk about, but I promise I won't keep it a secret from you, I'll tell you all about it this weekend. All right?'

'All right. Night-night, Mary.' He never requested her to tuck him up in Esme's house.

Ron spread cups and saucers and plates on the kitchen table while the kettle heated, watching Mary keenly out of the corner of his eye. 'You look real done-in, love,' he observed.

'I am, rather. It was an exhausting evening.'

'What did the teacher bloke say about Tim?'

Her cup was chipped; she sat rubbing her finger tip back and forth across the pitted rim, turning ways to tackle the subject over in her mind. When she looked up at Ron she seemed old and tired.

'Ron, I wasn't exactly truthful about why I took Tim to see John Martinson tonight.'

'No?'

'No.' Round and round the cup edge her fingertip moved; she lowered her eyes to it, unable to continue speaking while she looked into those wide blue eyes, so like Tim's in form and so unlike Tim's in expression. 'This is very difficult for me, because I don't think you have any idea of what I'm going to tell you. Ron, did it ever occur to you that it's going to be hard for me to take Tim if anything happens to you?'

The hand holding the teapot trembled; tea slopped onto the table. 'You've changed your mind, right?'

'No. I won't do that, Ron, unless you don't like my solution to our problem.' She folded her hands together in front of her cup and managed to look at him steadily. 'Tim and I have always had a very special relationship, you know that. Out of all the people he's ever met he likes me best. I don't know why, and I've given up even wondering about it. It isn't far wrong to say he loves me.'

'No, it isn't. He does love you, Mary. That's why I want you to be the one to take him after I'm gone.'

'I love him, too. I've loved him from the first instant I ever saw him, standing in the sun watching the concrete truck emptying cement all over Emily Parker's oleanders. I didn't know he was retarded then, but when I found out it didn't change anything, in fact it only made me love him more. For a long while I never attached any importance to the difference in our sexes, until first Emily Parker and then your daughter gave me some pretty rude shocks on the subject. You've always kept Tim sheltered from that sort of thing, haven't you?'

'I had to, Mary. With Es and me being so old, I knew there was a pretty good chance we wouldn't be around when Tim grew up, so we talked over what we oughta do while he was still a little bloke. Without us to watch over him, and him being as handsome as he is, it seemed as though he was likely to get himself into a heap of trouble if he ever found out what women were for while he was still young and the urge was strong. It was easy until he got old enough to work, but once he started with Harry Markham I knew it would be hard. So I went and had a talk with Harry, made it clear that I didn't want any of his blokes getting Tim into trouble or trying to wise him up about the birds and the bees. I warned Harry that if they tried anything I'd put the police on to them for contributing to the delinquency of a minor, and a minor who wasn't the full quid into the bargain. It was the only thing I asked, and I suppose they got their fun from tormenting him about other things, but I must say they was good about the sex business, even used to watch out for him and keep the women away. Bill Naismith usually comes most of the way to and from work with Tim, because he lives at the top of Coogee Bay Road. So between one thing and another, it's turned out fine. We been lucky, of course. There was always the chance that something might happen, but it never has.'

Mary felt the prickling march of blood suffuse her face. 'Why were you so adamant about it, Ron?' she asked, desperate to delay the moment of confession.

'Well, Mary, you've always got to weigh the pleasure agin the pain, ain't that right? And it seemed to Es and me that poor old Tim would end up getting more pain than he would pleasure from playing around with women and sex and all that. Mum and me thought he'd be better off ignorant. It's terrible true that what you never know you don't miss, and with him working so hard labouring it's never been a burden to him. I suppose it might seem cruel to someone on the outside, but we thought we was doing the right thing. What do you reckon, Mary?'

'I'm sure you acted in Tim's best interests, Ron. You always do.'

But he seemed to interpret her answer as noncommittal, for he hurried into a further explanation.

'Lucky for us, we had a good example right under our noses while Tim was growing up. There used to be a simple girl down the street from us, and her Mum had awful trouble with her. She was much worse off than Tim, only about fourpence in the quid, I reckon, and ugly too. Some rotten bugger took a fancy to her when she was fifteen, pimples and fat and slobber and all. Some men will hump anything. And she's been pregnant off and on ever since, the poor little dill, had one cock-eyed, hare-lipped ning-nong of a baby after the other, until they put her away in an institution. That's where the law's wrong, Mary, they oughta have some provision for abortion. Even in the state home people kept getting at her, and in the end they tied her tubes. It was her Mum told us whatever we did, not to let Tim get ideas.'

Ignoring Mary's soothing murmur, he got up and paced the room restlessly; it was painfully apparent that the decision taken all those years ago continued to worry him.

'There are blokes and sheilas who don't care if a kid is simple. All they're after is a bit of fun, and they sort of like the fact that they don't have to worry about the kid, because it isn't smart enough to chase after them and give them a hard time when they're sick of it. Why should they care? They reckon that the kid's so dill-brained it can't feel anything the way us ordinary people do. They'd kick it the way they'd kick a dog, smirking all over their faces because the silly ding comes back for more, wagging its tail, belly on the ground.

'But dill-brains like Tim and the girl down the street *do* feel, Mary, they ain't that far off the full quid, especially Tim. Good Christ, even an animal can feel! I'll never forget when Tim was a tiny little bloke, about seven or eight. He was just starting to talk as if he knew what the words meant . . . He come in with this chewed-up kitten, and Es said he could keep it. Well, not long after the kitten turned into a cat, it started to swell up like a balloon, and the next thing we knew, kittens. I was hopping mad, but lucky for me, I thought, she'd had them behind the bricked-up chimney in our bedroom, and I decided I'd get rid of them before

Tim knew anything about it. I had to knock out half the bricks to get at her, I dunno how she got in there in the first place. There she was, all covered in soot, kittens too, and I had Es breathing down me neck laughing her head off and saying it was just as well she was a black cat, you'd never notice the soot. Anyway, I grabbed all the kittens, took them into the backyard and drowned them in a bucket of water. And I've never regretted doing anything so much in all me life. The poor little bugger of a cat walked round the house for days, crying and howling and looking for her kittens, turning her head to look up at me with them big green eyes so full of trust, like, as if she thought I could find them for her. And she cried, Mary, she cried real tears, they rolled down her face just like she was a human-being sort of woman. I never thought animals could cry real tears. Jesus! For a while there I wanted to put me head in the gas oven. Es wouldn't talk to me for a week over it, and every time the cat cried, so did Tim.'

Pulling his chair closer to the table, he sat down again with hands outstretched. The old house was so quiet, Mary found herself thinking while Ron got himself together. Just the ticking of the old-fashioned kitchen clock and the sound of Ron swallowing. No wonder he hated it when he had known it so different.

'So you see, Mary,' Ron continued, 'if a cat can have feelings, so can a dill-brain like Tim, and more feelings, because Tim's not all that bad. He mightn't set the world on fire with his ideas, but he's got a heart, Mary, a great big warm heart just full of love. If he started in with a woman he'd love her, but do youse think she could love him, eh? He'd just be a piece on the side to her, that's all, and him just brimming over for her. I couldn't take it.

'Tim's got a real pretty face and a real pretty body, and there's been women – and men! – after him since he was twelve. After he was dumped, what do you think would happen to Tim? He'd look at me the way that poor bloody little cat did, as if he expected me to get his girlfriend back and couldn't understand why I wasn't even trying.'

A silence fell. Somewhere inside came the noise of a door slamming; Ron looked up and seemed to remember that Tim was in the house with them.

'Excuse me a minute, Mary.'

She sat listening to the loud monotonous clock until he came back, grinning to himself.

'Typical Aussie, that boy. Can't get him into more clothes

than necessary, and if he has half a chance he'll wander around mother-naked. He has a bad habit of coming out of the bathroom after his shower and walking all over the place without a stitch on, so I thought I'd better make sure he didn't come out here for something.' He looked at her sharply. 'I hope he behaves hisself when he stays with youse? No complaints?'

'He behaves himself perfectly,' she answered uncomfortably.

Ron sat down again. 'You know, it's a real blessing we're just working-class people, Mary. It's been easier to shelter Tim than if we'd belonged with the likes of Dawnie's man Mick. Them stuck-up snobs is harder to spot, more cunning like, men and women, but men especially, I reckon. Instead of drinking with dinkum blokes in the public bar at the Seaside, he'd be sitting in some pansy lounge with all the idle women and all the lisping fairies in the world. Our class has things better organised than that, thank me lucky stars. Black is blacker and white is whiter, and there ain't so much grey in between. I do hope youse understands, Mary, why we did it.'

'I understand. I really do. The trouble is that Tim's woken up, courtesy of the television set. He watched the love scenes and decided it was a good way to show me how much he liked me.'

'Oh, God!' Ron sat down abruptly. 'I thought we'd frightened him off it, I thought we'd scared the living daylights out of him so much he'd never try it.'

'You probably did a good job of scaring him off, but you see, he didn't really associate what he was doing with what you scared him away from. It didn't start off in his mind as a carnal thing. He just wanted to show me how much he liked me. In the process, unfortunately, he also found out how much he liked it.'

Ron was horrified. 'You mean he raped you? I don't believe it!'

'Of course not! He kissed me, that's all. But he liked it, and it's been preying on his mind ever since. I managed to convince him that between us it was forbidden, but he's awake, Ron, he's awake! It only happened once, I wouldn't ever let it happen again, but how can you or I blot it out of his mind? What's done is done! While there was no truth to what Dawnie or Emily Parker or anyone else thought it didn't matter, but ever since Tim kissed me I've nearly gone crazy wondering what on earth I'm going to do with him if anything happens to you.'

Ron had relaxed again. 'I see what you mean.'

'Well, I didn't know where to turn, who to talk to about it.

That was why I took Tim to see John Martinson tonight, I wanted him to meet Tim and then to give me his frank opinion on the whole situation.'

'Why didn't you talk to me, Mary?' Ron demanded, hurt.

'How could I possibly talk to you, Ron? You're Tim's father, you're too close to everything to be detached. If I'd talked to you first I would have nothing to offer you this moment beyond the facts, I'd have no direction to go and no solution. If I'd talked to you first we'd probably have come to the conclusion that there was nothing to be done save separate Tim from me. I went to John Martinson because he's had a great deal of experience with mentally retarded people, and he's genuinely concerned for them. I thought that out of all the people I know he was the only one capable of thinking of Tim first, and that's what I wanted, someone capable of thinking exclusively of Tim.'

'Okay, Mary, I see your point. What did he say?'

'He offered me a solution, and the way he presented it made me see that there's no doubt of it being the wisest thing to do. I told him that I thought you'd agree after you heard it, but I confess I'm not so sure in my own mind about that as I sounded when I reassured John Martinson.

'Whatever you say or think about it, I assure you I've already said or thought it, so nothing you can say will surprise or hurt me.' She held out her cup for more tea, anxious to have something to do. 'I'm forty-five years old, Ron, old enough to be Tim's mother, and I'm a plain, dowdy woman without any sort of physical attraction for men. What Tim sees in me is totally beyond me, but he sees it all the same. John Martinson says I ought to marry Tim.'

'Does he?' Ron's face was curiously expressionless.

'Yes, he does.'

'Why?'

'Chiefly because Tim loves me, and because Tim's a man, not a child. When he told me what he thought I should do, I was flabbergasted, and believe me I argued against it. It's like mating a thoroughbred with a mongrel, mating Tim's youth and beauty with me, and I told him so. Forgive me for saying this, but he answered that there were two ways of looking at it, that mating my intelligence with Tim's stupidity was just as bad. They weren't his words; he said, "If you're no fit partner for Tim, he's no fit partner for you." His point was that neither Tim nor myself is any marital prize, so what was so appalling about it? I still opposed the whole idea, chiefly on the grounds of the big difference in our ages, but he threw that aside too. It's me Tim likes, not the girl next door or the daughter of one of his workmates.

'What convinced me that John Martinson was right was something that hadn't occurred to me at all, and I'm sure it hasn't occurred to you either. We're both too close to Tim to see it.' She shook her head. 'Tim's a grown man, Ron, in that respect he's perfectly normal. John was quite brutally frank about it, he took me by the shoulders and shook me until my teeth rattled because he was so angry at my lack of insight and sympathy for Tim. What was the matter with me, he asked me, that I could deny Tim his right to be a man in the only way he can ever be a man? Why shouldn't Tim get as much out of life as possible?

'I'd never looked at it that way before, I'd been so concerned with what other people would think, how they'd laugh at him and tease and torment him because he'd married a rich spinster old enough to be his mother. But I'd completely overlooked the fact that he's entitled to get as much out of life as he can.'

Again she fell to exploring the chipped cup with her fingertip; Ron was concealing his reactions well; she had no idea what he thought, and as if to confuse her more he picked up the teapot to refill her cup.

'We've all heard of reverses. I remember once being very angry because one of the girls in our office fell in love with a paraplegic who refused to marry her. Archie knew the girl well enough to be sure she was a one-man woman, that there'd never be anyone for her but this man. He went to see the fellow, told him not to throw their chance of happiness aside because he wasn't a man in that one sense. And we all agreed that Archie had done the right thing, there was no reason why the girl shouldn't have married her man in a wheelchair. There's more to life than that, Archie told him.

'There is more to life than that, Ron, but what about Tim? How much is there to Tim's life, and how much could there be? Now that the opportunity has presented itself, have we any right to deny Tim everything he's entitled to as a human being? That's the crux of John Martinson's argument.'

'He really laid it on the line, didn't he?' Ron pushed his hands tiredly through his hair. 'I just never thought of it that way.'

'Well, I admitted the truth of his argument, I had to. But why me, I asked? Surely Tim could do better than me? But can he?

Can he really? Whatever I am, Tim loves me. And whatever Tim is, I love him. With me he'll be safe, Ron, and if in marrying him I can round out his life as much as it can ever be rounded out, then I'll marry him in everyone's teeth, including yours.'

Her feeling of teetering on the brink of a precipice had gone entirely as she talked; Ron watched her curiously. Several times he had seen her shaken from habitual calm, but never quite like this, so ringingly alive. One could not call her mousy in any mood, but mostly her plain good face was distinguished only by her strength of character. Now she seemed lit with a fleeting beauty that would disappear the moment her zeal died; he found himself wondering what marriage to Tim would do for her. Older and infinitely more worldly than Mary, he knew there was never an easy answer.

'Women normally live longer than men,' she continued eagerly, 'so there's every chance that I'll be with him for many years to come. I'm not so much older that my predeceasing him is a major consideration. He's not going to go off looking for some pretty young thing because his own wife is old and faded. I'm old and faded now, Ron, but it doesn't worry him at all.

'I thought about simply living with him, because in the eyes of most people that would be the lesser sin. But John Martinson is right. Marriage is better. If I marry him I have full legal authority over his life; Dawnie can never take him away. You see, Dawnie's been worrying me for some time. I don't think it's occurred to you how easily she could remove Tim from my custody the moment anything happened to you. Why should it occur to you? She's your daughter, and you love her dearly. But she doesn't love me at all, and she would never admit to herself that I'm better for Tim than she is. Your letters to her and Mick, your power of attorney, all those things mean nothing if Dawnie really wanted to make trouble. Upon your death Dawnie would become Tim's legal guardian in the eyes of any court in the land, no matter what sort of directives you left. I'm no relation, I haven't even known Tim very long, and our association is highly suspect.

'When you first asked me to take Tim, I didn't think beyond the fact that you trusted me so magnificently, but I think you're detached enough to see Dawnie in her true light. She loves Tim, but she hates me just that much more, and Tim would become the victim on her altar. John Martinson wasn't aware of the magnitude of Dawnie's enmity, but he hit on the only feasible solution in spite of it. I *must* marry Tim.'

Ron laughed wryly. 'Ain't life funny? You're right about one thing, Mary. People would understand it if you just lived together much quicker than they will your marrying. It's one of them queer situations where marriage is a crime, ain't it?'

'That's exactly the word I used to John Martinson. Criminal.'

Ron got up and walked round the table to put his arm about her shoulders, then he bent his head and kissed her. 'You're a fine person, Mary. I'll be real glad to see you marry my son. Me and Es couldn't have wished for a better answer, and I reckon she's cheering youse on.

'But it had better be soon, Mary, real soon. If I'm there to see it and I leave a testament to the fact that I approve, there's very little Dawnie can do. Leave it until after I'm dead and you don't have a leg to stand on. I oughta seen it for myself, but a man's always a bit blind about his kids.'

'That's why I had to bring the matter up tonight. I'm going to have to go into hospital for a few days to see to it that it's impossible for me to have children, but I think the marriage ought to take place as soon as possible.'

'Right you are! We'll go into town next Monday to get the licence, then youse can be married at the end of the week, I think.'

She stroked his scratchy cheek lovingly. 'I couldn't have asked for a nicer father-in-law than you, Ron. Thank you so much for understanding and consenting.'

24

In the end they decided not to tell Dawnie anything about the wedding until after the deed was done, but the day after Mary and Ron agreed on it she told Archie Johnson.

'Sweet suffering rock oysters, you're joking!'

It took some time to convince him that she was serious. And after the initial shock wore off he rallied and congratulated her sincerely.

'Mary love, I couldn't be more pleased for you. It's the oddest match since Chopin and George Sand, but if anyone on this old ball of mud knows what they're doing, it's you. I'm not going to make your life a misery by raising all sorts of objections because I'm bloody sure you've already thought of them for yourself. The only thing I'm sorry about is that after all these years of thinking I was safe I'm going to lose you. On that head I could cry.'

'Why on earth should you lose me?'

'Well, won't you have your work cut out looking after your Tim?'

'Heavens, no! I do need to take three months off almost immediately, no notice or anything, for which I'm very sorry, but I'm not going to give up work, nor is Tim. I think we'll both be better off getting out into the world among ordinary people. If we stopped working and saw no one save ourselves we'd both deteriorate.'

'I'd like to come to your wedding, Mary. I'm very fond of you, and though I've never met Tim I'm very fond of him, too, because he made such a difference to your life.'

'I'd like you and Tricia to come to my wedding.'

'When is it?'

'Next Friday afternoon at the Registrar General's offices.'

'Then why don't you begin your leave right this moment? If I have to put up with Celeste Murphy for three months I may as well face the music as soon as possible.'

'Bless you, but no thanks. I'll take Celeste under my wing until next Wednesday. That will be soon enough.'

Emily Parker heard the news gleefully. Mary invited her over after dinner that night, and told her.

'Lord love a duck, dearie, it's just what youse both needs. I'm tickled pink, love, I really am. Here's your very good health, and may youse live happily ever after.'

'Will you come to my wedding?'

'Ta, I wouldn't miss it for the world. Good luck to youse, Miss Horton, I'm real proud of youse!'

Mary also went and saw Harry Markham that night, after she managed to push Emily Parker back to the other side of the camphor laurels.

Harry stared at his visitor curiously, sure he had seen her somewhere before, but unable to place her.

'Do you remember renovating Mrs Emily Parker's house in Artarmon over two years ago, Mr Markham?'

'Yair, sure.'

'I'm Mary Horton, Mrs Parker's next door neighbour.'

His face cleared. 'Oh, right, right! I thought I knew youse from somewhere.'

'I'm not here on business, Mr Markham, I'm here to talk about Tim Melville.'

'Tim Melville?'

'That's right, Tim Melville. It may come as something of a shock to you, Mr Markham, but next Friday I'm marrying Tim.'

Poor Harry gurgled and gulped for a full minute before he found voice enough to squeak, 'You're marrying *Dim Tim*?'

'That's correct, next Friday. Under normal circumstances, having heard from Mrs Parker what sort of pranks you like to play on him, I'd be tempted to persuade him to find another employer, but he liked working with you and your men, so I'm happy to see him remain with you.'

Harry's eyes strayed past her to the huge Bentley parked at his curbside. He remembered now that she was accounted the wealthiest woman in Artarmon, and decided she was worth placating. 'Well, youse could knock me down with a bullrout, Miss Horton! This is quite a little bit of news, ain't it?'

'I'm sure it is, Mr Markham. However, I haven't much time and I'd like to be as brief as possible. There are a couple of things we must decide on right now. Firstly, do you wish to keep Tim in your employ if he takes three months' leave starting next Wednesday? Secondly, if you do wish to keep him in your employ, are you willing to keep your men in order on the subject of Tim's marriage?'

Still floundering, Harry shook his head to clear it. 'Crikey, Miss Horton, I don't know what to say!'

'Then I suggest you make up your mind, Mr Markham. I can't stay here all night.'

He thought for a moment. 'Well, I'll be honest with you, Miss Horton. I like Tim and me crew likes Tim. It's as good a time as any to do without him for three months because it's coming on summer and I can always find the odd university student or two as casual labourers, though it'll take a few of them to fill Tim's shoes, useless lot of snotty bastards they are. Tim's been with me twelve years and he's a bloody good worker. I'd have to look a lot longer than three months to find another labourer as cheerful and willing and reliable as Tim, so if it's all right with youse, I'd like to keep the little bloke.'

'Fine. As to my second point, I'm hoping you have the sense to understand that it would be very bad for Tim to be teased about his marriage. By all means go on with your practical jokes and the sort of ribbing Tim seems to accept as a matter of course. He doesn't really mind it. But the subject of his marriage is absolutely taboo, and I give you my word that if I ever discover you've embarrassed or humiliated him because he married a rich old maid, I'll break you and the members of your staff into little pieces morally and financially. I can't stop you discussing it among yourselves and as a matter of fact I wouldn't dream of doing so, since I'm sure it's a very interesting and intriguing morsel of gossip. But when Tim is around it's never to be mentioned, except to offer him the normal congratulations. Is that understood?'

Mary Horton was more than a match for Harry Markham; he gave in without a struggle. 'Yes, certainly, Miss Horton, anything you say, Miss Horton.'

Mary held out her hand. 'Thank you very much, Mr Markham, I appreciate your cooperation. Goodbye.'

Next on Mary's list was the gynaecologist. Having made up her mind what to do, Mary tackled the obstacles one by one in sequence, and enjoyed herself more than she had expected. This was her métier, doing things; she had no attacks of self-doubt, no second thoughts now that her mind was made up.

In the gynaecologist's office she explained the situation to him calmly.

'I can't possibly run the risk of a pregnancy, sir, I'm sure you see why. I presume you'll have to hospitalise me to tie off my tubes, so I thought while I'm in there and you're fiddling around with me, you might do something about the fact that I'm an intact virgin. I can't possibly endanger this relationship by evincing the slightest sign of pain, and I understand it's very painful for a woman to commence sexual activity at my age.'

The gynaecologist put up a hand to his face hastily to hide his involuntary smile; more than most men he was acquainted with Mary Horton's breed, for there were plenty of them working in Australian hospitals. Bloody dedicated old maids, he thought, they're all the same. Brisk, practical, disconcertingly level-headed, and yet for all that women underneath, full of pride, sensitivity, and a curious softness. His amusement under control again, he tapped his pen against the desk and hummed and hawed.

'I think I agree with you, Miss Horton. Now would you please step behind the screen there and remove all your clothes? Nurse will be in to give you a robe in a moment.'

By Saturday morning Tim was the only one left to tell. She had asked Ron not to mention the subject, but refused to take Tim to the cottage on his own.

'Of course you'll come with us, Ron,' she said firmly. 'Why should this make any difference? We're not married yet, you know. I can easily manage to get Tim off on his own and tell him.'

The opportunity came in the afternoon; Ron went to lie down for a while, winking broadly at Mary as he took himself off to his bedroom.

'Tim, why don't we go down to the beach and sit in the sun?'

He jumped up at once, beaming. 'Oh, that sounds nice, Mary. Is it warm enough to swim?'

'I don't think so, but it doesn't matter anyway. I want to talk to you for a while, not swim.'

'I like talking to you, Mary,' he confided. 'It's such a long time since we talked.'

She laughed. 'Flatterer! We talk all the time.'

'Not the way we do when you say, "Tim, I want to talk to you." They're the best sort of talks, it means you've got something really good to say.'

Her eyes opened wide. 'Aren't you shrewd? Come on, then, mate, no dilly-dallying!'

It was hard to rid herself of the intensely practical, energetic mood of the past few days, and for a while she sat on the sand in silence, trying to come down from her plateau of busy briskness. To adopt this attitude had been essential for her mental well-being; without it she could never have managed to say and do all that was required, for any sign of vulnerability in herself would have resulted in disaster. Now the hardiness was not needed, and must be discarded.

'Tim, have you any idea what marriage is?'

'I think so. It's what Mum and Pop are, and what my Dawnie did.'

'Can you tell me anything more than that about it?'

'Golly, I dunno!' He ran his hand through his thick gold hair, grimacing. 'It means you go and live with someone you didn't always live with, doesn't it?'

'Partly.' She turned to face him. 'When you're all grown up and you're not a little kid any more, you end up meeting someone you like so much that you think about going to live with them instead of living with your Mum and Pop. And if the person you like so well likes you just as much, then you go to a priest or a minister or a judge and you get married. You both sign a little piece of paper, and signing that little piece of paper means you're married, you can live together for the rest of your lives without offending God.'

'It really does mean you can live together for the rest of your life?'

'Yes.'

'Then why can't I marry you, Mary? I'd like to marry you, I'd like to see you all dressed up like a fairy princess in a long white dress the way Dawnie was and the way Mum was in her wedding photo on the dressing table in her bedroom.'

'Lots of girls do wear long white dresses when they get married, Tim, but it isn't the long white dress that makes you married, it's the little bit of paper.'

'But Mum and Dawnie wore long white dresses!' he maintained stubbornly, enamoured of the idea.

'Would you really like to marry me, Tim?' Mary asked, steering him away from the long white dress.

He nodded vigorously, smiling at her. 'Oh, yes, I'd really like to marry you, Mary. I could live with you then all the time, I wouldn't have to go home on Sunday night.'

The river ran on its way down to the sea, lapping and gurgling contentedly; Mary brushed a persistent fly away from her face. 'Would you want to live with me more than you want to live with your Pop?'

'Yes. Pop belongs to Mum, he's only waiting until he can go and sleep with her under the ground, isn't he? I belong to you, Mary.'

'Well, your Pop and I were talking about you the other night after I brought you home from Mr Martinson's, and we decided it would be a good thing if you and I did get married. We worry a lot over what will happen to you, Tim, and there's no one in all the whole world we like more than you.'

The blue eyes sparkled with light reflected off the river. 'Oh, Mary, do you mean it? Do you really mean it? You will marry me?'

'Yes, Tim, I'm going to marry you.'

'And then I can live with you, I can really belong to you?'

'Yes.'

'Can we get married today?'

She blinked at the river, suddenly sad. 'Not today, my dear, but very soon. Next Friday.'

'Does Pop know when it is?'

'Yes, he knows it's next Friday. It's all arranged.'

'And you'll wear a long white dress like Mum and my Dawnie?'

She shook her head. 'No, Tim, I can't. I'd like to wear a long white dress for you, but it takes a long time to make one and your Pop and I don't want to wait that long.'

Disappointment dimmed his smile for a moment, but then it bloomed again. 'And I don't have to go home after that?'

'For a little while you will, because I have to go into the hospital.'

'Oh, Mary, no! You can't go into hospital! Please, please don't go into hospital!' Tears welled up in his eyes. 'You'll die, Mary, you'll go away from me to sleep under the ground and I won't see you ever again!'

She reached out and took his hands in a strong, reassuring

clasp. 'Now, now, Tim! Going into the hospital doesn't mean I'm going to die! Just because your Mum died when she went to the hospital doesn't mean I'm going to die too, you know. Lots and lots and lots of people go into hospital and come out again without dying. Hospital is a place where you go when you're sick and you want to get better. It's just that sometimes we're so sick we can't get better, but I'm not sick like your Mum, am I? I'm not all weak and in pain, am I? But I went to see the doctor and he wants to make a little bit of me that's all wrong go all right again, and he wants to do it before you come to live with me so that I'm all better for you.'

It was hard making him believe her, but after a while he calmed down and seemed to accept the fact that she was not going to the hospital to die.

'You're sure you're not going to die, now?'

'Yes, Tim, I'm sure I'm not going to die. I can't die yet. I won't let myself die yet.'

'And we will get married before you go to the hospital?'

'Yes, it's all arranged for next Friday.'

He leaned back on his hands and sighed happily, then rolled over and over down the sloping sand until he ended in the bay, laughing. 'I'm going to marry Mary, I'm going to marry Mary!' he sang, throwing water all over her when she followed him down to the river's edge.

25

In honour of the occasion, Mary wore a peach tussore silk suit to her wedding, with a small peach silk hat and a modest corsage of tea roses on her lapel. The wedding party had arranged to meet on the Hyde Park side of Victoria Square, just across from the Registrar General's offices. Mary parked in the underground Domain lot and took the moving sidewalk from her car to the College Street exit, then walked across the park. Archie had wanted to drive her, but she had refused.

'I have to go straight from the wedding to the hospital, so I think I had better drive myself.'

'But you ought to let me drive you, dear!' he had protested. 'What do you think you're going to do, drive yourself home from the hospital when you're discharged?'

'Of course. It's a large private hospital run like a hotel, and I'm staying in much longer than is actually necessary so that I'm absolutely fit and well when I come home. I don't want to disappoint Tim by going home and not letting him come to stay with me very soon afterward.'

He glanced at her, puzzled. 'Well, I suppose you know what you're doing, because you always do.'

She shook his arm affectionately. 'Dear old Archie, your faith in me is touching.'

So she went to her wedding alone, and was the first to arrive on the park corner. Archie and Tricia came soon after. Mrs Parker puffed up in their wake wearing a startling confection of cerise and electric blue chiffon, and then Tim and Ron emerged from the subway entrance a few feet away. Tim was wearing the suit he had worn to Dawnie's wedding, Ron the suit he had worn to Esme's funeral. They stood in the clear bright sun chatting self-consciously, then Tim gave her a small box, thrusting it at her quickly when no one was looking. He was clearly nervous and unsure of himself; hiding the box with her hand, Mary led him a few steps away from the others and stood with her back to them while she undid the clumsy wrapping.

'Pop helped me pick it out, because I wanted to give you something and Pop said it was all right for me to give you something. We went to the bank and I took two thousand dollars out and we went to the big jeweller down in Castlereagh Street near the Hotel Australia.'

Inside the box lay a small brooch, with a magnificent black opal centre and a diamond surrounding, fashioned like a flower.

'It reminded me of your garden at the cottage, Mary, all the colours of the flowers and the sun shining on everything.'

Off came the tea roses, down they fell to the searing asphalt pavement and lay unnoticed; Mary took the brooch out of its velvet bed and held it out to Tim, smiling at him through a haze of tears. 'It isn't my garden any more, Tim, it's our garden now. That's one of the things marrying does, it makes everything each of us owns belong to the other, so my house and my car and my cottage and my garden belong to you just as much as they do to me after we're married. Will you pin it on for me?'

He was always quick and deft with his hands, as if they had escaped his psychic halter; he took the edge of her coat lapel between his fingers and slipped the sharp pin through the fabric easily, did up the safety catch and then the safety chain.

'Do you like it, Mary?' he asked anxiously.

'Oh, Tim, I love it so much! I've never had anything so pretty in all my life, and no one has ever given me a brooch before. I'll treasure it all my life. I have a gift for you, too.'

It was a very expensive, heavy gold watch, and he was delighted with it.

'Oh, Mary, I promise I'll try not to lose it, I really will! Now that I can tell the time it's beaut to have my very own watch. And it's so lovely!'

'If you lose it we'll just get you another one. You mustn't worry about losing it, Tim.'

'I won't lose it, Mary. Every time I look at it I'll remember that you gave it to me.'

'Let's go now, Tim, it's time.'

Archie took her elbow to guide her across the street. 'Mary, you didn't tell me that Tim was such a spectacular young man.'

'I know I didn't. It's embarrassing. I feel like one of those raddled old women you see gallivanting round the tourist resorts in the hope of acquiring an expensive but stunning young man.' The arm above his hand was trembling. 'This is a terrible ordeal for me, Archie. It's the first time I've exposed myself to the curious gaze of the public. Can you imagine what they'll all think in there when they realise who is marrying whom? Ron looks a more appropriate husband for me than Tim.'

'Don't let it worry you, Mary. We're here to support you, and support you we will. I like your Old Girl next door, by the way. I must sit next to her at dinner, she has the richest vocabulary I've encountered in many a long day. Look at her and Tricia there, magging away like old cronies!'

Mary glanced at him gratefully. 'Thanks, Archie. I'm sorry I won't be able to attend my own wedding dinner, but I want to get this hospital business over and done with as soon as I can, and if I delay until after dinner my doctor won't put me on his operating list for tomorrow, which means a wait of a week, since he only operates there Saturdays.'

'That's all right, love, we'll drink your share of the champagne and eat your share of the chateaubriand.'

Because there were sufficient witnesses in the wedding party, only one pair of fascinated eyes beheld the queer couple, those belonging to the officiating representative of Her Majesty's Law. It was quickly over, disappointingly shorn of ceremony or solemnity. Tim made his responses eagerly, a credit to his father's coaching; Mary was the one who stumbled. They signed the required documents and left without realising that the elderly man who married them had no idea Tim was mentally retarded. He did not think the match odd at all in that way; many handsome young men married women old enough to be their mothers. What he found odd was that no kisses were exchanged.

Mary left them on the same corner where she had joined them, plucking Tim's coat sleeve anxiously.

'Now you'll wait for me patiently and you won't worry about me, promise? I'll be all right.'

He was so happy that Tricia Johnson and Emily Parker felt like crying just to see his face; the only shadow to mar his day was Mary's abrupt departure, but even that could not depress him for very long. He had signed the little bit of paper and so had Mary, they belonged together now and he could wait for a long time if necessary before coming to live with her.

The operation made Mary sore and uncomfortable for a few

days, but she weathered it well; better, in fact, than her gynaecologist had expected.

'You're a sturdy old girl,' he informed her as he took the stitches out. 'I ought to have known you'd take it in your stride. Old girls like you have to be killed with an axe. As far as I'm concerned you can go home tomorrow, but stay in as long as you like. This isn't a hospital, you know, it's a bloody palace. I'll sign your discharge papers on the way out today and then you can leave whenever you want, this week or next week or the week after that. I'll keep stopping in just in case you're here.'

26

In the end Mary stayed five weeks, rather enjoying the quiet privacy of the old house on the Rose Bay waterfront, and rather dreading the thought of seeing Tim. She had not told anyone where she was going for her surgery except the dry little man who took care of her legal affairs, and the laboriously written postcards she got from Tim every day were all forwarded through the dry little man's office. Ron must have helped him a great deal, but the handwriting was Tim's and so was the phraseology. She tucked them away in a small briefcase carefully as she received them. During the last two weeks of her stay she swam in the hospital pool and played tennis on the hospital courts, deliberately accustoming herself to movement and exertion. When at length she left she felt as if nothing had ever happened, and the drive home was not at all taxing.

The house in Artarmon was ablaze with lights when she put the car in the garage and let herself in through the front door. Emily Parker was as good as her word, Mary thought, pleased; the Old Girl had promised to make the house look as though it was occupied. She put her suitcase down and stripped off her gloves, throwing them on the hall table along with her bag, then she walked into the living room. The phone loomed large as a monster in front of her, but she did not call Ron to tell him she was home; plenty of time for that, tomorrow or the day after or the day after that.

The living room was still predominantly grey, but many pictures hung on the walls now and splotches of rich ruby red glowered like the embers of a scattered fire throughout the room. A ruby glass vase from Sweden stood on the chaste mantel and a ruby-dyed fur rug lay sprawled across the pearl-grey carpet like a lake of blood. But it was pleasant to be home, she thought, looking around at that inanimate testament to her wealth and taste. Soon she would be sharing it with Tim, who had had a hand in its generation; soon, soon . . . Yet do I want to share it with him? she asked herself, pacing up and down restlessly. How odd it was; the closer she came to his advent the more reluctant she was to have it occur.

The sun had set an hour before and the western sky was as dark as the rest of the world, pulsing redly from the city lights under a layer of low, sodden clouds. But the rain had fallen farther west, and left Artarmon to the summer dust. What a pity, she thought; we could really do with the rain here, my garden is so very thirsty. She went into the unlit kitchen and stood peering out the back window without switching the kitchen or patio lights on, trying to see if Emily Parker's house was lit. But the camphor laurels hid it; she would have to go out onto the patio to see it properly.

Her eyes were quite accustomed to the darkness as she let herself noiselessly out of the back door, softly cat-footed as always, and she stood for a moment inhaling the perfume of the early summer flowers and the far-off earthy smell of rain, filled with delight. It was so nice to be home, or it would have been had the back of her mind not been consumed with the spectre of Tim.

Almost as if she could consciously form his image out of her thoughts, the silhouette of his head and body shaped itself against the distant, weeping sky. He was sitting along the railing of her balustrade, still naked and dewed with the water of his nightly shower, his face raised to the starless night as if he were listening raptly to the lilt of music beyond the limitations of her earthbound ears. What light there was had fused itself into his bright hair and clung in faint, pearly lines along the contours of his face and trunk, where the glistening skin was stretched tautly over the still, dormant muscles. Even the curve of his eyelids was visible, fully down to shield his thoughts from the night.

A month and more than a month, she thought; it's been over a month since I last saw him, and here he is like a figment of my imagination, Narcissus leaning over his pool wrapped in dreams. Why does his beauty always strike me so forcibly when I see him again the first time in a long while?

She crossed the sandstone flags silently and stood behind him, watching the column of sinew in the side of his throat gleam like a pillar of ice until the temptation to touch him could not be gainsaid a moment longer. Her fingers closed softly over his bare shoulder and she leaned forward to rest her face against his damp hair, her lips brushing his ear.

'Oh, Tim, it's so good to find you here waiting,' she whispered.

Her coming did not startle him and he did not move; it was almost as if he had felt her presence in the stillness, sensed her behind him in the night. After a while he leaned back against her a little; the hand which had rested on his shoulder slid across his chest to the other shoulder, imprisoning his head within the circle of her arm. Her free hand slipped beneath his elbow to his side, its palm pressing down against his belly and pushing him back harder against her. The muscles of his abdomen twitched as her hand passed across them caressingly, then became utterly still, as if he had ceased to breathe; he moved his head until he could look into her face. There was a remote calmness about him and the eyes searching hers so seriously had the veiled, silvery sheen to them that always shut her out while it locked her in, as if he saw her but did not see Mary Horton. As his mouth touched her own he put his two hands up to grip the arm she had linked across his chest, and they closed over it. The kiss was different from their first, it had a languorous sensuality about it that Mary found fey and witching, as if the creature she had surprised dreaming was not Tim at all, but a manifestation of the soft summer night. Rising from the balcony railing without fear or hesitation, he pulled her into his arms and picked her up.

He carried her down the steps and into the garden, the short grass hushing under his bare feet. Half inclined to protest and make him return to the house, Mary buried her face in his neck and stilled her tongue, yielding up her reason to his strange, silent purpose. He made her sit on the grass in the deep shadow of the camphor laurels and knelt beside her, his fingertips delicately touching her face. She was so filled with love for him that she could not seem to see or hear, and she leaned forward like a rag doll toppled by a careless flick of the finger, her hands splayed far apart and her head down against his chest. He held it there, pulling at her hair until it fell loose about her and her hands lay curled helplessly on his thighs. From her hair he passed to her clothes, peeling them away as slowly and surely as a small child undressing a doll, folding each item neatly and laying it on a growing pile to one side of them. Mary crouched there timidly, her eyes closed. Their roles had somehow become reversed; he had inexplicably gained the ascendancy.

Finished, he took her arms and propped them on his shoulders, gathering her against him. Mary gasped, her eyes opening; for the first time in her life she felt a bare body all along the length of her own, and somehow there was nothing to be done save abandon herself to the feel of it, warm and alien and living. Her dreamlike trance merged into a dream sharper and more real than the entire world outside the darkness under the camphor laurels; all at once the silky skin under her hands took on form and substance: Tim's skin sheathing Tim's body. There was no more than that under the sun, nothing more to be offered her on life's plate than the feel of Tim within her arms, pinning her against the ground. It was Tim's chin driving ribbons of pain from the side of her neck, Tim's hands clawed into her shoulders, Tim's sweat running down her sides. She became aware that he was trembling, that the mindless delight which filled him was because of her, that it mattered not whether hers was the skin of a young girl or a middle-aged woman as long as it was Tim there, within her arms and within her body, as long as it was she, Mary, to give him this, so pure and mindless a pleasure that he came to it unfettered, free of the chains which would always bind her, the thinking one.

When the night was old and the dim western rain was gone over the mountains she pushed herself away from him and gathered the little pile of clothes against her chest, kneeling above him.

'We must go inside, dear heart,' she whispered, her hair falling across his extended arm where her head had been. 'It's the dark before light, we must go in now.'

He picked her up and carried her inside immediately. The lights were still on in the living room; trailing her hand over his shoulder, she extinguished them one by one as he crossed to the bedroom. He put her down on the bed and would have left her alone had she not reached out to pull him back.

'Where are you going, Tim?' she asked, and moved over to make room for him. 'This is your bed now.'

He stretched out beside her, pushing his arm under her back. She put her head on his shoulder and her hand on his chest, caressing it drowsily. Suddenly the small, tender movement ceased, and she lay stiffening against him, her eyes wide and filled with fear. It was too much to be borne; she lifted herself on one elbow and reached across him to get at the lamp on the bedside table.

Since the silent meeting on the patio he had not spoken one word; all at once his voice was the only thing she wanted to hear, if he did not speak she would know that somehow Tim was not with her at all.

He was lying with his eyes wide open, looking up at her without even wincing in the sudden, drenching light. The face was sad and a little stern, and it wore an expression she had never seen before, it had a maturity she had never noticed. Was it her eyes that had been blind, or was it his face that had changed? The body was no longer strange or forbidden to her, and she could look upon it freely, with love and respect, for it housed a creature as live and entire as she was herself. How blue his eyes were, how exquisitely shaped his mouth was, how tragic the tiny crease to the left side of his lips. And how young he was, how young!

He blinked and shifted the focus of his gaze from some private infinity to the nearness of her face; his eyes dwelled on the tired, worried lines in it, then on the straight, strong mouth so sated with his kisses that its lips were swollen. He lifted one leaden hand and brushed his fingers against her firm, rounded breast gently.

She said, 'Tim, why won't you speak to me? What have I done? Have I disappointed you?'

His eyes filled with tears; they ran down his face and fell onto the pillow, but his sweet, loving smile dawned and the hand cupped her breast harder.

'You told me that one day I'd be so happy I'd cry, and look! Oh, Mary, I'm crying! I'm so happy I'm crying!'

She collapsed on his chest, weak with relief. 'I thought you were angry with me!'

'With *you*?' His hand cradled the back of her head, her hair slipping through his fingers. 'I could never be angry with you, Mary. I wasn't even angry with you when I thought you didn't like me.'

'Why wouldn't you speak to me tonight?'

He was surprised. 'Did I have to speak to you? I didn't think I had to speak to you. When you came I couldn't think of anything to say. All I wanted was to do the things Pop told me about while you were away in hospital, and then I had to do them, I couldn't stop to talk.'

'Your Pop told you?'

'Yes. I asked him if it was still a sin to kiss you if we were married, and he said it wasn't a sin at all when we were married. He told me about lots of other things I could do, too. He said I ought to know what to do because if I didn't I'd hurt you and you'd cry. I don't want to hurt you or make you cry, Mary. I didn't hurt you or make you cry, did I?'

She laughed, holding him hard. 'No, Tim, you didn't hurt me and I didn't cry. There I was, petrified because I thought it was all up to me and I didn't know whether I was going to be able to deal with it.'

'I really didn't hurt you, Mary? I forgot Pop told me not to hurt you.'

'You did magnificently, Tim. We were in good hands, your green hands. I love you so much!'

'That's a better word than like, isn't it?'

'When it's used properly it is.'

'I'm going to save it just for you, Mary. I'll tell everyone else I like them.'

'That's exactly how it should be, Tim.'

By the time dawn crept into the room and lit it with the clear, tender newness of day, Mary was fast asleep. It was Tim who lay staring wakefully at the window, careful not to move and disturb her. She was so small and soft, so sweet-smelling and cuddly. Once he used to hold his Teddy bear against his chest the same way, but Mary was alive and could hold him back; it was much nicer. When they took his Teddy bear away, saying he was all grown up and must not sleep with Teddy any more, he had wept for weeks with empty arms hugging his aching chest, mourning the passing of a friend. Somehow he had known Mum didn't want to take Teddy away, but after he came home from work in tears and told her how Mick and Bill had laughed at him for sleeping with a Teddy bear, she had steeled herself to do it, and Teddy had gone into the garbage can that very night. Oh, the night was so big, so dark and full of shadows which moved mysteriously, coiling themselves into claws and beaks and long, sharp teeth. While Teddy had been there to hide his face against they had not dared to come any closer than the opposite wall, but it took a long time to get used to them all around him, pressing down on his defenceless face and snapping at his very nose. After Mum had given him a bigger night light it was better, but he loathed the dark to this very day; it was deadly with menace, full of lurking enemies.

Forgetting he was not going to move in case he wakened her, he turned his head until he could look down on her, then slid up the pillow until he was much higher than she. Fascinated, he stared at her for a long time in the growing light, assimilating her alien appearance. Her breasts devastated him; he could not tear his eyes away from them. Just thinking about them filled him with excitement, and what he felt when they were crushed against him was indescribable. It was as though her differences had been invented just for him, he had no conscious awareness that she was exactly like any other female. She was Mary, and her body belonged to him as utterly as his Teddy had; it was his and his alone to hold against the inroads of the night, warding off terror and loneliness.

Pop had told him no one had ever touched her, that what he brought to her was foreign and strange, and he had understood the magnitude of his responsibility better than a reasoning man, for he had owned so little and been respected by so few. In the savage heat of his body's blind drive he had not managed to remember all Pop told him, but he thought, looking back on it, that he would remember more next time. His devotion to her was purely selfless; it seemed to come from somewhere outside him, compounded of gratitude and love and a deep, restful security. With her he never felt that he was weighed in the balance and found lacking. How beautiful she was, he thought, seeing the lines and the sagging skin but not finding them ugly or undesirable. He saw her through the eyes of total, unbounded love and so assumed that all of her was beautiful.

At first when Pop had told him he must go to the house at Artarmon and wait there alone for Mary to come home, he had not wanted to come. But Pop had made him, and would not let him return to Surf Street. A whole week he had waited, cutting the grass and weeding the flower beds and trimming the shrubs all day, then wandering the empty house at night until he was tired enough to sleep, with every light on to banish the demons of the formless darkness. He did not belong in Surf Street any more, Pop had said, and when he had begged Pop to come with him he had met with an adamant refusal. Thinking about it now as the sun rose, he decided Pop had known exactly what would happen; Pop always did.

That night the thunder had growled in the west and there was a stinging, earthy smell of rain in the air. Storms used to frighten him badly when he was a little boy, until Pop had shown him how quickly the fear went away if he went outside and watched how lovely it was, with the lightning streaking down the inky sky and the thunder bellowing like a mammoth, invisible bull. So he had taken his nightly shower and wandered naked onto the patio to watch the storm, disturbed and restless. In the house the bogies would have rushed gibbering at him from every cranny, but on the patio with the damp wind stroking his bare skin they had no dominion over him. And gradually the melting night had melted him; he had slipped into a senseless oneness with the unthinking creatures of the earth. It was as though he could see every petal on every dim flower, as though all the bird songs in the world flooded his being with a soundless music.

At first he was only dimly aware of her, until that beloved hand had seared his shoulder and filled him with a pain that yet was not a pain. He did not need to be able to reason to divine the change in her, the self-admission that she loved to touch him as much as he had yearned to touch her. He had leaned back to feel her breasts against him; her hand on his belly numbed and electrified him, he could not breathe for fear she would puff away. Their first kiss all those months ago had set him quivering with a hunger he had not known how to sate, but this second kiss filled him with a queer, triumphant power, armed as he was with what Pop had told him. He had wanted to feel her skin and could find only a part of it, frustrated by her clothes, but he had managed to command himself enough to do what had to be done, take them from her gently so as not to frighten her.

His steps had led him down into the garden because he hated the house at Artarmon; it was not his the way the cottage was, and he did not know where to take her. Only in the garden was he at home, so to the garden he went. And in the garden he felt her breasts at last, in the garden where he was simply another of its myriad creatures he could forget he was not the full quid, he could lose himself in the honeyed, piercing warmth of her body. And he had lost himself so for hours, alight with the unbearable pleasures of feeling her and knowing she was with him all the time in every part of her.

The sadness had come when she banished him to the house, and he realised they must part. He had clung to her as long as he could, carrying her small body within his arms and aching at the thought of having to let her go, wondering how long he must wait before it happened again. It had been dreadful, putting her into her bed and turning to go to his own; when she had drawn him back and made him lie beside her he had done so in numb astonishment, for it had not occurred to him to ask his Pop whether they would be exactly like his Mum and Pop and sleep together all through every night.

Then was the moment he knew he really belonged with her, that he could go down to the ground in the last, endless sleep safe and free from fear because she would be there beside him in the darkness forever. Nothing could ever frighten him again: he had conquered the final terror in discovering he would never be alone. For his life had been so very lonely, always shut out of the thinking world, always on some outer perimeter watching, longing to enter that world and never able to. He never could, never. Now it did not matter. Mary had allied herself to him in the last, most comforting way. And he loved her, loved her, loved her . . .

Sliding down in the bed again he put his face between her breasts just to feel their softness, the fingertips of one hand tracing the outline of a hard, tantalising nipple. She woke with a kind of purring noise, her arms slipping around him. He wanted to kiss her again, he wanted to kiss her badly, but he found himself laughing instead.

'What's so funny?' she asked drowsily, stretching as she wakened more fully.

'Oh, Mary, you're *much* nicer than my Teddy!' he giggled.

27

When Mary rang Ron to tell him that she was home and that Tim was well and safe, she thought he sounded tired.

'Why don't you come and stay with us for a few days?' she asked.

'No, thanks, love, I'd rather not. Youse'll be better off without me hanging around.'

'That's not true, you know. We worry about you, we miss you and we want to see you. Please come out, Ron, or let me pick you up in the car.'

'No, I don't want to.' He sounded stubborn, determined to have his way.

'Then may we come and see you?'

'When you go back to work you can come over one night, but I don't want to see youse before then, all right?'

'No, it isn't all right, but if that's the way you want it there's nothing I can do. I understand you think you're doing the right thing, that we ought to be left alone, but you're wrong, you know. Tim and I would be very glad to see you.'

'When youse go back to work, not before.' There was a tiny pause, then his voice came again, fainter and farther away. 'How's Tim, love? Is he all right? Is he really happy? Did we do the right thing and make him feel a bit more like the full quid? Was Mr Martinson right?'

'Yes, Ron, he was right. Tim's very happy. He hasn't changed at all and yet he's changed enormously. He's rounded out and become more sure of himself, more content, less an outsider.'

'That's all I wanted to hear.' His voice sank to a whisper. 'Thanks, Mary. I'll see youse.'

Tim was in the garden, repotting maidenhair ferns from the rockery. With a swing and a lilt in her walk that was new, Mary crossed the grass towards him, smiling. He turned his head and gave her back the smile, then bent over the fragile leaves again, snapping off a fine, brittle black stem below the spot where the frond looked pale and sick. Sitting beside him on the grass, she put her cheek against his shoulder with a sigh.

'I just talked to Pop.'

'Oh, goody! When is he coming out?'

'He says he won't come until after we've gone back to work. I tried to convince him he ought to make it sooner, but he won't. He thinks we ought to have this time to ourselves, and that's very kind of him.'

'I suppose so, but he didn't need to do it, did he? We don't mind visitors. Mrs Parker is always dropping in and we don't mind her, do we?'

'Oddly enough, Tim, we don't. She's a good old stick.'

'I like her.' He laid the fern down and slid an arm about her waist. 'Why do you look so pretty these days, Mary?'

'Because I have you.'

'I think it's because you don't always dress up as if you're going to town. I like you better with no shoes and stockings and your hair all undone.'

'Tim, how would you like to go up to the cottage for a couple of weeks? It's nice here, but it's even nicer up at the cottage.'

'Oh, yes, I'd like that! I didn't like this house much before, but it turned out to be real nice after you came home from the hospital. I feel as though I belong here now. But the cottage is my favourite house in all the world.'

'Yes, I know it is. Let's go right now, Tim, there's nothing to hold us here. I only waited to see what Pop wanted to do, but he's left us to ourselves for the time being, so we can go.'

It never occurred to either of them to look further than the cottage; Mary's grandiose schemes of taking Tim to the Great Barrier Reef and the desert evaporated into the distant future.

They moved into the cottage that night and had great fun deciding where they were going to sleep. In the end they moved Mary's big double bed into his room, and closed the door on her stark white cell until they felt like going into Gosford to buy paint for redecoration. There was very little to do in the blooming garden and less inside the house, so they walked in the bush for hours and hours, exploring its bewitching, untouched corridors, lying with heads together over a busy ant hill or sitting absolutely still while a male lyre bird danced the complicated measures of his ceremonious courtship. If they found themselves too far away to get back to the cottage before dark they stayed where they were, spreading a blanket over a bed of bracken fern and sleeping under the stars. Sometimes they slept the daylight hours away and rose with the setting of the sun, then went down to the beach after dark and lit a fire, revelling in the newfound freedom of having the world entirely to themselves and having no constraint between them. They would abandon their clothes, safe in the darkness from eyes out on the river, and swim naked in the still, black water while the fire died away to ash-coated coals. He would make her lie afterwards on a blanket in the sand, the urge of his love too strong to resist a moment longer, and she would lift her arms to draw him down beside her, happier than she had ever thought was possible.

One night Mary wakened from a deep sleep in the sand and lay for a moment wondering where she was. As thought came back she knew, for she had had to accustom herself to sleeping clasped in Tim's arms. He never let her go. Any attempt to move away from him woke him at once; he would reach out until he found her and pull her back again with a sigh of mingled fear and relief. It was as if he thought she was going to be snatched away by something out of the darkness, but he would not talk about it and she never insisted, divining that he would tell her in his own good time.

Summer was at its height and the weather had been perfect, the days hot and dry, the nights sweetly cooled by the sea breeze. Mary stared up at the sky, drawing in a breath of awe and wonder. The massive belt of the Milky Way sprawled across the vault from horizon to horizon, so smothered with the light of the stars that there was a faint, powdery glow even in the starless parts of the sky. No haze conspired to blot them out, and the leaching city lights were miles to the south. The Cross spread its four bright arms to the winds, the fifth star clear and sparkling, the Pointers drawing her eyes away from the still, waxy globe of the full moon. Silver light was poured over everything, the river danced and leaped like cold, moving fire, the sand was struck to a sea of minute diamonds.

And it seemed to Mary for a still, small space of time that she heard something, or perhaps she felt it: alien and thin it was, like a cry teetering on the edge of nothing. Whatever it was, there was peace and finality in it. She listened for a long time, but it did not happen again, and she began to think that perhaps on a night like this the soul of the world was liberated to throw itself like a veil over the heads of all living things.

With Tim she always spoke of God, for the concept was simple and he was uncomplicated enough to believe in the intangible, but Mary herself did not believe in God; she had a basic and unphilosophic conviction that there was only one life to live. And wasn't that the important thing, quite independent of the existence of a superior being? What did it matter whether there was a God if the soul was mortal, if life of any kind ceased on the lip of the grave? When Mary thought of God at all it was in terms of Tim and little children, the good and uncorrupted; her own life had driven the supernatural so far away that it seemed there were two separate creeds, one for childhood and one for full growth. Yet the half-heard, half-felt thing coming out of the night disturbed her, there was an other-world suggestion about it, and she remembered suddenly the old legend that when the soul of someone who had just died passed overhead the dogs howled, lifting their muzzles to the moon and shivering as they mourned. She sat up, clasping her arms about her knees.

Tim sensed her going immediately, waking when his gropings did not find her.

'What's the matter, Mary?'

'I don't know . . . I feel as if something's happened. It's very strange. Did you feel anything?'

'No, only that you went away from me.'

He wanted to make love to her and she tried to divorce herself from her sudden preoccupation long enough to satisfy him, but could not. Something stalked in the back of her mind like a prowling beast, something threatening and irrevocable. Her half-hearted cooperation did not disconcert Tim; he gave up trying to rouse her and contented himself with wrapping his arms about her in what she always thought of as his Teddy-bear hug, for he had told her a little about Teddy, though, she suspected, not all there was to know.

'Tim, would you mind very much if we drove back to the city?'

'Not if you want to, Mary. I don't mind anything you want to do.'

'Then let's go back now, right this minute. I want to see Pop. I've got a sort of feeling he needs us.'

Tim got up at once, shaking the sand out of the blanket and folding it neatly over one arm.

By the time the Bentley pulled up in Surf Street it was six o'clock in the morning, and the sun had long been up. The house was silent and seemed curiously deserted, though Tim assured Mary his father was there. The back door was unlocked.

'Tim, why don't you stay out here for a minute while I go inside and check by myself? I don't want to frighten or upset you, but I think it would be better if I went in alone.'

'No, Mary, I'll come in with you. I won't be frightened or upset.'

Ron was lying in the old double bed he had shared with Es, his eyes closed and his hands folded on his chest, as if he had remembered how Es was lying the last time he saw her. Mary did not need to feel his cold skin or search for a stilled heart; she knew immediately that he was dead.

'Is he asleep, Mary?' Tim came round to the other side of the bed and stared down at his father, then put out his hand and rested it against the sunken cheek. He looked up at Mary sadly. 'He's so cold!'

'He's dead, Tim.'

'Oh, I wish he could have waited! I was so looking forward to telling him how nice it is to live with you. I wanted to ask him some things and I wanted him to help me pick out a new present for you. I didn't say goodbye to him! I didn't say goodbye to him and now I can't remember what he looked like when his eyes were open and he was all happy and moving.'

'I don't think he could bear to wait a moment longer, dear heart. He wanted so badly to go; it was so lonely for him here and there was nothing more to wait for once he knew you were happy. Don't be sad, Tim, because it isn't sad. Now he can sleep with your Mum again.'

All at once Mary knew why his voice had seemed so remote over the phone; he had begun his death-fast the moment Tim left the house in Surf Street forever, and by the time Mary came home from hospital he was already weakening badly. Yet could it be called suicide? She did not think so. The drum had stopped beating and the feet had stopped marching, that was all.

Sitting on the edge of the bed, Tim got his arms under his father's back and lifted the stiff, shrunken form into his arms tenderly. 'Oh, but I'm going to miss him, Mary! I liked Pop, I liked him better than anyone else in the whole world except for you.'

'I know, dear heart. I'll miss him too.'

And was that the voice in the night? she wondered. Stranger things than that have happened to more staunchly doubting people without swaying their doubt . . . Why shouldn't the living cords which laced a being together flick softly against a loved one in the very moment of their unravelling? He was all alone when it happened, and yet he had not been alone; he had called, and she had woken to answer him. Sometimes all the miles between are as nothing, she thought, sometimes they are narrowed to the little silence between the beats of a heart.

28

Mary hated Ron's funeral, and was glad she persuaded Tim not to come. Dawnie and her husband had taken charge, which was only right and proper, but as Tim's representative she had to be there and follow the little cortege to the cemetery. Her presence was clearly unwelcome; Dawnie and Mick ignored her. What had happened when Ron told them she and Tim were married, she wondered? Since the wedding she had only spoken to Ron that once, and he had not mentioned his daughter's name.

After the sod was turned on Ron's coffin and the three of them moved slowly away from the graveside, Mary put her hand on Dawnie's arm.

'My dear, I'm so sorry for you, because I know you loved him very much. I loved him too.'

There was a look of Tim about his sister's eyes as she stared at Mary, but the expression in them – bitter and corroded – was one she had never seen in Tim's.

'I don't need your condolences, sister-in-law! Why don't you just go away and leave me alone?'

'Why can't you forgive me for loving Tim, Dawnie? Didn't your father explain the situation to you?'

'Oh, he tried! You're a very clever woman, aren't you? It didn't take you long to delude him as completely as you did Tim! Are you happy now that you've got your pet moron by your side permanently and legally?'

'Tim's not my pet moron, you know that. And anyway, does it matter as long as he's happy?'

'How do I know he's happy? I've only got your word for that, and your word's not worth two cents!'

'Why don't you come and see him and find out for yourself what the truth is?'

'I wouldn't soil my shoes by entering your house, *Mrs Tim Melville*! Well, I suppose you've got what you wanted, you've got

Tim all to yourself with the conventions nicely taken care of and both his parents out of the way!'

Mary whitened. 'What do you mean, Dawn?'

'You drove my mother to her grave, Mrs Tim Melville, and then you drove my father after her!'

'That's not true!'

'Oh, isn't it? As far as I'm concerned, now that my father and mother are both dead, my brother's dead too. I never want to see or hear from him again! If you and he want to make a public spectacle of yourselves by flaunting your sick fancies under society's nose, I don't even want to know about it!'

Mary turned on her heel and walked away.

By the time she got from Botany Cemetery to her house in Artarmon she felt better, and was able to greet Tim with a fair semblance of serenity.

'Is Pop with Mum now?' he asked her anxiously, twisting his hands together.

'Yes, Tim. I saw him put in the ground right next to her. You needn't worry about either of them ever again, they're together and at peace.'

There was something odd about Tim's manner; she sat down and examined him keenly, not alarmed exactly, but puzzled.

'What's the matter, Tim? Aren't you feeling well?'

He shook his head apathetically. 'I feel all right, Mary. Just a bit funny, that's all. It's sort of funny not having Pop or Mum any more.'

'I know, I know . . . Have you had anything to eat?'

'No. I'm not very hungry.'

Mary walked across and pulled him up out of his chair, looking at him in concern. 'Come out to the kitchen with me while I make us some sandwiches. Maybe you'll feel like eating when you see how pretty and dainty they are.'

'Little wee ones with all the crusts cut off?'

'As thin as tissue paper, little wee triangles with all the crusts cut off, I promise. Come on now.'

It had been on the tip of her tongue to add 'my love, my darling, my heart,' but somehow she could never bring herself to utter the wild endearments which sprang to mind whenever, as now, he seemed upset or lost. Would she ever find it possible to treat him wholly as the lover he was, would she ever manage to lose that rigid, shrinking horror of making a total fool of herself? Why was it she could only relax completely with him when they were secluded at the cottage or in their bed? Dawnie's bitterness rankled, and all the curious, speculative glances she and Tim got as they passed down Walton Street still had the power to humiliate.

Mary's courage was not the unconventional kind; how could it be? Having nothing as her birthright, her entire life up to the moment of meeting Tim had been designed to achieve material success, earn the approbation of those who had started out much better endowed. It could not come easily now to fly in the face of convention, sanctified by the law though her union with Tim was. While she longed passionately to forget herself, smother him with kisses and endearments whenever the impulse came, his inability to encourage her in a mature way made it quite impossible if there was the least chance of their being disturbed. Her dread of amusement or ridicule had even led her to ask Tim not to chatter about his marriage to anyone not already aware of it, a moment of weakness which she had regretted afterward. No, it was not easy.

As usual, Tim wanted to help her actively as she set about making the sandwiches, getting out the bread and butter, rattling the china noisily as he searched for plates.

'Would you find the big butcher's knife for me, Tim? It's the only one that's sharp enough to cut crusts off.'

'Where is it, Mary?'

'In the top drawer,' she answered absently, spreading a coat of butter on each slice of bread.

'Ohhhhhh! Mary, Mary!'

She turned quickly, something in his cry filling her with heart-stopping fear.

'Oh, my God!'

For an appalled second it seemed as if the whole room was blood; Tim was standing quite still by the counter, staring down at his left arm in unbelieving terror. From biceps to fingertips it ran pulsating rivers of blood, the outflow of a fountain spraying from the crook of his elbow. With the regularity of a time-piece the blood spurted in a vicious jet halfway across the room, tapered off, spurted again; a thin lake of it was gathering about his left foot, and the left side of his body glistened wetly, dripping its share onto the floor.

There was a roll of butcher's twine on a spool near the stove, and a small pair of scissors hanging on a cord near it; almost in the same instant that she had spun round, Mary ran to it and hacked off a piece several feet long, doubling and quadrupling it feverishly to make a thicker cord.

'Don't be afraid, dear heart, don't be afraid! I'm here, I'm coming!' she panted, snatching up a fork.

But he didn't hear; his mouth opened in a thin, high wail and he ran like a blinded animal, bumping into the refrigerator, caroming off the wall, the gushing arm flailing about him as he tried to shake it off, throw it away so that it no longer was a part of him. Her cries blended with his; she lunged at him and missed, pulled up short and tried again. Spinning in fear-crazed circles, he saw the door and made for it, plucking at his arm and screaming shrilly. His bare feet splashed into the pool of blood on the floor and he slipped, crashing full length. Before he could rise Mary was on him, holding him down, beyond any further attempts to calm him in her frenzy to tie off the blood supply to his arm before it was too late. Half sitting, half lying on his chest, she grasped the arm and wrapped her string about it above the elbow, knotted it securely and put the fork underneath to twist the cord until it almost disappeared into his flesh.

'Tim, lie still! Oh, please, please, Tim, lie still! I'm here, I won't let anything happen to you, only *you must lie still*! Do you hear me?'

Between panic and loss of blood he was done; chest heaving, he lay beneath her and sobbed. Her head came down until her cheek was against his, and all she could think of was the times she had prevented herself from calling him all those lovely, loving names, forced herself to sit calmly opposite him when she longed to take him in her arms and kiss him until he gasped.

There was a pounding on the back door, and the Old Girl's voice; lifting her head, Mary screamed.

'I heard the weirdest noises all the way over in me own house,' Mrs Parker babbled as she pushed at the door, then as she saw the blood-washed kitchen she made a sound halfway between a gasp and a retch. 'Jesus Christ!'

'Get an ambulance!' Mary panted, afraid to take her weight off Tim in case he panicked again.

Nothing Mrs Parker could say would persuade Mary to get up; when the ambulance arrived not five minutes later she was still on the floor with Tim, her face pressed to his, and the two ambulance men had to lift her away.

Emily Parker went with her to the hospital, trying to comfort her as they rode in the back with Tim and one ambulance man.

'Don't worry about him, pet, he'll be all right. It looked like an awful lot of blood, but I've heard people say that a pint of it spilled looks like ten gallons.'

The district hospital was only a short distance away, on the other side of the brick pits, and the ambulance reached it so quickly that Mary still had not recovered her powers of speech when they wheeled Tim away from her into casualty. After his fall he had seemed to lapse into a kind of stupor, not aware of her or of his surroundings; he did not open his eyes once, almost as if he was afraid of what he might see should he open them, see that horrible thing which had once been his arm.

Mrs Parker helped Mary to a seat in the elegant waiting room, chattering all the time. 'Ain't this nice?' she asked, trying to get Mary's mind off Tim. 'I remember when this was just a couple of little rooms squeezed between X-ray and medical records. Now they've got this grouse new place, real nice. All them potted plants and everything make you feel like it ain't a hospital at all! I've seen worse hotel lobbies, pet, honest I have. Now you sit there nice and quiet until the doctor comes while I go and find me old mate Sister Kelly, see if I can get a hot cuppa tea and some bikkies for youse.'

The admitting registrar came in soon after Mrs Parker had gone off on her errand of mercy. Mary managed to get to her feet, licking her lips in an effort to speak; she still had not uttered a word.

'Mrs Melville? I just saw the ambulance man outside for a moment, and he told me your name.'

'Tih-Tih-Tim?' Mary managed to say, shaking so badly she had to sink into her chair again.

'Tim's going to be fine, Mrs Melville, really he is! We've just sent him into the operating room to have the arm repaired, but there's no reason to fear for him, I give you my word. We've started him on intravenous fluids and we'll probably give him a pint or two of blood the minute we've got his type, but he's quite all right, just in shock from loss of blood, that's all. The arm wound isn't going to be too difficult to attend to, I've looked at it myself. A good clean cut. What happened?'

'He must have let the carving knife slip somehow, I don't know. I wasn't looking at him when it happened, I just heard him call for me.' She looked up pitifully. 'Is he conscious? Please make him understand that I'm here, that I haven't gone away and left him alone. He gets terribly upset when he thinks I've abandoned him, even now.'

'He's under light anaesthesia at the moment, Mrs Melville, but when he comes round I'll make sure he knows you're here. Don't worry about him, he's a grown man.'

'That's just it, he's not. A grown man, I mean. Tim's mentally retarded, and I'm the only person he's got in all the world. It's terribly important that he knows I'm here! Just tell him Mary's outside, very close.'

'Mary?'

'He always calls me Mary,' she said childishly. 'He never calls me anything but Mary.'

The admitting registrar turned to go. 'I'll send one of our junior residents in to take some particulars for the hospital records, Mrs Melville, but he'll be brief. This is a simple accident case, no need for too many particulars, unless he's got any health problems aside from his mental retardation.'

'No, he's in perfect health.'

Mrs Parker came back with Sister Kelly behind her bearing a tea tray.

'Drink this while it's hot, Mrs Melville,' said Sister Kelly. 'Then I want you to go along the corridor to the bathroom, take off all your clothes and have a good steaming bath. Mrs Parker's volunteered to go home and get you some fresh clothes, and in the meantime you can wear a patient's bathrobe. Tim's fine, and you'll feel so much better after you've soaked awhile in a good hot bathtub. I'll send a nurse to show you the way.'

Mary looked down at herself, only then realising that she was as covered in Tim's blood as he had been himself.

'Drink your tea first, while Dr Fisher takes some particulars for us.'

Two hours later Mary was back in the waiting room with Mrs Parker, clad in fresh clothing and feeling more like herself. Dr Minster, the emergency surgeon, came to reassure her.

'You can go home, dear, he's fine. Came through the surgery with flying colours, and now he's sleeping like a baby. We'll leave him in intensive care for a little while, then we'll transfer him to one of the wards. Two days just to watch him, then he can go home.'

'He must have the best of everything, a private room and anything else he might need!'

'Then we'll transfer him to the private wing,' Dr Minster soothed expertly. 'Don't worry about him, Mrs Melville. He's a beautiful physical specimen, really beautiful.'

'Can't I see him before I go?' Mary pleaded.

'If you like, but don't stay. He's under sedation and I'd prefer it if you didn't try to rouse him.'

They had put Tim in a huge, trolley-like bed behind a screen, in one corner of a room filled with a bewildering array of equipment that emitted muted clanks, hisses, and beeps. There were seven other patients, ill enough to trigger a momentary panic in Mary's mind. A young nurse was standing beside Tim unwrapping a blood pressure cuff from around his good arm. Her eyes were on her patient's face instead of on what she was doing, and Mary stood for a moment watching her obvious admiration. Then she looked up, saw Mary and smiled at her.

'Hello, Mrs Melville. He's asleep, that's all, so don't worry about him. His blood pressure's excellent and he's out of shock.'

The waxen pallor had gone from his face, leaving it, sleeping and smooth, softly flushed; Mary reached out to push the matted hair away from his forehead.

'I'm just about to take him down to the private wing, Mrs Melville. Would you like to walk along with me and see him put into bed before you go home?'

They told her not to visit him until the following day late in the afternoon, for he continued to sleep and Mary knew that her presence could be at best a vigil. When she arrived she found him gone from his room, away to undergo tests; she sat and waited for him patiently, refusing all the offers of tea and sandwiches with a polite, strained smile.

'Does he realise where he is and what happened?' she asked the ward Sister. 'Did he panic when he woke up and found I wasn't there?'

'No, he was fine, Mrs Melville. He settled down very quickly and he seems to be happy. In fact, he's such a sunny, bright person that he's become the ward favourite.'

When Tim saw her sitting in the chair waiting for him he had to be discouraged from leaping off his trolley to hug her. 'Oh, Mary, I'm so glad you're here! I thought I might not see you for a long time.'

'Are you all right, Tim?' she asked, kissing his brow quickly because two nurses were standing watching.

'I feel fine again, Mary! The doctor made my arm all better; he sewed it all together where the knife cut it, and there's no more blood or anything.'

'Does it hurt?'

'Not much. Not like the time a load of bricks fell on my foot and it got broken.'

Early the following morning Mary got a phone call from the hospital, telling her that she could take Tim home. Stopping only to tell Mrs Parker the good news, she flew to the car with a small case containing Tim's clothes in one hand and her breakfast toast in the other. Sister met her at the ward door and took the case, then ushered her into a sitting room to wait.

She was just beginning to become impatient when Dr Minster and the admitting registrar walked in.

'Good morning, Mrs Melville. Sister told me you'd arrived. Tim ought to be ready very soon, so don't worry. They won't let you out of this place without a bath and a fresh dressing and Lord knows what.'

'Tim is all right?' Mary queried anxiously.

'Absolutely! He'll have a scar to remind him to be more careful with carving knives in the future, but all the nerves to the hand are intact, so he won't lose power or sensation. Bring him to my rooms in a week's time and I'll see how everything is going. I may take the stitches out then, or leave them awhile longer, depending on how it looks.'

'Then he really is all right?'

Dr Minster threw back his head and laughed. 'Oh, you mothers! You're all alike, full of worry and anxiety. Now you've got to promise me that you'll stop flapping over him, because if you let him see you've been reduced to this sort of state you'll give him ideas and he'll begin to favour the arm more than he ought. I know he's your son and your maternal feelings are particularly strong because of his special dependence on you, but you *must* resist your tendency to cluck over him needlessly.'

Mary felt the blood welling up under her skin, but she pressed her lips together and lifted her head proudly. 'You've misunderstood, Dr Minster. Funny that it didn't occur to me, but I suppose you've all misunderstood. Tim isn't my son, he's my husband.'

Dr Minster and the admitting registrar looked at each other, mortified. Anything they tried to say would sound wrong, and in the end they said nothing, just got themselves to the door and slipped outside. What could one possibly say after making a gaffe like that? How ghastly, how absolutely ghastly, and how embarrassing! Poor, poor thing, how dreadful for her!

Mary sat in a haze of tears, fighting their tendency to spill over with every ounce of what strength she had left. Whatever she felt, Tim must not see her eyes all red, nor must any of those pretty young nurses. No wonder they had all been so open to her about their admiration for Tim! One said some things to mothers and quite different things to wives, and now that she thought about it they had indeed treated her like a mother, not like a wife.

Well, it was her own stupid fault. If she had been her usual calm, collected self throughout those agonised hours of waiting and wondering, it would never have slipped her attention that they all assumed she was Tim's mother. It was even possible that they had asked her and she had replied in the affirmative. She remembered the young intern coming up to her and asking if she was the legal next of kin, but she could not remember what she had answered. And why shouldn't they have assumed she was his mother? At her best she looked her age, but with the shock and worry of Tim's accident weighing her down she looked sixty at least. Why hadn't she used a personal pronoun which could have offered them some clue? How odd the quirks of fate; she must have said and done everything to reinforce their misapprehension, done nothing to dispell it. Mrs Parker must have done the same, and Tim, poor, anxious-to-please Tim, had absorbed her lesson too well when she had impressed on him that he must not rave about marrying her. They probably thought his calling her Mary was just his way. And no one had ever asked her if he was single or married; hearing he was not the full quid, they simply took it for granted that he was single. Mentally retarded people did not marry. They lived at home with their parents until they were orphaned and then they went to some sort of institution to die.

Tim was waiting in his room, fully dressed and very eager to be gone. Steeling herself to an outward calmness and composure, she took his hand in hers and smiled at him very tenderly.

'Come on, Tim, let's go home,' she said.